THE WEALTH

BY

RICHARD MARMAN

Published in England
by
ABELA PUBLISHING
Sandhurst, Berkshire, England

Email: Author@RichardMarman.com

Website: www.RichardMarman.com

ISBN 13: 978-1-92583-3-041

Republished in 2018 with Ocean Reeve Publishing

First Edition, 2017

DEDICATION

*This is book is dedicated to the charming
Seraglio Girls:
Sally and Elizabeth Marman, Brooke Carter,
Camille Moroney, Emma Livingstone, Lauren Jones
and Natasha Gardos
And to Norwegian beauty, Janniche Adolfsen whose
image graces the front cover*

Part One – The Mentor

Chapter 1	Morbac Forest
Chapter 2	Archer
Chapter 3	Mother of Fantasies
Chapter 4	Enta Geweore
Chapter 5	Urdec and Walter
Chapter 6	Night Work at Burgal
Chapter 7	Moor and Mire
Chapter 8	Velma
Chapter 9	Meeting the Threat
Chapter 10	Survival

Part Two – Eastern Journey

Chapter 11	Tremill Broch
Chapter 12	Jongarrat
Chapter 13	Weasel
Chapter 14	Ita Cay
Chapter 15	Beware – Corsair!
Chapter 16	Mountain Men
Chapter 17	Otillie
Chapter 18	Squire Redbone
Chapter 19	The Graveyard
Chapter 20	Henry's Plan
Chapter 21	Vipers' Nest

Part Three — Dambar

Chapter 22   The Dambar Block
Chapter 23   Simoom
Chapter 24   Henry's Battalion
Chapter 25   Girls of the Seraglio
Chapter 26   The Dambar Pit
Chapter 27   The Catacombs
Chapter 28   Spies
Chapter 29   Cohort
Chapter 30   Palo Innes

The Wealth

Part 1

The Mentor

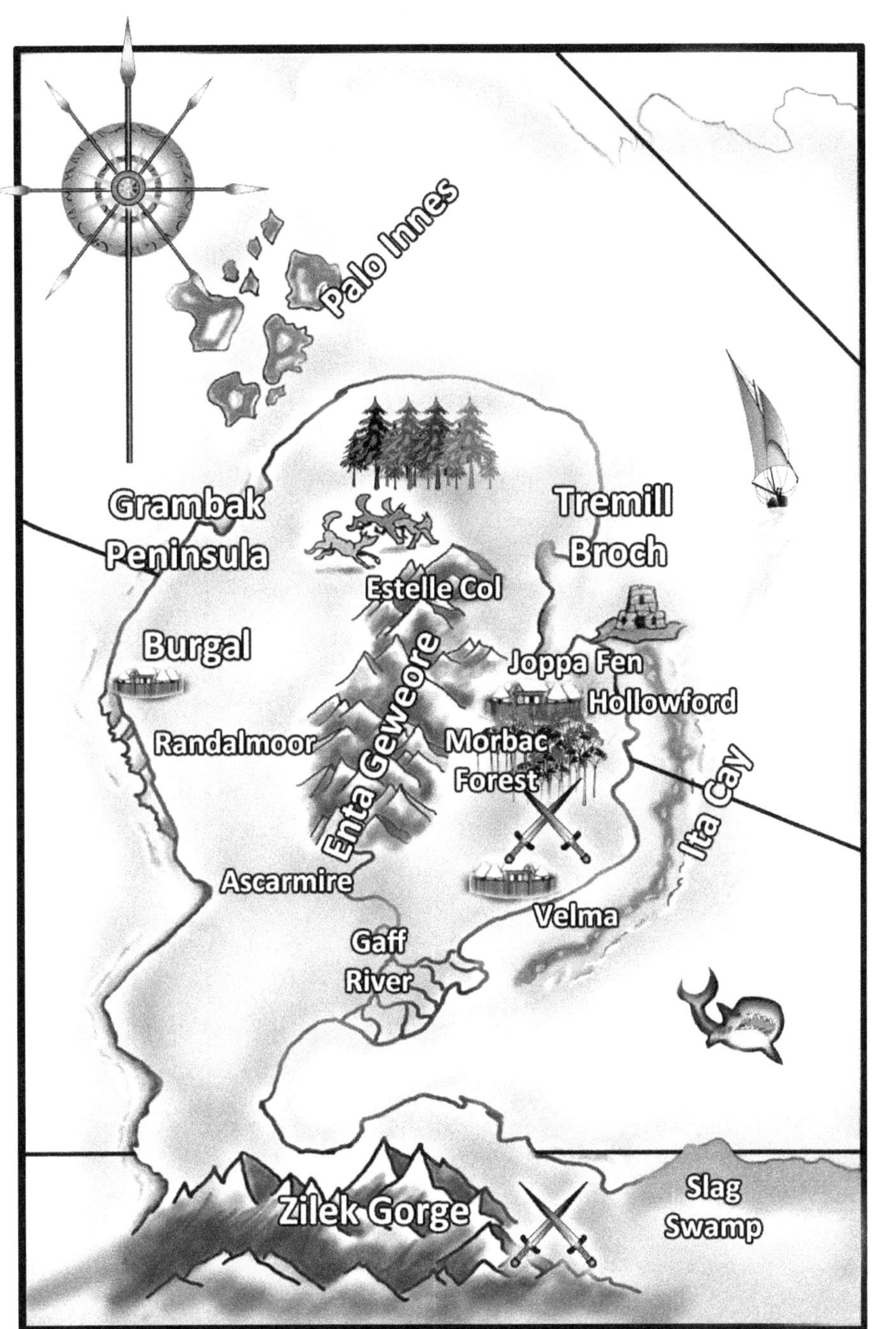

Palo Innes
Grambak Peninsula
Tremill Broch
Estelle Col
Burgal
Enta Geweore
Joppa Fen
Hollowford
Randalmoor
Morbac Forest
Ascarmire
Ita Cay
Velma
Gaff River
Zilek Gorge
Slag Swamp

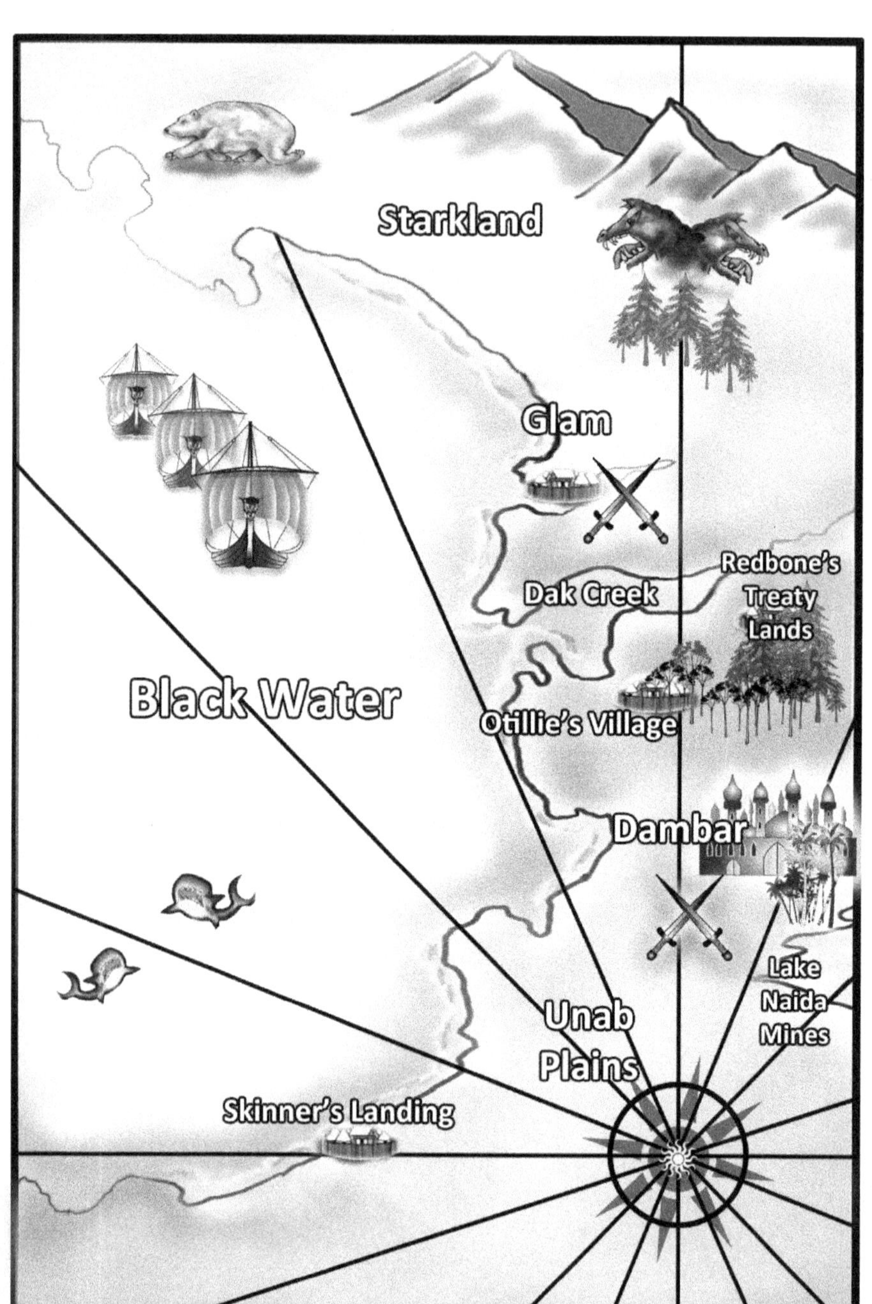

Starkland
Glam
Redbone's Treaty Lands
Dak Creek
Black Water
Otillie's Village
Dambar
Lake Naida Mines
Unab Plains
Skinner's Landing

I examine the
glinting ornaments
and stare in horror
at three ravaged bodies
lying before me.
Sensing a movement I slowly turn
to see a she-wolf. She snarls through bared fangs as
her back arches and she inches towards me.
I pick the broadsword from the
ground beside me and brace to meet her.
Yesterday I was secure and
carefree, but how quickly that has changed.

Chapter 1
Morbac Forest

Yesterday, Henry was alone in the forest at dusk. He thought the woods sombre and mysterious, yet a part of life that could neither be ignored nor avoided. Deepening shadows drew away from beech and birch trunks draped with ivy, moss, and mistletoe as a breeze scythed through their branches. Bulb shoots thrust through half-frozen earth in a green display with burgeoning hints of white, yellow, and blue against the grey-brown leaf mould. It was difficult to feel daunted with the coming of spring. This was the first clear weather after what had been a tedious winter, and Henry wanted to make the most of it to hunt.

He was not a hunter by trade, but indentured to his Uncle Edgar, the Hollowford Town blacksmith. Years before Henry's parents were murdered by raiding bandits, but nowadays Hollowford's yeomanry was better able to deal with brigands. Life had been peaceful in recent times. He became the smith's apprentice by default, as there was no one else to take him in. Edgar was stern, but mostly they got along. Today was Henry's day off, so he thought he'd try his luck at catching something extra for the stew-pot, especially as food had been rationed for weeks now. He carried a short bow made of layered spruce and had practised enough to be an excellent shot.

There were many encouraging signs that game was awakening from winter's grip and Henry had been tracking a deer herd for hours. If he returned with venison for the villagers, it would impress Chief Gareth, and it was always a good idea to stay on the right side of civic notables. But, he'd strayed too far to return home before dusk, and it looked as if he'd have to find a safe place for the night. He walked on until the forest opened into a large glade enclosed by beeches with an oak at its centre, standing like a lone sentinel. This was an ideal place to camp for the night, but Henry stopped short as he approached the tree.

A giant black boar was entangled in a briar patch beneath the branches, trapped while rooting about for any of last year's acorns. Everyone knew these animals were dangerous and this beast's growing anger and frustration as it battled the thorns made it even worse. It finally struggled free, leaving deep cuts across its jowls. No time was good, but this was an especially bad time to be spotted by an infuriated boar. Its nostrils flared as steam sprayed past its long, yellow tusks. The boar's coarse hair bristled and it charged.

Henry whipped an arrow from its quiver, nocked it, and drew the bowstring to his nose. Hitting a charging wild animal was chancy, but Henry's nerve held as he released. The shaft drove through the boar's eye. The boy reached for another arrow, but there was no time to shoot it. The boar slammed into him, driving all the air from his lungs. Henry crashed to the ground with the boar almost smothering him, but the arrow had penetrated its brain and the beast was dead. Only sheer momentum had finished the charge.

Henry struggled free. Not only was he worried about being crushed, but the beast's stench made him gag as blood oozed from its eye socket. The boy was battered and shaken, although he suffered no serious damage. He was amazed that he'd felt no fear during the charge, but realised there simply hadn't been time. Now he must decide what to do with his kill. There was no doubt the villagers would eat it, and the women usually butchered game quickly, but they were too far away. He could leave it and return to Hollowford for help, except night scavengers were likely to spoil the meat, so he'd just have to do the job himself. The arrow was damaged beyond worth, so he left it imbedded where it was and set to work. It was night when he finished, however a full moon bathed the glade in light. He'd done a fair job on the carcass, certainly well enough for the time being.

Then he heard the first wolf howl.

Soon joined by others, in no time the baying surrounded him. A pack had caught the scent of blood and they were on their way. Wolves were rarely troublesome, but a lone boy would have difficulty fending them off, especially if they were ravenous after lean pickings all winter. Usually they stayed in the high country of Enta Geweore and seldom hunted close to lowland communities. Henry thought of running and leaving them to it, but it was his boar and he was damned if he was going to give it up. The oak would serve well as a larder, so he began to heave the pieces of carcass into the lower branches. The boar's head was all that remained when the pack swarmed into the clearing.

There were two dozen, led by a monstrous grey wolf and its mate. Others followed in strict order of strength and prowess as was the way of the pack. Their eyes were ablaze and drool glistened from their jaws in the moonlight. The pack was desperately hungry.

Henry bolted for the oak with the last of his catch. He leapt into the tree just as the leading wolf bounded into the air after him. He felt its claws rake his back. His leather jacket protected him as he clambered to safety. The pack leader joined the others to polish off the boar's intestines, but it did not take long before their attention turned to the oak.

The wolves leapt at the lower branches where the boar meat balanced uncertainly. They grew bolder with each bound, and Henry was so worried he'd soon lose the lot that he threw the boar's head into the pack. They fell onto the prey in snarling bedlam until it was stripped to bare skull and they returned to the oak. He nocked an arrow to his bowstring and drew back. He couldn't miss at such close range and in brilliant moonlight. The arrow pierced the alpha-male's heart, killing it instantly. The pack fell onto it, but the leader's mate drove them back. The pack challenged her persistently, but she stood firm.

With the pack distracted, Henry moved his catch to the safety of higher branches. When he'd finished he clambered down a little way to see the she-wolf still fending the others off. They edged closer. Just as it seemed she would be overwhelmed, the pack appeared to lose interest and dashed away between the trees.

The lone she-wolf stooped over her consort, licking his disfigured face with a melancholy tenderness that Henry might have found moving under different circumstances. At last she flung her head back and with a lamenting wail followed the pack into the forest. She must accept fate and mate with the strongest remaining male who may have already claimed leadership over the pack.

Henry was in no hurry to climb down. He stashed his bow and arrows and wriggled into the fork of two stout branches, wedged securely in case he fell asleep. He dozed but was jerked awake by the sound of the wolf-pack baying close by. The howls changed to intense savagery as Henry imagined they'd tracked down some hapless prey. The cacophony was short lived and faded. Henry heard a few lonely wails, but at last the pack was heading back to its normal hunting grounds among the blue conifers in the snow-covered mountains. Hopefully, with the onset of spring and more plentiful game, they might stay there.

Henry settled in for the night.

Dawn sunbeams filtered through the tall timber as colour returned to the forest floor. A thin mist drifted upwards, but would quickly burn off and Henry knew there'd be no trouble finding his way home to tell the villagers, who would return for the boar. Following a narrow path, he soon reached the spot where the pack had made its kill, but it wasn't game they'd brought down. The corpses of three men lay in the centre of a clearing; or what was left of them.

The pack had ripped their flesh to the bone, but the victims had accounted for themselves well before they died. Several slain wolves lay where small scavengers and insects were already gathering to feast. A pair of broadswords and a dagger were discarded amid the carnage, so at least two of these men were warriors, judging by their weapons. Now Henry knew what had lured the pack away from his tree, confirming the wolves must have been famished to have attacked such a well defended trio. He was sure the pack showed no signs of rabies disease that occasionally maddened animals into unusual savagery.

He gingerly picked around the bodies, hoping to find clues to who they might be. They'd made camp, with the remains of a fire still smouldering, and there were also signs of horses that must have bolted before the warriors could mount up when the wolves arrived. Two cloaks lay crumpled where they had been cast aside, and their clasps caught Henry's attention. Gold medallions had been worked into brooches surrounded by amber, topaz, and curious blue stones Henry couldn't identify. These were not mere baubles, but valuable artefacts rarely seen in Hollowford. Chief Gareth's wife, Ayla, certainly wore nice jewellery, but she was the richest woman around. Trading in precious currency wasn't Hollowford's style, where a barter system was the normal order of business. Henry wondered why fighting men would own such treasures; he understood soldiers mostly squandered their wealth as soon as they came by it on rough wine and even rougher women.

There were no further signs of wealth, although Henry found a purse containing coppers, but that was all. He pocketed the coins. The golden discs were intriguing items and Henry wondered whether they were talismans from a strange tribe or the badge of a secret brotherhood. Chief Gareth might know something about them, as he'd travelled all over Grambak Peninsula, whereas Henry hadn't wandered very far at all. But if he showed the treasures to the chief, he might want to keep them.

He thought of burying the men, but knew it would take all day. It was better to bring help and the sooner the better, because the corpses wouldn't get any sweeter.

He turned to leave and froze. The she-wolf was crouching arch-backed before him. He could only think that she had returned to her dead mate and followed his scent back here. Why she came was a mystery. Perhaps she had been replaced by a younger, fitter female and had been driven from the pack. Whether she connected

Henry with the alpha-wolf's death didn't matter. Henry tucked the purse and brooches into the front of his tunic and seized one of the swords.

The wolf circled him with fluid hostility.

Where are the others? If they reappeared he was doomed. Sweat dripped from his brow as he held the sword uncertainly. He'd never formally trained in its use, other than sparring with other village boys using wooden weapons.

"I'm sorry," he whispered. "I know you were just hungry, but I have to eat too. If I could change things I would, and maybe these men would still be alive as well."

The wolf drew closer.

"I don't want to hurt you. I know what I did must seem wrong to you. Forgive me."

I'm talking to a wolf! What good will that do?

It did do some good, however. Henry inched towards the she-wolf, the sword raised in both hands. The wolf crouched before him and Henry was sure she'd attack, but she did not move. She bowed her head and her growling ceased. He lowered the sword and reached towards her with his free hand. He wasn't really sure why, but she appeared so vulnerable now, no longer the savage beast that threatened him with her pack. Whether the wolf felt Henry's regret, or merely thought the risk of taking him on alone was too great, would never be known. Had she been abandoned by the others and simply sought company and solace elsewhere? Was she acknowledging Henry as a surrogate for her mate? She raised her head and their eyes met. All the hostility was gone and she allowed him to stroke her back.

"Well, that's an interesting development," Henry said softly, "but you must go now because I'm heading home, and I don't expect wolves are welcome in Hollowford. Go on, scat!"

She seemed reluctant to leave, then abruptly leapt to her paws and bounded away into the forest. Henry realised why, hearing the jangle of spurs and bridles. With the ever-present threat of bandits in the forest, he left everything where it was and, still armed with the broadsword, headed for Hollowford with the medallions tucked in his tunic.

The glade droned with swarming flies as two mounted and warlike men approached. Their hair and beards hung in long braids and both warriors wore mail tunics, leather breeches, boots and plain metal helmets. Their indigo cloaks were drawn around them and held in place by similar precious ornaments to those of the dead men. Both riders were on their guard and drew their swords as they inspected the glade, peering into the forest before dismounting.

They poked around the bodies, taking particular interest in their abandoned cloaks.

"Something big 'appened 'ere," one of the men growled.

"Any fool can see that." The other spoke in barely more than a hiss.

"The wealth is gone," the Growl observed. "Someone took 'em."

"So I see," the Hiss replied. "Won't be 'ard to find. There's the trail. We'll press on."

They gathered the remaining sword, remounted, and began the hunt for Henry. Shortly after the riders disappeared, the she-wolf emerged and followed their path.

What is to become of the wolf now she must fend for herself?
Will she be lonely?

I think I'd better get some sleep.
Uncle Edgar wants me back at work tomorrow

Chapter 2
Archer

The thrill of last night's events had waned when Henry reached Hollowford. He felt worn out, although he'd come across the slain warriors' horses and rode one home while leading the other. It was mid-morning when he arrived.

The original village had formed around a crossing on a waterway called Hollow Tree Creek because of the ancient willows along its banks. In time a bridge was completed over the ford where an enterprising individual built a water wheel and mill house from which the village developed. A surrounding wooden palisade had proved useful in troubled years. Over time, when Gareth's militia had secured Hollowford's relative peace and the community grew to a small town, the posts were adapted for other, less martial purposes, such as extending the chief's feasting hall. Dwellings and stock pens now sprawled from the original fence boundaries. Pigs, geese, and chickens foraged, clearing up most of the village refuse. Enough land had been cleared outside town for crops, orchards, vegetable plots, and livestock.

Edgar was busy at the forge and ambivalent about Henry's return. He thought his nephew was a bit of a block-head, but was pleased to see him home safely. Henry showed some promise in the smithy and would graduate to journeyman in a few years, but after a restless night abroad, he wasn't much use for the rest of the day. He explained about the boar to his Aunt Thayer, who organised a party of villagers to take a cart into the forest and retrieve the carcasses. Several of Gareth's well-armed men accompanied them just in case the wolves showed up again.

Henry climbed to the loft above the forge where he'd arranged his bed of hay, goose-down pillows, and animal hides and soon fell asleep despite the hammering and clinking below. He awoke at dusk, just as Thayer's foragers returned with the boar piled high in their cart. They had buried the dead warriors where they lay. Henry hadn't realised just how huge the animal was, certainly big enough for all the villagers to have a decent meal. So Ayla persuaded Gareth to hold a feast in his hall the following night for everybody to celebrate a treat of fresh pork and the spring equinox passing. The entire village loved a party, so all and sundry raided their cupboards to see what they could contribute. Even after a long winter, they managed to gather vegetables, dried herbs and fruit, kegs of mead, cider and beer, salt, sugar beet, barley and other grains for baking bread and pies.

Amid the bustle, no-one noticed two travellers walk their horses to Clem Foster's inn. They concealed their weapons under saddle blankets and asked about accommodation for the night. Clem was a garrulous, portly fellow with a ruddy complexion, suggesting he favoured his own product.

"A place for the night?" he boomed, accustomed to being heard over the usual taproom chatter.

"Yeah, that's what I said," the man with a rasping voice replied, wishing this fool would make less noise about it. The travellers didn't want to draw attention to themselves.

"You'll be snug enough in the loft and the hay's clean. Stash your gear there while my lad takes care of your horses. You'll need a mug of porter by the sounds of you."

Clem Foster's consisted of the dirt-floor barroom where a fire blazed in the corner. Clem had once covered the floor with straw, but it caught alight one night and only the fierce stamping of his patrons prevented the inn from burning to the ground. Tables and stools were scattered with a few outside, where folk liked to sit on summer evenings. Casks of beer, mead, and cider were stacked along the back wall behind a serving counter.

Clem poured a tankard of black ale for his guests.

"We don't get many strangers hereabouts, especially before the warm weather," he declared.

"I suppose not," the Hiss replied.

"Rabbit stew, eggs, and fresh baked bread for supper tonight, if you've a mind. Two coppers each and that includes feed for your mounts. You can't ask fairer than that," Clem said.

The wayfarers handed over the money without haggling.

"Young fellow from here killed a great boar in the forest last night," Clem continued. "Came home all scratched about with a tale of wolves and dead men in the forest."

"Oh?" the Growl arched his eyebrows.

"He'll be in later, I'll be bound. Want to tell everyone about it."

"That might be interesting."

"Aye, you'd probably have stories to tell y'selves, you being travellers and all. Folk'll buy a round to hear a good yarn."

But the lure of free beer didn't appear to interest the strangers, who moved away and sat by the fire. Clem considered them a bit moody for his liking, but other customers were drifting in and he turned his attention to them.

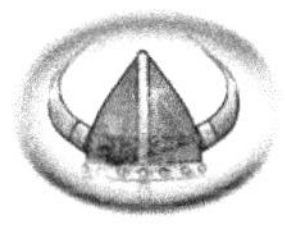

When Henry awoke he felt stiff and sore, but in good spirits.

"Clem Foster dropped by," Edgar said. "He reckons if you go over there and tell everyone about your adventures, it'll draw a crowd."

"He's too young to be hanging out with tavern riff-raff," Thayer declared.

"I drink with tavern riff-raff on occasion," Edgar reminded her.

"I'm not much of a drinker," Henry said nervously.

"Stick to small beer and you'll come to no harm."

Thayer suggested Edgar accompany Henry, but he declined, saying his nephew should savour the moment unassisted. He thought Thayer brewed superior beer to Clem anyway.

"But remember, you'll have to be up early tomorrow and ready for a full day's work," the smith added.

So Henry kissed his aunt goodnight and left for the inn.

"I suppose the time has come when he needs the companionship of men," Thayer said.

"Then it'll be girls," Edgar grinned, "and his troubles will really begin."

"I don't see that you have anything to complain about. In fact, now that we have the evening to ourselves, you might be quite happy having a girl around. I wonder if that is why you were so keen for Henry to go out alone."

She sat on his knee and placed her arms around his neck.

"I see my plan is working," he said.

Of course everyone at Clem Foster's wanted to hear Henry's story and he retold it several times as the night drew on. He accepted a few tankards and felt heady after a while. Even though he was enjoying the attention, Henry remembered his uncle's admonition and before too long bade everyone goodnight and headed home. He was feeling pretty smug about himself as he strolled through Hollowford's narrow lanes. A night hunting in the forest, close encounters with a boar and wolves, followed by an evening in the tavern made him feel far more grown-up than he'd been a couple of days ago. He was startled back to reality when a cloaked figure appeared from a corner, blocking his path. He was silhouetted but Henry could still make out the sword he carried.

The stranger's breath came in rasps as he edged forward, gliding, almost slithering. Henry spun around only to be confronted by another figure. The man's head was cloaked and his features hidden, but he too brandished a sword.

"Hold up there, boyo," the first man hissed.

"We can kill yer easy enough," his companion growled. "We're 'ere fer our property, we know yer gorrit."

"What?" Henry stammered. "I don't know what you're talking about."

"Liar!"

"To our way of thinkin'," Hiss added, "yer'll not wanna part from 'em valuables, so yer got 'em on yer and I sez hand 'em over right now."

Henry needed time to work a way out of this.

"I don't have them with me," he said. "I've hidden them."

But the two men weren't convinced.

"Then yer won't mind if we searches yer," Growl said, "and if yer're lyin', we'll kill yer out of hand."

Henry's eyes darted back and forth for a bolt hole. He lunged sideward to dodge Hiss, who grabbed him easily and struck him with the hilt of his sword. Dazed for a moment, Henry crashed to the ground. Hiss raised his sword. If Henry still had the amulets, it would be easier to retrieve them once he was dead.

Just as the sword swung, a shadowy form flashed before Henry and the she-wolf latched onto his attacker's forearm. He yelped as she snarled and savaged his wrist, but the warrior was tough and quickly flung her aside. She smashed into a wall and lay still. Growl grabbed Henry as Hiss returned to finish him off. He was about to swing his blade, but stopped in mid-stride. A tall, rangy figure entered the alley-way. He carried a double-bladed battle-axe, but wore no armour or helmet other than a chain-mail sark, cowhide leggings, and boots.

"This contest appears uneven, in my opinion," the newcomer observed blandly. "I heard there were a couple of strangers in town. I've been keeping an eye on you two, but lost you for a moment in these laneways."

Hiss was not about to debate matters and lunged at the stranger who anticipated something of the sort. There was no room to swing the axe so, after deftly avoiding Hiss's blade, the new-comer rammed the haft into his chest, knocking the breath from Henry's attacker and sending him staggering backwards. Henry recovered sufficiently to get to his knees, just as Hiss backed into him and was sent tumbling into Growl, who came to join the fight. The stranger saw the advantage and lunged just as Henry lurched to his feet and they crashed into each other with a bone-jarring thud that sent Henry reeling once more.

The attackers knew the commotion would soon draw others, so they fled into the darkness.

"Out of the way!" The stranger roared, shoving Henry aside.

The boy thumped into a wall, adding to his aches and injured pride as the stranger raced down several dead ends, but failed to find his quarry. He reached Clem Foster's front door where several patrons were spilling out.

"Two men, where are they?" he yelled.

"Out the back," Clem said. "They dashed inside, grabbed their gear, and leapt from the loft window into the stable yard."

Suddenly, two riders clattered past, knocking the stranger over, causing him to roll into bystanders. He cursed sharply as they hauled him to his feet before he stalked away to find Henry, still slumped in the alley with the she-wolf across his lap.

"Well?" the stranger demanded.

"Oh, it's you, Archer," Henry stammered.

"Yes, it's me," Archer replied without being particularly reassuring about it, because he was Gareth's reeve and in charge of village law-and-order.

Then he noticed the injured animal.

"Will your dog be all right?"

"She's a wolf."

"I wouldn't let that piece of news get around if I were you. Folk will skin her and peg the hide to a post outside town if they find out."

The wolf stirred and appeared to recover with only a few scratches to trouble her.

"Where did you get a wolf anyway?"

"In the forest last night."

"I heard about that and did you meet those two ruffians in the forest as well?"

"No, I've never seen them before, but the dead men out there looked just like them."

"Come on," Archer said, helping Henry to his feet. "You'd better come and explain things to the chief, and bring your pet with you. Has she got a name?"

"I haven't had time to think of one. What do you think about 'Bronwyn?"

"After your mother, is it?"

"Yes, do you think she'd mind?"

"No, she was much admired hereabouts. We all remember her in our own way, and you must do the same. Carry her memory with your new friend, Henry. It will please her spirit, I'm sure."

Normally Chief Gareth was a sociable fellow who liked to hold court with his retainers, but tonight he and Ayla had retired early. His daughter, Macayle, was supervising their three servant-girls clean up after supper. While her mother was a golden-tressed, flawless beauty, Macayle favoured her father's blazing red hair, emerald eyes, and uninhibited character. She was two or three years older than Henry, who adored her, but knew well enough she would never be for him.

Gareth kept a dozen men-at-arms who formed the nucleus of Hollowford's defences. They trained the village militia, who were chauvinists to a man when it came to protecting their families and property. Faranden, Archer's deputy, was the only other person around. He was muscular and blustery and Henry considered him to be a noisy bully, but he was a tough man in a fight and you don't want a sissy when it comes to standing up to marauders or savage beasts from the forest. Macayle flirted shamelessly with Faranden, but it was unlikely Gareth would choose him for her either.

A couple of Gareth's mastiffs snarled a challenge when they saw Bronwyn, but Macayle silenced them with a sharp command. She tossed them each a mutton bone and gave Bronwyn a couple of shanks to pacify any canine angst.

"Ah, our hero from the dark woods," Faranden announced, raising his drinking horn in a mock toast. "An honour indeed, sirrah."

"He's been having adventures closer to home," Archer said, "and getting mixed up in street brawls with a couple of rascals. They galloped off, but you'd better double the night watch and warn them to be extra alert."

Faranden nodded and left. Although he was enjoying Macayle's company, he knew better than to grumble in front of Archer. They both agreed it wasn't worth disturbing Gareth to report a minor altercation at the inn.

"Would you like a drink?" Macayle asked. "You both look as if you could use it."

She brought a pitcher of ale and two wooden mugs, eyeing Archer most of the time, but casting occasional glances towards Henry. They sat around a table, Macayle on a bench next to the reeve.

"So, what was that all about?" Archer said, straight to the point. "And don't even think about lying to me or I'll take over where those villains left off."

"That's pretty much what they said," Henry conceded.

He told the whole story of last night's adventure and concluded by taking the golden brooches from his tunic and placing them on the table. Macayle's interest transferred from Archer to the medallions. She beheld them wide-eyed and stroked the golden smoothness, entranced by the intoxicating quality of the objects.

"Nice," Archer assayed. "Very nice indeed. Can't say as I've ever seen anything like them."

"But how did they know I had them?"

"Most likely they knew those dead fellows in the woods and just followed you here, wouldn't you say?"

"I suppose so."

"They're beautiful," Macayle purred.

"The thing that bothers me is their strangeness. No one hereabouts crafted these for sure. I wouldn't mind knowing if any foreigners are prowling nearby, and more importantly, how many. There are no tinkers or gypsies in town right now, but I know someone who might help, so I'd better hang onto these for a while."

Archer placed the amulets into a pouch strung around his neck and tucked it under his sark. Henry looked concerned and Macayle pouted with disappointment.

"I'll probably be able to protect them better than you two," he sighed. "Anyway, it'll only be for a few days, and then you can have them back. I've got someone to see tomorrow, you can come with me if you don't trust me."

"Can I come too?" Macayle asked.

"I'm sorry. Even if I agreed, remember your mother wants you to accompany her to Tremill Broch for a spot of star-gazing. With unknown outlanders wandering about, your father may keep you here anyway."

Macayle pouted again. Her mother was fascinated by the stars and never missed a chance to study the heavens with the scholars and astronomers who lived at the Broch sited on an island to the north of Hollowford. Dean Merrick, Tremill's prime-wizard, had sent word that a once-in-a-lifetime extraterrestrial event was about to occur and Ayla couldn't wait to see it. Macayle shared her mother's enthusiasm, but the idea of riding to adventure with Archer and Henry sounded much more exciting.

"Can you ride, Henry?" Archer asked.

"I'm adequate," he replied. "I have to ride the mounts my uncle shoes to make sure the fitting is correct."

"Do you own a horse?"

"Actually, I own two now."

"Fair enough, we'll start tomorrow morning. Come on, I'll take you and your dog home, just in case those louts are still about."

"That's a wolf not a dog. You're not fooling anyone," Macayle said.

Bron is so quiet she can sneak about without anyone noticing.
Aunt Thayer nearly had a conniption this morning.
It woke us all.
Just as well, Archer is coming early

I have two horses now, a mare and a gelding
named Bella and Bruno.
I will take Bella today, she is the calmest.
Uncle Edgar will probably sell Bruno.
I doubt if he'll want the expense of feeding both animals.

Chapter 3
Mother of Fantasies

The following morning dawned cold with a drizzling mist that finally lifted to be replaced by depressing rain, so the forge was the place to be with its roaring fire. Bron had caused some consternation when Thayer came to rouse Henry and discovered a wolf in the loft. Luckily her shriek woke him and he explained before Edgar could grab a weapon.

"How will you stop her attacking our stock?" Edgar demanded.

"I don't think that's an issue.'"

Henry pointed to the remains of several rabbits Bron had hunted during the night.

"She seems quite tame now. I'm sure the only reason the pack attacked those travellers was because they were so hungry. With the snow melting and uncovering grasslands, rabbits are breeding again. There'll be no shortage of game."

"Be careful, Henry. If just one goose or lamb goes missing, it's the end of her."

But Edgar smiled and stroked the wolf, perhaps because she'd been named after his sister and the memory pleased him. He'd always called her "Bron" and the wolf became known in the same way.

Edgar had started work when Archer turned up. The reeve

wore a bearskin coat under his cloak with its hood drawn low over his brow.

"Morning, blacksmith."

Edgar straightened, nodded, and continued hammering.

"I've come for Henry."

"So he says. Although why, I cannot divine."

"He might remember something useful about the villains who attacked him," Archer explained, turning to Henry. "Rug up, son. It's sorely miserable outside, and bring your bow. Perhaps we'll see another boar."

"Thanks, Uncle," Henry said.

Edgar shrugged.

"Archer is Chief Gareth's reeve, so I'm bound to do as he bids. Mark him well and behave in his company. Make me proud that he has chosen you for assistance."

"Don't fret about Henry," Archer said. "He's attentive and not prone to waywardness. Events in the forest may signify or not, but we'd better find out. When I showed Gareth and Ayla the amulets, they were keen we should investigate."

Henry saddled Bella, who was stabled with Bruno beside the forge. Aware of his limited horsemanship, he chose the gentlest of the pair, although that was relative. Being warrior's mounts, both were spirited and required some persuasive handling.

Thayer supplied a muslin sack containing enough bread and cheese for them both. They mounted and disappeared into the forest, following a track shrouded by budding treetops. Water drizzled from above pooling in places or swirling away in streams. The clinging dankness was so different from before when, wolves and boars aside, Henry had enjoyed his hunting expedition. He drew his cloak closer, pulling the mantle further over his eyes.

Bron followed, often disappearing into the forest for short periods before returning to the trail. Archer didn't say where they were going. He was not inclined to conversation at all. Perhaps rain made him moody.

After a couple of hours' bleak trekking, the forest opened into a small, roughly cleared meadow that barely contained the encroaching wild-berry briars. Beside a small vegetable plot stood a hut made from cast-off timber, mouldy thatch, shingles, and crumbling masonry. The hut was built against an oak whose roots entwined the foundations so solidly they'd become part of the structure. Blue smoke curled languidly through the thatch, rose a short distance, then oozed downwards under the pressure of rain. Water casks, wooden buckets, plant pots, garden tools, and bric-a-brac were scattered close to the front wall, shaded by a small porch. Two wicker chairs had been placed there.

"Hello inside!" Archer called. "Anyone home? You can't be out in this weather. Come on, get off your rusty old backside. You've got visitors who've come all the way from Hollowford."

A muffled tirade followed from a voice that sounded like dry straw being set alight. Henry saw a gnarled, skeletal hand draw back the animal pelts that hung in the doorway. The oldest, least favoured, withered crone Henry had ever seen appeared. Her face was a skull of corrugated skin with a crown of tangled white hair. She was dressed in furs and waddled through the debris in her garden. She held a long shillelagh that she used alternately to steady her way and brandish in the air.

Small she may have been, but daunting nonetheless. Archer dismounted and, to Henry's surprise, stepped forward to embrace the harridan with genuine warmth. Hitherto Archer hadn't demonstrated much emotion about anything.

"Archer, you rogue," she cackled. "It's been so long since you've paid old Guilda a call, damn yer eyes. Been huddled up in the village with a gourd of porter and some buxom quean, I'll be bound, you neglectful scoundrel."

"It's your friendly, silk-tongued conversation I've missed mostly," Archer replied.

Henry knew of Guilda, the mysterious woman of the woods. Mother of Fantasies some called her. People spoke in awe of the spells and curses she could inflict with the help of a sinister hobgoblin who lived with her. Yet, she was known to tell fortunes accurately and dispense potions and charms that cured many ailments and bestowed fertility on brides seeking to become mothers. But this knowledge did not draw villagers willingly to Guilda because, even when she laughed, she seemed mildly crazy and a little scary.

Henry's uncertainty must have shown.

"Who do we have here?" Guilda said, eyeing him slyly. "A trembling field mouse perhaps. Or something for the cooking pot, maybe?"

"I'd watch my tongue if I were you, my only true love," Archer warned. "This is Henry, boar-slayer and wolf-tamer. Behave or I'll set him onto you."

"You call that a threat?" Guilda cackled through sparse teeth. "It's been longer than I can remember since young men felt disposed to set themselves on me."

"Pleased to meet you, madam," Henry said awkwardly.

"It's a polite one you have here, Archer. You could learn a thing or two from the lad. Put you horses under the shelter out back and come in from the rain, before we all die of ague. I've got mushroom broth on the boil, and there's plenty of cider.'

She was unconcerned when Bron padded beside her into the shack and settled close to the fire. Henry stabled the horses and joined the others. It was a bit smoky and the cluttered randomness continued with jars, potions, scrolls, books, and provisions stacked on shelves around the room. A labyrinth of cobwebs stretched across the roof into every corner.

Two beds stood on either side of the large room, a chunky wooden table and several stools occupied the centre. A bubbling cauldron hung over the fire and the soup smelt delicious. Guilda poured drinks from a firkin that lay against the wall.

"Drink up," she invited, "I have two more kegs stashed away, enough to last until apple-harvest when we can brew again."

It was tasty, made from fruit grown in Guilda's orchard deep in the woods. The apples also stored well and supplied her with a healthy supplement to her diet during winter.

"You should live in the village," Archer advised. "You wouldn't have to work so hard and you can beguile as many young fellows as you fancy."

"No, I think not. Folk may want my potions and cures at times, but I fear they'd have no time for an ancient like me."

"We do have other old people in Hollowford," Henry insisted.

"They'd probably drown me as a witch."

"You'd probably deserve it," Arched said.

"Don't you get lonely?" Henry persisted. Somehow Guilda didn't seem so sinister after you got to know her.

"True," she admitted, "but I have company at times and we had callers the other night. You and your kin up to mischief no doubt, Mistress Wolf."

Bron might have even looked a bit sheepish under Guilda's gaze.

"She's docile enough now," Henry said.

"Aye, a lone wolf would have little chance of survival," Guilda said.

"She catches enough food."

"Yes, and she'll live on small game all summer and autumn, but come winter when they're all buried snugly underground, she'll be hard pressed against anything bigger like a deer, unless it's old or sick. She might be lucky and find carrion, but who's to tell? It's not just food, you see. Wolves are sociable creatures that crave company. She'd rather be with you than be lonely. I'd say you've found a loyal friend there, Henry."

"She's proved that already. I think she's forgiven me for killing her mate."

"It may be that she just sees you as a stronger alternative. Wild creatures must be pragmatic. Life is short for many, so they don't have time to dwell on misfortune. We have mostly lost our contact with birds and beasts, but a few still hold onto that magical lore."

"The pack didn't harm you, it seems," Archer observed.

"Jongarrat led them away. He is one who has some skill with animals," she continued. "He's not back yet."

"I hope he's safe, I wanted to talk to him."

"So the truth is out, you blaggard! You've not come to visit me at all."

Archer had to do some fast talking to avoid Guilda's ruffled feathers, although teasing him was one of her favourite pastimes.

"Who's Jongarrat?" Henry asked.

"He lives here, you see," Guilda replied, but did not elaborate. "But, I sense it is you, Henry, with something on your mind. Do you want to tell me?"

Henry glanced at Archer, who nodded, so he quickly told

Guilda about his adventures. When he finished, Archer produced the amulets for Guilda to examine. She studied the treasures closely, squinting in the dim, smoky light.

"The runes are interesting," she said, "and the artisanship exquisite, but truth to tell, I've not seen the like before. As you say, Jongarrat may be able to help. He's always wandering far and wide."

"The scholars at Tremill Broch might know something," Archer suggested.

"Those buffoons with their heads in the clouds," Guilda retorted in a true assessment as the Tremill academics were fascinated by astronomy and astrology. "They wouldn't notice if the world caught fire around their precious island. Practicality isn't their strong point. These trinkets don't look like heirlooms to me. They're recently made for sure."

"Lady Ayla and Macayle set great store by Tremill Broch. Why they're travelling there soon to gaze at the sun and stars in some mysterious formation that only appears every hundred years, although how they know that is anyone's guess."

"Records, my boy. Almanacs, scrolls, and tomes by the score. They write down everything."

"Perhaps they've written something about the medallions."

Guilda merely shrugged.

"When will Jongarrat return?" Archer said.

"When the mood pleases him, it's his way," she replied, "but I might have a little something to relax you while we wait."

Guilda scratched among her phials, sacks, baskets and gourds. She placed a mixture of ingredients in a vessel and hung it on a spit beside the cauldron. The hut was soon infused with an intoxicating aroma that made Henry drowsy He was only half-aware of

Guilda's chant droning vaguely in the distance.

"Powder of eft skull and bantam blood,
Hawk's eye in brine to feed the brew,
Poppy seed and withered thyme,
Yarrow and mistletoe will do,
Nightshade and folk's glove,
Dried mandrake root, a pinch or two,
Star shine and moonbeams,
To charm our celestial dreams anew."

The ingredients morphed into an effervescent, clear liquid that fumed endlessly. Guilda doled the steaming mix into two bowls and passed one each to Archer and Henry. The lad looked doubtful, but Archer drew the concoction to his nose and inhaled, tossing his head backwards with closed eyes.

"Don't be afraid," Guilda crooned in Henry's ear. "The philtre will not harm you. Take up the vapours and sip the broth. You'll be rid of all woe for a while. See your friend Archer, I imagine you've never seen him so at peace."

Not that Henry had many woes, but Archer did look happy. Then again Archer wasn't exactly Henry's friend, so he didn't know how at peace Archer normally was. The reeve smiled and Henry was under the influence of the fumes by then. He breathed deeply and even sipped from the bowl. It tasted of mushrooms, herbs, and some unfamiliar flavours. Relaxed, he let his fancy drift where it chose. Henry became light-headed, his surroundings merged into hazy shadows and drifted away, only to rush back with acute clarity. The hut walls faded. He grew lighter, then weightless, and his body began to float. A feeling of freedom swept over him as he slowly rose and drifted straight through the thatched roof.

Soaring over the forest and finally above the clouds, he wondered absently where the rain had gone. The peaks of Enta Geweore emerged and he spied Hollowford and the northern wilderness through breaks in the weather, even glimpsing the sea beyond. He had never thought of water being there and had no idea of what terrain lay beyond Morbac Forest. There'd been no reason to go there, therefore no reason to think about it. Far off on the western shore, shrouded by mauve haze, he saw two glinting lights. Everything else faded to mist and he was only aware of the flickering orbs. They grew clearer until he identified them as medallions like the ones he found on the dead warriors. He made out each intricate design of swirling runes, so similar yet subtly different from the ones he knew. The gold and coloured crystals were mesmerising. They seemed to draw Henry, challenging him to come and claim them.

He hovered for a long time until, just as they emerged, the artefacts faded into drifting smoke. Henry didn't feel his descent, instead he simply found himself back on the stool. His mind cleared, leaving him mildly deflated as the euphoria drained. The hut was as he left it. Old Guilda was staring at him with amusement and rain still poured.

"Did you see me?" he asked.

"Yes, you've been right here all the time."

"No, you're mistaken. I flew through the roof, right into the sky. I could see everything for miles, even the ocean."

"The potion can do that, but you must use it sparingly or you may come to depend on the feeling."

"I saw more medallions."

"They might have just been these," she indicated the talismans on her table.

"No, they bore different signs."

"What are you babbling about, Henry?" Archer demanded, emerging from his dreams in a sour mood.

"I saw where the talismans come from, Archer. We must look for them on the west coast."

"It was a dream, just your imagination."

"Wait," Guilda said. "If outlanders have come, the western strand is a likely place to use."

She explained that the eastern shore of Grambak, where it joined a sea known as Black Water, was protected by a series of reefs called Ita Cay. Only mariners with sound local knowledge or foolhardy courage would attempt to navigate those shoals.

"Perhaps it's only a dream or possibly a portent, who knows?" Guilda said. "But, don't you think it's worth finding out?"

"You're right as always," Archer conceded. "I don't like the idea of strangers roaming about without knowing why."

So they talked on while sharing Guilda's soup, but left in time to be home before nightfall. They bid her farewell, promising to return before long.

"You're welcome to visit any time when you're hunting this way, Henry. Now that you see I'm quite harmless," Guilda called as she waved. "I'll tell Jongarrat you came by."

They rode back in silence. The rain was clearing and for a while the sun broke through the forest canopy. Bron disappeared again and returned with a large rabbit between her teeth.

As they neared the village, Archer turned to Henry.

"All right," he said, "if Gareth grants me leave to go traipsing around the countryside, you can come too, as my page or assistant, or whatever. Come on, we'll be home just in time for the feast."

We're home.
I stable Bella, wash and hurry to
Chief Gareth's hall.

I only hope Macayle will dance with me.
She's so pretty.

Chapter 4
Enta Geweore

Chief Gareth was an ample and enthusiastic man, whether feasting, carousing, hunting or waging war, he pursued them all with equal vigour. He'd reached an age when his flowing red hair and beard were flecked with grey. He always carried a double-bladed broadsword he'd appropriately named Goresax, which he wielded with bludgeoning effect. He was the bravest, toughest, most ruthless and cunning fellow around, which was precisely why he was chief. He sat upon his favourite chair with Ayla on his right and Macayle standing behind. Gareth's wife was a dozen years younger, sensually beautiful, serene, tactful, considerate, and charming. She was fifteen when she knew Gareth was the man for her, flirting with him outrageously and, even though every other Hollowford girl wanted to be his bride, she'd beguiled him completely. She begged her father to approach Gareth with a marriage proposal before another girl beat her to it. She needn't have worried, Gareth loved her and the negotiations were a mere formality. The wedding was held on Ayla's sixteenth birthday and the entire village grew to admire and cherish her. Macayle was Gareth and Ayla's only child, but hers was a difficult birth and, despite their enthusiasm, no other children followed. Even Guilda's potions proved futile.

When Henry and Archer arrived, the feast was in full swing

with the entire village crammed into Gareth's hall. A great fire blazed to roast the pork and vegetables. Other pots bubbled with tasty soups and sauces, while freshly baked loaves and fruit pies were stacked in baskets on the tables. Ale and mead flowed without restraint. The villagers dressed in their finest clothes, the ladies with embroidered gowns and the men in colourful tunics. The girls adorned their braided hair with spring blooms and were all in a coquettish mood. Everyone was having a great time.

"So you want to go roaming further, do you?" Gareth boomed, as it was not his way to whisper. "Fine reeve you are. Who will manage affairs while you're gone, may I ask?"

"Everything appears in order under your stewardship, lord," Archer parried glibly. Gareth didn't stand on ceremony. He was chief, everyone knew it, and no one challenged his authority. But, Archer enjoyed throwing in an honorific or two when wheedling his way round Gareth, although many villagers, including Henry, addressed their chief as lord out of respect and to keep on his good side.

"Flattery is it, you slippery-tongued scoundrel?"

"Why no, lord, just the plain truth and did you not agree that we best investigate any oddness close by?"

"The western strand is not close by."

"Indeed not, but we may not have to travel so far. And who knows, there might be more of Henry's precious lucre to be found."

Both Ayla and Macayle's eyes widened. They were girls who knew their priorities.

"Enticing baubles no doubt," Gareth conceded, "but their owners may not part with them willingly, and I do not believe we have yet stooped to highway robbery."

"Why, no such notion crossed my mind."

"Go where you must then. And while you're at it, see if you can spy out what the ruffian Olag Blackaxe is up to over at Velma."

Olag was the chief source of mischief for Hollowford. He led a large gang of cut-throats who constantly terrorised the town of Velma, where they made their winter quarters. Velma lay to the south and was squalid, vice-ridden and rat-infested, which suited the brigands handsomely. Hollowford folk seldom travelled there as it was dangerous and generally unprofitable. Blustery maybe, but Gareth was no fool. He was not much of a diplomat, but he was a shrewd strategist who knew the value of reconnaissance, especially when an enemy might become active as the weather improved.

"I can spare no one to go with you, mind," Gareth said. "I'll need Faranden to take over until you get back."

"I'll take Henry. He found the amulets after all."

"He could be useful and he is a boar-slayer now, but I daresay that's between you and the smith."

That was not entirely true, as chief Gareth could do pretty much as he pleased, although he did pay lip-service to the town council. The blacksmith's professional mystique afforded some privileges, but Archer omitted those niceties, making it sound like an order when he explained the plan to Edgar.

Feasting had put Gareth in an expansive mood and he allowed Archer to keep the medallions until they returned, but judging by Ayla and Macayle's expressions, Henry was just about resigned to losing them. Although Gareth would certainly consider compensation, Henry sullenly thought he should at least be given some choice.

"Enough business for tonight, Gareth dear," Ayla said. "Let's enjoy the festival."

So, Archer and Henry found a spot in the corner and Thayer brought them food and beer. Gareth made a short speech honouring Henry for providing the feast and everyone shook his hand, Macayle even kissed him on the cheek.

"Do you know much about swordsmanship?" Archer asked after the arrangements were made with Edgar.

"I've got a fine sword now. Uncle inspected it and said the workmanship was sound."

"That's not what I asked. Owning a weapon and being able to use it are not the same."

"I'm all right, I guess."

Henry could hold his own when practising with the village lads using wooden swords. Working in the forge gave him an insight into the balance and maintenance of weapons, but essentially his and Archer's idea of "all right" were two different concepts.

"I'm sure we'll have time for extra coaching along the way," Archer said. "Until then, let's hope any vagabonds we meet are either too stupid or hungry to cause trouble."

A troupe of musicians started playing bagpipes, flutes, rebecs, and drums so everyone turned their attention to dancing and singing long into the night. As Henry was the hero of the hour, Macayle was happy to dance with him.

Hollowford awoke late the next day, except Archer, who arrived just after dawn and roused Henry.

"C'mon, if you want to stay up and drink with the men at night, you can get up with the men in the morning."

Not that there was evidence of any other men up and about, but Archer didn't seem to think that was the point. They set out in weather that heralded an improvement. The ashen mist lifted and although thunder showers swept down the slopes of Enta Geweore, sunlight flashed earthwards through widening gaps of blue. Thayer once again provided food for their journey otherwise they carried only their weapons and the clothes they wore. Despite his name, Archer didn't always carry a bow, and this was such an occasion. He had the reputation of being a good shot, but said he'd leave the hunting to Henry, whom he acknowledged was even better.

They made their way into the foothills where the forest thinned and was replaced by scattered groves of spruce, maple, and aspen. Archer explained that Enta Geweore meant Giant's Work in an old language that few people spoke anymore. According to a legend, two mighty giants called Bull Brow and Staff Waver fell for the same girl. She was a virtuous little miss whose name was somehow forgotten with time. The titans felt disposed to fight for her and they were equally matched because no one was able to forge weapons big enough for them. So they stood a great distance apart and started hurling boulders at one other that piled high enough to form the mountains. The pits they dug to gather the rocks filled with water and became the seas that surrounded Grambak.

"Who won?" Henry asked.

"It turned out that neither was a very good shot so no real damage was done. Unfortunately, the noise they made gave the lass a headache so she ran off with a ship's captain to sail the southern oceans. She was never seen again. It was probably just as well, because what the giants planned for such a dainty maiden is anyone's guess. It appeared they were poor swimmers and unable to follow, so they skulked to the northern snow lands and that's where they remain as far as anyone knows."

"I've never heard that story before."

"You should get out more. Guilda knows scores of tales. I believe hundreds of legends are recorded in the library at Tremill Broch, the trouble is the wizards and scholars there aren't a very friendly lot. They're not over-fond of visitors, although they don't seem to mind Ayla and Macayle. Mind that wee minx Macayle can twist anyone around her little finger, she teases Faranden like mad."

"Aunt Thayer taught me to read and write, but I'm not much good at it."

"Like everything, it takes practice. I think I'd have the same problem as you. Why don't you keep a chronicle and record your adventures when we get home?"

"Aunt Thayer would like that."

Most Hollowford folk had neither opportunity nor inclination to embrace literacy, but Thayer thought it important. Edgar couldn't see the point, but he liked her to read to him from their small collection of books and admired her skill with numbers. She even kept a ledger recording the forge accounts.

They rode on until late afternoon.

"We'll camp yonder," Archer indicated a copse. "It looks like good shelter."

Although snow patches remained, there was ample grazing for the horses. Henry built a fire and gathered fuel to last all night. Bron proved invaluable and not only produced her own supper, but presented Henry and Archer with a plump rabbit each. Although Henry was capable of bagging game with his bow, she saved him time and effort. Having justified her presence, Bron settled by the fire. Water was never an issue as they crossed numerous mountain streams of wonderfully fresh snow-melt.

"It's always safe to drink from these streams," Archer explained. "No one is putting their grubby feet into the water — or worse."

Most folk believed Hollowford's community grew because aside from the creek, it lay above a spring of pure water that was accessed from a well. As the town grew, two more wells were dug, ensuring an ample water-supply. Lady Ayla had learnt from the Tremill scholars that village waste not consumed by pigs and fowls should be taken far from the water source, dried, and used as soil conditioner in the crop fields. As a result, Hollowford remained virtually disease-free and most people drank ale anyway, thus avoiding any risk of sickness. Even so, Henry believed mountain water tasted best of all.

Archer insisted they complete an hour's sword training every day. Henry was strong and possessed natural balance and agility. Despite his terse ways, Archer proved a patient instructor. Even though Henry often found himself on his backside, he was pleased with his improving skill. He was a fast learner and Archer was never able to fool him by repeating a ruse. Thus they practised amid the clash of tempered iron and vermilion sparks from their sword-blades.

"Enough!" Archer declared at last. "We'll chop ourselves to bits in the dark."

"Don't I have to learn to fight at night?" Henry gasped.

"There's little difference. You just have to be more on the sly."

They ate supper hunched around the fire. Henry discovered Bron liked having her neck stroked like a domestic dog. Guilda's observation was proving true and they were becoming close friends.

"Fighting is about conviction," Archer reflected as he tossed another log on the fire, sending a shower of glowing cinders skyward.

"Conviction?"

"Absolutely. Most people can learn the tricks of the trade. You know — thrusts, ripostes, parries, footwork, all the moves, and so on. You'll hear a lot of nonsense about honour and chivalry too, but in a stiff fight that's worthless. You beat your enemy any way you can. If it means sneaking up from behind and bashing his brains out, do it. It's not enough to dance around with fancy swordplay, although the basic skills are important."

"I hadn't thought about the motivation for fighting before," Henry admitted.

"It comes with the moment."

They talked for a while then took turns to guard the camp through the night, but weren't troubled by bandits or animals. Bron would not have let anyone approach without warning anyway.

The morning was brisk with only the occasional creamy cloud bubbling into the sky.

"We'll be among the mountains today," Archer said. "We go by way of Estelle Col. It's the only pass through."

They rode on. Kites and harriers soared effortlessly above them, some so high that they were mere specks. It reminded Henry of his dream in Guilda's hut. He envied the raptors' freedom until Archer said they spent all their lives searching for prey and were probably hungry most of the time. Spruce and mountain ash woodland grew between rocky outcrops to the sides of the pathway through Estell

Col. Archer scanned about before he reined up. He glanced back along the trail. Bron was equally ill-at-ease.

"Trouble, I'd say. Someone is following us," Archer whispered.

"Wild animals?"

"Wild men, more like."

"Shall we make a run for it?"

"Not yet. We don't know how many, and we don't want to go blundering into an ambush."

As they continued, the pass narrowed, but not alarmingly. Henry judged the tree-line to be just beyond accurate bow-range, which was comforting. He couldn't detect any movement in the woodland, but Archer was in no doubt.

"There are several of them, and they're singularly careless about stalking us."

They came to a bend in the trail where a figure stood. He was a scrawny, wrinkled, goblin-like fellow with an enormous hooked nose and large, pointed ears. He was mostly skin-and-bone, but stood haughtily with his head cocked to one side and one hand on his hip while lounging on his sword hilt. As Archer and Henry drew their horses to a halt his companions emerged from the woods. There were more than a dozen of them, scruffy and under-nourished, but armed with daggers, clubs and axes.

"Top o' t' mornin' to youse, sors," the ragged villain greeted pertly. "Tis a foin day to be travellin', now that it is to be sure."

"Indeed," Archer replied coolly, "if we're not delayed along the way."

"No, sor me darlin', we'd not be detainin' youse long at all and that's the truth. It's just a wee donation from your benevolence we'd be seekin'."

"How wee, rogue?"

"Well, sor, tis a moighty foin horse you'd be ridin', as I judge, and the boy's to be sure. A coin or two you'd be carrying, now wouldn't youse? In fact we can relieve youse of your entire burden, so we can, sor."

"You want to take everything we have?'"

"That, sor, I'd say is about the size of it."

"And if we choose not to make a contribution?"

"Ah, sor me darlin', that would be unfortunate, so it would. In truth we are men of commerce and abhor violence, but as you see there is a bunch o' us and only the pair o' youse."

The grinning bandits were closing in and contrary to their leader's opinion looked as if they'd commit murder for pure joy.

"Stay close, Henry," Archer whispered. "Do whatever I do and stay close!"

"Now sor, I think we've been civil long enough, what's it to be?" the goblin-man demanded.

"I'll tell you, sir," Archer said evenly between gritted teeth. "Either get out of our path or I'll drop you where you stand."

Archer drew his sword and dug his heels into his charger's flanks. The horse leapt forward and Archer drove his sword hilt onto the vagabond chief's skull with a crack and the scoundrel fell limply. Henry kicked Bella into action as well, all too aware of the babbling horde closing in behind.

They galloped around the bend and saw they were trapped.

A barricade of rocks and logs spread right across the pass at its narrowest point. It was as high as a man with no way around. The bandits must have taken days to build the barrier.

"We're going over! Stay with me!" Archer yelled without breaking his horse's stride.

Henry struggled to stay in the saddle. Bron detoured to the

side, disappearing beyond the tree-line, but Henry had no choice. The rag-tag charge was right on his heels. Archer was upon the fence in seconds and his horse hurdled across just clipping the top with its hind hooves. Bella may have been an ex-warrior's horse, but she baulked at the barricade, throwing Henry to the ground. He crashed into timber and rock, winded but unhurt, while Bella simply stood beside him.

Henry grabbed his bow from the saddle. Although his arrows were strewn over the ground, he gathered a couple, carefully aimed, and shot. He took one of the bandits fairly in the torso. His next arrow wounded another in the leg. The bandits' advance continued, although more cautiously. There was no time to retrieve further arrows, so Henry tossed the bow aside, drew his sword, and charged. He pitched into the gang of thieves, swinging the blade with both hands and cursing at the top of his lungs. With shuddering force, his first blow severed the arm of one villain. A second stroke landed against a skull, and another bandit shrieked as Henry's blade ripped across his belly.

But there were too many, and Henry was in danger of being overrun. Although, in the stress and excitement he didn't see it, another rogue fell with an arrow in his chest. The rest hesitated, then turned and fled in panic. Bron bounded back from the trees in time to give chase, snapping at their heels. The stunned leader staggered to his feet and stumbled after his companions with the two brigands Henry had wounded.

"Yeah, you want some more?" Henry bellowed. "Just come back any time. I'll be ready."

He called Bron, who abandoned the pursuit and trotted back to his side as he recovered his breath.

Henry turned and saw Archer poised with the bow he'd

discarded.

Three men lay dead before them, the one who'd been struck on the head and the two victims of Henry and Archer's arrows. In their malnourished condition, it was unlikely the wounded brigands would survive either, but Henry conceded he might not have been so lucky against fitter men.

"Thanks for the help," Henry gasped.

"It took me a moment to get back over the fence. I bagged one of 'em for you, but it looked to me like you were managing anyway. Now that's what I'd call conviction. You're a right little scorpion when your fire's lit, ain't you? Remind me not to get on your bad side."

Henry's blood cooled and the excitement faded. As he stared at the corpses, the realisation of what he'd done dawned upon him.

"Archer, I have just killed people."

"Yes, but they weren't very big…"

"No, I mean I just did it. I felt nothing other than I wanted to fight. It was like I lost control."

"You'd better get used to it because that's how things work out sometimes. Maybe we'll make a warrior out of you yet, and they were bad fellows after all."

There is so much to take in. I wonder if I shall remember later.
Forget, how can I forget what I've learned about Archer?
How does he take life-and-death so casually?
And what have I learnt about myself?
Am I going to be the same?
I mean hunting for food is one thing, but killing men..?

Archer says I should name my sword now it has tasted blood.
He calls his Avenger and his axe Skull-Crusher.
Not very subtle, I know, but Archer doesn't
seem to be a subtle fellow to me.
I chose Hornet-Sting and he agreed it is a good name.

Chapter 5
Urdec and Walter

They weren't bothered by wild men again as they crossed Estell Col and descended into open moorland beyond. It was a desolate place where relentless gales swept salt-spray a mile inland. The sight of the ocean was at first daunting, but magnificent. Its indigo deepness and breakers that battered the cliffs with a continuous roar was beyond anything Henry imagined. He also saw bleakness, suggesting life was a challenge in these parts.

They passed scattered shepherd crofts and fishermen's shanties. The occupants looked under-nourished yet still able to produce large quantities of spindle-limbed children. Dull eyes followed them. Whenever they asked about the amulets the response was uniformly brooding or down-right hostile.

"Friendly lot," Henry observed.

"They're just not used to strangers," Archer said with uncharacteristic empathy.

In time they came to Burgal, set by a cove cut into the cliffs. It was the largest settlement they'd come across on the west coast, but still just a group of squalid shelters flung together. The town did boast an inn, a simple structure close to the pebbly shore where fishing currachs were drawn up beyond the high-tide line. They left their horses in a stable beside the inn and entered. Sensing

Burgal's antagonism, Bron stayed close to Henry.

"Greetings, friend," Archer said to the landlord, a bald headed man who didn't reply.

"Folk hereabouts seem dispossessed of their tongues."

"We keep to ourselves, it works better for us," the innkeeper retorted.

"Not a lot of passing trade?"

"Nope."

"Then you're in luck, because my companion and I require board for the night. And how may I address you, my jolly host?"

"Name's Walter Rumple, if it's any business of yourn, and we ain't got no room."

Archer reached over the counter and grabbed Walter by his collar, hauling him half-way across the bar.

"Well, friend Walter, I suggest you find some, because I have no intention of spending another night in the wild when I can have a perfectly good roof over my head."

"Yer got money?" Walter gasped.

"Enough for your flea-pit, I daresay."

Walter thawed a little when Archer produced two coppers. It was generous, considering the standard of accommodation.

"And now, sir, a beverage for this young fellow and me, if you please."

Walter complied.

"Lived here long?" Archer probed, returning to his cheerfulness despite the landlord's truculence.

"All me life. Inn belonged to me pa."

"Then you must know what goes on around here, and you might just know something about these."

Archer laid the medallions on the counter. This had its risks as they were worthy of larceny with violence, but Archer judged any prospective thieves to be in poor condition. With Henry's help he could easily deal with them. Walter shuddered measurably at the sight of the artefacts.

"No, I ain't seen nothin' like 'em," he mumbled after a pause.

"Now that is a puzzlement, because the very sight of them seems to have put your teeth on edge."

Sweat glistened on Walter's brow.

"I tell you, I don't know nothin'."

"You'll forgive me if I'm not convinced, but we'll let that pass. If you are indeed so ignorant, perhaps there is someone we can ask, an alderman or chief, a village elder perhaps?"

"There ain't no one like that. Folk 'ereabouts does pretty much as they please, and minds their own business."

Archer heaved a sigh and glared at the innkeeper.

"Now, friend Walter, I've asked you civilly and I really don't want any unpleasantness, but I believe you know more than you're letting on. Tell me what you know or there will be unpleasantness. You're hiding something, Walter."

"No, sir, not me," Walter quaked miserably, "but, I tell you what. Go and see Urdec the druid, 'e's the man to see."

"A druid eh, pious little community are we? Very well, where can I find your druid?"

Walter explained the way. It wasn't far, so Archer and Henry left immediately with Bron beside them, following a muddy track towards the cliff tops. By then the sun was dipping to the horizon in a crimson ball. Dusk over the ocean was another new sensation for Henry, although the season of long twilights had begun and daylight would remain for several hours.

"Walter was very uncomfortable," Henry observed.

"I daresay he was worried about us running him through before we left. Wouldn't have taken much for me to do it either."

Henry felt their progress was being observed, although he saw no one. They came upon Urdec's home on the lee-side of the cliffs, giving some protection from westerly gales. A few stunted trees grew in a ring, but they were the only growth above knee-height anywhere near Burgal. Urdec's shelter stood in front of the arbour. It was made of stone, flotsam, and dead branches while peat turf covered the roof. A dozen man-high boulders formed a cromlech with the shack at its head. Henry knew that tree and stone circles were important for people who set store by spiritual ceremonies, so Urdec lived with a ring of trees behind him and a stone circle in front. Powerful symbols indeed.

Bric-a-brac surrounded the shelter, including bird feathers, animal bones and pelts, coloured stones, stag antlers, crude wooden statues, and scrimshaw carved into whale bones. Several tall poles stood with coloured rags, twines, and what looked suspiciously like scalps flapping from them. Bowls and pitchers were scattered around and a fire smouldered with unpleasant incense. There was no sign of Urdec, but something particularly caught their attention. Two medallions dangled from the post along with the other jumbled bunting.

"They're like my dream," Henry whispered.

"Just so, Henry, but we still don't know what they mean and right now that's not our immediate concern."

Bron bared her teeth and growled.

Men, women and children appeared from every shadow. They were armed with clubs, axes, daggers, scythes, sickles, hammers, and stout branches. Maybe they didn't look particularly well fed, but that was outweighed by determination, minacity, and sheer numbers.

Then Urdec appeared.

He stood on the wall, a bloated toad of a man dressed in a muck-stained surplice. His eyes bulged from a face of blubber as his pallid lips quivered, slobbering drool. His beard was mere wisps of white hair. Small animal skulls were draped around his neck and he carried a staff with the corpse of a hawk impaled on its end. His belly swelled, suggesting he was the only well fed person around.

"Behold!" he shrieked. "They stand thus, foul, wretched vassals of darkness. They will be judged, this degenerate offal of the depths. They seek to destroy, yet shall they be destroyed. In the name of the Great Triumvirate: Blowvane of the Sky, Great Orcbut of the Sea, and Bellous the Terrible of Earth, shall they be judged."

The raving continued for several tedious minutes. Urdec hurled curses upon the strangers, damning them to hideous and everlasting tortures for crimes against his gods who would surely be avenged, making Henry wonder what grim deities abided hereabouts. Whereas he respected the individual spirits of most living things, he'd never considered gods as being particularly interested in human affairs, so Urdec's entreaties sounded foolishly presumptuous. Nobody told gods what they should do.

The tirade left Urdec panting, but it had the desired effect on the villagers. They surged forward yelling for blood. Henry drew his sword, judging this to be a far different fight than seeing off a gang of half-starved ruffians. Bron snarled and braced for an attack, but to Henry's dismay, Archer turned and bolted away.

But he didn't go far. He was at the wall in a couple of bounds and hauled Urdec from his perch. Archer grabbed the druid's skull necklace and twisted it until he choked and his face turned purple.

Urdec struggled, but Archer drew his sword and held it to the druid's neck with enough force to draw a rivulet of blood.

"Stop where you are!" Archer bellowed just as the villagers were about to overwhelm Henry and Bron. "One more step and you'll need a new priest. I'll slit his throat and then some of yours, make no mistake about that."

The mob froze, but stayed poised menacingly close to Henry, and eyeing Bron warily.

"Call them off," he hissed in Urdec's ear, "or I'll part your head from your shoulders. For all your piety, I fancy you've no wish to meet your gods any sooner than necessary."

He flung Urdec forward, keeping a tight hold of his necklace.

"Cease!" the druid cried. "In the name of the Three Deities, put down your weapons."

After some hesitation, the crowd sullenly obeyed and moved away from Henry. It seemed the heat had gone out of them. Urdec, on the other hand, was in a mood of venomous loathing.

"The gods will be avenged," he snarled. "You have defiled their servant. There will be no peace for your folly. You are condemned to eternal agony and I rejoice for it."

More saliva dripped through his rotten teeth and onto his robe.

"Oh, pull yourself together, man," Archer said wearily. "We don't see why you wish us harm, because we don't plan to hurt anyone."

It didn't look as if they'd get any sense out of Urdec, but Archer hung onto him for insurance.

"I understand you have no chief," Archer addressed the crowd. "Is there anyone who will speak for you, a witan or village council maybe?"

There was a fair amount of mumbling and shuffling in the

crowd, followed by some head-nodding and back-slapping as Walter was gently nudged forward.

"Urdec normally tells us what to do," the innkeeper explained.

"I don't think he's up to it right now."

The crowd shook its collective head uncertainly. The immediate threat was past and the villagers mellowed noticeably, although Henry sensed their instability and knew they could easily flare again. Archer released Urdec, who scuttled back to his shelter and drew a cover across its entrance. Soon a baleful chanting was heard from within.

"I can't think straight with all that caterwauling. A good thump behind the ear should shut him up," Archer said, turning to make good his threat.

"Wait, lord," Walter stammered.

Archer turned back and raised his eyebrows, noting the inn-keeper's change in attitude.

"Come away back to my tavern. Our priest ain't 'imself at the moment, 'e's prone to vapours, but 'e'll be restored by tomorrow. It's best to leave 'im be for now."

"Why do you put up with him?" Henry asked.

"It's always been so," Walter said lamely. "It's the way we are, it's the way 'e is, it's as the gods decree."

There they go again, Henry thought, *who knows what gods want?*

Archer shrugged. If that was what they wanted, well so be it. He certainly needed to talk to someone sensible. The crowd had simmered down and beating their priest into silence might cause them to erupt once more. Above all, Archer felt like a mug of beer. So the procession marched back to Burgal, the villagers seemed far less hostile without Urdec's influence. There wasn't room for everyone, but many squeezed into the tavern while others hovered at the door. Walter opened the shutters and faces filled the window frames.

"My name is Archer, reeve for Chief Gareth of Hollowford, over Morbac Forest way."

There was a good deal of nodding at that, so obviously some villagers knew about Hollowford.

"My companion, Henry, and I came here peaceably, yet you'd have our blood for no clear reason."

"It's them things," Walter said, meaning the medallions.

"So they portend no good hereabouts?"

"That's right."

"Then how did Urdec come by a couple? Where did he get them?"

"It's raiders, y' see. They come two summers past and took our youngsters."

"Took them where?"

"Dunno. They just come at night and snatches maybe 'alf-a-dozen lads and lasses. They hide in the cliffs and nab young folk mindin' sheep. We got to take the flocks to pasture, see. Can't let 'em starve or we'd starve too."

"And the pastures are along the cliff tops?"

"Aye, first time we caught two of 'em before they got away in their currachs. They had them things round their necks. Urdec keeps 'em for spells and such to keep the raiders away."

"But they don't stay away?" Henry suggested.

"No, they're probably lurkin' around the cliffs right now with spring weather back."

"Do they take livestock?"

"Nope, just the young uns."

"They must eat something."

Walter shrugged and Henry felt the uneasiness of the folk around him.

"Maybe that's why they take the kids," he said.

Everyone exchanged looks, but no one wanted to pursue that particular line of thought.

"Have you tried to hunt them out?" Archer asked.

"Can't find 'em. There are 'undreds of caves and passages through the cliffs, plenty of places to 'ide, and plenty of spots to set an ambush."

"Parlous bunch of rascals, indeed. What about the two you caught?"

"Burnt 'em at the stake," Walter replied softly.

"And we all know whose idea that was, don't we?" Henry added.

"Did you happen to ask them where they were taking your people?" Archer said.

"Well, no. Urdec said we should destroy 'em right off. 'E told us the sea god must 'ave been offended some'ow and we was cursed. 'E said we 'ad to sacrifice the raiders to stop 'em comin' back."

"Which doesn't seem to have worked," Archer observed. "I cannot judge the will of your gods, but perhaps if you'd been less inclined to roast your prisoners they might have told you where they came from. I fancy too many hasty decisions are made around here. You were quite happy to see us sliced and diced not so long ago."

"But why are you 'ere? Where did you get them things?"

"We're here to discover the secret of the talismans. We found these two close to home and it appears the owners are trouble-makers, so Chief Gareth wants to know all about them. I guess it's up to us to find out."

"'Ow do you intend to do that?"

"Catching another couple of the raiders might be a good start."

"But 'ow?"

"Why, set a trap of course, and I think I know just what to use for bait."

By *what* Archer actually meant *who*.

Great!
What if I wasn't around?
I bet Archer wouldn't be out here alone.
I'm sick of being taken for granted by Mr High-and-Mighty!
I mean 'Archer', why is that even his name?
I'm a better bow-shot than him.

Wish I had it with me now, but he said I wouldn't need it.
He didn't want stray arrows flying around at night.
Worried I'd hit him, I suppose.

Chapter 6
Night Work at Burgal

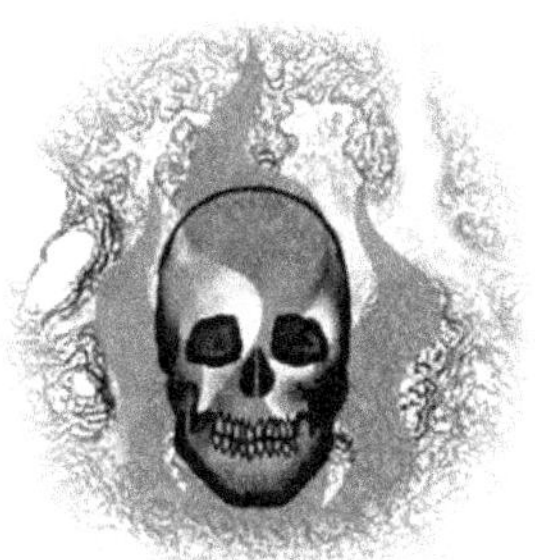

Henry shivered. It was midnight. It wasn't even as if Archer had asked. He just assumed Henry would agree with his plan. Well, next time Henry would be more assertive. Of course that was if there was a next time.

He trudged along the cliff top, herding a dozen sheep. Not being a shepherd, he wasn't very good at it, but Bron kept the flock bunched. There was ample moonlight and occasionally he peered below to see the eerie phosphorescence of pounding waves. Height might have bothered him, but there was more to worry about than a spot of vertigo. Fleas and all, Walter's loft seemed pretty inviting right now. Maybe there was no one up here. It was still early in the season.

But that wasn't the case.

Half-a-dozen spectres loomed like shadows, almost formless, certainly faceless under their black hoods. They rose from the heather and surged towards him. Henry drew his sword. They swarmed around him, nervously dodging as he swept the blade in a lethal arc. They were agile, but their flapping mantles hindered them.

They darted about, but weren't as aggressive as Henry expected. Perhaps they weren't used to resistance or Bron snapping at them, although she still had to dodge their weapons. One of them screamed as Henry drew first blood, but the jarring blow knocked him off balance. His attackers saw their chance and tackled him to the ground, piling onto him. Henry kicked and clawed, but they pinned his legs and arms and no amount of struggling would shake them off. Bron grabbed one attacker's cloak and tried to pull him away, but in the frenzy he took no notice.

"Archer!" Henry bellowed before a rag was rammed between his teeth. One of the mysterious figures drew a rope from his tunic and started to tie Henry's hands and feet.

Just when Henry expected to be dragged away to someone's cooking pot, the attackers relented. Chaos followed as Archer and the Burgal villagers arrived in a fighting mood. They laid into the midnight stalkers, but didn't have it all their own way. The strangers fought desperately and did some damage.

"Up you get," Archer said, cutting Henry free and hauling him to his feet.

The fight swirled around them, dissolving into individual struggles with each raider fending off a dozen villagers. A few Burgal men were nicked and bruised before they clubbed a couple of raiders to the ground while the others turned and ran, fading into the night.

"They're getting away!" someone yelled.

"Stop them!"

Damn right! Henry spat the gag out and raced after the escaping men who scattered and were soon lost except one. Henry wanted him so badly. It was heavy going and he stumbled over heather tussocks, but he was gaining. Just before reaching the cliff edge, Henry dived and grabbed the man's legs. They crashed to the ground, viciously wrestling and punching when other raiders reappeared with Bron snarling at their ankles.

Not again, Henry thought.

But, before they could overpower him, the ground gave way and they all plunged over the edge. Fortunately, the cliff was not sheer and they tumbled down to a shingle beach in an avalanche of peat-turf and scree. Henry clung to his opponent and thumped to a stop on top of him. That cushioned his fall, but the raider was winded and out cold. They rolled a little way and only stopped when a wave surged over them. The others staggered to their feet just as the villagers clambered down the slope. Seeing all was lost, they scrambled into their beached currach and shoved off. They rowed frantically and were nearly pitched over by breakers, but once they cleared the surf, someone hoisted a sail and they swept away to sea. The villagers hurled rocks after them with little effect, but the citizens of Burgal felt better.

Archer strolled onto the beach without showing any particular concern. Once again he hauled Henry to his feet, just as the last raider stirred.

"You're getting quite good at this," Archer said cheerfully. "Let's hear what this fine fellow has to say for himself if you haven't maimed him too critically."

"You're welcome," Henry snorted, *a thank you would be nice.*

He was cold and wet with a salty taste in his mouth, which surprised him because water wasn't supposed to taste like that.

The cloaked figure rose shakily to his knees and stopped when Archer placed the point of his sword to his throat.

"Go on then," the raider challenged, "finish me off."

"You seem in an uncommon hurry to die," Archer observed.

"Better a sword in the gizzard than frying at the stake."

Of course Urdec's method of dealing with kidnappers hadn't gone unnoticed and this raider obviously knew the risks. He didn't seem nearly as barbaric as Walter and Urdec had suggested. Their captive was a slightly built man only a few years older than Henry with flowing yellow, almost white, hair.

The villagers had suffered a few cuts and bruises, but nothing major provided their wounds didn't fester, which was a distinct possibility in Burgal. They had also recovered enough to start baying for the prisoner's blood and looked as if they'd tear him apart right there on the beach.

"There's been enough excitement for tonight, don't you think?" Archer said. "We'll take this rogue to the inn and look after our wounded. We're all exhausted, so let's get a couple of hours sleep and sort things out in the morning when everyone's calmed down."

They scrambled up the cliff, gathered the two other prisoners who'd been pretty badly roughed up by then, and returned to Burgal. No one noticed a stooped, lone figure following at a distance. Occasionally Bron turned and bared her teeth, but Henry called her and she loped after the villagers.

They secured the prisoners to a stout wooden pillar that supported the tavern roof before the villagers went home. Henry and Archer hoisted Bron into the loft then joined her. They fell asleep immediately.

74

Henry could have slept all day, but that wasn't an option. It seemed as if his eyes had just closed when Archer shook him awake.

"C'mon, Henry," he said, "the prisoners have gone."

"Escaped?"

"I don't think so. They were trussed up tight. Looks like Walter's gone too. I'm betting our friend Urdec slipped into town while we slept and nabbed 'em. I've got a bad feeling. The crowd was in a nasty mood last night."

They grabbed their weapons, dashed outside, and headed for Urdec's cromlech, but heard the commotion well before they got there. The whole of Burgal crowded around the stones, some people even perched on them for a better view. There was a great deal of jeering and fist waving. With everyone's attention drawn to the centre of the stone ring, they were unaware of Henry, Archer, and Bron approaching.

"What's going on?" Archer demanded, grabbing the nearest spectator's arm.

"See for yourself."

The crowd parted for Archer and Henry.

Urdec stood before the crowd chanting in a language Henry didn't understand, but to which the villagers regularly responded with a unanimous roar. The druid gyrated and gestured wildly, agitating the villagers into frenzy. Three stakes were driven into the ground behind Urdec with a prisoner tied to each one. Kindling and lumber were stacked waist-high around them. The villagers must have scoured Burgal for the combustibles.

Archer and Henry reached the centre. Urdec confronted them waving his staff while Walter stood beside the stakes, holding a firebrand.

"Stop this, Urdec!" Archer commanded. His only authority was his sword.

"You forbid me?" Urdec sneered. "How dare you hinder me in the Deities' work? These miscreants are condemned to fire. We will burn all who come until they come no more. You cannot stop us performing the will of the gods."

Who are these gods? Henry wondered. *If they were any good they'd have stopped the raiders coming in the first place.* He considered it best not to bother gods, because no one really knew how they'd react.

Archer drew his sword and, seeing the mood of the villagers, Henry did the same.

"Maybe so, but I've come a long way to learn about these amulets. I intend to find out today, so you will have to wait!" Archer replied.

Archer glared at Urdec, who hesitated, as did the villagers. They were naturally timorous, but their mood could swing quickly.

"I know you're angry," Archer addressed the crowd, "but anyone who tries to harm these men will have to go through me. Any takers?"

They shuffled and grumbled, but no one accepted the challenge.

"Watch my back, Henry," Archer whispered. "Yell if they get restless."

He turned and faced the staked prisoner before him. It was the same man Henry had captured. He was afraid, but determined to face death courageously. Their eyes met and Archer sensed his defiance, admiring him for that spirit at least. He pulled the medallions from his tunic and dangled them in front of the raider's nose.

"I want to know about these," Archer said softly. "These people think they're evil. I'm inclined to agree, and you're connected to them. As you can see, you have nothing to lose by telling me."

"As you say, I have nothing to lose," the man said through gritted teeth, "but by the same token, I have nothing to gain. I'm doomed to the fire, so let's save our breath and get it over with."

"This business has tried my patience enough," Archer declared acidly.

He raised his sword and as the prisoner flinched, the blade swept down and slashed through the ropes binding him. Archer grabbed his collar and marched him from the cromlech.

"He's as guilty as the rest," Walter challenged while Urdec was reduced to babbling gibberish.

"You can have him back when I've finished with him," Archer roared, barging through the crowd.

The villagers parted sullenly while Henry and Bron formed a rear-guard in case any of them grew daring. As soon as they were clear, Archer stopped.

"Now listen," Archer hissed in the raider's ear, "We can make a bolt for it and probably get away, but not until you tell me what these medallions are all about. You'd better be quick before Urdec riles them up again."

"So the Starkmen have come to plague you too," the prisoner replied enigmatically.

"Who?"

But he would say no more.

"You want information," he continued after a moment's pause, "and I can give it to you, but not until my people are safely away from here."

"That's impossible! Those vigilantes want your blood. Who can blame them? You stole their children after all."

At that moment, Urdec's patience was exhausted and he ordered Walter to light the fires. There was a sudden whoosh and the kindling blazed into life, followed by the crackling of a steadier fire. Both men at the stake screamed and the crowd roared with approval.

"For pity's sake!" the prisoner pleaded.

"Tell me what you know." Archer bellowed above the din.

"If you get us away."

"For you, yes. The others are lost. I can do nothing for them."

"Then you better take me back to die with them."

"And that would be really useful, wouldn't it? Henry, take this idiot back to Burgal fast as you can. If he causes any trouble, stick an arrow in his eye, he'll still be able to talk. Get the horses ready. Hurry!"

"What are you going to do?"

"Ease a little suffering."

Archer turned to the prisoner.

"Go with the lad and don't try to escape because he's a good shot with that bow. Now be off!"

The crowd was distracted by the horror before them, so Henry and his captive raced away unnoticed. And Archer marched back to the stakes.

Henry and the prisoner hurried along the path to Burgal. They weren't followed and they met no one. Everybody was at the executions. Henry bolted into the inn and grabbed their gear. He threw the saddles onto the horses and with the prisoner's help strapped the girths tightly. The only other animals in the stall were a dozen black-faced sheep.

"Can you ride?" Henry asked.

"I'll stay on."

"Get up behind me," Henry ordered "We're the lightest, so best for us to ride double."

"What about the others?"

"Trust me, there'll only be three of us."

Meanwhile, the crowd at Urdec's cromlech had turned ugly.

"They burn! They burn!" the druid chanted and the crowd echoed hypnotically. It took so little to whip them to insanity, but Archer was relying on their timid souls being easily daunted. The fires were firmly ablaze and the two victims were tearing at their bonds. Urdec beseeched his Austere Trinity to enhance their suffering in any way possible.

"Druid, this is barbaric!" Archer stormed.

"Do not trifle with the Great Ones' work, cursed heretic!"

Drool sluiced down Urdec's chin. He was beside himself with sanctimonious joy at the sight of human misery.

"The gods will not be defied! Do you not fear their mightiness?"

"Possibly, but I don't fear you, priest!"

Archer flung Urdec aside. He drew his sword and sprang towards the stakes. Disregarding the pain he slashed the blade through the flames. The first wretched captive died instantly, Archer's sword flashed again and the other raider joined him.

At least I made it quick. You may have deserved to die, but not to burn.

Urdec cursed and leapt onto Archer's back, his fist flailing. Archer tossed him off with no more than a shrug and the druid fell into the inferno. Urdec's surplice erupted in flames and fire engulfed him. He shrieked as he rolled clear, charring his hands as he tried to beat out the flames. The villagers stood stunned, frightened and confused, until several gathered their wits and rushed to their prelate's aid.

Archer dashed into the throng who scattered. They knew the power of his sword and fell over each other to run clear. People wailed as they were trampled in panic. Archer wished them no harm, but that wasn't going to stop him damaging anybody who stood in his way.

"After him! Don't let him escape!" Walter yelled.

Somehow emboldened by the furore, he rallied Burgal's folk as anger restored their courage. They gathered their weapons and ran pell-mell after Archer who was fitter, better nourished, and able to out-pace them.

Henry and his prisoner heard the crowd's steady roar that suddenly turned to a wail of hostile protest..

The prisoner clambered up behind Henry and led Archer's horse onto the path. They cantered towards Urdec's shelter to see Archer racing towards them with the entire village streaming after him. They screamed viciously as a hail of missiles — axes, farm tools, and rocks — thudded into the ground at his heels. The horses shied at the commotion and nearly threw the riders, but they hung on as Archer grabbed the reins. Despite the charger's prancing, he mounted, but the crowd was upon them. He battered villagers away with his sword hilt and Henry was forced to do the same.

"Go!" Archer roared.

"Which way?"

"Any way!"

The boy could be so thick at times.

The horses leapt forward with Henry and Archer swinging their swords and the prisoner hanging on grimly. They were nearly swamped as they reached Burgal. Walter grabbed Henry's stirrup and tried to drag him from the saddle. Henry saw the loathing in his face, who could blame him they were rescuing a child-stealer after all. Henry couldn't bring himself to kill Walter, but clubbed him effectively nevertheless. The innkeeper tumbled away and would nurse a sore head for days. Just as Henry thought they'd be overwhelmed, black-faced sheep stampeded into the crowd. Bron drove the flock, adding enough confusion to break up the villagers who tripped over each other as panicking sheep buffeted and trampled them.

The horses burst free and galloped away. A few Burgal hopefuls followed and threw rocks, but saw it was useless and gave up the chase. Only a tirade of curses pursued them as Bron, the horses and riders disappeared along a track that led south of Burgal.

Archer is furious!
I think he hates the fact that he slept while
Urdec and Walter stole his prisoners from the inn.

Our captive is a puzzle. He's not so different from me.
I mean after all he's done, he seems a likable fellow.
Not particularly warlike maybe, but when driven…

Chapter 7
Moor and Mire

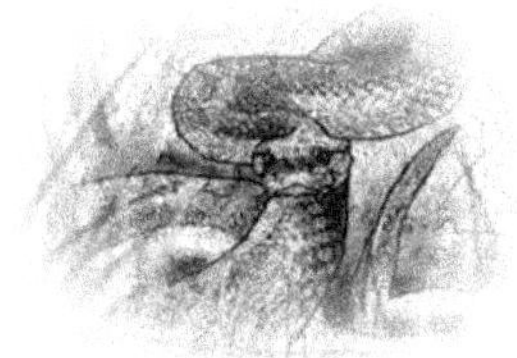

As they galloped away, Archer pulled ahead. Henry's passenger was indeed a poor rider and bounced around so violently they had to slow up in case he fell off. In time, Archer judged it safe to call a halt.

"We'll walk a spell and rest the horses," he said.

They travelled south and east for the rest of the day. Archer considered going back the way they'd come too risky, but was confident they'd find another way around Enta Geweore. He was in a sullen temper. The idea of being run out of town didn't sit well with him. At day's end they camped by a stream where Henry tried his luck fishing with little success. Their prisoner however, proved an expert angler and speared a dozen fish, which they roasted after tossing a couple to Bron. She preferred hers raw and polished off the heads as well.

Archer hadn't spoken to the captive all day, and Henry realised they didn't even know his name. His reticence may have been because he mourned his lost comrades, but kidnappers couldn't expect any sympathy.

"I'm Archer and this is Henry. What have you to say for yourself?" Archer, who was still in an ordinary mood, finally addressed the prisoner.

"My name is Edrid, from the archipelago of Palo Innes," the man said. "I am the leader there. My people call me 'prince."

"A prince indeed," Archer replied. "I wouldn't consider your behaviour particularly regal, your highness."

"The islanders gave the title to my father and I inherited it. I certainly don't deserve it."

"You don't seem so bad to me," Henry said.

"I don't sound too good either, do I?"

"Murdering innocent people? No, there isn't much good to be said about that."

"We haven't murdered anyone! Look, I'll explain. Palo Innes is isolated and that's how we like it. The islanders raise long-haired cattle, collect seabird eggs, and fish from our currachs. It's harsh, but we manage well enough. We don't bother anyone and no one bothers us. Not until the Starklanders arrived, anyway."

"You mentioned them before," Archer observed.

"Yes, and if you have those medallions, they're close to where you found them. They are their most treasured possessions. Starklanders admire their craftsmanship, precious metals, and coloured stones. They are currency. They represent their wealth."

So Edrid explained how the Starklanders arrived at Palo Innes. They came in their long, narrow ships, more by accident than design, swept by currents into a protected anchorage. The islanders had seen the ships pass occasionally, but the mariners had never found any sheltered coves before. Savage wolf heads were carved into pillars at the prow of their vessels. There were no wolves on the islands which made the ship totems all the more fearsome.

Before the keels scraped onto the beach, huge, fiery-bearded men leapt from the gunwales and surged ashore, subduing anyone in their path. Palo Innes folk weren't warriors by nature and they were soon driven back to Edrid's father's hall, forming a last redoubt. But the Starkmen didn't storm the defences. They probably didn't think it worth the effort. They simply rounded up anyone who hadn't made it to safety and carried them off.

Everybody on Palo Innes knew they'd return.

Of course they did, but the islanders posted look-outs and ran away into hiding. Eventually they were betrayed by an outcast known as Evil Queig, a ruffian who'd been banished to one of the outer islands for theft and paying unwanted attention to several island girls. He sailed his currach alongside the leading wolf-ship and showed the Starkmen a safe anchorage. After a series of spiteful skirmishes, the islanders were once again baled up in Edrid's father's hall, where the old man lay mortally wounded. The leader of the Starkmen stood before the hall dressed in leather and wolf hides and carrying a double-bladed axe. His name was Crag Daniek and he wanted slaves. He explained he could fight for them, but the Starklanders were pragmatic men and they'd just as soon make a deal.

"So you supply slaves and the Starkmen leave you alone?" Henry said.

"To a point," Edrid replied. "We can't beat them because they're better armed and ruthless. We're just fishermen and cattle-herders."

"So you come down the coast and pick up anyone you can," Archer surmised. "Sounds like a plan. I wonder where these rogues are from, or more to the point, where do they go?"

"Somewhere in the desolate north across the sea, but no one knows for sure. It's too dangerous and too far away."

"But, how did Urdec get the amulets?" Henry wondered.

"Two of the Starkmen came with us on the fist raid. They wore the medallions, they all do, and some have several. We were careless and the Starkmen over-confident. The villagers came in force. I'll give it to those pirates, they stood and fought while we ran away, they were overwhelmed by sheer numbers. No great loss, I suppose."

"Crag Daniek can't have been too happy."

"He didn't seem that bothered, just told us to have a ship-load ready for him when he got back or he'd make up the numbers from our folk. He does more often than not."

"You took a great risk going back to Burgal."

"That's where people are, and we were a lot more careful next time."

"And now the Starklanders have come to us," Archer mused, "but I wonder how. Maybe they got lucky and breached Ita Cay, or maybe they came over the mountains. Who knows, more to the point, why?"

"Let 'em come," Henry blustered, "Palo Innes may not breed fighters, but Hollowford does!"

Archer gave him a pained looked and they turned in for the night.

At sun-up they continued, keeping the silhouette of Enta Geweore on their left. Edrid decided to tag along as it was his only practical option. Archer was indifferent, but Henry was happy to have the company. He didn't slow them down as he doubled with Henry initially, but soon the way grew boggy and so covered with bushy copses that they dismounted and led the horses on foot.

"Won't your people wonder what's happened to you?" Henry asked. "How will you get a message to them?"

"Word travels along the coast. They'll find out in time."

"What if the Starkmen come back first?"

"We still post lookouts so the pirates don't always catch anyone. It depends on how determined they feel."

The journey took them through leagues of desolate, wind-swept heath land. It was tedious and treacherous going, but there were plenty of running streams, hares, and game birds in the area so they didn't go hungry or thirsty. There were no paths and they picked their way cautiously. They passed nobody and saw only one abandoned croft that had long succumbed to gales.

"I think this place is Randalmoor," Archer said, "but I've never been here."

"Can't see why not," Henry grinned. "It looks a right joyous spot to me."

Eventually the southern tip of Enta Geweore smudged the horizon. They made camp and Archer estimated they'd be in the foot-hills the following afternoon, but he didn't know what stood in their way.

Their dismal, smoky peat-fire gave little comfort, so they rose early after a cold night.

When the hills appeared tantalisingly close, they came to Ascarmire. It was a dreadful place of filth-ridden bog, black peat, and clinging mud. Putrid steam drifted from the quagmire, forming a rancid fog.

"Who farted?" Henry complained.

Archer glared at him.

Mosquitoes whined and occasionally they passed tensely coiled, malefic-looking vipers poised to strike. There were firm ways through the marsh, but their pace was slow. Jack-o'-lanterns winked in the mist. They were distracting and alluring, and Henry almost lost his footing several times as his concentration wandered.

"Do pay attention, Henry," Archer admonished. "It's just Will o' the Wisp up to mischief. Don't be lured by those light tricks, some say they're goblins' work and best left alone."

Archer was prepared to acknowledge the glowing magic. He'd seen plenty of strange folk in his travels, though never an actual elf or pixie, but wasn't taking any chances when it came to unexplained phenomena.

In time they grew used to tracking through Ascarmire and could divine safe paths. Then they stepped onto a large mossy turf area that looked secure enough. It was almost a small island surrounding by swamp, but it was their undoing. The island gave way under the weight of three men and two horses. The ground dissolved and they were pitched into the mire. The horses panicked, stamping what was left of the moss-island to shreds. The travellers tried to calm the animals, but it was impossible. They were waist-deep in muck and every time they tried to drag themselves free, they were sucked further down. Soon they were covered in black ooze and slowly sinking. The horses quietened, simply because they could no longer move, but fear blazed in their eyes. Only Bron remained clear of the water. She'd bounded to dry land in time and darted back and forth for a moment before disappeared into the fog.

"Wretched dog," Archer snarled.

"What do you think she can do?" Henry said. "I don't suppose calling for help will be any use."

"Can't make things worse," Edrid gasped and started yelling for all he was worth.

And then they discovered they had disturbed a nest of vipers.

The tussocks that now floated in pieces were their home and dozens of the serpents slithered into the water and headed towards the stranded travellers. Their banded bodies glided smoothly over the surface.

Sink, you monsters, Henry willed them, but they were expert swimmers and came straight for him. He wrenched Hornet-Sting free, but it was a hopeless task to wield it effectively. Archer had no more success. Henry was frantic not knowing which was worse, being sucked under clinging slime or stabbed by poisonous fangs.

They inched closer, with sinister, sibilant whispers as their tongues flicked forward. The horses sensed the danger and struggled again, stirring more mud and dragging them all deeper. The first of the lethal vipers glared at Henry with red eyes that pierced through him in an unblinking gaze. It floated and poised for a moment, its head oscillating as if sizing up its victim. It reared to strike, its huge jaws agape. Clear, pink venom dripped from its fangs.

Henry hauled his sword clear of the water, spraying slime towards the snake. It hesitated for just a second, but the swamp-water quickly settled and the serpent's head darted forward.

Henry groaned but felt no pain.

The beast exploded in mid-air inches in front of his face. With a whoosh and flash of steel, a huge axe-blade severed the snake's head and it spiralled away in a jet of blood. Two more blows hacked the reptile into writhing segments. Several other snakes sank into the swamp in death spasms, also destroyed by the axe.

Henry was mystified until he saw the axe-blade was attached to a long haft in the grip of a titanic figure. He was bigger than anyone Henry had ever seen. He stared at Henry before his attention turned to killing more snakes and driving the rest away.

His head was a rage of sandy-coloured hair and whiskers. He was dressed in bearskins with an untidiness that made him seem even larger. And he wasn't alone, another equally massive figure stood close by on one of the small, secure turf patches. The giants were almost identical. The second fellow was lounging on the hilt of a mighty claymore, eyeing his companion with mild interest, but offering no help. None was needed.

"Man, it's a fool thing to get stuck in the mud, hereabouts, and that's a fact," Henry's saviour observed sagaciously.

"Too right," the other giant replied vacantly, "Must've gone right 'stead of left back there. Boy, they're in trouble."

"Might've been all right over that away though."

"Or yonder towards rocks would be fine. Three men and two horses in the swamp's a bit daft, I'd say."

"Yeah man, it boggles the mind, don't it?"

"The hound's the only smart one."

The giants continued to debate the vagaries of the swamp while the three travellers and their horses slowly sank further. In their opinion, the extra wet weather lately hadn't helped the ground under-foot. And it was unusual to see so many serpents at this time of year. And them nags weren't the right animals to bring onto Ascarmire. But to be fair the paths did shift as often as not. And what a clever beast yon 'ound was to lead 'em back the right way. And...

And Archer'd had enough.

"Will you please shut up and pull us out before we drown?" he roared.

The giants stared at him. There was a pause as they considered the situation.

"Sure, be happy to," they replied evenly.

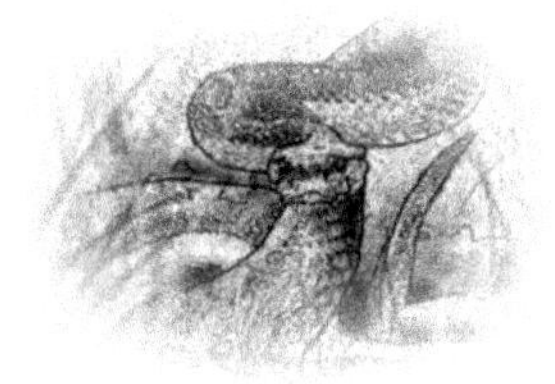

I fear Archer thinks less of me,
but at least he no longer despises Edrid.

It seems you must be killing someone to
impress Hollowford's reeve.

Chapter 8
Velma

The giants were surprisingly agile, moving through the swamp with ease. They deposited the mud-spattered wayfarers on firm ground and set about saving the horses, calming them with soothing whispers.

"You saved our lives. Thank you," Henry said.

"No bother," one of the giants replied.

"Our pleasure," the other said as they strode away.

"Wait. Please wait," Archer cried.

Now "please" wasn't a word Archer used often, and he'd done so twice today. The giants stopped, turned, and eyed him curiously. As Archer approached, their size was apparent. They stood more than a head taller than him, broadly muscular with skin the texture of tree-bark. They reminded Henry of fairground wrestlers and weight-lifting strong men who occasionally passed through Hollowford.

"I'm sure you're busy men, but we'd appreciate it if you'd guide us out of this marsh," Archer said

The giants shrugged and exchanged glances.

"Nope, not especially busy," the snake-slayer said. "You want out, we can take you. Where're y' headin'?"

"Hollowford. We're trying to get around the mountains. Randalmoor and this swamp proved more treacherous than we thought."

"Can be. We heard yer, but your 'ound led the way. M' name's Kimball and this here's m' wee sibling, Serlequin. Best if we lead them nags. Just follow on and watch yer step."

So they introduced themselves and fell in behind the giants, who were happy enough to answer questions, but tended not to volunteer information. It turned out they were twins and their mother, who lived further into the mountains, had a passing acquaintance with Guilda. They lived comfortably by fishing, hunting, and tending their vegetable patch and orchard.

Archer's company had been unlucky because they'd almost reached the edge of Ascarmire where the terrain turned to woodland. Kimball and Serlequin's cabin was not far, and they arrived before nightfall.

"Best stay 'ere t'night," Kimball suggested, "There's plenty of grub."

A hind hung from a trellis.

"Been there a week, reckon she'll be good and tender b' now and we've got beer."

They let the horses graze for a while, and then stabled them in a lean-to close by. Serlequin gave them some carrots, an apple each, and made sure the water trough was full to keep them going until morning. The cabin was roomy and they stashed their saddles and blankets on the floor. During supper, they discovered the twins had been born in Velma, but their mother had taken them to the hills after their father was killed in a knife fight.

"We go t' town fer a bit o' fun," Kimball said, "but not often."

"I'd imagine you can look after yourselves," Edrid ventured.

"We don't go looking' fer bother, but it tends t' come yer way in Velma."

"We are thinking of popping in to see what Olag Blackaxe is doing," Archer said.

"Sounds like it's trouble you want, so we'd better come along and hold yer hand. Sort of home-town advantage, you might say."

Next morning they set out.

Many of the town residents had left and formed small settlements scattered through the forest and pastureland south of Ascarmire. They traded among themselves, so brigands from Velma often waylaid travellers. Kimball and Serlequin thought they'd be safe enough as these highwaymen were merely cowardly bullies who'd be reluctant to tackle a well-armed party of warriors. Henry rather liked being considered a warrior.

Although they kept their eyes peeled, they saw no signs of outlaws and as they approached Velma, Kimball noted a singular lack of people. Even if not bent on larceny, there were always a few rough types and beggars hanging around town. Velma certainly had the look of squalor with a stench to match. Scores of ravens and brazen rats scavenged through the town refuse. Although there were no young men to be seen, a few nervous women, urchins, and old people hurried through the streets.

"Doesn't it strike you as odd there are no men-folk around?" Archer mused. "Even ale-soaked Velma rogues should be up and about by now."

"Suits me," Serlequin said.

Archer drew Skull-Crusher, his street-fighting weapon-of-choice, from his belt and held it ready, while Henry's hand hovered over Hornet-Sting's hilt.

"Anything odd doesn't suit me, but here's a fellow we can take on without too much risk,"

An old man dressed in rags sat by an inn door glaring at them.

"Wadda y'want?" the ancient demanded. "I've paid me tribute. There's nothin' left, so you're wastin' yer time."

"We're not Olag's men."

"Well, yer're too late, ain't yer? Blackaxe 'as taken everything I got."

"We're not going to rob you, old man. We just want to know what's going on around here."

"Well, it don't pay to blab, do it? Blackaxe don't care for folk blabbin' about 'is doin's."

"I may be able to adjust your attitude."

Archer produced a copper and held it in front of the old man's nose. He made a grab for the coin, but Archer whipped it away.

"Not so fast, my good fellow. You must earn it. What's going on around here?"

The old man looked uncertain.

"We won't tell Olag if you don't." Henry ventured.

"See Blackaxe 'as been gone a couple a days now, ain't 'e? Rum doin's been goin' on all winter, see. Sparrin' 'n' trainin' and forgin' weapons. Not like usual winter quarters when it's ale-guzzlin', bullyin', and fornicatin'. 'E's taken 'is 'ole bunch and 'eaded north with a great to-do."

"Where to?" Archer asked as the ancient seemed to have lost his reticence.

"'E don't confide in me, do 'e? But, it ought t' be plain enough. 'E's off to give Gareth a pastin', that's where 'e's gone."

They shouldn't have been surprised to hear Olag was on the prowl again, but to have taken his whole garrison was alarming. He probably had more than fifty thugs, with many of their spiteful scrubbers in tow who enjoyed a fight as much as Velma men.

Unfortunately, the old man's information was not entirely

correct. Not all Olag's ruffians had gone north. He left three burly fellows to keep an eye on things while he was away and they appeared around a corner. They were no match for Archer's group, especially when two were as formidable as Kimball and Serlequin, so no harm would have been done except they recognised Archer from past encounters. Their first thought was that Olag would want to know Gareth's reeve was sniffing around Velma, so they turned and bolted for the stables.

"After them!" Archer bellowed, tossing the coin to the old man and, axe in hand, raced in pursuit.

Kimball and Serlequin were fast, but their size was a disadvantage in Velma's maze of narrow alleys. They caught two of the escapees and subdued them with a few hearty thumps, but the third rogue disappeared.

"Where'd he go?" Archer demanded as he tried to shake some sense back into the stunned men. He received no reply, but heard the clatter of hoof beats close by. Leaving the giants to guard the prisoners, Archer, Henry, and Edrid raced into the next street to see the last Velma man galloping away. Bron dashed after the horse and attacked its hind legs. The horse reared, nearly throwing its rider. He clung on, but the horse stopped and pranced on the spot as Bron harried it, just managing to dodge the hooves.

"Shoot him, Henry!" Archer roared.

Henry wrenched his bow from his back, drew an arrow, aimed, and hesitated.

"Kill him!"

It wasn't as easy this time.

"Shoot!"

Edrid grabbed Skull-Crusher from Archer's hands, ran several paces and hurled it after the rider. The axe tumbled through the air and plunged into the fellow's back. He crashed to the ground and died instantly. When they reached the body, Archer stamped his foot onto the dead man's torso, gripped the haft and heaved Skull-Crusher free. He wiped the blade across the victim's cloak before handing it to Edrid with a nod of approval.

"You'd better hang onto this. You might have more use for it before too long. Looks like you know how to use it and you've got a horse of your own as well."

Archer eyed Henry, but it was impossible to judge his mood.

"Sorry," Henry mumbled.

"Like I said, killing comes with the moment. It's not always easy, so it's best not to dwell."

They discovered no more from the two other Velma men than the beggar had told them.

"We'll have to warn Chief Gareth and fast," Henry said.

Edrid grabbed the dead fellow's horse and they mounted up.

"Can you keep an eye on those two for a while?" Archer asked the giants.

"Yer might want us to come along with you," Kimball said.

"We're on horseback."

"Reckon we can keep up with them nags o' yours."

"What about them?" Archer indicated the prisoners.

"No problem."

Serlequin clouted them both back into unconsciousness, tied them with rope he found on a produce-wagon, and pitched them into a back-alley.

"Should keep 'em quiet long enough."

The giants were as good as their word and loped beside the horses looking as if they'd keep up all day. Archer's main concern was that they would fail to catch up and warn Gareth before Olag's surprise attack. Olag would certainly be able to run off a large number of livestock and kill many villagers, to a point where Hollowford might be too weak to retaliate. Olag's gang left an easy trail and were simply following the best path between Velma and Hollowford. So they were surprised when they came to Olag's camp a half-day march short of their destination.

The camp was established as if they were settling in. Olag had even erected a tent and his ragged banner bearing a raven's image dangled from a spear driven into the ground. Similar banners hung throughout the camp, although most of the ruffians simply lit cooking-fires and laid out their bedding beside them.

"Now why has he stopped?" Archer mused. "He must know that every minute's delay increased the risk of being discovered, and damned if he hasn't got over a hundred warriors there. More than I've ever seen before, so what's he up to?"

Archer stared at Henry in a very disconcerting way.

"We'll wait for nightfall and then see what we can find out."

"We?" Henry said.

"Well..."

"Why is it always me?"

"Because I know I can rely on you, Henry."

Archer's tone indicated Henry had some making up to do after the Velma incident.

"Anyway, who else? Kimball and Serlequin are going to be spotted straight away, Edrid's a stranger, and someone is bound to recognise me. That just leaves you, so do stop whining. There's a good fellow."

They left the path and melted into the forest, circling through the best cover to be close enough to observe the camp's routine. They waited until dark, checking when sentries passed. Kimball and Serlequin were all for braining a few skulls, but Archer warned against it. He thought it best to leave Olag's men undisturbed and avoid the risk of discovery.

When the coast was clear, Henry darted into the camp. Once within the perimeter, he calmed down. Everyone was concentrating on their supper pots and paid him no attention. He started when one the girls greeted him wantonly, but he managed a terse reply.

A brazier heated the front of Olag's tent and he was deep in conversation with several warriors seated on stools. His pet raven was chained to a perch by the tent opening. It turned and faced Henry who froze, but no one noticed him and he ducked into the tent's shadow. He edged forward as far as he dared. The raven fidgeted and flapped its wings, but Olag was engaged in a heated argument and ignored the agitated bird.

"We'll lose our surprise if we wait any longer," he insisted. "If we go now, we'll catch 'em nappin'."

"Yer don't 'ave enough men," a familiar voice said.

Henry recognised it at once. Growl!

"More 'n Gareth anyway," Olag retorted.

"A deal's a deal."

Hiss! Well, it wasn't surprising they were Olag's men, but what was that about a deal? No one would be foolish enough to make a deal with the Velma gang.

Henry inched closer and the raven struck in a squawking flurry of feathers. It judged the chain's length and darted at Henry just as he crept in range. He fended off the claws and beak, tripping over a guy-rope when he staggered backwards. He fell awkwardly, rolled and leapt to his feet. No time for stealth now, just head for the trees as the camp fomented around him. In the confusion, no one knew whether Henry was the threat or trying to help. He jumped over a cooking fire spilling a pot of scalding soup into the laps of a couple of warriors. Dodging others, he crashed into a line of horses that broke their tethers allowing them to stampede away. He careened into one of the guards, knocking him down. The Velma man tried to draw his sword, but Henry hurdled over him and raced for the forest.

"Catch him!' Olag roared. 'I want him alive!"

A dozen villains grabbed their weapons and leapt into pursuit. Henry heard their panting and cursing close behind, but there was no reason why he couldn't out-run them. Many of Olag's men wore heavy mail sarks and he was only lightly clad. He was probably fitter than most of them anyway, but he stumbled over a fallen log and crashed to the forest floor, stunned for a moment. Warriors closed in. He felt himself lifted to his feet and prepared for a stiff thrashing, although it didn't come.

"Off w'yer, laddie," Kimball whispered calmly, holding him by the scruff of the neck.

Henry ran. Uproar erupted behind him, but he didn't look back. Archer and Edrid waited with the horses close by. He leapt into the saddle and they galloped away.

"What about Kimball and Serlequin?" Henry yelled.

"Don't worry about them," Arched replied. "This is their idea."

After a mile or so, they reined up and waited until the giant twins caught up, having left a few sore heads among Olag's men. Henry looked nervously behind them, but there was no sign of pursuit.

"Them fellers gave up the chase a way back," Serlequin reported.

"Well done, but we'd better keep moving, if you're up to it," Archer said.

The giants exchanged glances, shrugged, and jogged along with the horses. They seemed to be enjoying the exercise and excitement.

"I saw those two warriors again," Henry said after they'd travelled a while. "The two men who attacked me were with Olag's gang."

"Not surprising really," Archer surmised. "Dung sticks together. C'mon, we'd better tell the Chief what we've discovered."

But gut-wrenching fear, I've come to know well.

Chapter 9
Meeting the Threat

Chief Gareth rose at dawn. For all his carousing, he rarely slept late and today he was going hunting. Ayla and Macayle were away at Tremill Broch. Although Gareth was reluctant to let them go, Ayla had stubbornly insisted and he only agreed after delegating four of his toughest warriors to escort them. She was not as fond of hunting as the chief anyway. To Gareth the moon and stars stayed pretty much the same. He appreciated the beauty of a clear night and was amazed when a comet had filled the skies some years ago, but for him, that was as far as it went. However Ayla enjoyed nothing better than stargazing at Tremill Broch.

After breakfast, Faranden arrived with Gareth's charger and mastiffs, leading a procession of a dozen villagers who had agreed to act as beaters and carried the chief's hooded saker and two peregrines. The hunt went well and they brought down several plump birds for Gareth's table along with plenty for all the beaters to take home for supper. They were about to call it a day when Archer's party found them.

"You appear to have gathered an entourage, reeve," Gareth observed and introductions were made with a quick explanation of their adventures.

"Olag is camped less than a day's march away with an army," Archer reported.

"You did well to out-run 'em. We'd better gather our folk to meet him. He might get discouraged if faced with a fight."

"They're staying put for now. It looks like a permanent camp."

"So what's he up to? Why lose the surprise?"

"Waiting for reinforcements, perhaps. Henry overheard them discussing something of the kind, but was discovered before he could gather any details."

"Who'd be fool enough to fall in with Olag's gang? Wild men from the forest?"

"There'd be no 'un from the forest that'd join 'im," Kimball advised. "Most folk hate 'im, y' see, and even vagabonds and brigands don't trust 'im."

"Then we'll go and give him a good thrashing and send him scuttling back to Velma," Gareth was positively drooling at the thought, there was always trouble when his mood favoured warfare.

"What if he plans to lure you to him for some sort of trap?" Edrid asked.

"Then, Prince of Palo Innes, he has succeeded and it will be all the worse for him."

Once Gareth's mind was made up, that was pretty much that. Henry voiced concern about the presence of Hiss and Growl, but Gareth was untroubled, confident Hollowford's militia would best Olag's men any day. It was Gareth's bold action that had reorganised Hollowford after many chaotic years at the mercy of forest raiders. Taking the fight straight to his enemies had proved a successful tactic in the past and he considered himself more than a match for Olag Blackaxe. The only worrying aspect of events was that the entire tribe was gathered, which had never happened before. Normally small gangs of Velma's finest ventured into the forest to cause mischief wherever the opportunity arose and could be seen off with a burst of discouraging archery

Without further discussion, they galloped to the village, leaving the indefatigable giants to keep an eye on Olag's movements. At their chief's call to arms, Hollowford's yeomanry sprang into action, donning their helmets, grabbing weapons, beer gourds, and food for a couple of days before mustering under Archer and Faranden's orders.

"It's as well Ayla and Macayle are safely away," Gareth conceded, but sent a youngster who knew the paths through Joppa Fen to warn them. He would have preferred they remained at Tremill Broch, but expected they'd return, because even if the day went well there would be injuries to nurse. Ayla and Macayle were the chief's family and knew their place was at Hollowford in troubled times. In their absence, Thayer took charge of the village womenfolk who loaded blankets, bandages, poultices, potions, salves, extra rations, and water kegs onto carts. No one expected to get away without casualties and, as additional insurance, the women included a considerable supply of extra weapons in case they needed to defend themselves. Although Thayer was confident Gareth would win the day, she was less sanguine about Henry joining the militia.

"He's too young," she told Archer.

"It's not his first fight, Thayer, and with four warriors away at Tremill Broch, we need every man."

"He's not yet a man."

"Man enough from what I've seen, I'd say. Don't worry, Edgar and I will keep a good eye on him."

In the middle of a battle, she wondered, but kept her thoughts to herself as men were often inclined to make promises they couldn't guarantee.

Hollowford's militia was formed in three companies of about thirty men each with Gareth, Archer, and Faranden leading them. They were all well armed with personal choices of broad swords, halberds, battle-axes, daggers, and spears. Their round, wooden shields were studded with iron spikes that also made them useful weapons. Edgar, mounted on Henry's other horse, Bruno, was armed with a sledge-hammer and rode with Archer so Henry, Edrid and Bron joined them. They wore an assortment of armour and helmets, but tied blue ribbons around their arms for recognition in battle and about a third of the warriors were mounted.

Gareth was not much of an orator unless bragging around the feast table, but he deemed the occasion worthy of a short speech.

"Men of Hollowford, Olag Blackaxe once again threatens our homes and families. If it's a fight he wants, it's a fight he'll get. I know you're all stout-hearted fellows, so let's go and give those Velma rogues the thrashing they deserve."

Realising that was all they were going to get there was a collective roar from Hollowford's yeomanry as they followed their chief south. There were no tears from the villagers, they were tough folk and knew fighting was simply part of survival in those parts. As the men disappeared, the carts followed to pick up the shattered remnants of battle.

Olag might have been a ruffian and a bully, but he wasn't an idiot and sent scouting parties to check the countryside between his camp and Hollowford. So he was aware of Gareth's arrival and not particularly bothered when his lookouts reported the approaching enemy. He estimated he outnumbered the Hollowford horde comfortably, and his options were limited in any event. If he withdrew to Velma, he risked being harried all the way by Gareth's force. He was well positioned on a ridge with his men spread across it, so they could not be out-flanked. Full of ale, mead and wine, they were a bellicose bunch who'd been spoiling for a fight all winter.

Olag stared across the shallow valley before him and up the ridge on the other side where he expected Gareth to emerge. A stream ran along the dell floor hindering an advancing enemy that would be at the mercy of arrow volleys. The forest thinned and his view was clear enough, although it was poor country for cavalry and this battle would be decided within the valley slopes. He signalled his men to withdraw from view beyond the ridge-line. Hiss and Growl joined him and he explained his battle-plan. He would stand alone on the hill-top and tempt Gareth to him. When the Hollowford militia was about half way up, Velma's army would boil over the ridge line, swarming down with the advantage of height to sweep the enemy away. The sun blazed from the side, favouring neither army.

Of course, no battle goes exactly according to plan.

But Gareth's force didn't barge straight into the trap as Archer and Faranden scouted ahead. There was no sign of Kimball or Serlequin, but they spotted Olag as he planned, standing against the skyline, his cloak billowing and tremendous in a bronze helmet with huge eagle feathers bolted to each side. His ragged standard flapped above his head, fearsome yet vulnerably alone, but Archer and Faranden weren't fooled for a minute. No one was going to take on an army single-handed, unless he planned single combat with Hollowford's champion, but that wasn't Olag's style. They rode back to the chief.

"I wonder what happened to your two big fellows, reeve," Gareth wondered. "You don't suppose they fell afoul of those blaggards, do you?"

Archer merely shrugged as it seemed unlikely anyone would best Kimball and Serlequin, but they'd been busy and even they needed rest. Perhaps they'd been surprised while they slept. He wasn't sure whether they planned to be participants or mere observers and, in any event, there was no time for speculation. The militia marched to the ridge in a clatter of weaponry and jingling riding hardware where Gareth halted and stood facing Olag. Hollowford's men fanned out to each side just as Velma's army was deployed. Gareth ordered his cavalry to dismount. Like Olag, he judged this dispute would be resolved on foot. And they waited.

"How long d'you reckon he'll just stand there?" Archer asked. "I judge his rogues are close behind him."

"They'll be well into their cups by now," Gareth said. "He won't be able to control them for long. Discipline and restraint ain't their strong points. Those men won't sit still all day. They'll either attack or go back to camp. Keep the men in view and make sure they stay off the booze. Tell 'em they've got courage enough."

"What will happen, Uncle?" Henry asked.

"It's not like a street scrap," Edgar explained. "There'll be a lot of yellin' and abuse to build up bravado and maybe scare 'em a bit. Most folk don't want to start a fight, but once it hots up they don't seem bothered so much. Stay close to me. You too, Edrid. Whatever you do, don't get separated."

Gareth was right; in less than half-an-hour Olag's men and many of their women started emerging all along their ridge under their ragged banners. They brandished weapons and shouted jibes at Hollowford's men, who howled insults back, daring the Velma army to come and take a beating. Henry wasn't so sure. There were so many enemy warriors. He tried to suppress his fear, waiting was worse than facing snakes, bandits, or wild boar, but maybe they'd lose heart and return to Velma.

Fat chance! Henry thought.

"They outflank us," Edgar observed, "So we'll have to form a shield-spear."

The militia had trained to form a wedged formation and push through superior numbers, thus breaking their line, but it was a manoeuvre with risks. Against disciplined warriors a wedge was vulnerable on its flanks, but against a reckless and untrained enemy the sides of the wedge could then turn and drive into the enemy line forcing them to defend in confusion.

"Velma louts are more interested in ale and slatterns," Edgar advised.

That old boy we spoke to seemed to think differently, Henry thought.

Finally, Olag stepped forward but ordered his men to stay put, cuffing a few heads to ensure obedience. He boldly marched down the slope and halted about half way to the valley floor.

"I believe he wants to parley, lord," Archer observed.

"Arrogant fellow, but I'd better go and see what the villain has to say." Gareth replied wearily. "Keep everyone alert and be ready for tricks."

As a token of good faith, Gareth rammed his huge sword, Goresax into the ground and armed with only a sharp-studded shield, marched to meet Olag. Most of his men thought it was an unnecessary and foolish gesture, but that was Gareth for you. He wasn't going to appear intimidated by someone he considered no more than a tavern brawler. Of course, no one was going to call him a fool for confronting Olag without a weapon, even though Velma's leader was leaning confidently on his own battle-axe. Gareth stopped level with Olag and they faced one another across the valley as the hill-top jeering ceased and both sides fell silent.

"Well met, Gareth," Olag growled, his voice carrying clearly as far as both ridges.

"So you plan to push me out of Hollowford."

"Oh no, I don't plan to evict you, I plan to kill you and take all you own. I plan to be Warlord of Grambak, and I shall especially enjoy your women."

Gareth was not to be goaded… Yet.

"And you think you're man enough for the job, you poxed spore of a Velma harpy and a jackass."

"Man enough to finish you, windbag. Blow all the hot air you like, flatulence won't carry the day, you know."

Henry paid little attention to the two leaders' exchange, but scanned the Velma horde for signs of treachery. It was not long in coming as a dozen archers crept forward on each flank with a clear shot at Gareth who was well within range.

"Lord, raise your shield!" Henry roared.

Instinctively, Gareth held his shield high as three arrows pierced its wood panels, but saved him while other shafts thudded around his feet. Olag saw his opportunity to quickly finish Gareth while he stood off balance. Raising his axe, he charged and his men followed, hurtling downhill and screaming their battle-cries. Henry raised his bow and fired an arrow into the ground in front of Olag, stopping him in his tracks, but Gareth wasn't out of trouble. Velma's army still poured down the slope towards him. The militia saw the danger and stirred to action. With Hollowford leaderless, Olag's ruffians saw a chance of routing their enemy.

"Wait!" Archer bellowed. "Not yet, men!"

Stay put, chief, I beg you! Make him come to you.

Gareth recovered and stood unarmed, but braced to meet Olag who advanced again. Henry drew another arrow, but Archer ordered him to hold fire.

"Let Olag come, Henry. See, the others follow now."

Henry stared at him in disbelief.

It's as if Archer does this sort of thing every day.
From what I've seen so far, I suppose he does.
It's just that he's so quiet.

Now Chief Gareth, you can always find him, even if you can't
see him, but Archer, you never hear him in a fight unless he's
giving orders.
Aunt Thayer is full of surprises too.

Chapter 10
Survival

"Gareth will have to fend him off long enough. You'll need Hornet-Sting now, lad," Archer said calmly.

Olag reached Gareth who'd stood his ground and swung his axe, the blade glancing off Gareth's shield. The chief used the shield to strike back, forcing Olag to duck and avoid its sharp studs. They started trading blows. Olag's axe sliced clunks out of Gareth's shield, which would soon be shattered to splinters, leaving the chief defenceless. Gareth would have to retreat, which was something he was unlikely to care for. Henry was appalled as the Velma horde surged towards Gareth. Their screams filled the valley in a frightening cacophony, yet Archer held the Hollowford men on their own ridge-line. As they approached, their faces could be seen contorted in a frenzied blood-lust as a fighting madness overtook them.

Velma's warriors were half-way down the hill when Archer let the militia loose.

"Now!" he roared. "Forward!"

He wrenched Goresax from the turf and led the militia swarming to war.

His timing was exquisite. Outnumbered maybe, but the militia had the advantage when Olag's army reached the stream and their pace slowed considerably as they splashed across before clambering up the other slope. They were almost upon Gareth when Hollowford's men crashed into them from higher ground.

The chief was having trouble defending himself until Archer tossed Goresax to his out-stretched hand. Gareth caught his sword and waded into the fight, battering Olag mercilessly. Hollowford's wedge ran out of impetus as the leading men reached the stream and were forced to fight in knee-deep water as Olag's army surged around them. Hollowford's yeomanry were now pressed back-to-back into two ranks. With the Velma army driving in on both sides there was no longer the advantage of elevation and Olag's greater numbers threatened to out-flank them. The solid shield-barrier held, although once encircled, Hollowford's army was in critical danger.

Henry's fear vanished in the chaos, blood, clashing steel, and screams of dying and maimed men and women. Spears drove through shields, piercing flesh and smashing bones as the fight became a matter of lunging, hacking, dodging, and hoping for the best. He ducked under a blade that swirled past and slashed at his enemy's legs, discovering they were vulnerable. A severed tendon immobilised a man instantly. Armed with Hornet Sting in one hand and a dagger in the other, it became his technique of choice. He lost all sense of Archer, Edgar, and Edrid's presence although Bron remained by his side. He heard Gareth roaring for his army to rally to him, but could not see him in the melee and he was aware that the barricade of shields was crumbling. A few Velma warriors broke through, but were cut down with no chance of quarter.

The battle dissolved into a formless struggle when Kimball and Serlequin arrived with a dozen wild men from the forest. Dressed in green and brown hunting gear, they carried an assortment of bows, spears, knives and clubs. The giants had abandoned their own weapons in favour of long, hardwood staffs that matched their height. This rag-tag band ran headlong into Thayer and the

Hollowford women who had caught up with their carts. It was uncertain who looked the most surprised as the two groups gazed at one another for a few seconds. Then the noise and commotion from the riverbed drew their attention and it was clear the militia was in desperate peril. Thayer eyed the giants, not knowing whether they were friend or foe, but a nod and a wink from Kimball reassured her. They looked more like outlaws than anything else to Thayer, but now was no time to be choosy.

"Well, don't just stand there, you big logs," she declared, "There's work to be done, and we'd better look sharp about it."

"Yes, ma'am," Kimball said.

He, Serlequin, and their woodland companions raced to the right while a score of women followed Thayer to the left. They grabbed every weapon from the carts then turned them around to serve as battering rams. They lurched down the hill to either side of the fight, striking Olag's horde from behind. Now it was the Velma brigands who found they were fighting on two fronts. The giants' ferocious strength was unstoppable as they bludgeoned men left and right with the great reach of their staffs so no one could get close enough to oppose them. Meanwhile the woodsmen had many old scores to settle. The carts crashed into the backs of Velma warriors, crushing several as they somersaulted to a halt and Hollowford's women desperately joined the bedlam of screaming, clashing steel and thumping impacts that now broke into individual contests surging along the valley floor.

Thayer found herself facing one of Velma's tattooed girls dressed in studded leather and armed with a stiletto in each hand. The young woman grinned as she brandished the knives believing she'd found an easy victim, but Thayer had often handled weapons in Edgar's forge and was comfortable with the sword she carried.

The girl lunged, but was over-confident as Thayer parried easily and in a single, fluid movement, swung the blade slashing her enemy's arm from wrist to elbow. The woman wailed in pain and disbelief as her knives dropped to the ground and she sank to her knees. The fight was over for her and she'd be lucky not to bleed to death.

Silly girl, just too young and reckless, Thayer assessed before turning to face other threats.

More personal conflicts raged now the wall of shields had disintegrated. Henry was faced with a charging spearman who lunged forward, but was distracted by Bron who snarled and crouched, poised ready to leap. Swift and fit, Henry easily dodged under the strikes of the Velma warrior, dived to the ground, and tumbled into the warrior's legs. Henry plunged his knife through one enemy foot and hacked at the other with Hornet Sting severing the toes and totally crippling his opponent. Henry leapt to his feet and cast around for further danger, which of course was everywhere on the battlefield.

Gareth was in trouble. The problem with being a leader in a big fight is that every enemy warrior wanted to claim the honour of killing you. It was not simply vainglory that drove men to that aim. With their chief dead, an enemy was likely to become disheartened and easier to beat. To this end, Gareth found himself surrounded by half-a-dozen warriors and it was only his tenacity that kept them at bay. In any event, the battle was now so fluid it was doubtful whether either side really knew where their leader was.

Luckily, Velma's army was now bewildered by Kimball, Serlequin, and Thayer's attack and unsure which way to turn to meet the new hazard, not to mention their rapidly mounting casualties. Henry broke through the cordon that surrounded

Gareth and joined him in fending off the enemy. Archer and Edgar carved savage roads through the battlefield, while Edrid was doing some serious damage with Skull-Crusher. Faranden, swinging his halberd with devastating effect, was in his element buffeting his way through the fight, roaring and cursing as he battered enemy warriors aside or drove the weapon point home. Many Velma men fell under their onslaught until, bewildered and terrified, Olag's army broke and bolted from the field in disarray. Some abandoned their weapons as they fled, leaving the wounded staggering and crawling as best they could.

With a cheer, the Hollowford folk raced after them, cutting down stragglers until, fearing they'd break into small, random groups, Gareth and Archer called them back. It was only then Henry realised what a grisly mess surrounded him. Half a dozen Hollowford men lay dead and twice that many were wounded, some groaning pitifully, others silently numb with shock. *How can I be so tired? The fight was over so quickly and I'm so thirsty!* He slowly came to his senses and saw, to his surprise, Thayer in the midst of the wounded, binding the arm of a wounded, weeping Velma girl. He staggered over fallen warriors and hugged her.

"Auntie, what are you doing here?" he gasped.

"Saving your skin, by the looks of things," she replied with astonishing matter-of-factness. "Now go and find you uncle. See that he's safe and help anyone you can."

"You fought in the battle..?"

"Of course I did. Oh, those Velma hooligans make me so angry with their dreadful behaviour. Look at this poor, wee lass — she's only here because she followed their bad example. I think she'll mend then I'll take her back with me and try and make something of her."

Henry shook his head and stumbled along the river-bed, how he wanted to drink the icy water, but blood swirled in crimson streaks and he dared not risk it. He clambered over what he took to be a corpse, when an iron hand grabbed his ankle. Olag Blackaxe lay half submerged with his blood oozing steadily into the stream. Henry raised his sword, but Velma's chief held him firmly until Henry saw the amulet holding Olag's sodden cloak. He wrenched his foot free, crouched beside the Velma chief and ripped the brooch away. Their eyes met.

"What are these talismans?" Henry whispered. "Who gave this one to you?"

"You're the boy my louts told me about, ain't you?"

Blood gurgled between Olag's teeth, his lung was pierced and death awaited.

"Got the better of me, I'll admit. …but…tell Gareth…'e may have won this battle…but 'is troubles are just beginnin'…"

Olag's voice trailed to a gasp and with a final spasm he sank face-down in the creek, spluttering a few, final bubbles before he died.

"Well, well, found yourself some more loot, have you?"

Faranden stood over him, looking particularly jealous and Henry wondered if he'd be challenged for the prize. Obviously Faranden considered it, but simply strode away to pick over the bodies of fallen enemies hoping to find something of value or practical use. The rest of the militia and women folk were also combing the battlefield or tending the wounded, and carrying them to those carts that remained undamaged.

I'd better show the clasp to Lord Gareth, Henry thought absently.

Velma had lost over a score dead and an equal number of

prisoners crouched in a wretched group. The women and younger
boys would return to Hollowford and be indentured to those
who'd lost family, repaying them with a few years hard labour.
The remainder, who were beyond rehabilitation and certainly a
future threat, were shown no mercy and quickly executed. There
was no sign of Growl, although Hiss was among the captives. He
wanted to make a deal, thinking he could negotiate his life for
information. Gareth however, was not in a particularly clement
mood.

"Hanging's really too good for you," Gareth opined.

"Drawing and quartering perhaps, lord," Archer suggested
urbanely. "Castration maybe, although I've discovered they favour
the stake in the west."

Gareth, Archer, Edrid, and Henry hunkered down beside Hiss.
Bron joined them and remembering how he'd treated her, snarled
with intent. Henry stroked her ruffled coat and she settled a little.

"Now," Gareth began evenly, "I want some answers. No
messing about, just the truth. Otherwise, I'll start chopping bits off
you and feed them to the wolf here."

Hiss nodded.

"So what stirred Olag up so much to risk this venture?"

And this is what Hiss told them…

The previous autumn, a Starklander wolf-ship was caught in a
foul storm off Ita Cay near Velma. The vessel washed onto
jagged shoals, but fortunately for the mariners, although badly
holed, remained intact. They waded ashore to be met by Olag and

most of his gang, who rightly saw the castaways as a serious and well-armed threat. So to avoid a fight, Olag decided to help repair the wolf-ship and send the strangers on their way, realising they wouldn't try anything as foolish as broaching the reef again. There was ample timber to fell and Olag even drafted a local carpenter whom the Starklanders quickly put to work.

Of course, Olag was intrigued by the sleek craft and was soon asking questions about the ship and its crew. The leader, Crag Daniek, was happy enough to explain who they were, that they made their living from the sea (although he failed to mention precisely how), and ship-wrecks were common enough to be considered an occupational hazard. Olag became effusive and invited the Starkmen to Velma, but Crag Daniek refused, not wishing to stray far from their ship. He was suspicious of Olag anyway. They waited for high tide and kedged the boat off the reef into protected water. During the week it took to repair the vessel, Crag Daniek and Olag sized each other up. Every sunset they sat around a beach campfire sharing gourds of wine or mead and talking well into the night. Olag boasted that he controlled the entire peninsula, although Crag Daniek, who had a pretty shrewd idea of its size, didn't believe him.

"So yer reckon yer gorrit all under control, but yer must 'ave enemies," he suggested.

"Only Gareth at Hollowford, north of 'ere," Olag conceded.

"Rich, is 'e?"

"Fattest settlement anywhere around."

"Be lottsa booty then?"

"Livestock, supplies, and women ripe fer the pickin'. 'Is missus is a right looker. I've 'ad me eye on 'er fer ages."

"What's stoppin' yer?"

"Not enough men. I probably got more than 'im, but 'e 'as 'is snoops out and I'd need a surprise attack."

"Pity we couldn't raid from the sea with that reef in the way."

The use of "we" wasn't lost on Olag.

"You thinkin' of an alliance?"

Crag Daniek inclined his head slightly.

"What do you have in mind?" he asked.

Olag had explained the reef ended at Tremill Broch just before cliffs rose on the northern coast of Grambak. The tower stood on a lone, sandy island linked to the mainland by a causeway that was only exposed at low tide. Tremill Broch housed scholars and wizards, but no warriors; easy pickings. Olag was sure the Broch housed treasure and had always wanted to raid it, but Hollowford stood in the way. Perhaps the island could be reached from the sea as it was just clear of the northern tip of Ita Cay.

So a plan was hatched. Crag Daniek suggested the Starklanders would return in spring to attack Tremill Broch and Hollowford from the north while Olag would lead a southern assault overland. Crag Daniek left two men with Olag while the remaining Starklanders sailed away, carefully negotiating Ita Cay at high tide. As a sign of good faith, he also left several of the valuable talismans. Growl and Hiss won one each from Olag, who was a poor gambler. So when spring arrived, Olag assigned one of his men to accompany the two remaining Starklanders north to meet Crag Daniek and guide them through Joppa Fen, which could be perilous. Unfortunately for them, they were the victims of the wolf pack that Henry discovered. Olag had also ordered Hiss and Growl to follow at a distance just in case of treachery.

Gareth had heard enough. Although he hoped word had reached Ayla and Macayle and they were hurrying back to Hollowford, he took all his mounted men, including Henry, Archer, and Edrid, with him to escort his family home. Edgar and Thayer took charge of transporting the Hollowford dead and wounded. Accompanied by a few sobbing widows, they trudged home. Kimball and Serlequin proved expert herbalists and bathed everyone's wounds with natural antiseptics. Their strength helped enormously in recovering the carts and carrying the injured from the battlefield to join the procession back to Hollowford.

With Olag destroyed, the foresters who accompanied the giants were free to resume their solitary, mysterious lives in peace. They disappeared as suddenly as they had appeared. The Velma slain were left where they lay for scavengers. Indeed, kites were already circling overhead while wolves and bears would not be far away. Hiss was still securely trussed to a tree when Gareth's company rode past.

"What about me?" he cried.

"Now the way I see it," Archer replied with some relish, "you're tied nice and tight and it's going to take some time to get loose. You might do that before predators arrive, but then you might not."

And they galloped away.

The Wealth
Part 2
Eastern Journey

So the race is on and every second counts.

The sky is alight.

No one rests, Gareth won't let them.

Chapter 11
Tremill Broch

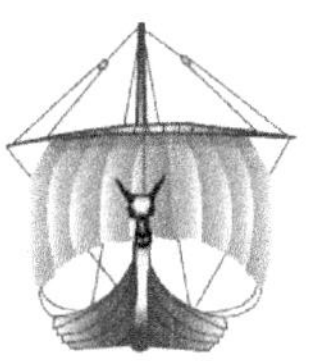

They rode through a night ablaze with shooting stars and thunder flashes that felt like sinister omens, even if no one knew why. By dawn, their horses were exhausted as they entered Joppa Fen. It was time to dismount and lead the animals anyway, as the fen, although not the putrid morass of Ascarmire still needed care through its wetland paths. With the first hint of sunlight, the thunder clouds dwindled and the meteor shower faded. A chorus of bird calls heralded dawn as flocks of geese, ducks, and waders took flight ahead of the riders. Frenzied insects swarmed and were harried by squadrons of darting birds, including the first swallow and swift arrivals. Joppa Fen's lakes abounded with swans, moorhens, eiders, and egrets, while blue kingfishers perched on willow branches, occasionally plunging after small fish.

The party ate and drank on the move, only stopping occasionally to allow the horses to drink lake water. Gareth urged them on, his doubts growing by the moment. Perhaps Crag Daniek's raiders, having experienced one shipwreck, would be reluctant to venture into unfamiliar shallows. Or perhaps their navigation would go awry, but that was mere wishful-thinking. By mid-morning, the fens gave way to sand dunes and salt-grass that was heavy going until they reached the flat, hard-packed beach along Ita Cay lagoon. The thirty horsemen thundered northwards with sea spray cascading as the waves surged past their horses' hooves. Henry loved the coast, its wild freshness and the roar of crashing surf that defined the ocean's might. Puffin colonies roosted in the dunes and thousands of birds flapped out to sea for their morning catch.

Tremill Broch stood at the very tip of the reef. Henry had no idea how far they must travel, but sensed the growing urgency of the other riders, especially when they spied a distant smudge of smoke ahead. Gareth spurred his redoubtable charger into a final effort when a lone figure appeared as a speck on the beach. As they drew closer, they saw it was a boy of eleven or twelve, bare-footed and dressed in a drenched, ragged robe. He was exhausted and staggered to a halt looking terrified as Gareth's horsemen halted in front of him. Archer once again surprised Henry by dismounting and taking the quaking boy firmly, yet gently, by the shoulders to steady him. He was Basil, the messenger Gareth had sent to warn the Broch of danger.

"Relax, young man. What news do you have for us?" Archer asked softly, but the boy could only shake his head as tears welled in his eyes.

"Speak up. Is all well at the Broch?"

"Oh no, lord," Basil spoke in barely a whisper. "Evil has come to Tremill Broch… Raiders from the sea!"

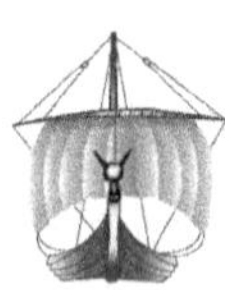

Just prior to dawn, three sleek, black forms glided inshore on a tide. They were long, shallow draft, lapstraked vessels, low set in the water with barely half a fathom of free board along their gunwales. There was no wind now and the crews furled each ship's single, square sail allowing the craft to drift to shore with the current and guided by occasional steer board adjustments and oar strokes. The boats were manned by three score heavily armed warriors clad in mail and wearing bronze helmets, all with ox horns, eagle feathers, wolf and snake effigies, or animal skulls attached.

The sea was calmer here where the top edge of Ita Cay disappeared into a series of sand banks, which still posed the hazard of grounding ships, although with little danger of breaching their hulls. The surf abated as well and rolled off the reef in long swells that dissipated to mere ripples lapping the shoreline. Crag Daniek stood at the prow of the leading wolf-ship and peered ahead as the silhouette of Tremill Broch loomed into view, illuminated by thunder flashes and shooting stars. The original stone tower, consisting of several galleries connected by a spiral stairway to the battlement-encircled roof, was centuries old. Two wings and several cottages and store-houses were added over time. An austere spot, only a few stunted bushes surrounded the buildings. Crag Daniek studied the sea as the first, pre-dawn light rays flashed across the surface enabling him to judge where the channels lay. Evil Queig, the traitor of Palo Innes who stood beside him, was also an expert mariner and could read the waters as well as anyone.

The warriors fairly bristled for action and stowed the sweeps in a single, practised movement then shuffled restlessly as they took up their weapons. Crag Daniek's pet sea-eagle perched on the wolf's head, unhooded, but tethered. The corsair leader kept the erne to catch sea birds for nothing more than his amusement to see the prey ripped to grizzly shreds on the ship deck.

Queig's face twitched with a tic of anticipation. He was no longer the underdog. In the company of Starkmen, this was his first chance to indulge his natural malevolence. He was quite looking forward to it, especially if he faced someone smaller and weaker than himself — not to mention unarmed — which pretty much fitted in with the Starklanders' attitude. He had become one of them and looked the part with long straggling blond hair, much the same as the raiders who were usually fair or red-headed, although Crag Daniek's mane was as black as his heart. Queig was smaller than the others, but tough, sinewy, and carrying no spare fat at all.

"There she lies, Guv," Queig announced, "just like Olag said."

"Looks quiet enough."

"Might be trickery…"

"With this lot on board, they'll be bleedin' sorry, I tell yer. Everyone ready?"

"Yeah, Guv, they're spoilin' fer a scrap."

The keel of the first wolf-ship nudged the shore and the raiders piled out, splashing into the shallows. Crag Daniek admonished them to silence. He wanted total surprise. The other ships were right behind the first and warriors poured over the gunwales following their companions in search of blood. They surged across the sand and smashed through the Broch's main entrance, startling a couple of scribes who were busily recording the night's celestial events. Most of the two-score scholars were indeed awake, having spent the night observing the sky activity. They scattered before the Starkmen, but there was nowhere to run. The tide was still too high for the causeway to be of use. They were either cut down with swords and axes or bludgeoned unconscious by clubs and maces.

Gareth's four warriors were asleep after watching the night sky for hours and rose groggily, scrambling for their weapons. They stood no chance and were hacked to death within minutes, although some of the scribes escaped through the Broch's confusing passages. The Starkmen ransacked the rooms, destroying scrolls, potions, medicines and scientific equipment with wanton delight. Some of the scribes made a bolt for half-a-dozen coracles drawn up beyond the high-tide line, but they were either captured or massacred. The Starkmen bundled another helpless group into a corner, where Crag Daniek grabbed the nearest, quivering figure and dragged the poor wretch to within an inch of his face.

"I could kill yer," he snarled, "but the fun's gone out of it as there ain't a decent fight amongst the lot of yer. We're pirates, see, and we don't like to 'ang abart. So tell us where yer treasure's 'idden or I'll slice yer bleedin' nose off."

The scribe was too terrified to speak and only his lower lip trembled along with a drool of saliva. Crag Daniek was never long on patience and simply cracked his fist onto the poor fellow's head with such ferocity that his spine snapped and he sank to the slate floor. The warrior chief didn't waste time, but grabbed another wretch from the group of hostages.

"Now see what 'appens to them what shuts up when they should bleedin'-well blab. I can keep this up all day, so where's yer loot?"

"There's nothing here," one of the scribes found the courage to address Crag Daniek, who turned and glared at him, releasing his captive.

"Yer bleedin' liar…"

"No lord, w…we have nothing of value here. J…just books and chronicles and medicine. There is no gold or jewels, we are scholars, not kings, and have no use for treasure."

That made no sense at all to Crag Daniek. Of course everyone had a use for wealth, and he was about to run the scholar through, when Dean Merrick appeared. He'd been on the tower roof with Ayla and Macayle, who were so preoccupied with the meteor shower in the pre-dawn, western sky, that they failed to see the wolf-ships approach and only realised the danger when they heard the commotion below. He urged the women to a ladder set against the Broch's outer wall reaching to the roof of an adjoining out-building. He then gathered half-a-dozen small sacks from a storage cabinet at the top of the staircase before descending to the Broch's lower chamber.

Dean Merrick cut an imposing figure standing aloof on the top stair overlooking the chamber. He was tall and ancient, some folk said over a century old, but nobody really knew and he'd certainly been at Tremill Broch far longer than anyone else. His white beard flowed to his waist over a crimson dalmatic embroidered with multi-coloured trim. He carried a staff, but didn't seem the sort of person to use it as a weapon.

"What is the meaning of this?" Dean Merrick boomed in a deep voice that in no way suggested an old man and with such authority, that Crag Daniek swung around eyeing the chief wizard for a moment. Then he smiled.

"The meanin' of this, you blitherin' old fool, is pretty bleedin' clear if yer ask me. We're robbin' yer, ain't we? Now tell us where yer treasure's 'idden or we'll kill the lot of yer."

"Would you presume to anger me further, pirate Be gone!"

Crag Daniek threw back his head and roared with laughter, followed by his men.

"Now that 'as me quakin' in me bleedin' boots, that does. You think I'm scared of an old man with a stick?"

"Oh, this stick..?"

Merrick raised his staff and swept in around the room as gouts of flame flew from its tip. More flashes followed, accompanied by small explosions and billowing, blue smoke. The scribes took the chance to scamper into hiding, leaving the Starkmen spluttering in smog as the chief wizard descended the steps and started thumping pirate skulls with his staff. Crag Daniek raced towards Merrick, but was driven back by two shots of flame that seemed to come from the wizard's finger-tips.

"Beware, sorcery, everyone outside!" Crag Daniek ordered and barged through the portal where daylight had well and truly arrived. His men were only too glad to follow and they milled around as smoke poured from the Broch. Dean Merrick remained inside to tend his wounded colleagues, content that he'd scared the raiders off, for a while at least.

They are such superstitious, simple souls, he thought, *to be fooled by a few mummer's tricks with saltpetre, charcoal, sulphur, and a flint. Mind you, it takes practice to toss flaming powder around without burning your fingers off.*

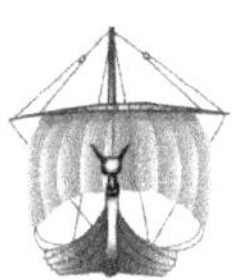

Ayla and Macayle clambered down the ladder and slid off the thatched roof below, hoping to make it to the coracles, but sinister figures swarmed over the island and there was no way to reach the shore without being spotted. Also, that avenue of escape was closed when the raiders upended all the coracles and smashed their frail hulls. They saw Basil on the mainland side of the causeway, waiting for the tide to ebb sufficiently to wade across. He stood horrified at the devastation on Tremill Island until the Starkmen spotted him and fired several arrows that thwacked into the beach at his feet, forcing him to turn and run. He wisely kept running. With the raiders momentarily distracted, Ayla and Macayle ducked inside one of the storage sheds. They found kegs and sacks of produce that looked as if they had already been ransacked by the Starkmen, so they restacked as much as possible before crouching behind the barrier they'd made.

Crag Daniek was in a fury as he staggered from the Broch, his eyes smarting and red from the black-powder smoke. He ran straight into Evil Queig who'd been rampaging through the store-rooms with a group of pirates.

"Ain't nothin' 'ere, Guv," Queig reported. "Just some grain and turnip sacks that we've stowed aboard the boats."

"No bleedin' treasure," Crag Daniek roared. "That lyin' worm Blackaxe'll pay for this, I'll wring 'is bleedin' neck next time I see 'im. Well, if it's a fire that old fart wants, it's a fire 'e'll get. Burn this cursed place to the ground!"

There was plenty of combustible material lying around and soon the Starklanders were setting alight anything that would burn. The Broch was made of stone and the raiders' reluctance to go back inside made it safe enough, but all the other buildings were wood and thatch and they soon blazed fiercely, including Ayla and Macayle's hiding place.

"We can't stay here," Ayla gasped. "We'll either choke or roast to death. Let's try and swim for it. The tide's going down, so it won't be so far."

"It's our only chance," Macayle agreed. "The smoke will hide us."

They kicked aside their protecting bales and raced for the shore through the swirling smoke and straight into Evil Queig. No one knew who was more surprised, but Queig, who was alert and had a fondness for pretty girls, grabbed Macayle. She kicked and wrestled so it took all his attention to hang onto her. Ayla pounded him with her fists, screaming abuse at the top of her lungs, which drew the attention of other pirates who seized her, although it took three of them. Queig finally wrestled Macayle to the ground and a couple of Starkmen helped him to haul her back to the wolf-ships, by which time Crag Daniek had decided to cut his losses and head back to sea on the ebb-tide, especially when one of his warriors reported riders approaching.

"'Ow many?" he demanded.

"Dunno, Guv. 'Ard to tell, but enough to cause trouble and they look the business. They'll be able to ride across that causeway anytime now."

"Yeah, this place ain't worth fightin' for. C'mon let's get outta 'ere."

Crag Daniek reached the wolf-ships with the last of his raiders just as Queig was scrambling on board with Ayla and Macayle, who weren't going quietly.

"What yer got there, Evil?"

"Two pretties if ever I saw 'em, Guv. Looks like it weren't a dead loss after all."

Crag Daniek heaved both women over the stern gunwales and they tumbled into a very unpleasant bilge that held several inches of stale, garbage-ridden brine. Ayla leapt to her feet and began screaming at Crag Daniek as he vaulted aboard the wolf-ship. He slapped her with the back of his hand, sending her sprawling again with a trail of blood seeping between her clenched teeth.

"Shut up!" he raged, and then turned his attention to his crew.

Four men used their huge sweeps to kedge the ship into deeper water until the other oarsmen took over. They rowed the vessels aft-first to gain enough sea-room to turn them and hoist the sails. The Starkmen ignored Ayla and Macayle, considering a good belt across the mouth was enough to subdue any woman. But Ayla and Macayle weren't any women and they knew their chances were now very limited and dwindling by the second.

"Quick," Ayla hissed, "over the side!"

Once again they sprang to their feet and scrambled to the gunwales, only to see a line of oars pounding into the surf. If they jumped they risked being battered to death, but there was no choice and not a moment to spare. Evil Queig noticed his prizes about to escape and yelled from the prow, alerting the oarsmen, who stopped rowing and held their sweeps parallel to the water out of sheer habit. Macayle leapt onto the aft oar and danced from one to the next until she reached the forward oars, but lost her balance and plunged into the sea. Ayla was a split second behind her, but it was a split-second too late and just enough time for the rear oarsmen to grab her legs and drag her screaming and struggling back on board.

Macayle's head bobbed to the surface just clear of the oar-blades, she was not a particularly strong swimmer, but she swam with all her might. She realised that her velvet cloak was pulling her down and quickly unclipped the clasp letting it float free, leaving her in just a light shift and much better able to stay afloat. Crag Daniek grabbed a bow and fired an arrow that slammed into Macayle's shoulder. She shrieked and sank beneath the surface, leaving a smear of blood dissipating across the sea. Ayla screamed abuse at the pirate chief, but she was held by two burly Starkmen and helpless to act. The crews drew the oars on board as the ships veered with the current before hoisting the sails and slipping away to sea.

Gareth's riders surged across the causeway as the last of the sea water washed away, so even Bron was able to bound along with little difficulty. They galloped into a scene of fire, smoke, and death. About ten of Tremill's scholars had been randomly slaughtered and their bodies lay scattered in bloody heaps. Dean Merrick met Gareth at the Broch's main entrance, his face grim but calm in view of the carnage.

"I fear you are too late, lord," he said, "but perhaps your men can help douse the fires."

"Ayla and Macayle," Gareth cried, "where are they?"

"I'm sorry, lord, they were stolen. Your men were taken by surprise and have all been slain."

Gareth's grief and rage were immeasurable, but what could he do? The smoke was clearing and they saw all three sails disappearing to the eastern horizon. The Hollowford men began a clean up while Merrick tended his wounded colleagues. Henry and Edrid scoured the island in search of clues to where the pirates were bound, but of course there were none. They reached the shoreline in as much despair as Gareth. All Hollowford loved Ayla and Macayle and now they were gone and there was no way of finding them. Then Henry noticed a movement close to shore, a weak floundering figure with blood seeping into the current and what looked like a dozen large grey fish circling it the shallows.

"Dog fish," Edrid announced, as Henry gave him a puzzled

look. "Small sharks, they are common and normally shy, but the blood has drawn them."

Henry had never seen sharks before, but of course Edrid was a marine expert. The dogfish were perhaps half the size of a grown man, but they looked dangerous. He drew Hornet-Sting and waded through the waves. Bron bounded in beside him trying to catch the smallest dogfish. Henry slashed at one of the sharks inflicting a deep, bloody wound that drove it away. The others followed, seemingly not particular what blood attracted them. Then he turned his attention to help Edrid drag the body from the water.

"Lord! Lord Gareth! Archer!" he yelled with all his might. "Come quickly. Please!"

"She's lucky the ebb-tide didn't sweep her out to sea, but she's still a very sick girl," Dean Merrick announced, rather unnecessarily in Henry's view, as anyone could see that. Macayle lay ghostly pale on a pallet with her shoulder bound with clean linen. "I've removed the arrow. Luckily the head and shaft came out cleanly, but a couple of dog-fish bites haven't helped. It's all I can do. I'm afraid I'm more an alchemist than physician,"

"I'll salvage a wagon from one of the sheds, lord," Archer said softly. "We'll take her home now."

Macayle is so sick.
Dean Merrick may have removed the arrow completely
and the wound is clean, but the dog-fish bites fester.
They are only, small cuts, but don't heal
and she has a terrible fever.
No one knows what to do, but bathe her with cold water.
Please recover, Macayle, I couldn't bear it if you died.
Why have such violent times come to the Peninsula?
Archer says times are always violent.
Tribes only get along if they must to combat a greater threat.
He likes individuals well enough,
but is pretty cynical when considering people in general

Chapter 12
Jongarrat

Everyone believed the previous night's flaming sky had portended such disastrous events, there could be no other explanation. Henry took Basil home and explained to his mother how brave he'd been before returning to Gareth's hall, where a glum party hovered around Macayle's bed. Thayer applied cool compresses, but her fever continued. Even Kimball and Serlequin's herbal brews proved ineffective.

"I am at a loss," Gareth admitted dismally. "How can we find my Ayla? How can we heal Macayle?"

No one answered. The wolf-ships had gone, leaving no clue and even Edrid was vague about where the Starkmen came from. It wasn't as if they'd told anyone. Hollowford folk weren't mariners and Edrid's islanders only fished close to shore, their currachs were no match for wolf-ships.

"Where have they gone?" Gareth cried in frustration.

"They're goin' 'ome."

The group turned as Guilda entered Gareth's hall, accompanied by a stocky figure who had spoken. He barely came to her shoulder, but there was nothing comical about his tough, weather-beaten, bearded face. He was dressed in leather breeches and boots with a coat of otter pelts and carried a knap-sack strapped across one shoulder and a water gourd over the other. An axe and a dagger were tucked into his belt. He also carried a long staff and looked like he knew how to use it. In all, he appeared to be a man who relied on self-sufficiency for long periods.

"So you've returned from your woodland wandering, Jongarrat," Gareth sighed. "We have grim tidings."

"Aye, I heard, Gareth," Jongarrat didn't bother with honorifics, he was any man's equal. "But first things first. You'd better let Guilda have a look at your wee girl."

"Word gets around the forest," Guilda said. "I thought I'd be needed after your fight."

She examined Macayle and announced she was infected by the shark bites. Guilda produced an efficacious poultice from her bag, which she applied to the wounds.

"Be off with you all. You're only in my way," she ordered. "Thayer, I'll come and help the others when I've tended Macayle."

Guilda seemed unconcerned about the outcome. She certainly had no intention of bleeding Macayle, saying the poor girl had lost enough blood already, but she had confidence in her medicine. That proved correct. By evening, Macayle's fever broke, after which she slept peacefully until dawn. While his daughter rested, Gareth held a council-of-war in his main hall. All his warriors were present including Kimball, Serlequin, Edgar, and the mysterious Jongarrat. Even Henry and Edrid were allowed to sit in. Guilda and Thayer took a break from nursing battle casualties and joined the company for a while.

"What can you tell us?" Gareth asked Jongarrat directly.

"You're up against a tough gang who'll take Ayla back to Glam first."

"Where?"

"It's their hide-out across Black Water."

"What will they do with my wife?"

"Keep her as a slave maybe, or sell 'er. Starkmen like gold and I'd say she's worth a fair bit."

It was a compliment in its way, but Henry thought Jongarrat could have been more tactful, although Gareth showed no offence.

"Then we must go and rescue her," Henry declared.

"Yeah, right, sonny," Jongarrat said dismissively. "How're you gonna cross the sea with no boats, no one to build 'em or sail 'em, except our islander, here."

"Is there a way around or does the sea stretch to the edge of the world? Surely it can't go on forever?" Archer asked.

"You could go overland, but it'd be through Zilek Gorge and that's a good way to end up dead. The Corbin Brethren guard that pass, and they'll kill anyone who tries to get by just out of spite. Some say they're cannibals, which I fancy is true 'cause there ain't much to eat up in the mountains. Want to end up in someone's cooking pot do you, Gareth?"

"That tattooed girl from Olag's gang said as much," Thayer explained. "She was born into a Corbin tribe before being sold to some Velma thugs. She'll confirm they're ruthless, barbaric, and treat everyone mercilessly, including their womenfolk and children. She preferred Velma and never wants to return to Zilek."

"Sounds about right to me," Jongarrat added smugly.

"We'll take the militia and make short work of any mountain rogues."

"Whoa there, Gareth. Weren't you listening? Firstly, as Thayer said, the Corbin ain't just a pack of bandits. The pass is narrow and a few good fighters can hold off your army. You'd have to provision and resupply a horde and I don't think you've the resources fer that. The only chance is a small group, maybe half-a-dozen to sneak by, but..."

"How will so few take on the Starklanders?" Archer asked with his usual sceptical precision. "We could hire mercenaries, I suppose."

"Don't expect help from no one and I weren't thinkin' of heroics, man, just buyin' her back before they sell her off. You better take them trinkets young Henry found and any other baubles you've got. It might be a harsh trade."

Even Jongarrat was tactful enough not to mention in what condition Ayla might be, if they found her, and no one else wanted to think about it at all.

"Then we'll do it, dammit!" Gareth declared and Henry knew that was the last he'd see of his treasure, but if it brought Ayla back, then he was happy to part with the talismans.

"We?"

"You've been there before it seems to me. We need you to guide us, name your price."

Gareth wasn't much of an asker, which was a poor tactic when dealing with someone as rambunctiously independent as Jongarrat.

"I ain't got a price," the dwarf-man replied peevishly, he'd provided information and felt his obligation fulfilled. "Guilda needs me here. What about your tattooed girl?"

"She's in no condition to travel," Thayer said quickly. "Her wound will take weeks, even months to heal and, from what she told me, she'd rather die than go back."

Guilda thought Jongarrat's excuse was pretty lame anyway.

"I'll be fine," she said. "You wander off half the time anyway and I'm needed in the village for a bit until all these folk mend. Go on — help Gareth get his woman back."

"Look, it's just not for me...the other side of Black Water, I mean," Jongarrat said enigmatically, but explained no further when pushed. Gareth, Edgar and Archer tried to entice him with wealth, including the precious talismans, an endless beer supply, and even a couple of the captured Velma girls, but Jongarrat wasn't interested. Finally Guilda appealed to his better nature, although he insisted he didn't have one.

"If for no other reason, go for the sake of poor Macayle, who lies sick and without a mother."

"There're plenty of folk who get by without mothers…"

But Guilda just glared at him and Henry felt a pang of hurt.

"All right," he sighed, "I'll guide you if it'll shut everyone up. Choose five of your best, Gareth. Get 'em kitted and make sure they understand they might not be coming back. We leave first thing tomorrow. Everyone bring bows and as many arrows as you can manage. We might need some long-range protection."

Gareth gave orders to Archer and Faranden, his rage now channelled into cool, diligent preparation with steely determination, and beware anyone who stood in his way. Jongarrat left the hall and headed for Clem Foster's inn.

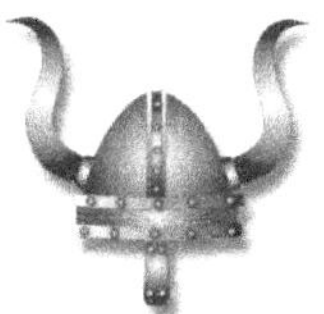

Gareth would have gone on his own, but Archer and Faranden were liegemen and bound to do what they were told. Kimball and Serlequin agreed to accompany them out of curiosity, a mood for mischief, and because they were decent fellows who wanted to lend a hand. Jongarrat knew Guilda wouldn't give him a minute's peace if he changed his mind, so he was resigned to the task, making a contrast to the others, but no one was going to mock their incongruity. Although the giants seemed amiable enough, who was going to make fun of a fiery, well-armed dwarf?

Henry moped at being left behind. He'd found the amulets after all, but Gareth was intractable and Jongarrat insisted a party of six was ideal, big enough to deter trouble but stood the best chance of going unnoticed. Any more and the venture was doomed from its start. Jongarrat warned that horses would also prove a liability in Zilek gorge, so they walked. They left armed to the teeth and Edrid returned Skull-Crusher to Archer, saying his need was now undoubtedly greater. The whole village turned out to see them off.

Henry sulked for a while and it hadn't help when Faranden drew him aside before the warriors left. Faranden suggested in no uncertain terms that the boy wasn't so smart now and had been put firmly back in his place. But Henry cheered up because Macayle recovered quickly, although she fretted terribly for her parents. So he brought her spring flowers every morning to cheer her up.

"Do you think they stand a chance of finding mother?" she asked while he sat beside her.

"Don't worry, they're as tough a group as you'd ever want to meet. If anyone can it's them, but your father could be away for months. I just wish there was something we could do, I hate feeling so helpless."

"I think I'd despair if I lost them..." she hesitated. "Oh, I'm sorry, Henry. It was thoughtless of me."

"No, it's all right, I miss Mum and Dad, but it was so long ago now, I sometimes don't seem to remember them. It saddens me when that happens, I suppose, but it eases the pain of losing them. I've got used to it by now. Anyway, I have Aunt Thayer and Uncle Edgar and I love them as much as any parents."

Realising he was supposed to be comforting her and not the other way around, he went on to talk about other things, including Edrid who had disappeared without a word to anyone. Macayle's arm was bandaged neatly in a sling and she took short walks with Henry and Bron, restoring colour to her cheeks and strength to her body. Edrid returned a few days later and was delighted by Macayle's recovery. They celebrated with a pitcher of small beer outside Clem Foster's, including Bron who lapped from a wooden bowl and enjoyed the taste.

"I haven't thanked you two valiant paladins for rescuing me," Macayle said coyly, kissing them lightly on the cheek in turn. "Dear Henry has been so attentive, but you seemed to have deserted me, Prince Edrid."

"I've been exploring," Edrid announced, "talking to people."

"Talking about what?" Henry challenged.

"Boats, among other things. I took a trip back to the coast."

"What, back to Burgal?"

"No you goose, the Ita Cay coast. I found someone who might help us. His name is Anshelm the Angler, and he knows all about boats."

"Well, he would," Macayle said, "he's a fisherman, but he's an old hermit who doesn't talk to anyone. He lives in a shack along the beach below Tremill Broch, but I've never met him."

"He talked to me," Edrid said a little smugly, "fisherman-to-fisherman, so to speak."

"And how is that of interest?"

"We're going to build a currach and sail after those villains."

"You're mad!" Henry cried, "It would be suicide."

"No, think about it. I've spent all my life on open water, I've built dozens of coracles and currachs and I'm a good sailor..."

"Nothing modest about him," Macayle grinned, nudging Henry in the ribs and wincing as she jarred her wounded shoulder.

"I'm just stating facts," Edrid sighed.

"And then we take on the entire Starklander clan. Great plan!"

"No we find 'em, hide in a cave or somewhere, and stake out the lay of the land, then sneak in and rescue Ayla, just like you did at Olag's camp."

Yeah, and look how that turned out — me running for my life, Henry thought, but let it slide noticing Macayle staring wide-eyed at Edrid. She was revising her opinion of him dramatically.

"There will probably be islanders there to rescue too," Edrid continued, "and it's a way of atoning for past deeds."

"You didn't have much option, if you ask me," Henry reminded him sympathetically.

"Nevertheless, I behaved dishonourably and Palo Innes men lie dead for it. I'm duty-bound to find my lost people, alone if no one will help me."

"Of course we'll help you," Macayle said and placed her hand over his, much to Henry's chagrin.

"Yes, Edrid," he agreed, "you're not going off crusading all by yourself."

And once the decision was made he became just as enthusiastic as Edrid, at least they were going to do something. Now Macayle was looking at him with the same warmth she showed the Prince of Palo Innes.

"I told Anshelm we'd visit him tomorrow."

"That's fine," Henry said, "Aunt Thayer told Uncle Edgar to give me time off from the forge to look after Macayle."

"And what a good job you're doing too," she smiled for the first time in days.

So the three companions set out the following day. Macayle, not content with her docile palfrey, was mounted on Bruno who she handled expertly, while Henry favoured Bella and Edrid still rode the horse from Velma. By now the animals were used to Bron, who bounded along beside them. Guilda judged that an outing would improve Macayle's health and be a diversion to cheer her up. In her opinion people, either recovered quickly or died. She was pleased to announce Macayle fell into the first category. There was a trail to Anshelm's beach-shack used by one enterprising fellow who'd struck a deal with the fisherman to trade all his spare catch — mostly for beer — and sell it to Hollowford goodwives. This established a monopoly which suited Anshelm, who'd rather deal with one person than dozens. The angler's shanty was set into coastal dunes where two upturned coracles and a number of paddles lay close by, alongside nets hanging from frames while lobster pots, coiled rope, long-lines, driftwood, and other salvaged flotsam were plied randomly. The shack was weathered by salt spray, but in good repair and its wooden shingles all nailed securely in place.

"Why do loners have so much stuff?" Henry wondered. "This looks like Guilda's place."

"Might come in handy, even if he never uses it, eh?" Edrid quipped.

"Oh, very droll, young scallywag. Very droll indeed" Anshelm said, emerging from his hut. "It ain't like I can borrow or trade with neighbours if I need summut, so I keep what I find, don't I?"

He was wiry and muscular with a face that reminded one of

grainy wood etched by sun, surf, and wind. A leather patch covered one eye, but the other was a piercing, pale blue. His age was hard to determine, but his flowing hair and beard were completely white. He seemed rough, but grinned through brilliant white teeth although a couple were missing, and was not at all the grouchy recluse they'd expected.

"Morning, Anshelm, I'd like you to meet my friends, Henry and Macayle from Hollowford."

"G'day to you young 'Enry, and to you, miss," Anshelm greeted civilly. "Edrid 'ere tells me you've a notion to go a-sailin'."

They dismounted and gathered around a fire where two iron pots gave off the inviting aromas of fish chowder and unleavened bread. For all his solitude, Anshelm was sociable on his own terms, proving a cordial host and as he was expecting them, he'd prepared lunch. He explained he lived in isolation because he discouraged others from settling on the shore and competing for fish, but dinner guests were quite a different matter. He poured them each a bowl of soup and broke the hot loaf into quarters. Henry had to admit he couldn't remember when he'd tasted anything as good. Bron, who wasn't particularly fussy, finished off a bucket of fish heads.

"There ain't so many fish as you can just keep 'ookin' 'em outa the sea. You can only take so many or there'll be none left for next year. Others 'ave tried, but didn't 'ave much luck, their lines kept getting' tangled, nets broken, 'oles in their coracles and suchlike," he smiled wickedly. "Nope, they didn't 'ave no luck at all."

"Edrid told you about Tremill Broch?" Henry ventured.

"Yup, rum doin's fer sure. Poor buggers never did no real 'arm and gets whacked anyway, just don't seem fair, do it?"

"You know we want to go after the raiders."

"So Edrid said, but what d'you reckon you can do?"

"Rescue Ayla and sail away, Edrid knows how to handle a boat, but it'll have to be sturdy and big enough to carry provisions for a few weeks."

"And you plan to take on the Starkmen?"

"No, silly," Macayle said, "We'll have to be sneaky."

Henry and Edrid exchanged glances because it was the first they'd heard anything about her going, but they both remained silent and if Anshelm noticed, he gave no indication.

"Now young Edrid 'ere is used to wild seas from what 'e tells me, so I don't doubt he can 'andle a boat. But goin' beyond the reef is a risky business. You sure you want to take it on?"

They all nodded.

"They don't call 'em 'igh seas for nothin'. There're storms that'll smash a boat to splinters and Orcas, sharks, and who-knows-what swimmin' about out there. You've gotta exercise caution, aye caution's a good plan."

"We know all about sharks…"

"What them little dog-fish? Wait till y'see a great white. They're monsters, all teeth and a bad attitude."

But Henry was determined.

"In that case," Anshelm said, "I don't mind givin' yer a hand, and I've got something to show you when we finish our soup."

After their meal, they washed the bowls and spoons in seawater, leaving them to dry on a bench. Anshelm explained that salt seeped into the wood and improved the flavour of the next meal.

"I'll remember that," Macayle, who fancied herself as a good cook, said.

He led them inland to where a copse stood among the dunes.

"Now if yer wanna build a ship, yer can't start from nothin', yer need materials, see."

Pulling back some branches, he revealed a stash of wooden planking, iron fittings, ropes, turn-buckles, cleats, and even a large sheet of stout canvas. The significance of this collection was not lost on Edrid, although Henry and Macayle weren't quite as excited about what looked suspiciously like a pile of junk.

"It's a start," Edrid said cautiously. "Where did you get all this from?"

"The Starkmen," Anshelm replied slyly. "When they come ashore last fall-season, I went down fer a look. Them Starkmen and Velma folk was so busy choppin' wood and fixin' up the busted ship, they was exhausted by day's end. They didn't notice stuff disappearin' each night and they left loads behind. That seemed a waste, so I brought it back 'ere bit by bit. Used some of it to repair me own 'ouse and boats."

"A start maybe," Henry said, "but even I know we'll need much more than this."

"Ye'll need 'elp no doubt. You'll 'ave ter do some persuadin', but there's carpenters and a cooper in town, and a seamstress and cordwainer fer the sheets and sails. Yer uncle's a smith, 'Enry, that'll come in mighty 'andy."

By then it was too late to return to the village, so they piled the fire with driftwood and settled down for the night. Mackerel were chasing bait-fish close to shore and Anshelm netted a dozen, which they baked for supper. After their meal, while they chatted about the harmony and vagary of life on the coast, Anshelm produced a piece of whale bone and resumed carving an intricate design into it that Macayle admired greatly. He chatted enthusiastically about boat building in general and their project in particular.

"You seem keen to build the boat," Macayle observed.

"It's a change, y'see. 'Ceptin' the weather, most days be much the same 'ere-about, so somethin' different is an amusement, ain't it?"

They turned in early and were up at first light for the ride back to Hollowford for some serious negotiating with the villagers.

So for no other reason than a fisherman's boredom
we had found a valuable ally.
I was wallowing in self-pity,
but thanks to Edrid we're actually doing something.
Gareth might not think I'm good enough for his quest,
but we'll see who's good enough.

CHAPTER 13
WEASEL

Gareth soon lost patience at their progress and strode ahead. Kimball and Serlequin kept up easily, while Archer, Faranden, and Jongarrat followed knowing, determined as he was, Gareth would tire and slow down. Jongarrat reminded him their journey was not a matter of days, but weeks or months, and they'd need a solid, steady pace to keep going.

In time they returned to the battlefield, now filled with squabbling crows, kites, wolverines, and foxes. Larger scavengers such as wolves and bears had come and gone leaving slim pickings for the rest. There was no sign of Hiss and whether he'd escaped or fallen to predators was unclear. The carrion-feeders flapped languidly skyward or slinked into the forest as the travellers passed, but only a few returned when the coast was clear, because there was nothing worth coming back for. Rats and bugs would complete the cleanup, leaving the forest pristine with only ragged strips of cloth and rusty chain-mail to mark the fight. Even that would decay in time.

Olag's camp was predictably deserted, someone had even released his irritable raven, but the marquee remained, providing shelter for the night. Spring storms raged regularly now and thunder growled continuously. More downpours threatened when they reached Velma so, hostile as the town might be, they needed to find somewhere dry. No one had bothered to bar the gates and

Gareth led his men through, striding forward with Goresax drawn and ready. Technically he was now Lord of Velma, but its citizens might not necessarily agree.

"There are plenty of ale 'ouses, Gareth," Jongarrat said, indicating a doorway close by. "This un's probably the best. It's not great mind, but better than outside tonight."

"You seem well informed," Gareth observed.

"I get around."

The inn reminded Archer of Walter's place at Burgal, same dirt floor, bare ramshackle furniture, ale and mead casks against the wall, and a ladder leading to a loft covered with straw and probably infested with fleas. A fire glowed in a stone grate with an inefficient flue so smoke veiled the barroom. A handful of unsavoury looking drinkers sat inside, but quickly made themselves scarce. Two hooded figures were deep in discussion with the proprietor before darting through the back door, leaving him fidgeting behind the bar. His face was ashen, with baggy eyes that seeped a yellowish puss, while his long, hooked nose, tangled hair, and stringy moustache gave him a twitching, weasely appearance.

Gareth eyed Jongarrat who merely shrugged.

"Like I said, it's the best place in town."

"Oh indeed, lord," the weasel oozed, "Best beer and victuals on the peninsula, oh yessir."

"I'll wager Clem Foster might contest the point, but we'll need food and lodging tonight and jugs of porter right now."

"Coming right up, yessir," Weasel said.

The party gathered around one of the tables, pulling up chairs and stools while Weasel placed drinks before them. The dark beer wasn't the best they'd tasted, but it wasn't poison either, so the first round quickly slaked their thirst.

"There's pork stew on the boil," Weasel said as he brought more drinks. "Very fortifying, yessir. Just what travelling gentlemen like you need, yessir. And where might you be bound in these troubled times?"

"We are bound about our own business," Archer replied acidly.

Weasel was becoming garrulous, now he realised the strangers weren't going to rob him or wreck his place, but Archer's tone restored him to his normal, shifty self. There wasn't enough room in the loft for them all, so Gareth, Serlequin, and Kimball made themselves comfortable on the floor while Archer, Jongarrat, and Faranden shared the garret. Weasel even provided furs and extra straw for the floor.

"Want you to be comfy," he said with a wink. "Sleep nice and sound tonight if you've a long trip tomorrow."

During the evening, the back door cracked open and a figure beckoned Weasel, who crept through the exit and held a discussion in heated whispers with four men, including the pair he'd spoken to earlier. One of the others spoke in barely a hiss, while his companion's voice was a deep growl. Weasel was agitated and plainly unhappy when he returned to the barroom. In time, Gareth's party took turns at the privy, before turning in and were soon snoring deeply. Weasel waited until he was sure they all slept soundly before snuffing out the remaining candles and slipping through the back door, leaving the fire to smoulder with enough warmth for the night, but also ensuring the front entrance stayed unbolted.

Some time past midnight, Hiss and Growl made their move, leading two dozen furtive shapes along the shadowy alley towards Weasel's tavern. One of the men carried a pot of animal fat and smeared the hinges before silently easing the door ajar. A shaft of moonlight laced across the barroom floor, but none of the sleepers stirred. More men slipped into the tavern and soon the three forms on the floor were surrounded. The intruders raised their clubs and weighed in mercilessly. But something felt wrong, and they stopped almost immediately as their victims simply dissolved into a flurry of down, straw, and pulverised animal pelts. They realised they were battering hide-covered straw bales and not flesh and bone. Suddenly a flint sparked and a torch flared to life illuminating Gareth and Jongarrat beside the bar.

"Oh dear, dear me," Gareth chided shaking his head wearily. "You must think us the simplest of men."

As he spoke, Archer and Faranden dropped from the loft, axes swinging and slew two men each as Jongarrat and Gareth leapt into action, killing half a dozen Velma thugs who were hard pressed to defend themselves in the cramped barroom. The attackers turned to flee, but were jammed in the doorway or crashed into others who were trying to get inside and escape a dreadful commotion in the street. Kimball and Serlequin had left via the back way and waited in the shadows before following the waylayers to the tavern and now attacking them from behind with a vengeance.

"Don't hold back, lads!" Gareth yelled as he drove Goresax through a Velma gut. "They had harsh plans for us!"

Archer was the first to hack his way outside to find the alley scattered with dead and wounded, while a couple of survivors staggered away nursing injuries that would likely prove fatal. Hiss and Growl lay among the dead.

"Well lookee there," Archer observed, "it's the talkative fellow from our last fight, seems his pal released him in time after all. Got their just desserts all right. Henry will be pleased after they knocked him and his wolf about."

"I'm pleased they turned up before we really fell asleep," Serlequin added.

There was a great deal of scuffling and yelling from inside before Faranden came through the door dragging Weasel along. The innkeeper showed remarkable agility, and it was all Faranden could do to hang onto him. The big warrior slapped Weasel a couple of times subduing him to twitching whimpers.

"I grabbed him as he tried to slip out the rear. He should have known we'd be suspicious when he didn't lock the door in a cesspit like Velma."

"Now, was robbery the reason for this, or is there a more sinister motive?" Gareth asked quietly. Turning to Jongarrat, he indicated the bodies that littered the doorway and street.

"What do you make of this lot? Just Velma trash?"

The dwarf inspected the dead men and agreed that indeed appeared to be the case, with the exception of two men who wore distinctive, full length robes and their faces and arms were completely tattooed with swirling images.

"Corbin renegades," Jongarrat muttered, "come to town for a taste of sin mebbe, or to spy out future victims, who knows?"

"Noticed 'em when we arrived and they seemed pretty chummy with this fellow," Faranden growled, twisting Weasel's collar until he choked while pressing a dagger to his throat for good measure.

"No...I...know...nothing..."

"You seem to know how to plan murder and theft."

"No…they made me…said they'd kill me if I didn't help…"

"And we're going to kill you because you did help."

"No, please, lord!" Weasel quaked in Faranden's grip. "Now I can help you, lord, guide you. I've been to Zilek."

"And what makes you think that's where we're going?" Gareth asked.

"The little fella there," Weasel said, which bristled Jongarrat's hackles as he wasn't much shorter than the inn-keeper. "He blabbed about the Corbin… All Velma knows you're Chief Gareth from Hollowford. You come from the north going south…so it stands t' reason."

"Shrewd little negotiator, ain't he?" Faranden sneered. "But we've got a guide already, so I might as well run him through right now."

"Wait, it's been years since I came through the gorge," Jongarrat admitted. "He might be useful, and we can keep an eye on the sneaky little rat."

"Well, do you think you have knowledge enough to save your wretched life?" Gareth asked and Weasel nodded vigorously. "All right, but make one wrong move and you're dead. Tie him up, Faranden, and let's at least get some sleep for the rest of the night."

Jongarrat might have considered himself off the hook as he'd only said he'd guide the party through Zilek Gorge and committed to nothing beyond there, although Gareth assumed he'd lead them all the way to Glam. Now they had another guide he considered heading back, but dismissed the thought as he knew Guilda would only give him grief and send him after Gareth again. Normally she was good company, but in a bad mood, well…

Some of Weasel's bravado returned the next day as he led them south and he thought of ways to stir up trouble. He dawdled until Faranden nudged him with his halberd point, muttering a few profanities about where he'd shove it if Weasel didn't get a move on.

"You're all going to die anyway," the innkeeper warned. "No one gets through Zilek the brotherhood don't want to."

"Jongarrat did," Archer observed, "and now we have two guides."

By and by, the company reached the Graff River estuary, which was a vast flood plain similar to Joppa Fen with fewer pathways. At times they trudged through sucking quagmires of mud or waded waist deep across ponds and lagoons. No silent wetland, the buzz and chirps of amphibians, reptiles, and insects filled the air. As men were rare hereabouts, wildlife wasn't particularly shy. Flies and mosquitoes hung around in droves. Slapping them away just added to the travellers' fatigue. Fortunately they crossed the worst of the Graff Delta tributaries in a day and found firm, dryish ground to make camp. Seemingly endless, tall grass-covered plains sprawled ahead where antelope herds grazed. With such an abundant supply of game, the travellers were unlikely to go hungry.

Questioning Weasel further proved discouraging. He became stubborn and even boldly antagonistic once he sensed Gareth might bully him, but was unlikely to kill him out of hand. That was more of a Velma practice. He only repeated that the gorge was patrolled by warriors whose sole purpose was to rob and murder anyone foolish enough to pass by. Jongarrat had confirmed as much. Archer and Gareth thought there would hardly be sufficient travellers to make the Corbin even the meanest living until Jongarrat explained Zilek wasn't just a single pass. Hundreds of chasms and ravines stretched far to the south. He remembered experienced guides, who either knew how to dodge or pay off the Brotherhood, made a fortune leading traders and small caravans through the labyrinth of mountain passes. It seemed they specialised in small, valuable merchandise including gemstones, spices, and especially desirable slaves, where the profits were as high as the risks. However, there were always men ruthless enough for such enterprises. Ironically, along with extensive surrounding wetlands, Zilek Gorge was the bastion that kept Grambak Peninsula isolated and protected from marauders.

They took several days to cover the savannahs that at first appeared to be flat and easy to traverse, but were riddled with gullies, rabbit burrows, and hidden creek-beds, so they made no better time than through the Graff River Delta. Finally the purple scar of the Zilek Range smudged the horizon and Jongarrat called a halt, suggesting it would be the last chance for a fire and hot food. Although it could take days to reach the mountains, smoke would be visible for leagues and there was no sense in announcing their arrival.

Small herds of antelope continually broke cover, and the party had no trouble bagging a small buck for supper. They roasted the whole animal and planned to use the left-over cold meat to supplement their rations until it was once more safe to hunt game and start another fire. As they sat around the campfire, Jongarrat explained his plan.

"It's too easy to get ambushed in the gorge, so we go over the ridges," he said. "It's hard goin' and colder, but nothin' to a bunch o' tough troopers like you, eh? I'll lead and mebbe remember the way from years ago. Weasel 'ere can warn us where the Corbin camps are, 'cos I reckon 'e knows a lot more than 'e's telling'."

"They lives in caves. There's dozens of 'em, 'ow am I supposed to find 'em all?" Weasel protested.

"You'll manage," Faranden grinned, "because if you miss one, you'll be of no further use and we'll toss you over a cliff. It's as simple as that really. Quite an incentive, I'd say."

Two days later, they approached the Zilek foothills where scattered trees spread a refreshing shade as the days became noticeably warmer. There was still plenty of running water and they all replenished their water gourds.

"Best to rest for the afternoon," Jongarrat announced, "There won't be any stoppin' once we're in them mountains."

High upon a granite tor that marked the entrance to Zilek Gorge, a lone sentinel scanned the northern plains towards Graff River. A long mantle protected him from sun and wind, its grey colour providing perfect camouflage against that rocky terrain. The cowl was wrapped around his mouth and nose, hiding the swirling tattoos covering his face. He stood motionless with the patience of an experienced hunter, staring through deep brown, almost black eyes. Little escaped his notice. In time he was joined by another grey-robed, tattooed tribesman who stood silently beside him.

"Peace to you, brother," the first lookout finally greeted.

"And to you, brother," the other warrior replied. "Death to

intruders."

"Death to intruders," the first tribesman echoed, peering into the vast emptiness below. "I cannot be sure, but there might have been a movement on the plain."

"An animal herd perhaps."

"I could not divine."

"Our brothers from the northern scout are due to return at any time."

"Perhaps, but they made no signal."

The newcomer shrugged.

"There is food prepared," he said.

"That's welcome," the first sentry said, turning towards their camp, "Blessing and honour upon your family."

"And to yours. Death to intruders."

"Death to intruders!"

*I have also
discovered
you can't
trust girls
for a second!*

Chapter 14
Ita Cay

Henry needn't have worried, everyone from Hollowford pitched in to help. It was that kind of community and they knew they'd either be dead or enslaved by now except for Henry and Archer's warning about the Velma attack. Edgar accepted their story that Edrid wanted a boat to sail home, which was plausible enough. Folk trouped across to Anselm's hut in groups to see what they could do, so he had more visitors in a week than during his entire life on the beach.

Villagers used coracles and rafts for stream fishing, but no one had actually built a sea-going craft and they all wanted to be part of the project. After consulting Anshelm, Thayer even drew a plan that met with the fisherman's approval. There was some discussion over design and construction materials, mostly between Anshelm and Edrid. A few townsfolk made suggestions that were usually met with a nautical scowl, but occasionally they contributed something worthwhile.

George, the village master-carpenter turned up with a journeyman and two apprentices, pulling a cartload of timber, adzes, saws, awls, nails and mallets. They set to work, guided by Edrid or Anshelm. A cheerful fellow from the cordwainer's shop generously supplemented Anshelm's store of seal pelts with a stack of cured animal hides to cover the boat frame making a water-tight, leather hull.

Edrid explained what iron fittings were needed and Henry went to work at the forge. Thayer oversaw a number of Hollowford goodwives who stitched a pair of stout, canvas sails and a cover to protect the stores from salt spray. Joe, the cooper, provided a tun for water storage and three firkins to hold salted meat, vegetables and bread. A pair of woodsmen felled suitable timber and hewed a massive, solid block. They bored a hole through the wood slab to hold the mast before bolting it to the keelson. In the evenings, some villagers stayed at the beach rather than make the long trek back home at night. They built a grand bonfire and enjoyed a meal with some ale, making a pleasant diversion from the thought that they might not see their beloved chief and his wife again. Everyone knew good leaders were hard to find and they had the best in Gareth and Ayla.

By default, the village headman's position fell to Edgar. The job mainly entailed keeping Gareth's warriors out of Clem Foster's tavern and ensuring they continued their patrol and guard duties. If they resented Edgar's new-found authority, he had his strength and sledge hammer as back-up so they obeyed him. As temporary chief, Edgar also found himself mediating village disputes. While the squabbles were normally petty, they proved frustrating and time consuming, although folk started calling him "mayor," which he quite liked. He came to realise Gareth did a lot more than just sit around his hall feasting. It didn't help his temper that Henry was away boat-building when he was needed at the forge, but Thayer said the battle must have affected the boy and he needed time by himself.

"By himself!" Edgar raged, "Half the wretched village has gone to the coast with him."

But Thayer knew how to settle Edgar and persuade him to see things her way. He was a gentle giant, after all, and not prone to lingering anger or moodiness.

"Give him a little while," she said softly.

"It is a slack time at the forge, I guess," he conceded, as she poured him a beaker of ale one evening. Although, with the arrival of spring, there would be plenty of ploughs and hand tools to be sharpened or fixed. It was just as well neither of them knew what Henry was really up to.

We could describe the entire boat building, but it's enough to say the vessel progressed quickly with so many helping hands and Edrid's knowledge. It turned out to be a sleek craft based on a stout wooden keel, stem and stern posts, ribs and spaced hull-planks with long, dry reeds packed tightly between them. The single mast bore a foresail rigged to a short bowsprit and a lateen mainsail. The boat comfortably accommodated up to half-a-dozen people along with supplies and spare gear. Boiled pine resin covered the hull, painted in several layers to stretch the hides, ensuring a water-tight seal around any joints. Edrid had even installed a tiller, rather than a steer board, that made rudder control much lighter. Initially, quite a crowd of villagers camped beside Anshelm's hut, but as the major work was completed and only the more fiddly tasks remained, they drifted back to Hollowford and their home responsibilities.

Eventually, only Edrid, Henry, Macayle and Bron remained, but everyone promised to come back for the launching. Edrid was content and declared the boat better than anything he'd built on Palo Innes. In all fairness, resources were scarce on the islands and he had far more materials to work with on Anshelm's beach. The boat now rested on the high-tide line, ready for its maiden voyage with two pairs of oars and four rowlocks installed on the gunwales to help negotiate any difficult currents before reaching open water.

"What're ye plannin' on callin' her?" Anshelm asked as he covered the stores with the canvas sheet. "You gotta name her. Fer luck, see."

A debate followed, but Macayle settled the matter simply.

"Why not *Seawind*?" she said. "I mean, the sail drives her through the sea and the wind drives the sail."

"Aye, that'll do," Anshelm said as he tied his finished scrimshaw to the stem-post. "Yer need a figurehead mind. It don't have to be big, but it means the ship has a spirit. The sea has to know that. There ain't no way she'll let a dead thing float on her fer long."

Henry and Edrid thought *Seawind* was a bit girlie, and would have preferred something like *Wave Thrasher* or *Surf Crusher*, but didn't mention it. They also discussed how useful Anshelm would be if he sailed with them, but he hadn't said anything about going and seemed happy to have just been involved as a shipwright. Anshelm had never attempted anything remotely as sophisticated as *Seawind* and was anxious to trial her, but as far as he was concerned, inside Ita Cay Lagoon was far enough. He explained, even though *Seawind*'s draft was shallow, they'd have to wait until the turn of high tide next morning when the sea level inside the reef was deep enough to sail without running aground.

"There won't be a test run," Henry announced as they shared lunch.

"Don't talk daft, boy," Anshelm scoffed. "This ain't no coracle. Even Edrid here ain't built nothin' as grand as *Seawind*. There's bound to be adjustments needed in the rigging, yards tightening, and such."

"What's the rush?" Edrid said.

"Every day we waste will make it harder to find Macayle's mother, but don't you see — if Edgar finds out about this, there's no way he'll let me go. We stock the boat today and go on the tide tomorrow."

"Stock up with what?" Macayle demanded.

"Water's no problem. We'll easily fill the cask from streams nearby, and there's enough salted fish and gammon here for weeks, as well as vegetables for days."

"Ain't you forgetting them's my stores?" Anshelm pointed out.

The problem was that Archer and Gareth had taken the talismans and Henry was left with no negotiable currency. One of the brooches would have bought Anshelm's soul, let alone a few bushels of groceries, but Edrid was a shrewd persuader.

"Surely you're coming with us," he said, although Anshelm stared at him blankly. "Of course you are," Edrid continued slapping the fisherman's leathery back. "Who'd pass up an opportunity of a life time, especially not a bold mariner like yourself? Why skippering this craft is going to be the most joyous experience of all. The sailors back home would give an arm just to handle *Seawind* for a day."

"I'd be skipper..?"

"Why yes, who else? You know the reef, I can't think of anyone better to handle the tiller. You said yourself things were pretty dull around here, so now's your chance for a little adventure."

Oh, smooth, Henry thought, *you wily rascal Edrid, you've touched his vanity, bravo. Although "a little adventure" might be understating matters.*

"*Seawind* will easily fit four," Macayle declared and three heads turned to her.

"Four?" three voices said in unison.

"There are four of us, aren't there? Five including Bron."

"You can't be serious," Henry said. "You're not coming. Your shoulder hasn't healed."

"It has just about. See, I can move it like before. I could punch you in the nose."

"It's far too dangerous."

"Ayla's my mother!"

Macayle turned to the others with a desperate gaze, but Edrid and Anshelm simply shook their heads.

"It won't do, lass," the fisherman said gently. "The open sea is no place for women. It's hardly a place for men."

She looked defiantly at Edrid.

"I'm afraid I have to agree with them. Palo Innes men sail boats, their women are busy enough on land."

"My father's the chief, so you have to do what I say."

"No," Anshelm replied, "we have to do what *he* says, and I can guarantee he'd have our hides if we took his daughter sailin' in an untried boat."

The argument raged back and forth, but finally Macayle gave up.

"If that's the way you feel," she wailed, "I'll go home. I hate you!"

She leapt onto Bruno's back and cantered away without another word. Bron looked puzzled and distressed by the argument.

"Go with her, Bron," Henry said, waving after Macayle. "See

she gets safely home. Go on girl, scat!"

Bron hesitated, eyeing Henry uncertainly, but with a little more urging she seemed to understand and loped away.

"That went better than I thought," Edrid sighed.

"She hates us," Henry murmured. It was a devastating blow. "It couldn't have been worse."

"She'll get over it. Had to be said anyway, women aboard is bad luck fer sure, there just weren't no way she was goin'," Anshelm said, a little harshly in Henry's opinion. "Cut tother horses loose and they'll follow her to Hollowford. C'mon we'd better get *Seawind* loaded if we're goin' at first light. Them townsfolk'll be disappointed at missing her maiden voyage."

Henry and Edrid exchanged glances and smiled, they had their skipper. They pushed *Seawind* below the high tide line, and then moored her so she'd be afloat on the morning tide, but not drift away. A shore breeze was usual at dawn which was best to fill the sails and help them cross the reef quickly. The next task was stowing supplies, fishing tackle, and weapons, including Henry's bow and several full quivers scrounged from Bob the Fletcher, then drawing canvas across the stores, securing it with tie-down lines. There seemed a huge amount of bric-a-brac including bowls, knives, spoons, creels, even a couple of leather buckets they could fill with seawater to keep any fish they caught fresh longer. Anshelm was meticulous when checking everything onboard, saying they'd need to be self-sufficient and there would be no going back for anything they'd forgotten. Edrid explained the cargo also acted as ballast and would help steady *Seawind*. With a final check they were satisfied and, after supper, turned in.

Henry found it hard to sleep, regretting what he'd said to Macayle, but regretting so much more what she'd said in return.

He missed Bron as well. She was a true friend, but she'd be better off on dry land. He'd no idea how a wolf would react at sea. Come to that, he had no idea how he'd feel either. The vastness of the task ahead was daunting on the eve of their adventure and misgivings flooded through Henry's mind, more doubts than he thought a human could possibly manage. He tossed long into the night, but eventually fell asleep to the sullen growl of breakers pounding the reef. The waves they'd have to face at dawn.

Edrid shook Henry awake.

"C'mon, let's go," he urged. "The tide's about to turn, there's no time to lose."

The morning was fresh and breezy, which Edrid and Anshelm seemed cheerful about. There was enough wind to fill the sail, but not so blustery as to prove treacherous. They clambered aboard and, while Henry and Edrid manned the oars, Anshelm cast off and settled onto the transom bench to handle the tiller.

"We got two choices," he cried. "Either head north and navigate them sand bars at Tremill Island or take a short cut through Ita Cay. There's a breach in the reef close by."

He estimated the chance of going aground was greater through the shifting sandbanks, but the risk of dashing against the rocks would be far more devastating. Impatient to be in open water, Edrid favoured the reef option and Henry agreed because it would save precious time. Anshelm shrugged and steered for a gap in the reef. About then Henry realised he knew nothing about sailing, even his rowing was erratic, and he often missed strokes, although he was a fast learner.

"What am I supposed to do?" he yelled.

"What you're told, laddie!" Anshelm called back above the surf's roar that now filled their ears. "Right now, just swing them oars!"

Soon they approached the channel that ran out to sea. It looked hardly wide enough for *Seawind* and the current ripped through at an alarming rate.

"Ahoy, Edrid, standby the foresail and hoist her when I say. The wind's following so we'll be blown right out to sea. Belay them oars, Henry!"

Belay?

"Stow 'em, y' lubber. Bring 'em aboard."

Lubber?

But he hauled the oars in and dropped them beside the pair Edrid had abandoned for the foresail sheets. There was nothing more he could do.

"Hoist away!" Anshelm bellowed and Edrid heaved on the line.

"Lend a hand, laddie," Anshelm ordered.

With two manning the sheets, the sail billowed and they felt themselves sucked forward into a maelstrom of white water between the rocks. *Seawind* pitched forward and dipped viciously before smashing into a sea swell that battered against the outgoing current, sending salt-spray as high as the masthead and drenching everyone on board. Even above the ocean's roar, Henry heard a scream that must have come from the mass of seabirds that swirled above them. Water sloshed ankle-deep in the bilge while Anshelm wrestled with the tiller. The current dragged them relentlessly towards a rocky doom despite the fisherman's efforts. Edrid trimmed the foresail to catch the best wind. Just as they were about to crash into the reef, another swell rushed from the sea and surged between them and the rocks, driving *Seawind* back into the channel centre, but swamping the boat even more before sweeping them dangerously close to the other side of the passage.

Henry grabbed an oar and jabbed at the rocks, fending them away, but he slipped and fell awkwardly, bruising his back. Fortunately, the oar dropped inboard. He dragged himself to his feet, clutching anything to steady him. They were nearly through the channel when another wave battered their gunwales, tipping *Seawind* so violently Henry thought he'd be thrown overboard. He clung to the mast as tightly as he could, although the wood had been planed smooth and was now drenched and slippery.

Then a roller, so great it blocked the horizon, welled up from the deep and reared before them as *Seawind* plunged into the foaming wall of water. The wave smashed aboard and swamped the boat to the gunwales before surging away into Ita Cay. *Seawind* was past the shoals and surf, but wallowed badly with bilge water knee deep, making her freeboard so low even small waves lapped over the sides, threatening to sink her. The vessel was now such a dead weight the foresail had insufficient force to pull her through the waves and, despite an outgoing tide, breakers slowly dragged her back to the reef.

"Tie off the sheets, Edrid!" Anshelm called as he steered *Seawind* to face the swell. "Man the sweeps, lively now. Henry, bail her out!"

Edrid waded to the centre bench, refitted his oars and frantically rowed, but made no extra headway. Henry grabbed a floating bucket sloshing about amid the debris and bailed for all his worth, but so much water poured in, what he heaved overboard hardly kept pace. It seemed useless. Suddenly the canvas covering their cargo burst open and Macayle staggered out, spluttering seawater. She found the other bucket and started bailing too, while Bron lay on top of a keg looking decidedly ill. Working frenetically, they started making headway and, agonisingly slowly, the bilge water-level dropped, allowing the foresail augmented by Edrid's rowing to draw *Seawind* away from the beckoning shoals. No one said a word until the vessel was completely drained and *Seawind* picked up speed and glided out to sea. They slumped onto the benches, exhausted. Henry, Edrid, and Anshelm stared at Macayle in disbelief.

"What?" she said with a shrug, rubbing her aching shoulder.

"Are you mad?" Henry sighed. "This is no place for a girl."

"You think so, do you? You'd be at the bottom of the sea if I hadn't been here to help, so don't give me any more of your boy rubbish!"

"She has a point," Edrid said, smiling at Macayle. He was actually glad to see her, but Anshelm had other ideas.

"There ain't no goin' back through the channel now," he observed. "But mark me, no good can come of this. None at all."

But *Seawind* handled beautifully, leaving Anshelm with only one thing left to say.

"Hoist the mainsail, lads."

*I can't believe the variety of life in the ocean.
Anshelm and Edrid say you can eat just about
everything you catch.*

*You can even harvest sea weed! Anshelm adds it to
his fish stews and they taste fabulous.
Why, there are so many fish they could feed the
whole world for ever.*

CHAPTER 15
BEWARE - CORSAIR!

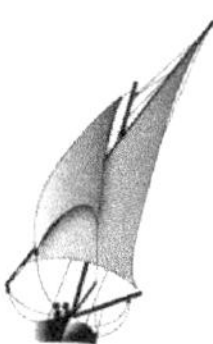

Anshelm was in a grim mood, women and ships simply didn't mix, even though he referred to all vessels as her. He couldn't really throw Macayle overboard, although he mentioned that option, only to received hostile looks from everyone including Bron, who was recovering a little. Anyway, no one felt like taking their recalcitrant stow-away to task. It wasn't worth the tongue-lashing they'd receive.

"I can't see that's there's any real harm done," Edrid conceded.

"One more mouth to feed…"Anshelm grumbled.

"Two actually," Henry corrected, nodding towards Bron.

"She don't seem up to scoffin' much grub right now."

Anshelm handed the tiller to Edrid, went forward, and untied his scrimshaw from the stem post. Without a word, he hung the carving around Macayle's neck, securing it with an untidy knot. It was quite small and sat well against her breast, like a piece of jewellery. Macayle fingered the whale bone and liked its smoothness and design.

"You wear it when you're on board, lassie," Anshelm said quietly, hoping the charm's favours would somehow outweigh any evil a girl might attract. She thanked him as she had admired the piece while Anshelm was carving it and considered it more a gift than a ward. Henry and Edrid exchanged puzzled looks, but Anshelm said no more before returning to the tiller. He was aware that *Seawind* no longer had a figurehead, and that couldn't be good.

In any event, there were other issues to contend with. Although they'd breached Ita Cay, serious sailing lay ahead. *Seawind* caught the wind gracefully, allowing Anshelm to manoeuvre her sleekly through the ocean's vagaries. Navigation by the sun and stars was no problem. Anshelm and Edrid had done plenty of night sailing, although they admitted normally close to shore in gentle conditions by moonlight. They'd both studied the heavens and knew the passage of constellations, but Macayle was the true expert after so many lessons with Dean Merrick.

"That's all very well," Henry said, "but what happens if it's cloudy."

"I've got this, see," Anshelm replied and took a small, metal rod from a leather thong around his neck and dangled it in front of them. The shaft of glistening alloy spun several times and pointed north. Anshelm spun it again and it settled in the same direction.

"Nice trick," Edrid observed.

"No trick, sonny. Me old dad give it to me before he died. Called it lodestone, he did. We keep it pointin' on the larboard bow and we'll be headin' due east."

Larboard? Henry stared at him blankly.

"Left, laddie, when ye're lookin' forr'd," Anselm said. "Steerboard's t'other side."

That was all very well as far as it went, but took no consideration of currents and wind drift. Edrid was best at reading the deep tides after years of judging treacherous seas that swirled around his archipelago home. Meanwhile, Macayle embraced the task of purser, re-stowing their cargo, clearing up *Seawind* and organising food rations. Edrid ran several long lines aft with lures he'd asked Henry to fashion from polished steel at the forge. It wasn't long before a couple of hefty pelagic hunters clamped onto the hooks.

"Won't be going hungry at this rate," he beamed smugly.

"Yon metal 'ooks may be stronger, but they'll rust soon enough. Bone or 'ardwood's best."

A fishing tackle discussion followed that didn't interest Henry, so he stood at the prow and coaxed Bron to join him now she was used to *Seawind*'s rhythm and no longer suffered sea-sickness. She even appeared to be enjoying herself and started padding up and down the deck. The occasional dousing with salt spray didn't bother Henry; its freshness was so exhilarating. A dolphin pod gambolled across the bow, much to Henry and Macayle's amusement once Anshelm explained they weren't dog-fish. A large shark streaked by, but the dolphins challenged it, stemming its curiosity and driving it away.

"Dolphins and sharks don't make happy neighbours," Edrid said. "A big 'un'll eat a small dolphin if it gets the chance, but won't take on a whole bunch."

Peering ahead, Henry spied a speck on the horizon speeding towards them, morphing into a huge white bird that skimmed the surface occasionally dipping one of its wingtips into the white-caps. It drifted with such ease that its wings barely moved, as if cushioned by the tiny passage of air between its belly and the sea. The bird's size and elegance staggered Henry, who judged the wingspan to be more than a man's height.

"Albatross," Edrid declared.

"Aye," Anshelm agreed and smiled at last. "Now that's a good omen."

"It seems so lonely out here," Macayle said. "I wonder if it will guide us to land."

"I don't think so, miss. It's their nature to patrol the ocean for years. Some say they're never off the wing and only seek dry land to mate and raise their young. Legend has it there's a huge colony on an isle at the edge of the world that's just covered white with 'em at breedin' time."

The albatross circled *Seawind* several times and then flew eastwards convincing Macayle it was showing the way.

"The ocean is a wonder" she declared. "I can't see why people haven't sailed here before."

"Gettin' out here ain't that simple. Look what happened back at the reef, lassie," Anshelm admonished. "And men *have* been here. Don't forget the raiders."

"Still, I could live like this forever," Macayle effused.

"We do," Edrid said. "Although we don't usually venture too far from land. There are so many fish, and we are only a small community."

"Are you really a prince?"

"That's what people call me. It's just a name, like folk call your father chief. He's earned the right to the title, but I'm not sure about myself."

"You will if you free your people."

They stood together in silence, not awkwardly, but at ease with their new friendship.

"Look!" Henry cried from the bow.

They stared high in the sky to see a sea eagle beating its ragged wings in a hover directly above the albatross that spotted it and started to weave gracefully to confuse the raptor.

"It's a long way from shore for an eagle," Edrid observed. "They're like us and don't venture out of sight of land. It won't attack the albatross, though, it's much too big."

But even as he spoke, the predator swooped onto its prey. The albatross was agile, but no match for the erne with its advantage of height and incredible speed as it plunged towards the sea. It raked the albatross's back, shedding feathers and blood into the ocean. Victim maybe, but the sea wanderer possessed a massive beak and snapped at the eagle as it soared away. The respite was short and the erne attacked again, but this time the albatross was ready. Although talons ripped into it again, the albatross swung its beak and clamped onto the eagle's legs, shaking the raptor which was now in danger of being dragged into the sea. Sensing its peril, the erne screamed and hacked at the albatross's eyes. It broke free just as the albatross splashed onto the waves, but as it staggered away, one of its taloned feet remained in the albatross's beak and a thin trail of blood dripped from the ravaged stump. The albatross lay on the water with its great wings spread limply, barely holding it afloat.

"Dammit," Anshelm muttered. In a day of bad omens, this was the worst.

He steered *Seawind* to the fallen bird and when it came alongside, Henry and Edrid lifted it on board, avoiding a few snapping protests. The bird was exhausted and badly mauled. Edrid folded its wings and placed it in a creel at the bottom of the hull. Bron showed some interest, but the albatross still had a couple of nips left and the prudent wolf kept her distance. The bird sank into the creel, its head drooping and looking quite forlorn.

"Will it live?" Macayle asked.

"Dunno," Anshelm said. "Wild beasts either heals themselves or dies—ain't much we can do about it but keep the lines out and make sure it's got plenty of grub. Then we wait. Weren't natural for the eagle to attack—that bird's been trained to kill just for sport."

The albatross remained in the basket that night and recovered by morning. Its wounds had lost their lividness and it stopped its belligerent snapping when it realised the boat crew meant no harm. Macayle even hand-fed it when its appetite returned. The bird was insatiable and Bron had to be quick to ensure she got a share. Occasionally, the albatross flexed its wings, pushing anyone aside with its immense span. It slept for much of the time, but often raised its head to look around as they sailed on in fair weather over smooth, rhythmic swells. As lookout, Henry was first to sense the change. The ocean surface started shimmering into a continuous, pulsating froth. As *Seawind* drew closer, the water boiled into a maelstrom of leaping, silver specks flashing past. The sea was almost a solid mass of small darting fish.

"Bait fish!" Edrid said. "Sardine swarms with hunters after them."

As he spoke, vast flocks of gannets and guillemots gathered overhead and plunged into frenzied shoals of sardines, dragging their prey back into the air to be harassed by skuas trying to steal a meal. The sardine swarm was chased by just about every other predator in the sea. The fizzing sea of frenetic bait fish was so vast they seemed to be spread forever. Sharks and dolphins forgot their differences and herded the swarm into gyrating balls, and then picked away at them until most were gone. *Seawind*'s crew watched in fascination, even Anshelm and Edrid were mesmerised.

Suddenly, the ocean erupted so close to *Seawind* she was swept aside and her crew all hung on to avoid being tossed overboard. A monstrous, gaping mouth spewed up from the depths, swelling as it scooped thousands of sardines in a single gulp. Macayle screamed and buried her head into Edrid's chest, while Henry and

Anshelm stared, unable to take in the gigantic spectacle. Bron howled in fear and the albatross flapped frantically to stay on board. The grey monster dropped below the surface in a spray of water that almost swamped *Seawind*. Panicking fish continued surging all around them before drifting away as the sardine host moved on. The monster reappeared, but at a distance and soon they were clear.

"A kraken," Henry whispered, his knuckles white from gripping the gunwale. "Who would have thought they could be true? We're lucky it didn't swallow us whole. Sharks are bad enough, but I hope we don't run into another one of those…"

Big brute no doubt, but not a kraken and quite harmless, Edrid thought, grinning while keeping his arms around Macayle. *But let Henry think what he likes.*

Macayle released herself from Edrid's embrace, staring into his eyes with uncertain feelings.

"Come on," she said. "Let's bail this water or we'll sink before we reach land."

"Aye," Anshelm observed, "yon birds ain't albatrosses and they'll need to return to roost. Land won't be far off."

The sun sank over their stern as Anshelm lit a lantern to illuminate his lodestone. The albatross left them in the night, no one knew whether it slipped into the sea or flew away, but it vanished as suddenly as it had appeared. They did not see it again and felt a loss, hoping it had enough strength to resume its lonely flight clipping the wave tops.

But their chagrin was short-lived when Henry spied a grey fleck along the horizon in predawn's glow, just before the sun blinded their view. The landfall loomed closer as the sun rose. Light flooded onto sheer cliffs rearing from the shoreline. Ocean swells, gentle enough in open water, now released their fury as they dashed against this rocky coast.

Anshelm sailed as close as he dared to the cliffs that were pitted with caves, small crevices, and grass-tufted ledges teeming with nesting gannets, guillemots, and razorbills. Their shrieks filled the sky and could be heard for miles. In places narrow streams cascaded over the cliff tops, trailing mist all the way to the bottom, leaving a moist sheen on the rock face.

"There ain't no climbing yon cliffs," Anshelm observed dully.

"Where can we land?" Macayle asked but only received a shrug in reply.

According to Anshelm's lodestone, the coastline ran more-or-less north-south, so they took advantage of the prevailing south-easterly wind and steered northwards, taking care not to drift too close to shore. All morning, the basalt wall stretched endlessly, except for isolated fissures, far too narrow to provide a suitable anchorage.

"If we don't find somewhere by dusk," Edrid said, "we'll have to go back to sea. We don't want to be close to those cliffs at night."

They discussed how far they'd press on before cutting their losses and heading south. The irony of turning about just short of a landfall wasn't lost on anyone, but at that moment it didn't matter what they decided.

It was Bron who gave the warning. *Seawind*'s crew was so intent on finding a landing spot, they were oblivious to the wolf-ship bearing down on them, her crimson sail billowing with the wind's full effect and her crew rowing in unison. Crag Daniek stood under the fearsome figurehead, nursing his wounded sea eagle that perched uncertainly on his shoulder. The pirate boss had no way of knowing how his pet was crippled, but he was out for revenge and he wasn't particular on whom. Right now he had a small boat in his sights, a nice soft target. Crag Daniek turned and bellowed orders to his crew as he marched to the stern and took over the steer board, forgetting his eagle that launched itself to the top spar, hobbling on its one sound leg before balancing.

"It's the ship that took mother," Macayle wailed.

"And that's Crag Daniek at the helm with Queig beside him," Edrid confirmed.

"Can you see her?" Macayle asked in desperate hope.

"They'll have put her ashore before now," Edrid said.

"Oh, what has become of her.. ?"

"What'll become of us, more like," Anshelm growled. "C'mon Edrid, Henry, man them yards. We got some sharp shiftin' t'do."

"Heave to, damn yer eyes," Crag Daniek roared, "or I'll run yer down!"

"What then? You'll kill us," Henry yelled back.

"Not her, we won't," one of the pirates called after spying Macayle. A chorus of ribald comments followed as half the crew abandoned their oars and clambered over their fellows to leer at her. They were a fearsome lot with braided beards and matted hair that spewed from under their helmets and tossed in the wind.

None seemed to recognise Macayle. Apparently all potential slave girls looked much the same to them. Crag Daniek and Queig cuffed and kicked the rovers back to their sweeps and they fell to disciplined rowing once more, but the disruption was enough for *Seawind* to duck under the wolf-ship bow. *Seawind* stood a good chance of escaping, she was fleet and her lateen sail caught the wind more sweetly than the wolf-ship's square rig. Also a small boat wasn't much of a prize and hardly worth chasing down.

But Henry had other ideas.

He reached for his bow and nocked an arrow. They swept so close to the wolf-ship, the range was only yards as Henry aimed for the pirate leader, but as he released the arrow *Seawind* rolled in the wolf-ship's bow wave and the shot soared high. The bolt thumped into the spar impaling the ill-fated eagle's remaining talon. The bird screeched with rage and tumbled from its perch wrenching the injured claw free, only managing to recover and flap away just in time to save itself from crashing into the ocean. A gang of skuas saw its plight and harried it mercilessly, driving it towards the cliffs where hunters and prey disappeared in a mass of swirling sea birds. They heard Crag Daniek bellowing every dire threat imaginable.

"Oh, good shot" Anshelm said. "Now you've really vexed 'em. Look!"

Sure enough, the wolf-ship was driving towards them with her sail once again taut to the wind and the oarsmen pulling with all their might.

"Sorry," Henry mumbled. "I was aiming at Crag Daniek."

"Aye, well, try *hittin'* him next time."

But the Starklanders had hooked their round shields to the gunwales for protection and Henry's next shot simply thudded harmlessly into one.

"Yer'll pay fer that, you bleedin' cur," Crag Daniek yelled, brandishing a clenched fist. "Ernie were me best bird. Row, me brave louts, or I'll have yer backs in tatters! Ram 'em, carve 'em into fish bait!"

The wolf-ship came straight for *Seawind*, crashing through waves sending salt-spray high into the gaping jaws of the figurehead then dripping from its fangs like drool. *Seawind* was sleek, but the wolf-ship was designed for fast, hit-and-run sailing and, aided by a score of seasoned rowers, there was little chance. Anshelm avoided disaster twice, but each time he was driven closer to the cliffs in a cunning cat-and-mouse chase. Henry and Macayle rowed while Edrid trimmed the sails, but it was a puny effort against the wolf-ship's might. Although, in time the pirates would tire giving *Seawind* a chance to slip away. Queig, an arch sailor, moved to the wolf-ship bow, sizing up Anshelm's skill and anticipating his next move.

Finally *Seawind* drew just too close and Queig yelled for Crag Daniek to pull the steer board hard over. He was a brute of a man, but it still took all Crag Daniek's strength to veer the wolf-ship. Then Queig ordered the larboard rowers to ship their oars and the starboard side to heave on the sweeps with all their might. The wolf-ship came about almost completely on its axis with its prow now pointing straight into *Seawind*'s beam.

The wolf-ship drove right into her.

She was a tough little boat, but finally out-stalked, and no match for a wolf-ship, she crumbled to flotsam as its solid clinker hull ploughed through her, leaving only wreckage in its wake. But the wolf-ship didn't sail away unscathed. Several of its strakes snapped, dangerously puncturing the hull which allowed water to pour through.

"Lively, yer swabs," Crag Daniek cried. "Get canvas over the side and plug that bleedin' hole!"

The damage was not fatal, but the wolf-ship now lay perilously close to the cliffs and the pirates were far too busy rowing, bailing, and fitting canvas over the breach to give *Seawind* or her crew any further thought. Only Queig glanced back for a second, but could make nothing of the wreckage. The Starkmen reefed the sail to slow their vessel and stem the water flow as they limped northwards.

"At least them buggers are at the bottom of the briny," Crag Daniek growled. "Teach 'em to shoot Ernie, 'e were a fine bird. Yer didn't see nothing behind, did yer, Queig?"

"Naw, Guv, them's deaduns all right."

"Good… Teach 'em…me best bird…"

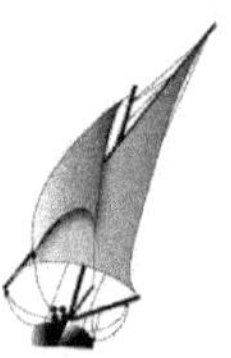

Poison, sacrifice, endurance.
Great men, great deeds.

But is there no end to self-righteous zealots?
The world seems full of them
And they're always causing trouble.

Chapter 16
Mountain Men

When Gareth's band of adventurers camped in the shadow of the Zilek Mountains, Weasel escaped during the night. He was tightly bound, but somehow wriggled free and slipped away during Faranden's watch. Everyone agreed they were better off without the oily rascal, who was probably scuttling back to Velma so there was no point in chasing him. He'd proven useless so far and Gareth regretted bringing him at all. Hopefully a bear or wolf pack might find him before he reached town. It was Faranden's extra diligence rather than negligence that allowed Weasel to flee. Assuming their captive was secure, the big warrior scouted beyond the camp ensuring no enemies prowled about, allowing Weasel to simply sneak off while he was away.

"It was only because you were so mean to him," Archer said to Faranden, who didn't find it particularly droll.

Weasel had planted a scorpion into Faranden's pack before he left, and it crawled up his arm when he reached inside for his breakfast rations. He flicked it off sharply enough, but it landed on his thigh, nipping him with its pincers before its tail flashed and sank into flesh. Faranden ripped the arachnid away, leaving its barb imbedded below his skin. Jongarrat prised the sting free and assayed it wouldn't kill Faranden, although venom was soon well into his bloodstream. He would stay infected for some time, possibly days.

Matters didn't improve as they climbed into Zilek's foothills, where hostility pervaded at every corner in the form of sharp rocks or thorny succulents. Jongarrat's insistence that they avoid pathways and trek along the ridge-lines slowed their progress further, which infuriated Gareth who was in a hurry as always. Clouds hung over the mountains and a missed footing became increasingly perilous as they gained altitude.

"The Corbin watch down there, see," Jongarrat whispered. "Even in this rain, it's safer up here. If we run into anyone at least we won't be at their mercy from above, but we must be quiet for now."

They climbed on, avoiding thorns, venom-spitting puff adders, more scorpions, and hordes of voracious bull-ants, until finally even the toughest life vanished, surrendering to cliffs and scree alone. Fog clung to them like a dank shroud and, although they drew their cloaks closer, iciness seeped through to their bones. The ledges they traversed narrowed, forcing the warriors into single file. Still the stout-hearted pride of Grambak yeomanry marched on uncomplaining, even Faranden who was suffering most.

"It was just a little bug," he muttered as he grew light-headed. His thigh swelled and turned livid, but he was tough and kept up, though he frequently stumbled. Eventually, even his strength failed as he lagged behind and had to be helped by his companions, whose lungs were also gasping for breath in the thin atmosphere. The extra burden of Faranden soon took its toll.

"We'll have to rest..." Archer whispered. "Just wish… it wasn't here on this mountain top."

Gareth merely grunted, in his view their progress was far from satisfactory.

"A bit further..." Jongarrat rasped. Altitude was having its effect on him as well. "Path levels off as I remember…should find a cave…need shelter up here."

He was acutely concerned about their slow pace because it made discovery more likely, but Faranden was delirious by then and only Kimball and Serlequin's strength kept him from pitching to his death. The weather cleared, which made matters worse in a way, as they could see the precipitous drop and the trail that snaked like a thread so far below.

"I ain't ready for you yet," Faranden gasped as a group of vultures spiralled aloft in the updrafts that swept through Zilek Gorge. Their attention was on carrion rather than fever-ridden warriors, but that could change.

Jongarrat's memory proved correct and the ridgeline levelled, but remained perilously narrow, twisted, and crumbling underfoot. They found a cave far earlier than Gareth hoped and far higher than Jongarrat cared for, but both agreed they must stop. Faranden could go no further. The cave was just large enough to shelter them all for the night. Faranden's wound was so swollen with pus, that Jongarrat was forced to lance it, which gave some relief though his fever still ran high. Faranden drifted into fitful sleep while the others huddled together for warmth and ate cold rations.

"Beats me how you crossed here by yourself," Archer said to Jongarrat.

"I never said I was alone. Nope there were others, but I'm the only one alive now. Who's to say this time will be any different?" he added, looking Gareth squarely in the eye.

There's nothing longer than a night so cold you can't sleep, but at least they kept guard between moments of dozing from sheer exhaustion. However, everyone's spirits lifted considerably in the morning as Faranden was much improved and Jongarrat assured him he'd recover completely. As a result they pushed on, but Faranden still limped and once again they camped early when they found a suitable cave. They'd descended from the highest escarpments and felt, if not warm, at least less cold. Jongarrat confirmed they'd past the worst terrain, but still had leagues of tough going ahead.

"Sorry to hold you up," Faranden said sheepishly.

"Wasn't your fault," Gareth said. "That scorpion would have killed anyone else."

"But I let Weasel escape…"

"Good riddance," Kimball and Serlequin chimed.

The next day wore on at their torturous pace as Faranden's leg still bothered him, but was vastly better than the previous evening. At this rate, he'd be fully recovered in a couple of days. Jongarrat scouted ahead, cautiously inspecting caves and crevices for Corbin warriors bent on foul-play. But the mountains appeared deserted to the point where Gareth challenged the wisdom of sticking to the ridgelines rather than the much easier pass below. Jongarrat merely grunted and said Gareth could go where he damned-well pleased, but he was sticking to the high ground.

They descended further where grass and scrub reappeared while the numbness in their fingers and toes eased with the returning warmth. Finally, the ground broke up and it became impossible to maintain the high ground, but Jongarrat surmised that if they couldn't use the ridge lines, then neither could anyone else. They found a path that looked promising although still narrow with a long drop on one side. Then all of a sudden they had a bit of luck when Archer spotted a herd of mountain goats.

A dozen animals grazed on the precarious slopes just above the trail and raised their heads as the travellers approached, but resumed feeding when Jongarrat signalled the company to freeze.

"Lunch, my lord?" Archer whispered.

"Think you can bring one down without it falling off its ledge?"

"I should be able to get up above 'em and bag one. It'll either drop where it stands or fall onto this trail and you'll have to catch it."

"Don't worry about us. You shoot it and we'll catch it," Jongarrat said.

Now that sounded all well and good, but stalking nervous mountain goats needed patience, which wasn't Archer's strong suit. He slung his bow and quiver across his back and clambered up the slope beside the trail. The goats eyed him suspiciously whenever he moved, so he spent long periods motionless until the herd settled and he was able to reposition himself in short stages. The saxatile pasture looked sparse, but it must have suited the goats because although they were alert, they didn't flee.

At last, he reached a point above the herd that placed it between him and Gareth's group, so even if any bolted, Faranden, who was a sound bowman, would have a shot as well. He edged closer to within range. From his vantage point, he saw the high trail they were following, glimpsed Gareth's group partially hidden behind boulders, and scanned the valley that was deserted right down to the canyon floor.

He sighted on a young buck and drew back the bow-string with some regret. There was a nobility and grace about the creature and Archer admired the tenacity of anything that survived in such harsh surroundings. But they needed food to maintain their strength, and Jongarrat had told him there were large, spotted cats that hunted in the mountains the goats might fall prey to,, and dammit the wind was picking and…

Archer caught the flicker of movement from the corner of his eye and knew wuthering wasn't the cause. The herd sensed it too and scattered, using seemingly impossible trails or leaping from ledge to ledge to reform at a safe distance.

Two or three dozen men moved to meet Gareth's group along the trail. They were heavily robed against the weather and sunlight flashed off metal suggesting their aggressive intent. Archer looked beyond the Hollowford men and saw more figures clambering along the trail behind them. Although the warriors were forced to travel single file, Gareth was hemmed in on both sides. Archer cupped his hands and bellowed, but his warning was swept away on the wind that now howled and blasted clouds of abrasive dust. Archer called again, but grit caught in his throat and it was useless anyway, so abandoning care, he careened down the slope causing a small avalanche.

Jongarrat felt the danger first — just a sense amid the wind that had whipped up to cover most sounds. He leapt to his feet and drew his sword.

"Corbin!" the dwarf hissed.

In an instant, the others were standing with weapons poised and braced for battle just as the Corbin were upon them. The sight of five well-armed and prepared warriors brought the attackers to a halt, those behind colliding with the leaders, nearly pitching them into the canyon. With the ambush's impetus stalled, the Corbin milled around uncertainly, having planned on a quick spot of butchery. Their grimy robes, vital for survival on Zilek's heights, were now flayed in the wind, hindering their movements. And among the group who'd arrived from behind was none other than Weasel, prancing about and ranting in triumph.

"See, it's them. I told you. I was right."

"Silence, fool!" the Corbin leader commanded, standing at the head of the band. He was bearded, but hard to make out shielded by his robe and scarf masking his face.

"Ha! Ha!" Weasel gloated, pointing at Faranden. "Not so smart now are you? Not such a big man anymore? That bug bite slowed you down plenty. You'd have got through if you'd gone fast. Slowed up and gave Corbin time to gather."

"I said, 'quiet!'" the Corbin leader snarled, cuffing Weasel soundly, which did the trick. "Surrender, infidel. I am Bagsha Grimhand, Corbin Master. Your presence on our sacred glebe is an affront to the one-god who demands retribution for your desecration."

"One-god, is it?" Gareth jeered, "Hardy seems sufficient to me."

"Sacrilege! You dare defy the sacred word of the one-god!"

"Let's you know what's on his mind, does he?" Gareth goaded Bagsha. He generally tolerated piety, but discouraged druids and their dogma from Hollowford, considering them distracting and impractical. Most, like Urdec, stayed away, many preferring life as hermits, which suited Gareth fine.

"Enough," Bagsha snarled. "Cede or die."

"Cede and what?"

"Bondage. It is the one-god's will."

"Speaks to you personally, I gather? Thank him for the offer, but slavery ain't our style."

"Then die!"

"That ain't our style either."

Bagsha, now enraged beyond reason, surged forward but halted as a gurgling sound came from beside him. Weasel stood frozen to the spot, grabbing the arrow shaft impaling his throat as blood poured over his fists and down his arms. He stayed erect for seconds before crumpling to the ground. Bagsha stared at the body, momentarily giving Archer time to unleash two more arrows, taking out a Corbin warrior with both. They pitched screaming into the canyon and could be heard wailing to the bottom. Archer slung the bow across his back, jumped from his perch. Drawing Avenger which he judged the best weapon in the circumstances, slashed across the back of one warrior and skewered another. He was hacking a path through before the Corbin realised his presence and turned to meet him.

While Archer diverted the Corbin's attention, Gareth launched forward to challenge Bagsha at the head of the other bunch. The Corbin Master met the attack with a skilful riposte and the two leaders locked in battle. Only one or two others could squeeze past and they had to be mindful of Goresax and Bagsha's scimitar that sliced indiscriminately.

They were met with deadly force by Kimball, while Serlequin and Faranden faced the opposite group who were now fighting two fronts just like Gareth's band. Jongarrat proved agile and lethal as more wounded Corbin plunged over the edge, whether their wounds were fatal was immaterial at that stage. The battle raged in confusion with the Corbin's greater numbers at no immediate advantage, except they'd eventually win by attrition.

"This way, lord!" Archer bellowed. "Fight through to me. The way is clear beyond!"

The warrior beside Bagsha shrieked, then groaned, then made an inhuman sound as Kimball's axe cleaved him from crown to chin. The Corbin advance faltered. Faranden and Serlequin forced their way past the remaining mountain men between them and Archer, while Kimball and Gareth formed a solid rear-guard and Jongarrat dealt with any random threats. They were clear, leaving a trail of butchery and charging Corbin baying for blood. Backing slowly along the high trail, Jongarrat assumed the lead with Archer on guard for any surprises. And so they fought on, but the conflict was taking its toll and Gareth knew they'd tire before long, especially Faranden who again limped badly. The path ran noticeably downhill, helping their progress, although it gave the pursuing Corbin the advantage of elevation. Occasionally, Kimball and Gareth would surge forward and drive the attackers back with serious wounds and sudden death.

Then the path flattened and split in two, but a horde of robed warriors swarmed towards them along the right fork, leaving no alternative but the left. The two groups merged at the junction and charged with renewed confidence, bolstered by the reinforcements. Six men against a hundred was never going to have a favourable outcome and Faranden knew it. He burst past Gareth and Kimball and held the advancing Corbin at bay. The path was still narrow and the drop just as fatal, but he saw it widened a short distance away and the risk of being surrounded greatly increased. And it wouldn't take the Corbin long to work out they could clamber along the high ground and pitch rocks and spears onto the fugitives.

"Go on, lord!" Faranden cried. "It's our last chance to hold them on this narrow path."

Thwack!–A Corbin fell to his halberd.

"I don't leave my people," Gareth yelled.

Swish, thunk!–Another Corbin head rolled as the decapitated

torso slithered over the edge and tumbled away.

"My leg won't bare me further, but I can stand fast and keep 'em busy."

Splat!–The halberd point drove into a Corbin gut.

"I'll not leave you!"

Slice, clang, thump!–Another victim collapsed screaming with blood gushing from his groin.

"You must, or we all die. I let Weasel escape, this is down to me. It is my right to repay that mistake. Now go!"

Crash!–The halberd blade smashed a shield to shards, severing the owner's arm.

"I'd have given you Macayle when we returned, you know," Gareth said.

The sound of panting!–A breather as the Corbin paused to regroup. Faranden grinned.

"Lord, she was never yours to give. She'll choose her own man, and I know it's not me. Now be gone. Here they come again."

Each of the five remaining warriors clapped Faranden on the shoulder in a silent farewell before racing along the path. But even as they escaped, Jongarrat knew they were going the wrong way.

The Corbin crept closer to the lone warrior. They were cautious with no one game to make the first move, until Bagsha Grimhand ran one of his own men through, spurring the others to action.

"Come on, you pansies. Let's be having you," Faranden roared. "You've seen how real men fight. Now you'll see how a real man dies. How many of you will it take, eh?"

It took a great many and gave Gareth's company time to get clean away.

"**I**t is done, master," one of Bagsha's warriors reported. The Corbin leader had taken a supporting role in Faranden's defeat and now stared at the score of dead and wounded piled around his shredded corpse. It had been mutilated after a Corbin blood-lust, where each man, including Bagsha, cut off a portion of flesh. They recognised a formidable warrior when they fought one, and wanted to consume a piece of him to infuse part of his potency into themselves. There was always hunger on Zilek's sparse mountains anyway.

"But, the others are long gone."

"It is of no importance," Bagsha grinned, slyly running his tongue across his lips as Faranden's blood dripped into his beard. "They're heading for the graveyard, and the muggers await. Come, we'll follow to ensure none escape."

Don't give up – Don't ever give up hope
But so many people in this world live in fear.
Hollowford is fortunate to have Chief Gareth with
stout fellows like
Archer and Faranden to defend it.

I never realised how vital it is to defend your home.
I've learnt that weakness is exploited at every turn.
Yet in all this barbarity, occasionally kindness is found.

Chapter 17
Otillie

Henry burst to the surface. After spewing a gallon of seawater he still reckoned half the ocean sloshed inside his gut, but fortunately his lungs were clear. He was a strong swimmer, but in a grand old funk when he looked around and saw nothing. No *Seawind*, no wolf-ship, and worst of all, no companions! Then a wave rolled away and he glimpsed the wolf-ship's red sail before it disappeared behind another swell and vanished completely. No other heads bobbed on the surface, there wasn't even any wreckage in sight.

"Anshelm! Edrid! Macayle! Bron!" he yelled.

There was no reply and calling out only allowed waves to splash down his throat, forcing him to turn his head and avoid more incoming surf. As a particularly large wave dipped past him, he spied cliffs ahead and swam towards them, although a landing spot seemed hazardous if he found one at all. He discovered salt water to be more buoyant than the rivers he was used to and swam strongly, yet the coast appeared no closer. In time he tired, finding the movement of his arms and legs increasingly difficult and he grew apathetic.

Whatever, I'm only going to get my brains bashed out by the rocks anyway.

It was all too easy to let lethargy engulf him, hallucinating about Hollowford in summer, calm streams and gentle countryside, about his family, friends, and a happy home. Drowsiness overwhelmed him and he started to sink.

Happy life, well, you won't see that again at this rate. Pull yourself together.

He struggled back to the surface and ploughed on.

What's the point? Edrid, Anshelm, Bron, and Macayle are probably dead by now.

Once again, his will to fight waned, but it would all be for nothing if he simply gave up, so back to the surface he came. It was then he realised Hornet Sting was still strapped to his waist. Although not heavy, the sword was enough to make the difference between swimming or drowning so he considered abandoning it to shed weight. As he struggled to discard the weapon, the cliff-face that had seemed so distant suddenly reared up and Henry was swept into a current that formed an inshore whirlpool. It dragged him towards the ocean-savaged rocks, but before he could be dashed to death he spiralled helplessly into the vortex centre.

And down he went.

He battled against the tide, but he might just as well have saved his strength, the water enveloped him, and his lungs ached for air. But the whirlpool had a purpose and that was to feed a blow-hole in the cliffs. The underwater world was a blur, but Henry glimpsed a pin-prick of light far above that he was blasting towards.

Some believe you see a light before you die...

The wave spewed through a rock fissure and tossed Henry a fathom into the air, suspending him for a second before he dropped back into the blow-hole, meeting a second wave that cushioned him and washed him onto a narrow, shingle ledge in a grotto below the rock opening. There he lay, bleeding and bruised, in a phosphorescent beam of light, stunned and exhausted as other smaller waves lapped and ebbed, leaving him half-submerged at the water's edge. And it wasn't long before the local denizens discovered him. Beginning with a few clicks that grew into a scraping, shuffling cacophony, thousands of crabs, drawn by the scent of blood, swarmed over Henry for a feast. He groaned, but was just too weak to resist as the crustaceans' claws went to work.

"Shoo! Scat!" a girl's voice snapped as she edged through the blow-hole, taking care not to slip on the slimy, algae-lined rock. She was about Henry's age, lean almost to the point of gauntness, but with a kindness in her eyes which softened her features, although they also mirrored a deep sadness. She reached Henry and the crabs scattered into rock-pools and crevices.

"He's here, Dad," she called. "Quick, before the next gusher comes!"

"Probably nothin' left but fish bait," an old man grumbled, but scrambled into the cave anyway. Old and equally under-nourished perhaps, but he scaled the grotto wall nimbly enough. He stood over Henry and started rifling through his tunic finding nothing, so he turned his attention to Hornet-Sting and the dagger. As he gripped the hilt, Henry groaned and in a reflex grabbed the old man's arm, although he was barely conscious. Shaking free, the old man jumped back.

"He ain't dead, Dad," the girl gasped.

"No, he ain't. C'mon, let's clear off before he comes round and decides to use that there pig-sticker.'

"We can't leave him. He needs help."

"Ain't got no money to pay for it."

"He's strong. He can work."

"Don't look so strong to me. The only reward for helpin' him'll be cut throats. It don't pay to meddle these days."

"I'm staying; you do as you please."

"Don't be daft, girl. Another big 'un'll be along any moment and wash you away. He don't mean nothin' to you."

"So it's finally come down to the price of everything, has it?"

He paused for a moment, shrugging before scrambling into the open.

"Yes, it has."

The girl turned her attention to Henry, wiping scraps of kelp from his face with the hem of her shift, and shaking him vigorously.

"Oh, do wake up," she cried. "We must hurry. The next wave'll be along any time and we have to get out of here."

Her urging worked and Henry jerked upright, his eyes snapped open, and he stared at the girl in disbelief.

"Am I dead..?" he stammered.

"No, of course not. What a silly thing to say, if you were dead, you wouldn't be able to speak to me, would you?"

"Some people believe maidens carry people into the sky when they die…"

"Hush, we don't have time…Oh no…"

"What?"

"Another wave!"

A sullen growl filled the grotto as water sucked out of the underwater channel, building into the next line of surf surging towards the cliffs.

"We'll drown," the girl wailed.

"Not if I can help it. I've drunk enough ocean for one day."

Henry drew Hornet-Sting and wedged the blade deeply into a rock crevice.

"Put your arms around my neck and hang on tight. Don't let go for anything, even if you think you're strangling me."

He placed one arm around her waist and pulled her closely to him, finding a sound footing just as the sea unleashed its fury. With a roar, a wave flooded into the grotto as a needle-blasting mixture of air, salt, and water. Fortunately not a solid barrage of sea, or Henry would never have held onto Hornet-Sting. After the fountain died, a greater peril of being sucked out through the underwater entrance remained, but the wave's power was spent and the sea ebbed, leaving two soaked, frightened but alive, young people clinging tightly to each other.

"Now will you hurry?" the girl demanded.

"Hurry it is, yes miss," Henry gasped, wrenching Hornet-Sting free and, forgetting his exhaustion, clambered onto the rocks above. Once safely above the high water line, he sank to his knees while the girl crouched beside him and, to his surprise, started giggling.

"That was fun," she said.

"I admire your notion of amusement hereabouts," Henry replied, staring into her green eyes that sparkled and seemed less melancholy now. "You saved my life," he said, after regaining his breath and composure. "Thank you. My name's Henry."

"Pleased to meet you, Henry, I'm Otillie. I live with my dad in the woods back from these cliffs."

"Where is he?"

"He's gone. He thought you'd do some damage with your sword."

"Why would he think that?"

"It's the way things are around here. It pays to be cautious."

"I'll remember that, but how did you find me?"

"We were on the cliffs gathering gannet eggs when the wolf-ship sailed past and we saw you sucked into that blowhole. You were lucky it was only a little wave…"

"Little wave?"

"Yep. Some spray way into the sky. Any bigger and you'd have been dashed onto the rocks and that would be that."

As if to prove her point, another jet shot through the blow-hole, showering them with spray.

"Did you see anyone else?"

She looked puzzled.

"In the sea, I mean. I had three friends and my wolf with me."

"Sorry, I didn't see anyone else…and…you've…got a wolf."

He nodded, although had a wolf was more accurate.

"You're not from around here, are you?" Otillie said. "We don't keep wolves as pets."

"It's unusual back home too. I come from Grambak across the sea," he replied absently, pointing vaguely to the west and then told her his story while she listened wide-eyed, without interrupting once. He just blurted it all out, as if to unburden his grief. Someone had once said talking things over helped, but he didn't feel any better afterwards.

"I must find them!" he concluded

Henry leapt to his feet and raced to the cliff edge, scattering protesting gannets and guillemots. He peered into the surging waves, but there was nothing to see. He scrambled over rocks and even scaled down the cliff-face, thinking he saw some wreckage, but it was the imagination of futile hope. Birds squawked around him and the bolder ones lunged at him while others swooped at his head, but he didn't notice as grief consumed him. What a hopeless quest it had been, ill conceived, and badly carried out–what had they been thinking? Four naïve adventurers taking on the

Starkmen, it had been lunacy from the start.

He examined every nook and crack in the rocks. Sometimes the cliffs reared high above the sea and in other places dropped dramatically, almost to the water's edge where waves washed over granite covered with grey-green slime and brown kelp. And it was in one of these crags that Henry saw wreckage and a glimmer of hope.

"I have to go down and see," he said to Otillie, who'd followed him patiently, occasionally eating gannet eggs as she went.

"Don't be silly," she admonished. "It's slippery and dangerous. I'm not rescuing you again if you fall into the sea."

But he didn't listen and clambered down to the wreckage. It was treacherous going and he lost his footing several times, but stubborn determination made him grab onto clefts in the rock and save himself. Fortunately limpets and barnacles clung to the surface between the tide lines and their roughness allowed a better grip.

The wreckage was the smashed remains of one of *Seawind*'s strakes wedged into the cliff and that was all. He examined the wood and even stroked its smooth surface as if he might derive comfort just by touching something connected with the boat and his friends. Then he noticed the leather thong attached to Anshelm's scrimshaw snagged on the plank. The whale tooth was intact and wedged so securely, Henry needed some effort to yank it free.

He turned the ivory over in his fingers and cast about him for any clues of life. Macayle had been wearing this when they were attacked, but there was no sign of her, so it must have been torn from her neck as *Seawind* broke up. He couldn't bear the thought of what injuries she must have suffered. He realised no one could have made it ashore here and survived a battering from the surf.

Henry stayed and examined the rocks with intricate care. He found nothing else, although he searched until several waves surged dangerously over his legs. Finally, recognising he risked being swept out to sea, he pocketed the scrimshaw and made his way back to the cliff top. He slumped to the ground and sat with his head in his knees weeping so wretchedly even the sea birds stopped bothering him.

Sorrow was nothing new to Otillie, but she was unsure how to deal with this strange boy's misery. She had no answers for him, death was death, it came all the time, even in her bleak world you simply enjoyed what moments of happiness you could. To her just being free to roam the shore with a belly full of gannet eggs was enough for now. She crouched beside him and placed her hand gently on his shoulder.

"You'd better come home with me," she said.

'Don't dwell' I keep remembering Archer's counsel.
Yes, I can just hear him now.

'Move on boy, what's happened has happened.
There's nothing you can do to fix it.'
The trouble is I'm not Archer.

Chapter 18
Squire Redbone

"Our place isn't much, but it's safer than here," Otillie said. "We'll gather some eggs along the way. Don't mind all the squawking and the smell, but watch out. Gannets will peck when they're disturbed. Only take one from each nest and leave single eggs be. There will be plenty, but it's a pity they don't lay all year round."

Chickens lay all year – what's wrong with keeping chickens? Henry thought.

They trekked along the cliff top through the raucous, guano-reeking gannet rookery, stopping to pick eggs from tightly packed nests. They did indeed have to dodge many affronted guardians. Henry received the worst of it as he was constantly distracted, scanning the coast for signs of *Seawind* or her crew, but he saw nothing. When Otillie's knap-sack was full, she led Henry inland through wildwoods to her village. Briars encroached along the path and when Henry complained about the thorns, Otillie explained they bore enough berry-fruit in autumn to last through winter so she didn't mind.

"Do many folk live around here?" he asked. Maybe someone had rescued his friends.

"It's not that sort of country. The Starklanders have driven most folk away. They tolerate us because we've nothing left to steal."

"What do you know about the Starklanders?"

"Mostly they're pretty stupid. My dad says there used to be

several settlements close by, but the Starkmen were greedy and took everything — food, slaves, ale and mead, so people starved or simply disappeared. We're the last. If they'd left enough for us to continue, they'd have been able to demand a tribute every year, but now they have to roam the high seas to get what they want."

"But even they must have a home, a base."

"Oh yes. They live in a fortress on Glam Island, some way north. They don't like the briar country much either."

"I can understand that," Henry said, pulling a couple more thorns from his tunic.

"But we still fear them. They are unpredictable and deceitful. They're just as likely to burn our village and kill everyone for fun."

"Why don't you do something about it?"

She laughed and said he'd see for himself.

"Well, why do you stay, if it's so hard?"

"You're too inquisitive, which isn't generally a good thing around here. Where would we go anyway, Glam? The southern desert or the wild mountain lands in the east? At least we get by here."

Shortly they came to Otillie's village, consisting of a handful of shanties reminiscent of Burgal down at the heel. There was no sign of life; no poultry scratching around — hence the gannet egg harvest — or livestock pens — no playing children — no chief's hall — no inn, just grey shacks shrouded in wood-smoke. There was no greeting other than a few, furtive peeks through window shutters or hessian curtains. Otillie led him to her hut, which was indistinguishable from the rest. She pulled aside the jute sack that covered its entrance.

"Not much, I'm afraid, but it keeps the rain out…sometimes."

"I dunno, there's an old woman who lives down our way

whose place is just like this," Henry grinned.

Otillie's dad was seated on a stool in front of their smouldering fire. He leapt to his feet when they entered and grabbed Otillie, shaking her violently.

"Are you mad, girl?" he hissed. "What do you think you're doing bringin' him here?"

"I couldn't just desert him…"

"Leave her be," Henry said. "I don't mean you any harm."

"Maybe not," the old man snarled, "but who knows what trouble you've brought with you?"

He released Otillie, who rubbed her aching shoulders and shrank beside the fire. Her dad glared at them both before storming out.

"Is there any way to convince him I'm not a threat?" Henry asked.

"Not now. Later perhaps. Now you need food and rest. We have turnip soup. It's hot and will fill you up."

Although turnip wasn't Henry's favourite vegetable, Otillie added wild herbs, kelp, and salt scraped from shoreline rocks to the brew so it tasted fine along with a plateful of boiled gannet eggs. Exhausted and with his belly full, he fell asleep on a pile of straw in the corner. The hut may have been smoky, but he was at least warm and comfortable. He slept all day and through the night.

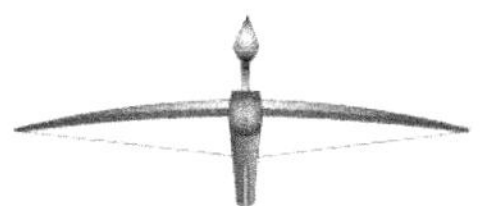

"**H**enry! Henry! Wake up," Otillie urged. "Oh, do wake up, you lazy lump! Dad stayed out all night, and I think he's gone to tell the Starkmen about you."

It was still dark, but dawn was not far off.

"What...?"

"It's the only thing that would keep him out in the forest after dark."

"Why?"

Henry was awake now.

"Because he's frightened they'll find out anyway. This way he hopes he might get a reward."

"From the Starklanders? I don't think so."

"Well, if not a reward, at least no punishment. They only know one kind of punishment. Come on, you'll have to hide in the woods until it's safe."

"Glam to the north, desert to the south, east sounds best."

"But that's Squire Redbone's territory, he's forbidden entry. There's a treaty."

"We'll just have to take our chances. Let's go."

"No. I'll wait for my dad."

"No way. You were the one who rescued me and that's who they'll kill first. Your dad'll be safer with you gone."

They grabbed a little food and, as they dashed through the village, torches flickered in the wildwood behind them. The Starkmen would arrive at any moment. Otillie knew the woodland tracks and they slipped away just as the first pirates burst from the forest. They headed straight for Otillie's hut and ransacked the place in seconds. Finding nothing, they tumbled terrified folk from their beds and started roughing them up.

It didn't take them long to discover where the fugitives had gone. Even at that time of morning they found several witnesses who were easily bullied into providing the information. In moments they were hot on the trail, bellowing for the blood of the boy who'd maimed Crag Daniek's favourite hunting bird.

"That was quick," Otillie whispered. "They must have anchored in Dak Creek just to the north. I think their ship needed repairs."

"Sssh…Just run," Henry admonished. "Save your breath."

They hardly noticed the thorn scratches as they dashed for safety. It was a steady climb and in time, brambles and undergrowth gave way to more open pine forest. For a slightly built girl, Otillie had extraordinary stamina and Henry often found it difficult to keep up until she stopped abruptly.

"We're here. Redbone's land," she said with a hint of dread in her voice.

"Looks harmless enough," Henry said, "and we just ran out of choices."

Shafts of daylight lanced through the forest, illuminating half-a-dozen helmeted warriors closing in behind them, the Starkmen had caught up. Henry grabbed Otillie's hand and they ran on as the northern warriors drew their weapons and fanned out through the pines. Whooping and yelling in triumph. The fittest warriors raced to the sides and then ahead of Henry and Otillie, who grew tired and slowed noticeably. Beer-swilling louts Starklanders might be, but this group was fast enough and those who rushed ahead turned to block the way. Henry and Otillie were now surrounded. They stood back-to-back as Henry drew Hornet-Sting and passed his dagger to Otillie whose only other weapon was a fallen pine branch.

"Well, well, well, what 'ave we 'ere?" the leading pirate sneered through a forest of red whiskers and broken teeth.'

"Couple 'o runaways, says I," another Starklander opined. "Now the guv'll be real pleased to get hold of this young brat after what he done to Ernie."

"I've done nothing to any Ernie!" Henry cried. "So leave us alone!"

"The guv's hunting bird, yer goose. It ain't good fer nothin' now and the guv'll wanna talk to you about that."

"You'll never take me alive."

"Suit yerself," the leading Starkmen sighed. "We'll kill yer now and maybe keep the girl a while, although she looks a mite skinny to me."

He moved forward like a snake, but Henry had fought enough battles to be ready for him and fended off the attack, slashing back as Hornet-Sting drew first blood. The Starklander cursed and staggered back, but others took his place. Otillie was nimble and dodged several warriors, inflicting some damage with the branch that shattered after a couple of hefty thwacks, leaving her with only the dagger and her wits. They were both driven back to a single, large pine trunk. Two Starklanders levelled their spears and with a scream charged towards Henry and Otillie bent on finishing them off there and then.

Henry braced for the agony when the two spearmen grunted and fell bristling with what appeared to be very short arrows. The Starklanders turned to meet the threat, but more missiles rained down with deadly accuracy and, in seconds, the entire pirate gang lay dead or badly wounded. Silence and absolute stillness descended on the forest, except the grunts of the wounded men and a call from a distant cuckoo. Then movement stirred as a dozen squat figures moved cautiously towards Henry and Otillie. The dwarf-men were mostly red-haired with flowing beards and hostile expressions. They each carried a cross-bow — something Henry had not seen before — and several bolt quivers. They picked over the dead Starkmen for plunder, finishing off a couple where necessary. Their leader approached Henry, glaring at him, but with a hint of curiosity. He stood just below Henry's shoulder, but was stocky with muscles tight as oak and hard as steel.

"Thank you," Henry said, thinking civility a wise option, "That was wonderful shooting, and very timely."

"And who's t' say you don't get the same," the dwarf challenged. "There's a treaty, y' know and you've broken it."

"He didn't know," Otillie pleaded, "We were desperate. They were going to kill us."

"So I saw. Be silent, girl!"

"I haven't made any treaty with you," Henry challenged.

"Don't matter," the dwarf snapped dismissively, "The squire don't fancy strangers in his part of the forest. There've been too many rum doings hereabouts lately."

"Who's the treaty with?" Henry asked.

"Everyone. It's understood, so push off before I let you have it."

"We can't go back, Crag Daniek will kill us."

"Can't help that, ain't none o' my business."

"Then why save us in the first place?"

"Weren't savin' you. They were treaty breakers and they knew it, so that's what they get. Now hop to it, before I get annoyed."

Henry turned to Otillie and took her by the arm; there was no point in arguing with a bunch of trigger-happy fellows who'd proven they were good shots.

"Come on, Otillie. We'll think of something. Cantankerous little fellows, aren't they. Reminds me of Jongarrat back home…"

"Wait!" the dwarf leader said. "What do you know about Jongarrat?"

"I know him, that's all."

"You'd better come with us then."

The dwarves didn't elaborate, but formed a protective column ahead and behind their captives as the procession marched away. They weren't in any particular hurry and it was easy-going, even for Otillie, who was shaken and scared, but she was a plucky girl and bore hardship bravely. Henry returned Hornet-Sting to its scabbard as no one attempted to disarm him, while Otillie kept the dagger. They left the pines behind and descended into an oak and beech filled valley coursed by clear creeks and rock pools. Grouse and partridge occasionally flapped from cover and several deer dashed across their path. Between the trees they passed small, recently ploughed fields lying ready for the first season's planting. A number of goat herds grazed at the forest edge tended by groups of children. Finally they came to the dwarf village that reminded Henry of Hollowford on a smaller scale.

"Yeah, mind yer 'ead goin' through doors," the leading dwarf said, actually smiling.

The villagers showed a lot of curiosity and many followed Henry and Otillie as they approached a large cottage in the centre of town. It was a neat building with colourful spring bulbs blooming in window boxes and pots along a porch that ran the entire length of the house. A dwarf relaxed on a rocking chair on the porch, eyeing the approaching strangers with interest. He was middle-aged and his hair and beard were streaked with grey.

"We found these trespassers," the leading dwarf announced. "We killed a dozen others. Starkmen!" He spat as he said the word.

"And you spared these two?" the grey-hair observed. "How uncommonly clement of you, Anvil Cornfoot."

"This un says he knows Jongarrat," Anvil Cornfoot explained. "Thought you might be interested."

"A perceptive observation indeed."

The two dwarves didn't appear to be friends, but that was possibly just their normal manner. The grey-haired fellow turned to Henry and Otillie and grinned as laughter lines spread from the tips of his eyes to every corner of his whiskered face.

"Welcome," he greeted cheerfully, "I am Redbone, village squire and the forest conservator."

But Henry barely heard him as his eyes gazed upon Macayle, Edrid, and Bron who stooped through the doorway onto the porch.

"Where's Anshelm..?"

Although they were overjoyed to see him, their eyes gave the answer.

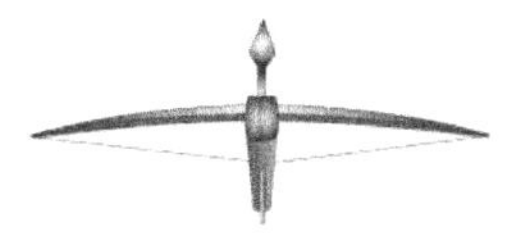

Can this be the stuff of legends?
A dwarf confronting a host of dragons?

Sounds about right to me.
The chroniclers at Tremill Broch certainly think so.

224

Chapter 19
The Graveyard

The five survivors from Zilek Gorge hurried down a sloping path that made their pace easier, but the temperature and humidity rose to a cloying intensity. Fortunately, tree-cover now shaded their trail, but dense undergrowth smothered the path and they had to hack their way through. Jongarrat relinquished his task as guide, complaining that, as they'd gone the wrong way, he was as much in the dark as anyone. At first Gareth thought anything was better than the mountain pass, but after struggling through tangled vines and bush for hours, he wasn't so sure. They were all drenched with sweat and quickly using their water supply.

There was no time for regrets about Faranden — it was done. He was a warrior and met a warrior's death. It was an occupational hazard, and there was no point dwelling on it. Most galling was that they were not men who took retreating well. Gareth had told Bagsha as much and he meant it. Jongarrat's grizzling didn't help and when Gareth told him to shut up, Archer and the giants thought there'd be a confrontation. After a brief nose-to-chest stand-off, Jongarrat obeyed and marched sullenly on, venting his frustration on the thickening jungle. There was evidence of a path, but it had not been used for a long time.

They made a cold camp that night, but slept poorly. Storm clouds developed in the afternoon and rain poured all evening. Considering snow had barely thawed on the peninsula, the atmosphere was oppressively hot here, but they'd travelled many leagues south and the land was low-lying. Nevertheless, Jongarrat remembered the climate was normally mild hereabouts and they must just be experiencing an unseasonable heat-wave. The rain forest was alive with sounds including a howl that Jongarrat identified as one of the large, spotted cats that hunted at night. With no fire to drive off predators, the wayfarers stayed alert, although they sensed movement and sometimes saw eyes reflected in lightning flashes, the big cats passed them by. Unfortunately, leeches proved more trouble than carnivores and had to be cut out, drawing blood and swarms of flies.

"Can it get any worse?" Archer asked rhetorically.

"We come the wrong way. What d'you expect?" Jongarrat snapped, but everyone ignored him.

It was about as wrong as they could get as they'd come to Slag Swamp, a mosquito-infested, mangrove-packed bayou that stretched endlessly along the southern coastline of Black Water. There was no choice but to turn inland and try to find an easier way around. They waded through knee-deep, brackish water for half a day until they came upon dry land and trudged eastwards. Their spirits improved when they found a trail. They followed it for hours, even Jongarrat cheered up and whistled a jig as they picked up the pace, feeling it was the best progress they'd made for days. And all went well, until they reached a riverbank.

The river was not particularly wide, but trees that lined the banks were festooned with scores of skulls dangling in grotesque bunches. Crows massed and perched on top of the skulls, which they'd picked clean while other birds shrieked from the tree-tops. Everyone was alert and wondering if the skull-laden totems meant hostile folk lived in the area, or just people with a very peculiar way of dealing with their dead.

"Sacrifices?" Gareth wondered. "It has the look of ritual."

"Who knows?" Jongarrat replied. "Executions maybe. We could still be in Corbin territory for all we know. Maybe that's what they planned for us if they'd caught us. C'mon, let's get across this river."

He took a step, but just before he splashed into the water, Archer grabbed him by the shoulders and flung him sprawling on his back. The water erupted as a massive, green saurian with teeth-ridden jaws agape clambered onto the bank and lunged at Jongarrat. The beast was three times as long as a man, swift both in and out of water and only Kimball's quick thinking saved the dwarf. As the reptile's jaws were about to latch onto Jongarrat, Kimball brought his axe smashing onto the creature's skull. Blood oozed from the wound, but its hide was so thick, even Kimball's strength wasn't enough to kill the beast.

It roared and rolled back to the water's edge and quickly sank from sight. Within seconds, dozens of other saurians were drawn by the smell of blood and surged towards the stricken reptile. They tore into it without mercy as the river boiled blood-red. The monsters rolled as they ripped pieces from the wounded animal, exposing their yellow bellies and thick, scaly tails that could stun a man with a single blow. The carnage was quickly over, with nothing remaining except a pool of blood and fragments that drew schools of fish to devour the scraps, even though they risked being scooped up by the lizards.

Gareth's warriors withdrew to a safe distance and stood staring at the river that had returned to its original tranquillity.

"Well, well, now that's an unexpected development," Jongarrat said.

"What are those things," Gareth asked, "dragons?"

"Call 'em what you like, Gareth," Jongarrat replied, "I know 'em as muggers, but I don't know what the blazes they're doing here. Mostly I've heard they live in the hot country way down south."

"Seems hot enough to me," Serlequin commented.

"No, they need heat all the time. There must have been a huge flood that brought 'em here and left 'em stranded, which means they'll be hungry. I've got a feeling the only things keeping 'em alive are what was attached to those heads. I reckon that's how the Corbin get rid of enemies they don't fancy themselves."

"We'd better see if we can get past them to the south," Archer said.

As they trudged along the bank, the muggers simply followed, cruising silently with just their raised eyes and nostrils visible and an occasional ripple from their powerful tails that propelled them with ease. When their scaly bodies did rise above the surface, they looked rather like floating drift-wood, a perfect camouflage.

As the day drew to a close, Gareth ordered the company to move safely away from the river and make camp. This time they lit a fire — the bigger the better in Jongarrat's view — to deter muggers and cats. The muggers continual bellowing meant no one slept much, but in the morning they thought their luck had turned. The river was tidal and reduced to a trickle. Scores of muggers lounged on the mud-flats with their jaws agape, while an army of white egrets strutted around them and confidently pecked away between their teeth. Everyone exchanged glances and shrugged.

"You know they're just lying there," Archer observed. "Looks to me this is the ideal time to get around them. They don't seem so inclined to move when they can't swim."

"They need the sun to warm 'em up," Jongarrat said. "Which way do you want to go, Gareth?"

"Is it just me, or are yon beasts grinning?" Kimball pondered.

"Hard to tell through all them flamin' teeth," his brother replied.

As the muggers stretched as far as they could see, Gareth sent the twins to reconnoitre in either direction along the bank. Neither was gone long before they both returned with bad news.

"We're surrounded," Kimball reported. "Corbin, crashing through the bush. They're still back a way, but more are arriving all the time. They're in no hurry, just waiting at a safe distance, probably hoping the muggers'll finish us off so we don't kill any more of 'em."

"Between a rock and a hard place," Serlequin confirmed. "Pity we couldn't pick the muggers" teeth like yon birds and just amble past.'

"Maybe we can't go around them now, but if we're careful, we might get past 'em." Gareth said. "They seem calm enough to me, and a stiff thump with a sword blade should sort 'em out, don't you think?"

They all nodded. They were warriors after all, so fending off a bunch of over-sized lizards shouldn't pose any great challenge to them. But then they heard a roar of turbid water as a tidal-bore swept from the sea up the river-bed. The egrets flapped into tree perches ahead of the rushing water that wasn't huge, but a rapid surge that left the warriors stranded on the bank. The muggers had no difficulty as the wave washed over them. Several strong tail sweeps maintained their position until the river settled where they seemed content to float lazily just below the surface.

"So now we're really trapped," Gareth surmised. "We'd need

wings to get over that lot."

"Over!" Jongarrat declared. "That's it. Over."

"We can't fly, remember!"

"Not fly…over. Archer, can you get an arrow into the top of that big fig-tree on the far bank? The tallest one."

"Yes, easy."

"We'd better be quick then," Jongarrat said and explained his plan.

The Corbin warriors closed in, hidden behind undergrowth, but there was no doubting their presence. They howled war-cries and taunts, as much to build up their own courage as to dismay the enemy. They didn't have a clear view of the riverbank and several braver or less patient souls crept forward, but were promptly dealt with by Kimball and Serlequin who, despite their size, moved silently through the bush.

"Them big fellers ain't gonna hold 'em off forever," Jongarrat surmised. "Let's get to it."

He and Archer clambered as far they could up one of the large fig trees that lined the bank. They quickly unbraided a rope to only a couple of strands and secured one end to an arrow shaft and carefully coiled the twine to prevent it snagging while Jongarrat wound the other end around his wrist.

"Think it'll be long enough?" he asked.

"Better be," Archer replied. "But who knows how the twine will affect the arrow's flight?"

"Just hit the tree and stop making excuses.'"

Archer drew the bow, aimed, and shot. The arrow flashed through the air and thudded high into the trunk on the opposite bank, while the twine spiralled away behind it. Jongarrat drew in the slack so it spanned the river and spliced another length of rope to the twine.

"Looks thin, don't it? Hope it'll hold my weight," he said.

"It's short range, so the arrow's wedged tight, but are you sure you want to do this?'"

"Got a better idea? The Corbin ain't gonna wait for Kimball and Serlequin to pick 'em off one by one. They'll come in force, and I judge pretty soon. When I'm across I'll pull the main line over. Just don't let go of your end."

Jongarrat tossed the rope over a branch, dropping the end to Gareth, who tied it around his waist using his weight as an anchor. Without a further word, the dwarf launched himself hand-over-hand across the river, locking his ankles around the rope for support. The line sagged despite Gareth's bulk and Jongarrat dipped dangerously close to the muggers as he reached the river centre. A couple of the reptiles reared out of the water towards him, just missing his back.

As he passed half-way, the space between him and the muggers grew, but it meant extra effort to climb to safety. And he would have done it too, Archer's arrow remained firmly impaled in the tree, but the twine slipped free and Jongarrat plunged into the river, splashing down in water deep enough to break his fall, but a few yards short of the bank and right beside a mugger. He drew his dagger and plunged it into the reptile's spine and hauled himself onto its back. The wound was only slight and it easily flicked him off into the tightly packed animals that closed in. He landed on another mugger, quickly steadied, and hopped agilely across the backs of two more, closely avoiding their snapping jaws before reaching the safety of the far bank.

He raced for the fig with several snarling saurians lumbering after him and clambered into the tree just before they caught up. Although he was pretty sure they couldn't climb, he wanted to put as much distance between himself and the monsters as possible, so he scrambled to the top branches.

He reached the arrow that was stuck in a branch almost at the peak of the canopy, but in his haste he'd forgotten the rope and their escape link was broken. He sat panting for a moment, and then sensed that he was not alone. Slowly he raised his head and stared into the hypnotic eyes of the largest boa he'd ever seen draped across the upper branches. Its tongue flickered with interest only inches from his face.

Gareth saw Jongarrat dash to safety. With great relief until he noticed the abandoned line floating on the water. Archer realised Jongarrat had no chance of retrieving the rope and hauled it back. They both grew concerned when there was no sign of the dwarf and, worse still, Kimball and Serlequin returned reporting the Corbin were massing in large groups as their yelling increased. With no other ideas, Archer tied the twine to another arrow.

Hope this works. I'll put the shot as close to the other one as I can.

The rope snagged on the first attempt so Archer spent frustrating moments pulling it in and re-coiling it. The second shot proved successful. The arrow disappeared into foliage as the life-line arched gracefully between the tree-tops. Then nothing. The rope hung limply over the river and there was no hope that the arrow or the two-strand twine would hold any of the larger men's weight. They were still trapped.

"Looks like it's cross the river, weapons at the ready after all," Gareth conceded, but now the water was at least chest high in the centre and there was every chance they'd have to swim some of the way with no hope against the reptiles in their element.

Then the line began to tighten. The thin cord first, followed by the thick mountain rope that inched across the river and finally spanned the gap. Archer tested it by tugging sharply to confirm the link was secure. They expected Jongarrat to yell or at least wave to confirm he'd attached his end, but there was no signal from the far side.

"What the blazes is he playing at?" Gareth fumed. "This is no time for stupid games."

"We'll just have to trust him," Archer conceded. "The rope is strong enough for us all now."

According to plan, Archer strapped his bow across his back and carried as many arrows as he could. Serlequin took the rope-end from Gareth while he and Kimball stood guard. With the rope now firmly secured at one end and well anchored by Serlequin at the other, Archer stayed well above the milling reptiles and was soon across. He reached the tree-tops where Jongarrat crouched, his forehead glistening with sweat.

"Well done," Archer said, clapping him on the shoulder and without waiting climbed down to the tree base. The muggers had returned to the river so he was safe enough. Unslinging his bow and nocking an arrow, he stood ready to discourage any attacks with a few accurate shots.

Gareth followed without incident.

"A little communication would have been nice," he hissed at Jongarrat, who simply rolled his eyes upwards indicating the serpent just above their heads. Archer's second arrow had landed right between the dwarf and the boa. Fortunately, judging by its swollen belly, it was digesting something large enough to satisfy it for a month. So it wasn't interest in dwarves.

"I get along fine with most beasts," Jongarrat whispered, "even big, dangerous ones, but I hate snakes. They're just plain sneaky."

Gareth drew Goresax that he'd strapped across his back.

"Don't worry, I'll stay here and deal with the serpent if it causes trouble. You join Archer, two bows are better than one."

Jongarrat had lost a couple of arrows in the river, but still had enough to be useful. He left without another word.

Kimball was next and despite Serlequin's efforts, the line dipped dramatically with the giant's back barely clearing the surface. The muggers stirred and cruised in circles, which encouraged him to hasten and he too clambered to safety. Gareth untied the rope and tossed it over the stoutest branch, dropping it to the ground. Kimball now acted as the anchor as Archer signalled Serlequin to climb the tree opposite them and fasten his end to a stout branch.

Serlequin was barely up the tree when the Corbin seemed to sense it was safe to charge. They burst from the bush and streamed onto the bank, their cloaks abandoned in the heat and their tattooed bodies dripping sweat. The muggers showed some interest, which slowed their charge.

The Corbin were well armed and surely there were enough of them to see the muggers off, but they were a cowardly lot at heart and baulked at the water's edge. At first they just looked baffled by the vacant bank, but it wasn't long before they discovered tracks surrounding the tree. Serlequin had just secured the rope and was hauling himself across when the Corbin let out a collective roar and started hurling weapons at him. Archer and Jongarrat sent several arrows into the crowd, bringing down four warriors and sending the others scuttling for cover. But, it wasn't long before they recovered and brought archers of their own into the fight.

At first the tree canopy protected Serlequin and spoiled the Corbin warriors' view, but as he reached the centre, he became very vulnerable indeed. A dozen arrows whistled past him as he dangled helplessly, but the threat urged him on and he hauled his great weight with renewed speed. At that moment, half-a-dozen Corbin warriors gathered the courage to storm the tree.

Archer and Jongarrat brought down two of them before they reached the foot of the trunk, but the others clambered up and started hacking at the rope-end with battle-axes. It only took a few hefty blows to sever the line and under Serlequin's weight it flicked away with a whip-crack. The giant thumped onto the muddy bank with such force that his breath shot from his lungs. He lay stunned as the muggers surged towards him. It only took seconds for him to recover, but by then he was surrounded.

He drew his axe.

Until then, Archer and Jongarrat had been diverted by the Corbin warriors across the river and it took Gareth and Kimball a moment to reach the ground. They were about to charge to Serlequin's aid when a hail of missiles showered down from the far bank. The river edge was now crowded with men roaring abuse and hurling spears, so the four fugitives dived for cover. Archer and Jongarrat once again fired arrows into the mob, but more missiles rained in, slamming into the mud around Serlequin's feet. The first salvo missed the giant, but impaled several muggers only inches away. The animals thrashed as blood sprayed from their wounds, drawing others who fell upon the injured reptiles. The distraction gave Serlequin just enough time to turn and bolt towards the big fig-tree. He plunged for cover, landing squarely on top of Jongarrat, nearly knocking him out.

The others untangled them and all five gave the Corbin a farewell gesture before racing from the riverbank as a last volley of spears and arrows rained down. Bagsha Grimhand stormed through his gang, cuffing them for the cowards they were. He was furious at the men who'd cut the line, saying it was their only way after the fugitives. Even when they pointed out the escapees would have surely cut the line on the far side, he still wasn't satisfied and tossed a couple of men to the muggers in pure spite. Bagsha paced the bank in frustration until more saurians moved towards him, forcing the entire Corbin tribe to beat a hasty retreat into the forest.

The muggers resumed their languid cruising while the boa remained on its perch and birds, along with other wild creatures, returned to continue Slag Swamp's sluggish routine. The graveyard failed to claim any peninsula-men that time.

We're so close; the Starklanders camp is not far.
But, what to do now?
How am I supposed to deal with this?

Where the blazes are Gareth and the others?
It seems I have all the questions and none of the answers.

Chapter 20
Henry's Plan

For someone who'd only been hugged occasionally by his Aunt Thayer, Henry found he enjoyed the experience, especially when Macayle just about squeezed the wind out of him. Edrid shook his hand until it ached, and Bron slobbered over his leg, which he was prepared to overlook under the circumstances. Otillie and the dwarves were forgotten until he remembered he'd been rescued too, and introduced her. At any other time Otillie might have been over-awed by Macayle, who acted like a lord's daughter when she was in the mood, but now appeared as dishevelled as any lowly peasant.

"I found this, I think it's yours now," Henry said, handing her the scrimshaw.

She took it and sadly replaced it around her neck exposing some livid bruising she'd suffered during the shipwreck.

"Anshelm couldn't swim, you know," she said. "Odd, isn't it? He lived so long by the sea and never learnt."

"We hung onto a piece of wreckage, but we couldn't reach him," Edrid added. "I suppose it's a fitting end for a seaman. I don't think he knew much about it."

That wasn't exactly true, but Edrid thought he'd spare Henry the details of a desperate man's panic as he thrashed futilely in the waves, cursing them all for persuading him to join such folly.

"Can't see how there're any preferences when it comes to

dying," Anvil Cornfoot commented to no one in particular. "You'd have gone the same way if'n some of our folk hadn't fished you otta the briny."

And that was the truth. Edrid and Macayle had clung to the largest floating part of *Seawind*, managing to hoist Bron across it where she lay with her paws dangling into the sea. The flimsy raft drifted northwards until they were swept into a boiling lagoon at the edge of Dak Creek, surrounded by sheer cliffs with no way of escape. Redbone's men were returning from a fishing trip when they spotted the trapped castaways.

They rigged tackles and pulleys before several dwarves lowered themselves to the water. It was a risky business, but dwarves were competent builders and engineers who enjoyed a challenge. They placed slings around the half-conscious survivors and hoisted them to the cliff top, then carried them to their village, fed them, tended their injuries, warmed them up and put them to bed. The presence of a wolf was unnerving at first, but they grew used to Bron, especially as she proved to be quite friendly.

"Let me get this straight," Henry said. "You fellows risked your lives to save Edrid, Macayle, and Bron, but were going to skewer us full of arrows?"

"It's the principle, don't you see? You were trespassing, they were in distress..." Redbone began.

"Don't you think being chased by half-a-dozen blood-thirsty pirates is in distress?"

"Well, you have a point, but...Macayle is a great beauty, there's no doubt. It would be such a waste..."

"Otillie's beautiful too..."

He hadn't expected to say that and everyone smiled, especially Otillie, while Macayle eyed him with amused curiosity.

"Oh, I think fair or plain, Anvil would have shown equal gallantry and I don't reckon he would really have shot you, would you Anvil?"

But Anvil Cornfoot's expression was inscrutable.

"I suppose we were lucky so many rescuers were around," Edrid said.

"Gannet season brings folk to gather eggs," Redbone said. "But now you've been reunited, it's time to tell us about Jongarrat."

"Obviously you know him," Henry replied.

"He's my brother."

"He doesn't look much like you really…I mean, except for size."

"Times change people. He's been away for years."

"According to Guilda, he's been with her on-and-off forever."

"Guilda?"

"She's an old, magic woman who lives near our town…" Henry explained everything he knew about Jongarrat and his life on Grambak Peninsula. "…I've no idea what made him travel so far. He's really a bit secretive about that," he concluded.

"When our father died, Jongarrat was to be squire, but the position didn't sit well with him. He's no diplomat, as you know. In the end, he caused more arguments than he settled and — well, not to put too fine a point on it — he was booted out and I took over. Naturally, he was pretty bitter about that and eventually left with several companions, saying he'd seek his fortune elsewhere. No one actually wanted him to go, they just didn't want him to be squire any more, but I can understand how he could take something like that personally.'

"I don't know about making a fortune or what happened to the others, but Guilda said he was content enough. They get along anyway."

"I'm sure everyone would be happy to see him back again."

"You might get the chance to find out. He's coming with five of our toughest warriors to try and get Macayle's mother back from the Starkmen — if we don't beat them to it."

It was time for lunch and while Macayle and Otillie helped Beatrice, the squire's wife, in her kitchen, Redbone showed Edrid and Henry around. Despite his truculence, Anvil Cornfoot accompanied them and listened while Henry told his story.

"So you plan to go and beat the pants off the Starklanders with two men, a girl, and a dog. I can see how that will work," Cornfoot observed.

"I admit we haven't thought it all through yet, but we have to do something," Henry replied lamely. "And Bron's not a dog, she's a wolf."

"There are less than a hundred of the villains," Redbone assayed. "Not that many really, especially after Anvil here disposed of a few more. Apparently they're outlaws from their own lands way across the western oceans. A tough breed by all accounts, but this mob is truly feral. Hard men to stop, I'd say."

"Anvil's men didn't have much trouble, although the Starkmen seem to have laid waste to everywhere else around here," Henry observed.

"We protect ourselves and it's up to other folk to do the same. You know there are still enough people in the area to outnumber the Starkmen, but it's a matter of resolve."

"Even if we only go and spy out the land and wait for Chief Gareth, it'll be something."

"Wise choice," Cornfoot agreed.

"The idea of three of us trying to spirit Lady Ayla away from the pirate stronghold is ambitious," Edrid admitted. "But there are still Palo Innes folk to rescue if there's a chance."

"Good luck with that then," the squire said. "But remember, Glam is a fortress. It's sited on an island at the mouth of a fjord. The only way across is by ferry, and that's guarded day and night."

"You seem to know a lot about them. Will you help us?" Henry asked.

"We know enough to keep out of their way," Anvil Cornfoot said.

"I think Anvil is right," the squire added. "We can defend our own lands, but our role is to conserve this forest and not meddle in other people's feuds."

"We shall go anyway," Henry declared and Macayle nodded, she was close to finding her mother and didn't want the search to lose momentum.

They returned to a table laid out with culinary treats, venison stew, roast pheasant, hot bread, fried onions, carrots, and green vegetables, along with cider and elderberry wine. Otillie stared wide-eyed at the feast.

"Everyone tuck in," Beatrice said, sitting next to her, "especially you, dear."

They did the meal justice, which pleased Beatrice, and spent the afternoon lazing on Redbone's porch. Otillie's stomach gurgled for a while, but settled down in the end.

"We'll head back to your village tomorrow, Otillie," Henry said. "Maybe we can get some help there."

But she looked doubtful.

As evening approached, Beatrice shooed the men away to give Macayle and Otillie privacy. She boiled water and filled a tub for the girls to bathe while she washed and dried their shifts. She also supplied a brush and comb as they chatted and giggled, taking turns untangling each other's hair before decorating the tresses with daisies and marigolds. After dressing in clean clothes, their transformation from vagabonds to young ladies was complete. Even Anvil Cornfoot agreed they looked "nice," so the girls both kissed him on the cheek. And, for the first time that she could remember, Otillie felt safe with friends around her.

Beatrice, who was not only a fine cook but an able seamstress, suggested the girls needed something sturdier to wear for traipsing around the forest, and sat up late sewing and adjusting breeches, tunics, and boots to fit them.

"Not very lady-like," she conceded, "but far more practical."

The following morning, they woke to find Redbone gone, but Beatrice sat by the fire stirring a pot of porridge that hung from a trivet over the embers. She smiled and indicated a pile of wooden bowls and spoons on the table, which was also laden with platters of bread and bantam eggs.

"The squire has duties in the forest. He bid you 'goodbye' and wishes you well," she said with a certain finality.

After breakfast, they were surprised to find Anvil Cornfoot waiting on the squire's porch. He had honed Hornet-Sting to a razor-edge and pointed to a small arsenal of weapons lying by the steps including several bows, axes, knives, swords, and a couple of full arrow quivers.

"Help yourselves," he offered.

Although Edrid had returned Skull-Breaker to Archer, and it

would have been lost it in the wreck anyway, the prince favoured a battle axe. So he chose one along with a dagger and a bow. The girls settled for a sword and a stiletto each. Henry took a bow to supplement Hornet-Sting. They decided against cross-bows as there was no time to practise and Cornfoot admitted they took a bit of getting used to and were slower to reload than a conventional bow. He nodded with approval at their selection then wrapped the remaining weapons in sacking and placed them inside.

"Thanks, this is quality stuff," Henry said, recognising fine forge-work when he saw it, but then the dwarves were good at that sort of thing as well.

"Squire reckons you'll need 'em before you're finished. He also told me to give you this."

Cornfoot handed Henry a hunting horn tied with a leather strap. Henry took the horn, eyeing it doubtfully, and then placed it around his neck and gave the dwarf a questioning look.

"It's a signal horn," Cornfoot explained. "Blow if you get in a fix and dwarves will lend a hand, if they can. It's a totem, wear it and you'll pass safely through our lands. Don't want to get skewered after all the trouble you've been through. C'mon, we'd better get cracking."

"We?"

"Yep, I'll guide you through the woods or you'll be lost in no time."

They strapped their weapons on and farewelled Beatrice, who provided them each with a knapsack full of provisions and a water gourd. Anvil Cornfoot led all day with only a couple of short stops to eat and rest. He was remarkably nimble, moving through the undergrowth with ease while Bron seemed to enjoy bounding along beside him. Henry and Otillie stayed with the pace, but

Edrid and Macayle struggled.

"I'm a fisherman, not a forester," Edrid complained during one of their breaks. "It makes you wonder why dwarves are short. I mean, sure they're a bit stocky, but they're just like us only smaller."

"No, I hadn't thought about it. They just are," Henry replied.

"I don't think so. It's the forest that's made them what they are. Look how agile our friend Anvil is compared with us clunking about. They've had to adapt to live here. They've been moulded by the land."

"So you're saying people change?"

"Yes, they need to suit where they live, except I don't know about Starkmen," Edrid said, and then added, "Macayle looks very fetching in her new clothes, don't you think?"

Henry glared at him, but conceded Macayle would look fetching even in rags.

They reached Otillie's village at dusk and saw at once that all was not well.

The place had been ransacked and was deserted. What little the villagers owned was scattered on the street, and at least half the buildings were now smouldering heaps of rubble. A flock of ravens clattered around, scavenging in the rubbish.

"Dad!" Otillie called. "Where are you? Oh, come out please. It's me Dad, I'm home."

There was no response, but while they cautiously investigated the shanties that still stood, Bron was distracted to the village edge and stood at bay, growling at a slight movement in the briars.

"Ambush?" Edrid hissed.

"I don't think so, stealth ain't Starkmen's style," Cornfoot said.

"Come out, whoever you are," Henry ordered, drawing his

bow. "Right now or I'll let you have it."

"Don't shoot," a voice called from the undergrowth after a pause. "The Starklanders have gone…for now."

"All right," Henry said, but kept his bow ready.

The villagers straggled from the forest, scared, ragged, hungry, cold, and thoroughly miserable. Some bore bruises from beatings and all suffered cuts and scratches. They gathered around Henry's group with a mixture of hostility and trepidation.

"What happened?" Otillie demanded, but no one was inclined to answer. "Where's my dad?"

"He's dead, girl," an old man finally said wearily. His lip was so badly swollen he barely whispered and his white beard was stained with blood.

"Where is he?"

"I dunno. Starklanders came for this young fellow here," he nodded towards Henry. "Your dad brought 'em from Dak Creek. They got all steamed up when they discovered you'd got away and killed him in spite. Things got even worse when the thugs they sent after you didn't come back, so they started tearing the place apart and beating folk up. We took off quick-smart, but not before a few of us got thumped about.'

"Come on, we'll find him," Henry said and it didn't take long.

Otillie's dad lay in a crumpled, pathetically frail bundle by their burnt-out shack. She knelt beside him and cradled his fragile body, tears streaming down her cheeks. Macayle placed her arm around Otillie's shoulder, but the girl was heartbroken.

"He wasn't bad," she sobbed, "but he wasn't strong either. He just wanted to keep me safe, and now look what's happened. Oh, Henry, I wish we'd never found you. Please go away before anything else happens."

But with night approaching, there was nowhere to go, so they stayed. Everyone spent a cold night around fires fuelled with debris, and in the morning Henry, Edrid, and Anvil Cornfoot helped with the clean-up. They buried Otillie's dad in a plot at the village edge and stood in a forlorn group until the other villagers drifted back to their repairs.

"So what now?" Edrid asked. "I guess we'd better head off, we're not welcome here."

"I've got a plan," Henry said.

They squatted in a circle while Henry explained what he had in mind. Using a twig, he scribbled a map in the dirt, checking with Anvil to see that his bearings were correct. Finally, they rose and stretched their legs.

"That's it, then?" Edrid said.

"Pretty much, what do you reckon?"

Edrid shrugged.

"Don't look at me. I'm just an observer," Anvil Cornfoot said.

Henry eyed him suspiciously.

"Well…yeah… The squire asked me to keep an eye on you in case you got into trouble. But I ain't gonna stop you. It's your necks after all."

"Right, let's get 'em all together and see what they have to say."

How do I rally Otillie's people?
They've seen so much suffering and their spirits are broken.

On the other hand, what have they got to lose?
But, it'll be up to me to get them going.

Chapter 21
Vipers' Nest

It took some time to gather the villagers, mostly because they were reluctant to be gathered. There was work to do and they wanted to get on with it, but Henry, Edrid, and Macayle pestered them until they all formed a group in what remained of the town-square. Otillie had softened a little and helped persuade them to at least listen to Henry. They were indeed a forlorn lot, noticeably short on young people, and many were sickly or infirmed in some way. Obviously the Starklanders had stolen all the able-bodied villagers and Henry hoped this would be his trump card.

"Aren't you sick of this?" he asked them. "How long have the Starkmen been terrorising you?"

No answer, just tacit sullenness.

"Years," the same ancient who'd spoken earlier finally replied. "But older folk can remember when they weren't here."

"And look what they've done in that time," Henry said. "They've stolen your food, carried off your young people and killed anyone who got in their way or just for fun. Looks to me like life could be fine here, but you need young, healthy folk for that. If this goes on much longer, you'll all starve or die from illness."

"What do you expect us to do about it?" the old man challenged, accompanied by a great deal of head-nodding.

"Get 'em back, of course, and get back at the Starkmen."

"How? Look at us."

"The dwarves told me there aren't that many Starklanders — less than a hundred — and there are six mighty warriors on their way from my home."

Henry neglected to mention he had no idea where these mighty warriors were or when they might turn up, but no one gainsaid the point.

"And what if we fail?" someone mumbled from the crowd.

"Then we fail, but what is your alternative?"

"We survive."

"Living like mice, without a shred of dignity — dashing into the forest every time you hear a rustle in the undergrowth — your bellies aching from hunger and your children dying of plague because they don't have the strength to fight disease — your homes ripped apart every time the Starkmen feel like a spot of vandalism. I can see how you enjoy surviving."

"It's easy for you to say, you don't live here."

"Yes, but if I did I'd have the grit to fight back. Think of Otillie's father. Don't you want your young people back? Isn't there a spark left here?"

Apparently not. Even though they hung their heads, they still turned and shuffled back to what they were doing, leaving Henry fuming.

"Nice try," Edrid said. "You're quite the little orator at times, but I guess we're on our own."

"Some odds," Henry grumbled. "Two men, a girl, a dwarf, and a tame wolf..."

"Forget the dwarf, I'm just an observer," Anvil reminded him.

"Cheer up," Edrid said. "We've always got Gareth and his crew to rely on."

Maybe, but when or if reinforcements would arrive was

problematic.

"Let's get going," Macayle said. "We're not doing any good here."

So they said goodbye to Otillie and left half their food with the village. It was only a token gesture with so many mouths to feed, but it was all they could think of.

Anvil Cornfoot confidently led the way through the wildwood. It wasn't long before they reached Dak Creek. They scouted the banks, discovered the wolf-ship had sailed away, and they looked for a place to ford. Moving inland, they found a spot and clambered down to the water's edge. There was plenty of fallen timber and driftwood close by, so they lashed pieces together, making a raft that allowed them to cross with nothing more than wet feet. They dragged the raft above the water line, knowing they'd probably need it to re-cross the river, possibly in a hurry.

The thorn bush relented on the far side of Dak Creek, turning to conifer forest which made travelling easier. When they camped, they felt confident enough to light a fire and spent a comfortable night close to the embers. During the afternoon, Bron caught rabbits and partridges for supper.

"Useful having a wolf around," Cornfoot observed as he roasted the prey while Bron gnawed some small rodents she fancied as appetisers.

"A few people have said that," Henry replied.

"You like her, don't you?" Macayle asked Henry as they warmed their hands.

"Who, Bron? Of course I do."

"No, silly. Otillie."

"Oh… She saved my life and…yes…I thought she was nice. I'm sorry how things worked out, though."

He didn't want to talk about it. Macayle was digging in areas he'd rather avoid. Liking people was fine, but look what happened — Anshelm was dead, and so was Otillie's dad. When he liked people, tragedy seemed to strike, and he certainly liked Macayle. So he changed the subject. He thought he'd had a birthday in the last week, but couldn't say exactly when as he'd lost track.

The following day, they set off at a brisk pace and the forest was alive with early summer activity. Blue jays, cuckoos, and woodpeckers all added to the woodland chorus, while red squirrels bounded through the tree-tops. Deer herds grazed between trees, heralding a good food supply so Bron didn't need to hunt smaller prey. They hadn't travelled far when Anvil Cornfoot signalled a halt and placed his finger to his lips. Henry drew his bow and the others stood ready for trouble. The dwarf froze for a moment then crept back along the path for a short distance before returning.

"Quick, off the track," he hissed. "Someone's following us — a large bunch as I figure it."

How Anvil had sensed the danger was a mystery, but Henry remembered some people, including Archer, were acutely aware of their surrounds. They ducked behind trees and bracken and waited. In moments they heard the noise of people tramping along the trail with no particular caution. Starkmen...? No...

Every able-bodied individual from Otillie's village marched along the trail armed with pikes, scythes, staffs, hatchets, axes, a sword or two, and even a fair number of bows. And Otillie was leading, striding ahead and urging the others to hurry up.

"What do they want?" Edrid whispered.

"Dunno," Henry replied softly, although the villagers were

making enough noise that it was unlikely he'd be overheard. "To finish us off in case we cause trouble at Glam?"

"You going to find out?" Anvil Cornfoot asked.

"Suppose so, if we let 'em pass, we'll only catch up later."

"Be careful, Henry," Macayle added.

How exactly? Henry thought, but rose from cover and strode onto the path just as Otillie approached. He didn't draw Hornet-Sting or nock an arrow to his bowstring, which might have been a good idea if the crowd wanted trouble, but he didn't think so. His fears were instantly dispelled when Otillie stepped forward and hugged him, while the villagers smiled and waved.

"We thought about what you said," she began. "You were right. Of course, we can't let things go on the way they are. It ain't no life, so we'd like to join you—if you'll still have us. We all agreed. We've brought all the food we could, to keep our strength up."

Henry eyed their bundles of turnips uncertainly and hoped they could do better than that along the trail.

"Otillie's a very persuasive girl," the old spokesman said. "She bullied us left, right, and centre. So here we are — everyone who is strong enough to make the trip. There's a bit of fight left in us yet.'

"Well, ain't that a turn up for the books," Anvil Cornfoot said as he and the others emerged from cover. "How did you folk get across Dak Creek?"

"Same as you," the old boy replied, "built a couple more rafts and ferried everyone across, even left a line over the river to make it easier going back."

"Let's get going then," Henry said, mindful of keeping up their enthusiasm.

Armed with a staff, Otillie nudged Macayle aside and marched beside Henry. Macayle simply smiled and joined Edrid who, although pleased with the arrangement, said nothing. He just looked smug. Anvil Cornfoot explained the path led directly to Glam, so he didn't have to guide them. He took up the rear guard, ensuring there were no stragglers and, more importantly, that they were not being followed.

On the third day, they reached Glam without incident and well-fed on roasted game. The Starklanders appeared to be content in their lair and weren't roaming abroad. Anvil Cornfoot had fretted about security when they lit evening cooking-fires, but his fears were unfounded. Henry held the company back some distance from Glam while he, Edrid, Anvil, and Bron went to reconnoitre. Macayle came too, saying it was her mother who'd been captured after all, and Otillie just said she was coming. The old boy, whose name was Julian, and had been a respected elder in more halcyon times, took charge and made a good job of organising the villagers. Some civic pride seemed to be returning already.

Glam was set in the centre of a fjord. A steep path led from the cliff-top to a ferry terminal that was the island's only access, other than by sea. The adventurers found a vantage point to observe the fortress without being spotted. The ferry was guarded by two rather bored sentries, who lounged on battle-axes. A tow-rope sagged into the water, leading to a barge moored to the island docking pylon. The stronghold itself was surrounded by a wooden palisade, but it was in disrepair with many stakes missing and completely open on one side where storage sheds, make-shift shelters, animal pens, and a barracoon stood.

The gate by the ferry mooring was open and unguarded. Three wolf-ships, which appeared to be the Starklanders' entire fleet, were docked at the far side of the island. The sails were furled, suggesting the pirates were not planning another raid soon. The main hall was built of pine logs covered with a thick thatch, with a stone-walled kitchen close beside it where smoke lazed through its shingle roof.

Beyond reared a massive white-peaked wilderness that the Starklanders had claimed as their territory; although why they wanted it was anyone's guess.

"There she lies," Anvil Cornfoot announced. "Whatcha plannin' to do about it, Henry?"

"There's an awful lot of activity going on. Look at all those folk running in and out of the cook-house."

"Feasting and boozing around here most nights, I'd expect. Starkmen don't do much else."

"Now that's a useful piece of information, I think we'll make our move before Otillie's people change their minds."

"You've got a plan?"

"Yep, but someone's going to get really cold and wet," Henry replied, staring straight at Edrid.

Midnight.

They'd watched Glam fortress until it was dark, but were still able to make out a little from torch lights on the island. The festivity was in full swing by nightfall, judging from the bustle of slaves between the kitchen and great hall.

"It's risky, y'know," Cornfoot hissed. "They might still outnumber us."

"Maybe, but we're sober. You don't have to come," Henry replied, but was rather comforted by the dwarf's use of us. "I thought you were just an observer."

"I was, but I wouldn't miss this for the world."

"Good, then stop whining. Anyway, Edrid's going to even things up."

The Starkmen were well into their cups and a raucous chorus drifted across the fjord.

> *"We are the Starkmen,*
> *Strong as can be,*
> *We fear no man,*
> *On land, river or sea.*
>
> *We are the Starkmen,*
> *Put us to the test,*
> *With Sword or axe,*
> *We'll show who's best.*
>
> *We are the Starkmen,*
> *Warriors all are we,*
> *All men fear us,*
> *On land river and sea."*

It was all dreadfully conceited stuff and went on relentlessly, but Henry was able to gauge the enemy's condition as the singing progressed. They'd been at it for five hours so he judged they were blurry to a man. It was time to move.

Anvil Cornfoot showed Henry how to drive a dagger through a man's jugular and finish him off quickly and quietly. They went ahead and easily dealt with the two guards, who were half-asleep, and dumped their bodies into the fjord as the villagers advanced. Edrid put his toe into the water and gasped. He was barefoot and stripped to a light shirt and breeches with an axe strapped to his back and a dagger tucked into his belt.

"Don't be such a sissy," Henry whispered.

Edrid just looked mean until Macayle kissed him on the cheek.

"Stay safe," she said softly, although it seemed a forlorn hope, considering what he was about to do.

"I will. Give me an hour. I hope they don't change the guards before then."

"We can deal with that," Henry replied.

Half the villagers volunteered to go with him, but he was the best swimmer and the current deceptive, so he chose to go alone, saying he was less likely to be detected that way. The sea around Palo Innes was warmed by a southerly current, but the fjord still contained a fair portion of ice-melt, so Edrid found it bitterly cold. Fortunately, Glam was no great distance and Edrid swam strongly with pent-up hate to urge him on.

Personal hygiene wasn't the Starklanders top priority and refuse floated close to Glam. Edrid just had to swim through it although the tide swept most waste out to sea sooner or later. There were no sentries patrolling the island when Edrid dragged himself dripping and shivering onto the rocks, but a Starklander staggered through one of the breaks in the palisade to the shore and relieved himself, nearly hitting Edrid in the process.

In a single, fluid motion Edrid drew his dagger and drove it into the pirate's kidney, then pitched the body into the sea. He glanced around and ducked behind a lumber pile, but the splash did not cause suspicion. He crept to the ferry and, discovering it unguarded, released the raft from its mooring and pulled on the tow rope. His signal was answered and he delayed only long enough to see the ferry being hauled across the fjord by the villagers.

Edrid bolted for the barracoon and found over thirty prisoners huddled against the cold where only a few thin planks served as shelter. Half were islanders and they recognised their prince immediately, the rest were the strongest from Otillie's village. The gate was bolted and held by a stout padlock, but Edrid smashed the wooden frame with his axe and entered the barracoon. Hushing their excitement, he told them Henry's plan.

"Can you get hold of any weapons?" he asked the prisoners.

They knew of a couple of stashes on the island, so Edrid instructed several people to gather as many as they could, arm everyone, and meet him back at the barracoon. The slaves had managed to make a meagre fire which was probably all that kept them alive. Edrid made three torches from rags. He gave one each to three of the strongest men and they headed for the wolf-ships. The boats weren't guarded, but Edrid killed two drunken Starklanders sleeping it off where they had collapsed. The hulls were laden with bric-a-brac and Edrid ordered his men to pile anything flammable in the centre, especially oars and sails. They also found kegs of pitch used for caulking and poured that over the deck then crouched in the bilge and waited.

Henry, Otillie, Macayle, Bron, and Anvil Cornfoot were in the first wave to land safely on Glam and immediately sent the ferry back for reinforcements. There was certainly still some activity from the hall, but far more subdued than the earlier debauchery.

"We have to check no slaves are inside," Macayle said. "I'll go."

"That's not part of the plan," Henry hissed. "It's far too dangerous."

"Oh, and I feel really safe out here. My mother might be in there, and they won't notice just another serving-girl."

"Just wait then. It won't be long. I'll tell you when to go. We've got to time this just right."

The next ferry load arrived, and as the raft was towed back for another batch. The night sky filled with blazing orbs as fire arrows sank into the hall's thatch, immediately erupting into flames. The villagers had proved pretty good shots and the blaze quickly took hold of the entire roof and smoke began swirling.

"Now!" Henry said to Macayle, as the last group of villagers stormed ashore, leaving only a handful on the far bank.

She dashed to the door that joined the kitchen and slipped inside. The great hall was rank with the stench of wood-smoke, stale beer, and flatulence as the last of the revellers lounged around on benches, guzzling from wooden steins and drinking horns. The atmosphere inside was so thick that no one had noticed the smoke from the roof so far, but it wouldn't be long before its effect was felt even here. Food scraps and spilt ale covered the floor, and the last of the platters were being cleaned up by half-a-dozen remaining captives. They were all girls about Macayle's age who endured the Starkmen's groping as they went about their work. Many bearded drunkards were draped across the tables, snoring. There was no sign of Ayla.

Macayle joined the task of clearing up accompanied by some unwelcome familiarity, but was able to whisper to the other girls to leave the hall and not come back. Some looked worried, but Macayle assured them the Starkmen were hardly likely to notice in their present state and nodded to the roof where smoke was now streaming down. She was about to sneak out when Crag Daniek grabbed her.

"Where d'yer think yer going, girlie?" he demanded, belching ale-sodden breath.

"For…more porter, lord," she stammered.

"Don't need booze. Come here and I'll show yer what I need."

She pulled free and tripped over a fallen stool in her haste, while Daniek lurched to his feet. He seemed amused rather than angry.

"You wanna play games, girl. Well I can play games too."

He staggered after her. Drunk or not, he was fast. It was no contest. In a few strides, he reached Macayle and dragged her to her feet.

"Well, what 'ave we got 'ere?" he growled as he pulled her towards him. "Pretty little minx, ain't yer? But hang on, ain't I seen yer somewhere before?"

"Where's my mother, you great buffoon? What have you done with her?"

"Oh, yeah, I remember now. The feisty looker we got from that bleedin' wizard tower. Well darlin', she ain't here, but you are and I think I might enjoy that."

Once Edrid saw the fire arrows, he ordered his companions to set light to everything. With the help of the pitch, flames roared to life and soon the boats were well ablaze. The sails were first to go and Edrid tossed any spare oars overboard to ensure the vessels' immobility. There would be no escape to sea for the Starkmen. He and his three companions raced back to the barracoon where the others waited and were now armed with an assortment of weapons. The serving girls joined them, shivering and nervous, but still calm.

"We have friends guarding the front so kill any pirates who come out this way," Edrid hissed. "No mercy. We've no time for prisoners, understand?"

They all nodded. This was the kind of talk they wanted to hear after the abuse they'd endured.

Early summer's dawn was just a hint in the eastern sky, but the blazing roof gave plenty of light.

Where the devil is she? Henry thought.

He drew Hornet-Sting and, leaving Anvil Cornfoot in charge at the front, raced around the hall where burning debris began tumbling from the ceiling. He cannoned into Edrid, who confirmed Macayle had not escaped with the other slaves. They exchanged glances and crashed through the door, just as the smoke finally stirred the Starklanders into action.

"The bleedin' roof's burning!" someone yelled and the pirates bolted for both portals. Henry and Edrid were barged aside by the human tide, sending them tumbling and winded as several Starkmen trampled them in the stampede.

Anvil Cornfoot formed the villagers at either side of the main entrance and the escaping Starklanders were simply cut down as they tried to dash past. Otillie's people found new strength and fought like demons. Some Starklanders made it through the cordon, but, as they generally only had their fists for protection, did little harm in return. The panic-stricken survivors clambered onto the ferry until it nearly floundered, hauling on the rope to cross the fjord and kicking away any late-comers who tried to board, leaving them wallowing in the shallows where the villagers fell upon them.

Knives and axes slashed mercilessly. Soon the fjord ran red to the screams of the dying, while corpses drifted seawards on an ebb tide. As the ferry reached the far shore, the villagers who had fired the roof drew their bows and shot a hail of missiles with deadly accuracy from such short range. A second salvo left a pile of dead and dying pirates bristling with arrows and groaning their last breaths.

The released slaves were doing similar damage at the rear door, although several Starkmen wrested some weapons from them and fought back. The Starkmen were easily beaten as the door only allowed them to exit in ones or twos. Other crowding Starklanders pressed from behind and jammed the opening. Half-a-dozen Starkmen were trampled to death or close to it. The islanders were out for revenge and only a handful of pirates made it to their ships, which were now well alight and no means of escape. Some dived into the water, where they either drowned or froze, while a few made of stouter stuff turned to meet Edrid's people, but seriously outnumbered, they stood no chance. Some Starkmen begged for mercy, but it was no use. What did they expect? The islanders heeded their prince's instruction and gave no quarter.

Henry staggered to his feet, dazed and disorientated in the choking haze. The hall was a total mess with benches, stools and table-wear strewn everywhere, while some pirates still lay unconscious on the floor or slouched in corners. He spotted Crag Daniek hunched over a long table, pinning Macayle beneath him. Whether his intention was homicidal or carnal, he'd lost all reason and seemed oblivious to the chaos around him or the danger from falling embers.

Henry charged, battering Crag Daniek aside while Macayle scrambled free. But he was a huge man and didn't move far before recovering. Henry raised Hornet-Sting to strike, but Crag Daniek was too quick for him. The Starklanders had left their weapons pretty much where they dropped and many were scattered on the floor. Crag Daniek grabbed a two-handed broadsword he favoured and came to meet Henry. Meanwhile, bleeding from a gash on his temple, Edrid staggered to his feet and Macayle rushed to his aid as more burning timber collapsed from the rafters. Sparks flew up where they landed and the fire spread to anything flammable in the hall.

Henry had developed into a fair swordsman, but Crag Daniek's immense strength behind the glaive forced him backwards. It was all he could do to parry the constant battering. Crag Daniek, relying on brute force and not style, swung a mighty cross-cut that Henry dodged, but felt the blast of air as it brushed past. The blade smashed into a bench, sinking deeply into the wood. Crag Daniek cursed as he planted his foot to heave the glaive free. It jerked away as Henry swung Hornet-Sting and the blades clashed only inches from Crag Daniek's face.

But Henry was forced back again and swung a low stroke after ducking below another sweep from the broadsword. The blade sliced into the pirate's thigh and he jerked momentarily, but still stormed at Henry, madder than ever. Crag Daniek now limped as he favoured his sound leg and Henry took full advantage of his wound, flicking Hornet-Sting's point deftly into the dripping gash.

But Henry had darted too close to Crag Daniek's long reach and the pirate swung his fist into the side of Henry's skull, knocking him senseless. Henry crashed across a bench and crumbled to the floor, his head spinning. Crag Daniek was over him in a couple of bounds, despite his bleeding thigh. Towering over his enemy, the glaive arched through the air and down towards Henry. The sword smashed into an axe blade as Edrid leapt into the fight. The blade scraped along the axe-haft and slid through Edrid's left wrist, severing his hand.

Edrid stared blankly for a second then dropped to his knees beside Henry, who was drenched with pulsating jets of blood. Somewhere, miles away, Henry thought he heard Macayle scream as he stared up at Crag Daniek, who raised his broadsword again.

Then Otillie was there. She leapt onto Crag Daniek's back. Clamping her legs around his waist, she grabbed his hair, jerked his head back and drew her dagger across his throat. Crag Daniek dropped the glaive and clutched his throat. He reeled and crashed down in front of Henry and rolled onto his back. Otillie hung on until he hit the floor then leapt aside.

"That's for my dad!" she screamed at him, her eyes maddened with hate.

Macayle ripped the sleeve from Edrid's shirt and bound it tightly around his wrist until the bleeding stopped.

Crag Daniek lay dying as his life-blood poured away and filled his gullet.

"Where's Ayla?" Henry cried. "What have you done with her?"

Despite everything Crag Daniek actual smiled.

"Dambar…" he croaked, blood oozing between his teeth. "…My sword…"

"What? Not likely."

"My sword…must die with it in my hand…to go to the feasting halls…of the gods…"

Henry grabbed Crag Daniek's sword hilt with both hands and plunged the blade into the pine-wood floor leaving it quivering only inches from the pirate chief's outstretched fingers.

"Get it yourself," Henry hissed.

With the last of his strength, Crag Daniek lunged for the sword, but only managed to slash his fingers as he uttered a last, gurgling prayer to his distant, one-eyed god.

"I don't know whether that counts," Henry muttered bitterly over the dead Starklander.

Suddenly, Anvil Cornfoot stood beside them. He grabbed a fallen fire-brand and rammed it into Edrid's stump to cauterise the wound. Edrid was too shocked to scream, but Macayle gasped at the horror of sizzling flesh.

"Get out!" Cornfoot yelled. "The roof's caving in."

They hauled Edrid up and dragged him to the doorway as beams crashed down, just clearing the portal when the hall collapsed and flames shot out, blasting their backs. They escaped with only minor singes and Anvil Cornfoot's beard smouldering.

A few Starklanders survived the blaze and butchery, but they were left summarily dangling from the nearest branches high enough for the purpose. In some cases, it was clemency, considering the injuries and burns they suffered. There were five villagers to bury, two had just been unlucky and fell to random blows from the Starklanders, but the other three were found hacked to death mysteriously close to the wolf-ships. No one saw them die. Other than cuts, a few burns, and bruises, everyone else was in good shape except Edrid, who'd lost a lot of blood and was in a poor way.

So the party of villagers and emancipated islanders built a stretcher and bore Edrid away from Glam, watched by the lone figure of Queig, who'd used a battle axe to smash through the hall's structure and stealthily deal with three villagers before slipping into the fjord and swimming ashore. Henry led the party, fretting at the delay when the villagers raided any storerooms that remained undamaged, but conceding they needed food for their return journey. Crossing Dak Creek also took time, but finally they entered dwarf territory with Henry blowing his hunting horn for all it was worth.

The Wealth

Part 3

Dambar

*Macayle is devastated that we didn't find her mother
on Glam Island.
And she grieves for Edrid.
But Otillie's people were magnificent.
Anvil Cornfoot says some people just need a little
shove to achieve great deeds.
But what has become of Lady Ayla and what did
Crag Daniek mean by 'Dambar'?*

Chapter 22
The Dambar Block

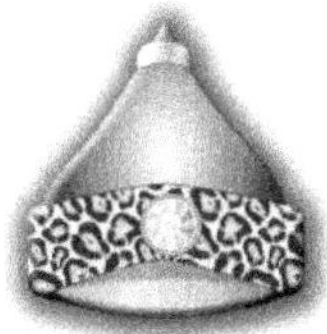

What indeed? Many bold deeds were done in her name, but what had become of Ayla? After her capture, she lay weeping in the bilge of Crag Daniek's wolf-ship as it sailed from the blazing wreckage of Tremill Broch. The pirates were in a foul mood at losing Macayle and having little to show for their raid. Crag Daniek was probably maddest of all, but realised it was pointless taking his rage out on Ayla. She was, after all, a beauty of possible high value. He placed her between two burly oarsmen with orders not to move an inch.

"Now stop yer blubbering, woman," he said. "You ain't escapin', so just make yer mind up to the fact."

"What d'yer reckon, Gov?" Queig asked. "I've seen younger."

"Yeah, but what a looker, and a blue-eyed blonde t'boot. Too good for this lot. But we know where she'll be appreciated, eh?"

He hailed the other two ships and ordered them back to Glam then turned to Queig.

"Set a course for Skinner's Landing. Haul them yards and hoist the mainsail, yer blaggards. Put yer backs into it, we might even make something outta this trip yet."

So they sailed southeast to the only landfall along the coast of the Great Unab Plains. To the south lay the quagmires of Slag Swamp and the entire west coast of Unab was a barrier of vast cliffs with only one mooring–Skinner's Landing–and that was hardly a safe haven.

Ayla pulled herself together, because she was not about to wallow in self-pity, nor let these villains see her distress. Even so, her heart ached for Macayle, but was there a chance that she'd escaped safely? She must never give up hope. Sailing was a cold business, however, and she was not adequately dressed for bracing winds and sea spray. Queig supplied her with a fur robe and draped it around her, allowing his hand to wander in the process. She brushed him aside, but drew the cloak tighter despite its feral state.

"Don't want ya gettin' cold, me lovely," Queig leered. "Ain't no one gonna be interested in a wench with a runny nose."

They sailed for several days, until cliffs reared above the horizon as they approached Skinner's Landing. It was nothing but a fissure where the rock-face had succumbed to pounding surf and tumbled into a pile of rubble, forming a stony beach. To the Starklanders' credit, they were fearless mariners and manoeuvred their ship with daring skill. Crag Daniek ordered the sail to be struck and they negotiated the wave-lashed rocks with oars until the hull scraped ashore. Breakers still battered the wolf-ship and she surged dangerously, until the entire crew secured a rope and kedged the vessel safely beyond the high-tide line, taking up nearly all the beach area.

Queig heaved Ayla over the bulwarks where she landed knee-deep in water. It appeared he was no longer interested in her well-being now they'd reached their destination and there she stood, wet and shivering.

"Guardian!" Crag Daniek bellowed above surf's roar. "We ain't got all day, damn yer!"

That wasn't quite true, because the Starkmen were in no

particular hurry, but shortly a few heads appeared as dots at the cliff top, followed by a rope ladder that tumbled to the beach, unfolding as it went. Without hesitation, Crag Daniek clambered upwards.

"Bring her," he said to Queig.

"You don't honestly expect me to climb on that thing?" Ayla said, not because the thought was so daunting, but she was determined to delay the pirates whenever she could.

"I'm pretty sure that's what he meant," Queig said, pointing his dagger at her. "And I've got this to prod your pretty little rump if you don't get a move on."

Put that way, Ayla had no choice but to grasp the hemp ladder-lines and haul herself upwards. The wind picked up as they climbed and the ladder swayed enough to make Ayla gasp, although Crag Daniek forged ahead and Queig seemed quite at ease. Her foot missed a rung and she slipped, but held onto the lines. Queig was close enough behind to support her and prevent her falling. As she reached the top, two pairs of hands helped her over the cliff's lip and onto her feet until she regained her breath and composure.

"Well done," Queig winked. "Y'know, we've had women baulk on that line, and we've had to hoist 'em up in a sling, kicking and wailing all the way. Better if you can make it by yourself. Much more dignified, don't you think?"

She was about to fire a salvo of abuse at him, but what was the point? She needed a cool head rather than indignant protests. The two men who held her were curiously dressed in grey robes, turbans and scarfs drawn over their faces, exposing only their eyes. Ahead stood an austere, flat-roofed, stone building with a narrow door and only slits for windows. Shacks, stables and store-houses were scattered close by. The surrounding landscape was just as unwelcoming. Sand dunes and rock spread to the horizon, sparsely interspersed with succulents and the sagebrush, although some areas were ablaze with the spring blooms of desert flowers.

A rather fastidious figure bustled from the building, hitching his robe as he minced towards Crag Daniek. He was short, bald and obese, and when he spoke it seemed as if he had too much saliva in his mouth and gulped continually to avoid drooling.

"Gweetings, Gwag Daniek, what an unexthpected pweather, I musth thay," he oozed. "Welcome, gweat thir, and how may Olgawic-y-Ithlad be of thervithe today?"

"Not much quantity-wise to be sure," Crag Daniek admitted, indicating Ayla.

"Oh, my, jutht the one?" the trader looked genuinely disappointed.

"Yeah, but this is quality merchandise, not yer usual island chippies. You'll get twenty times more for her than the thick-headed churls we've been handling lately."

Now, Olgaric-y-Islad was a wily merchant, despite his obsequious ways. Slave-trader, mercer, spy, arms-runner, and usurer were all his stock-in-trade; in fact, anything that turned a quick profit. He wasn't fussy who suffered in the process. He'd sized Ayla up immediately, knowing the taste for fair haired rarities in Dambar, but wasn't going to tell this foul-mouthed barbarian that.

"Come, wet uth take tea and dithcuth thith in gweater detail, my fwiend."

They entered the building, where a steaming pot brewed with an aroma Ayla found pleasant, but could not identify. She remained standing while the others sat on quilted cushions around a low table as two slaves dispensed tea in small cups. Wine casks were stacked against the walls and a couple of jaded young women hovered in the background.

"Now, wet me thee," Olgaric said slyly.

He rose and pawed Ayla carefully. She baulked, but was restrained by his assistants and she sensed his interest was purely professional and not prone to lust.

"Get uthed to it, my dear," Olgaric whispered. "You no longer own anything, including yorthelf."

But he was done with her and turned to Crag Daniek.

"My, my," he clucked. "Thee ith a beauty, no qwethtion and in pwime condithion, it'th a pity you haven't anything younger though. The market ith difficult you thee, now thtwong wads for the mineth I can move quickly and at a good pwithe."

"Now listen, yer oily crook," Crag Daniek growled, "last time I brought you a ship-load of broad-backed oafs and all yer could talk about were getting yer 'ands on some women. Well, here's a beauty. She's all I've got because I'm holdin' back thirty or forty mine-fodder at Glam till the price gets better."

"Oh, thir, mine workerth are alwayth in demand, but the marketh change tho and the pwice fwuctuateth. I can give you five medallionth for her and that ith cutting out my perthentage altogether."

"You think I came down in the last shower?" Crag Daniek sneered. "If you offer five straight off, then she's worth at least twice that."

"Oh, no thir, I would not twick you…"

And he rambled on about hard times and a depressed market, you see, and overheads and taxes were extortionate these days, and everyone was tightening their belts and cutting back on luxuries. Crag Daniek bickered back in turn that he had to face storms, shipwrecks, hostile islanders, sea monsters, and goodness knew what else…and Ayla had taken all she was going to.

"Shut up, you infernal rogues!" she snapped. "I am not a piece of meat and I will not tolerate this. I am a chief's wife and demand to be treated as such…"

"Queig, take 'er outside and shut her up," Crag Daniek said, "but no marks, mind."

So Ayla was marched outside and restrained by Olgaric's heavies who knew how to handle rambunctious slaves without bruising them. When Queig returned, the haggling was still in progress, but it looked as if Crag Daniek was making little headway.

"Can I have a word, Guv?" Queig suggested and whispered in his boss's ear.

"Tell yer what, old boy," Crag Daniek said, returning his attention to the negotiations. "Seeing as it's such a bother; we'll take 'er on to Dambar ourselves and save you the trouble, eh?"

"But, it ith a long and dangerwous journey, think of the twibethmen. I know you're keen to thail home…"

"Oh, we're in no hurry, and I can take 'alf me crew for protection. The rest won't mind waiting here; I know you've got a good stock of booze and a few scrubbers to keep 'em happy."

Crag Daniek's observation was correct. Although the medallions were their chief source of wealth, they were so highly prized that the pirates wouldn't part with them unless absolutely necessary. They were cashed up in other ways. Loot was generally gathered in a free-for-all and the Starkmen had plenty of lesser coins and trinkets to trade for booze and slutty bargirls.

"That won't be nethethary, thir. I'm confident we can come to thome awangement."

Crag Daniek finally settled for eight medallions, although Olgaric would have paid twenty. Dealing with ignorant barbarians was child's play to the trader. The pirate boss stashed the loot inside his bear-skin tunic and left. Olgaric's guards had manacled Ayla's ankle and chained her to a post.

"My husband will tear you limb from limb when he catches up with you," she hissed.

"Yeah, yeah, whatever. But you'll be off directly," Crag Daniek said. "Olgaric ain't likely to 'ang about."

"Off where?"

"Dambar, of course. You're for the auction block. We're going to stay here for a bit and enjoy ourselves."

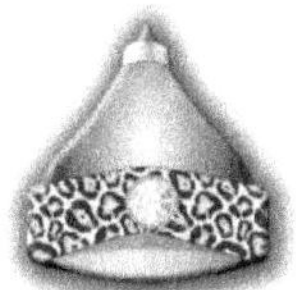

Like most peninsula folk, Ayla was unaware of Dambar, having been protected by isolation, marshland and rugged surrounding terrain. But she knew instinctively she wasn't going to enjoy the experience. Olgaric's minders paid no attention to Ayla's protests and transferred her to a wheeled cage and secured the shackles to the wagon frame. The sun blazed with an unfamiliar intensity as they started across the Unab Plain, but at least the cart's canvas roof provided shade. Four mules drew the cart, led by a whip-cracking teamster.

Olgaric was mounted on a tall, humped animal he called a dromedary and was accompanied by twenty heavily armed retainers, who looked like they meant business. It was fractious, foul-smelling, and prone to drooling, but Olgaric, for all his pasty unfitness, controlled the animal expertly. He proved garrulous and happy to educate Ayla about local geography and human demographics. The guards needed to be well armed and tough as nomadic tribesmen roamed the plains, exacting tribute from anyone they could bully.

Indeed, the desert was covered with tracks and they often saw groups of robed riders in the distance. They were mounted on sure-footed, small horses that managed well in rough country. But Olgaric's minders deterred any attack and the tribesmen kept their distance. Ayla quickly realised her complaints were falling on, if not deaf, certainly indifferent ears and saved her breath after a while, fuming in silence.

Hanging was too good for these villains. Who did they think they were? Who did they think she was? Gareth would have them flayed alive and their gizzards drawn when he found her... If he found her.

After a week of blazing days and freezing nights, they approached the gates of Dambar and the sight took Ayla's breath away. Its sheer size was astonishing with spires and minarets towering impossibly high within the citadel wall. Dambar stood in isolation above the surrounding desert, but beyond sparkled the vast expanse of Lake Naida that supplied the city's water and supported a fishing fleet. The imposing gates were guarded by a platoon of guards wearing light leather kirtles, casques decorated with coloured plumes, and carrying oval shields and scimitars. The bodies of a dozen miscreants dangled from gibbets bolted to the city wall, swaying as they were savaged by swarms of crows and buzzards. Obviously Olgaric-y-Islad was well known, and his party entered the metropolis unchallenged.

As she passed through the city portal, Ayla's rebellious mood turned to despair. Dambar was huge. How could anyone possibly find her in this teeming labyrinth? The walls seemed impregnable and sentries checked all strangers. It appeared she was being held by a city favourite, so anyone opposing him would be discouraged. She passed through narrow streets engulfed by an architectural hodgepodge of luxury villas, humble shanties, market stalls, stores, and taverns with over-hanging upper stories where strumpets lounged in windows, touting to the crowd below.

"Looks like Olgaric's brought some competition," one yelled, blowing kisses to the slave-trader and his escort. The streets and alleys swarmed with pedlars, buskers, footpads, opulent merchants, and urchins all shoving and babbling at once. Wealth and squalor rubbed shoulders in a maelstrom of commerce and pilfering. And amid the stench of animal droppings, garbage, cooking oil and sweat, ornate gardens were placed to neutralise the city's human exhaust. A blonde barbarian was a source of great interest and a crowd of gawkers followed the wagon. Olgaric's home and place-of-business was sighted at the edge of one such urban oasis. It was a modest, but comfortable villa with a walled courtyard covered by vines and shade-trees. Servants rushed from the house and fawned over their master, who instructed them to take Ayla inside while he dismissed his retainers.

Once within the sanctuary of his walls, Olgaric clicked his fingers (pretty much his primary means of communicating with minions) and two nervous, young women scuttled forward, having developed the skill of always looking busy.

"Pwepair her," he commanded and that was all.

The maids led Ayla to a rear quadrangle with a spa of steaming water in its centre, supplied by an underground thermal spring. Here she was bathed, preened, combed, manicured, massaged with fragrant oils, and finally dressed in a simple, pristine-white shift. She enjoyed the experience and it felt wonderful to be truly clean again. Sadly, she sensed her euphoria was just a respite.

"Oh, yeth," he purred when she was presented to him. "Tho much better."

"Now you've had your fun, I've just about had enough of this," Ayla stormed. "I demand to be released."

"I'm thowwy, but that jutht ithn't pothible."

"Why not?"

"Becoth you are to be thold at the market. I have alweady thent word to the wicheth wards and thity burgerth that the thail will pwothede in an hour."

"Do you really think I will submit to such an indignity?"

"You mutht thee you have no choithe."

"Just try me."

"Come willingwy or have my boyth dwag you."

"And how will the sale go if I act the shrew?"

Olgaric had heard it all before. He was unimpressed. "It matterth little, the pwithe will be the thame, but the man who buyth a threw will beat her altho."

Ultimately, the point was moot. Olgaric clapped his hands and two of his burly louts entered and, although she remained unshackled, led her through the city throng to the Dambar Block. Olgaric's message had got around and a crowd was gathering. Finely dressed mercers, abacus-shuffling clerks, factors, fine nobles–borne to the scene in ornate sedans–and the usual idlers all jostled for a vantage spot. The block was a raised platform that the city fathers thriftily used for executions between market days. Barracoons surrounded the block containing unfortunates either sold or destined for sale. Slaves were traded individually or in groups: scholars kidnapped from their studies in distant academies for their scientific and mathematical skills; black-skinned giants from the southern reaches of Unab destined to toil to their deaths in mines or galleys on Lake Naida; women fated for household service, child care, and the bed-chamber; hairy barbarians and dwarves snatched from the edges of Redbone's forest to be exploited in circuses or as royal amusement. And, so many children.

Olgaric's prestige was confirmed when other traders deferred to him as he took the dais immediately. Ayla was placed centre-stage, where she stood erect with her head held high. She was a noble woman after all and cowering wasn't for her. Olgaric nodded his approval as it displayed his product to the best advantage.

"My wards, wadies and gentlemen, thitithenth of Dambar. I have only one wot for your pweasure today, but thuch a beauty. A fair-haired maiden from the far north, a puwe dewight!"

Maiden? Ayla actually smiled, if only briefly.

"A thpethial purchathe, gentlemen, a wawity not to be overwooked, come thirth. Do I have an opening bid?"

A hubbub ran through the gathering as the mercers discussed what certainly appeared to be a unique purchase. More mature perhaps, but a stunning woman nevertheless, and experienced...? They knew Olgaric was a crook, but it looked like he'd found a winner this time.

"Give us a look," a fat monger yelled.

"Yeah, let's see what we're getting."

"Wouldn't buy a pig in a poke."

More ribald comments followed and Olgaric turned to Ayla, although he lost much of his earlier confidence when she glared into his eyes.

"Don't even think about it, lizard," she hissed through gritted teeth. "Touch my robe and you won't walk for a week, and I daresay your siring days will be over."

Olgaric baulked. He recognised pure malice when it faced him and realised Ayla would die rather than be shamed before the Dambar mob. But he had a brace of tough minders who'd do his dirty work for him. He motioned them forward to a heightening roar.

Then silence.

The crowd parted as a nobleman strode to the dais followed by a troop of spear-toting infantrymen. He was not particularly tall, about Ayla's height, but walked with such majesty and presence you just had to take notice. He was dressed as a warrior; a black double-headed eagle was embroidered on his tabard and a scarlet cloak flowing in his wake. A falchion hung from his ermine-fringed baldric and golden torques encircled his upper arms. His beard was clipped in the Vandyke style favoured by many Dambar men.

"I'll take her," the noble said and Ayla's heart leapt.

Oh bravo, I am rescued.

He took a purse from under his tabard and tossed it to Olgaric, who caught it expertly but looked doubtful as he assayed its weight.

"You have a problem?" the noble challenged.

Olgaric hesitated, but the noble's steely gaze convinced him the deal was unnegotiable.

"Oh no, ward, no gweat thir, none at all."

"Good. Bring the woman."

The lord turned and strode back through the crowd. Two soldiers escorted Ayla behind him so quickly she was nearly dragged off her feet, but managed to keep up without tripping as they marched from the Dambar block.

"My lord," she cried, "Thank you for rescuing me from that wretched pig, but I beg you please slow down and tell me where we're going."

The noble stopped abruptly and faced her and Ayla found herself staring into the most pitiless black eyes imaginable.

"Woman," he said quietly, yet with such latent menace, "you are neither in a position to thank me nor slander the name of a worthy Dambar citizen, nor make demands of any sort. So it behoves you to keep your mouth shut! I am Count Lud Maslovaric, colonel-in-chief of the Dambar Cohort and grand chancellor to Duke Percival IV, palatine ruler of Unab. I have procured you because I believe it may please him. You are now his vassal with no privileges, no rights — only abject obedience. The duke is intolerant of all else. I do hope I have made myself clear otherwise your stay in Dambar will be very unpleasant and short indeed."

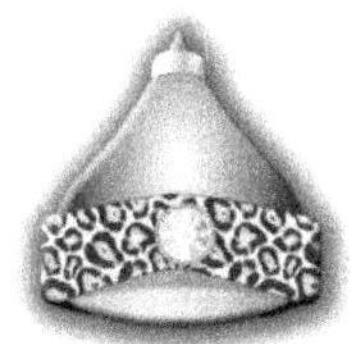

*Yes, all will be well when Chief Gareth and Archer arrive.
They'll be here soon…*

CHAPTER 23
SIMOOM

But was help on the way? Gareth, Jongarrat, Archer, and the indefatigable giants trudged on. Leaving the mosquito-ridden, energy-sapping edge of Slag Swamp, things seemed to be picking up. Gone was the black, clinging sludge underfoot as the ground became firmer and their pace quickened. They were feeling pretty smug about having bested the Corbin, who proved not to be so mysteriously evil after all, just desperate, disorganised, and not entirely sane. Unfortunately, as the dense swamp and clinging vines cleared, more sun baked down and water became scarce. Small antelope herds appeared occasionally in the bushland, not only providing food, but also leading the travellers to the isolated oases in the area.

Before nightfall, they found a small valley where a spring flowed from one end to the other. Shrubs and small trees covered the valley floor and as game seemed unusually tame, Archer had no trouble bagging supper. They gathered enough kindling and wood to last all night, lit a fire, and prepared their meal. The plant foliage smoked a little, giving off an aroma of mixed herbs and spices that was so pleasant the travellers couldn't resist breathing deeply and piling the fire higher.

"Grub smells good," Archer said as Jongarrat turned the meat on a spit he made from green branches. "Didn't know you were such a good cook."

"Yep, probably the best in the world."

"A chef even," Kimball said.

"A chief chef," Serlequin agreed.

"Hold it, I'm chief," Gareth protested.

"But not chief chef," Archer said, "or you'd be chief chef chief."

Now, this discourse should have been a warning that something was not altogether right. Even in Gareth's feasting hall and with a belly full of mead, they'd have made more sense. They all grew more cheerful and less coherent as they tossed more fuel on the fire, spraying sparks everywhere. Though not particularly amusing, they found this hilarious and they laughed without restraint. Kimball and Serlequin staggered to their feet and using their formidable strength, ripped more branches from nearby bushes and hurled them onto the fire. Soon they were all at it, causing an immense blaze that was in danger of spreading into a bushfire. Luckily, they caught the urge to dance before the fire got out of control and cavorted around their camp, singing at the tops of their voices. The sight of five warriors prancing around, silhouetted against the flames may have been droll, but they were unquestionably vulnerable and making enough noise to draw the attention of others.

Which they did.

A dozen riders watched from the ridge line. Normally they would never have gone undetected, but Gareth and his companions were far from normal by then, and in no state to post an effective lookout. The riders dismounted and observed with interest. They were dressed for life on the harsh Unab Plains with loose pants, robes, and mantles drawn across their faces as the smoke redolence drifted towards them. They exchanged glances and although their faces were covered, amusement showed in their eyes. Their leader led them away to the valley edge, where they camped well clear of any effect from the fumes.

Grambak's warriors partied long into the night until, exhausted, they collapsed where they stood and slept well past dawn. When they finally stirred the fire had died and the smoke abated, but their heads throbbed and their bodies felt drained of energy. They shivered in the morning chill, seeming to feel colder than normal, so Archer gathered more of the remaining tinder to replenish the fire.

"You know, I wouldn't do that if you ever hope to get out of this valley," a voice said with a rich, deep accent. It was very unlike the way Grambak folk spoke, but clear and easy to understand. "And oh, didn't we make fools of ourselves last night?"

Their weapons were scattered where they had been abandoned, which was unfortunate because they were surrounded by grinning tribesmen. Gareth however, was not disposed to humour.

"Who the blue blazes are you?" Gareth demanded, swaying uncertainly as he faced the tribal leader.

"More to the point, who are you?" the man replied, dropping his scarf and revealing a handsome, olive face with a smile of pure white teeth. "I'm from around here, but you clearly are not."

Gareth and his warriors just looked puzzled.

"Only someone truly ignorant would pile that concoction of dreams together. Why, there were enough intoxicants floating around last night to knock out an army. I'm surprised you woke up at all. I bet you feel awful."

The tribesman broke some branches off various bushes and showed them to Gareth.

"This is a Valley of Enchantment, and you were certainly beguiled. Nearly all plants here possess magic properties to make you feel at ease, on edge, clever, or slow, depending on what you use. I rather fancy you tried the lot. We smuggle this stuff to slaves at the Nadia Mines. It's all they have to live for, and that's not usually long."

Gareth's men looked at the stranger sheepishly. Carousing in a tavern was one thing, but to have totally lost control of their senses was another.

"Allow me to introduce myself; I am Gunthred Vy, Chief of the Clan Vy, nomads of the plains."

"I am Gareth, Chief of Hollowford, and I'm not in the habit of making a fool of myself."

"Indeed, then you must take care. There are other enclaves like this one, and you're hardly dressed or mounted to deal with Unab. It's blistering hot by day and bitterly cold at night and goodness knows how you'll fair if a simoom comes along.'

"Simoom?"

"You'll know when you see one."

"Thanks for the warning; I think we're discovering the perils hereabouts."

"We heard you miles away and frankly, I'm surprised you've got this far."

"We're bound for Glam on the northern coast. My wife was snatched by raiders and we plan to get her back or die in the attempt."

"The latter seems most likely to me. You're going in the wrong direction."

"How's that? Our guide, Jongarrat here, says we must travel with the sea on our left. It is, I believe, only a few leagues from here."

"Oh, he hasn't misled you, but if the lady you seek is a fair-haired beauty then Glam is not your destination."

Gareth glared at Jongarrat who shrugged.

"If my information is correct," Gunthred Vy continued, "a wolf-ship brought a single prisoner to Skinner's Landing sometime past now; a remarkable woman with golden hair much prized in Unab. We observed the trader's caravan that took her to the city, but it was too well guarded for us."

"You could have rescued her?"

Gunthred Vy stared at Gareth incredulously and slowly shook his head, conceding she'd have been no better off in his hands than Olgaric-y-Islad's, but he wasn't going to tell Gareth that.

"Life is difficult in the desert, we do what we must."

"What city?" Archer asked.

"Why, Dambar, of course," the nomad replied. "It is the centre of all trade for hundreds of leagues."

"Then that's where we'll go," Gareth said.

"Do you think that's wise?" Gunthred Vy arched his eyebrows.

"Undoubtedly not, but if we must go to Dambar to rescue my Ayla, then that's what we'll do. Perhaps you'd be kind enough to guide us, if you don't have pressing matters elsewhere."

"I'll go part way, but that is all. The Duke holds my son, Ebony Vy, hostage to ensure we stay clear of the city, behave ourselves, and pay our taxes. We usually get the money from fat Dambar factors anyway. Keeps the economy circulating, you might say."

Gunthred Vy instructed his men to return to their camp where there was work to do. He waited for Gareth and his men to gather their weapons and kit, but not before Jongarrat collected samples of seeds from the valley for Guilda to use in her herbal remedies. Kimball and Serlequin gathered some too, hoping they'd be able to grow the plants just for fun.

"Fill your gourds," Gunthred Vy advised. "It's a long way between water holes."

Gunthred Vy led them to the coast where they found a path to the north.

"You don't need me anymore," he said. "This trail leads to Skinner's Landing; follow the road to the west from there. You'll find several wells along the way and be at Dambar's gate in a week."

They reached Skinner's Landing easily enough, but Crag Daniek and the Starklanders were long gone. The proprietor and his rather worn-out bargirls confirmed Ayla had indeed been there, but would have reached the city by now. They spent the night, taking turns to stand guard in view of their Velma experience. They were unmolested apart from the enterprising harlots, although the travellers' response to their advances remains unrecorded.

The following morning, they replenished their water supply, bought some fresh loaves, and dried venison before heading along the western road. They managed their water with care, eking the supply between wells and estimated their rations would last until they reached Dambar.

The fifth day was oppressively still. By noon, the sun was so intense they were forced to stop and take shelter under a coppice of scrubby acacias in a small gully encircled by a stone ridge. It wasn't much, but provided some relief and by mid-afternoon, they felt inclined to press on again. As they returned to the road, the air remained still and a brown haze shimmered across the horizon ahead. It grew rapidly and soon a dust cloud filled a quarter of the sky. Just ahead of the storm was a speck that developed into a rider galloping towards them, frantically whipping his dromedary to go even faster. The Unab Plain which seemed so lifeless erupted as rabbits, antelope, bobcats and all manner of birds bolted from cover and fled to the east. The rider didn't slow as he approached.

"Simoom!" he cried, racing past the travellers. His voice was almost lost as the afternoon stillness was shattered by a roaring gale that swept in from the west.

"Take cover!" Gareth yelled, and they all dived back into the gully. They hunkered down together and drew their cloaks over their heads as sand whipped at them with stinging ferocity. The wind intensified as did its voice, howling to a nearly deafening crescendo. Sand and grit surged against the travellers and was soon waist deep. The coppice was filling up and there was no chance of digging a way out. It was impossible to lift their cloaks as the sand would blast into their eyes, blinding them in no time. They just had to sit it out. To make matters worse, the simoom blew with malicious vagary, coming from one way, then another, and sometimes from several directions at once, while scree constantly drifted higher. They tried to shake the growing debris away, but even Kimball and Serlequin's strength was no use as the sand simply packed tighter around them and more gathered before they could sweep it away. They tried to clamber free, but the simoom blasted them back with sheets of sand that stung like ten thousand wasps. Their movements were seriously limited in any event, as they needed to cling tightly to their cloak hoods to prevent them billowing loose and leaving their heads unprotected. Jongarrat's size put him in greatest danger of being smothered and for a while they managed to lift him until he reached their head-height, but by then the sand weighed so heavily they could do no more. When the build-up reached their necks they were practically immobile and the blizzard of sand kept coming.

By the time it reached chin-level, they couldn't move at all.

Then the simoom died as suddenly as it had begun.

So the five warriors were virtually buried alive and, with hoods covering their faces, they were suffocating. The sun emerged and baked down, although the acacia scrub gave a little shade. They were wedged solid and unable to wrestle a way out. Their breath came in pants and sand encrusted their mouths and nostrils. No one spoke; it was just a waste of energy and only invited more sand as well as swarming flies. With the flies came ants, beetles, scorpions and raptors that seemed to have found good hiding places or ways of dodging the simoom. Vultures, buzzards, and kites circled overhead and several even perched on the few acacias that had not been uprooted. The scavengers waited, but wouldn't have to do so for long.

The birds grew bolder and started ripping at the cloak-hoods. As their faces were exposed, the travellers screamed and rocked their heads frantically. The creatures backed off, but not far. They skulked around, but at least the trapped men could see their fate. Jongarrat muttered something about desert cats, jackals, and wolf-packs, but no one took any notice as they grew thirstier and more disorientated and would soon lose consciousness allowing the predators do as they pleased.

Just as the raptors regained their boldness, they surged into the air and lumbered away with a raucous flurry, leaving feathers and down floating in their wake. The clatter of hoof-beats and jingle of bridle hardware had scared them away as a cavalry troop armed with lances, falchions, and carrying oval shields cantered along the road from the east. Their commander was richly dressed in sparkling mail, a purple cloak, flowing pantaloons and a fur-rimmed casque upon his head. He signalled his troop to halt beside the gully.

"Take a look," he ordered and two troopers hastened to examine Gareth's group.

"They're all alive, lord," one reported.

"Dig 'em out then, and we'll see what they have to say for themselves."

That took some time, because the soldiers weren't equipped for excavation. Digging with their hands and shields, they eventually got the job done and dragged the travellers free. Kimball and Serlequin were a challenge, but with much of the sand cleared away, they were able to wrench themselves out and stagger to safety. With some water down their throats and a good dusting off, the warriors quickly recovered, although they were still unsteady on their feet.

The troop leader dismounted and squatted beside Gareth and his companions.

"Now what do we have here?" he asked in an urbane voice with the same thick Unab accent they'd heard before. "You might like to explain why I shouldn't have left you there for the buzzards."

"I'm Chief Gareth from Hollowford," Gareth explained yet again. "I'm on a quest with these men."

"Oh, it's a chief, is it? Can't say you look much like a nobleman to me."

"I'll fight you like one.'"

"Oh undoubtedly, lord," the cavalryman said, raising his palms in mock submission. "We certainly have no shortage of nobles in Dambar. The duke creates new peerages when he fancies raising more taxes. It's amazing how much people will pay for a title.'

"I earned mine with my sword."

"I'm sure you did," the cavalryman continued with infuriating condescension. "But, a quest you say. What would that be, if I may be so bold?"

"I seek my wife carried off by brigands, and I have information she has been taken to Dambar. These warriors are Grambak Peninsula's best and they will help me retrieve her."

"They certainly come in all shapes and sizes on your peninsula, but this is your lucky day. My troop and I come from Dambar and it will be our pleasure to escort you there. It's not far and you can ride a spell until you regain your strength.

"We are indeed fortunate you came by," Archer said suspiciously.

"No mystery, sir," the cavalryman said. "Many come to grief in a simoom so we followed the storm to see what's left. Vultures circling overhead are always a dead give-away."

"Very commendable of you, I'm sure."

"Not at all. It is our duty to protect Dambar citizens. We rely on merchants and caravans to keep trade alive. And of course, there's a recovery fee, or if we're unfortunately too late, salvage rights."

"You'll be disappointed in us then," Gareth said warily, knowing he must keep their wealth secret to use when negotiating Ayla's release.

"No matter," the cavalryman replied glibly. "Glad to be of help. Unab can be a dangerous place, especially if you fall foul of tribesmen."

"Gunthred Vy offered us no harm. In fact he was very helpful."

"I'd have thought you were more than capable of dealing with one crazy old rascal."

Gareth considered Gunthred Vy was not particularly old, crazy, or alone, but said nothing. It was best not to offend anyone and avoid local differences that might be fomented by his opinion. The cavalryman sent two riders ahead with word for the city seneschal to prepare accommodation for his guests. He had not yet introduced himself, but Gareth pressed him.

"Why, I am Count Lud Maslovaric," he replied, "I do beg your pardon, I'm so used to people knowing who I am."

Good, an important ally, Gareth thought, but Jongarrat and Archer remained chary, although the giants were happy to accept the count at face value. They weren't complex thinkers and he'd dug them out of the sand, so that was good enough for them.

Dusk fell as they approached Dambar and the city brilliance affected Gareth and his companions just as it had Ayla. There was a last-minute bustle of merchants, mummers, livestock herdsmen, carriages, and produce-carts entering the city gate before they were closed for the night. The peninsula men had never seen such a throng. Even on market day in Hollowford the crowd was minute compared with Dambar's multitude. They stared in amazement, which Maslovaric shrewdly noticed.

"Trade, sir," he announced gesturing towards the city. "It's what generates wealth, knowledge, and culture. It permits leisure to explore higher ideals, develop art and music. It is what makes us civilised."

It was impressive no doubt, although the city smell wasn't particularly civilised and could not be ignored. Fatigue and trauma had left Gareth and his men prepared to tolerate the odour and just relieved to be spending the night under a roof. But, they were not nearly as alert as they should have been. Even Archer and Jongarrat didn't see the danger as they entered the city. They were on foot now, which made any sort of visibility almost impossible.

The sentries snapped to attention as they passed through the main portal that clanged shut behind them. The city mass was almost overwhelming as Maslovaric's troopers pressed through. Other soldiers joined them to help clear the way. What they failed to notice were the platoons that fell in behind and when they entered a square it seemed oddly vacant, containing no market stalls or trading booths that cluttered every other quarter of the city. As they reached the centre of the plaza, troops rushed from side allies, behind doors, and leapt through windows. They hurled nets over the travellers, dragging them to the cobblestones. Soldiers piled in with a will and battered the peninsula men into submission. Despite a desperate struggle, the nets restrained them and even the giants were subdued. Their wrists and ankles were shackled and they were dragged to their feet with Gareth bellowing treachery and foul-play at the top of his lungs. A crowd had gathered and cheered at the spectacle until Maslovaric ordered silence.

"Oh, do stop complaining," he said to Gareth. "Do you really think I have time to run around after a bunch of barbarians, but you may be of some use? And you can forget about your precious Lady Ayla, she is unavailable and will remain so."

"You know where she is?"

"Always have, but don't worry; she's safely in the duke's hands."

Gareth wrestled free and would have dragged Maslovaric from his saddle, but half a company of troopers pounced and hauled him away. The count snapped his fingers and a junior officer rushed forward and saluted.

"Take them to the cages!"

So they were led away, kicking and struggling, assisted by spear points, whips, and clubs all the way.

"A bit of spirit is good considering what the Count has in mind for you," the officer conceded.

"And what's that?" Gareth snarled.

"You'll see, but it seems to me you've come a long way just to die."

The soldiers manhandled them through lane ways, up and down stone steps, and through archways and gates until they came to the city keep, a granite bastion that towered above the outer walls. Turrets soared even higher where standards flapped languidly, bearing the duke's heraldry. An iron portcullis opened and they were hustled through into the dank, dark bleakness of Dambar Gaol. They clattered along more stairways and passages before coming to a chamber with corridors leading away to prison cells. In dim torchlight, the chamber was strewn with manacles, braziers with associated branding irons, a rack, impaling spikes, whips impregnated with metal splines and a number of unidentifiable objects, although their purpose was clearly apparent.

A scrawny, ferret-faced man met them, attended by two burly heavies, all muscle with shaven heads glistening in the torch light. The turnkey carried a bludgeon that he tapped into his palm.

"Howdy, gents," he greeted. "Always a pleasure to welcome new guests. My associates and I are at your disposal and we'll endeavour to make your stay as unpleasant as possible."

He nodded, indicating a holding cell at one end of the chamber.

"In there," he ordered the troops, who flung the grid-door open and heaved the travellers inside. They landed, bruised and full of wounded pride, but otherwise unhurt. The cell was rank with stale straw, and foulness pervaded from a pit in one corner that served as their latrine. Rats scuttled along the walls and massed in corners. For all their size, Kimball and Serlequin couldn't abide rodents and started kicking them towards the pit, but mostly the rats simply dodged clear.

"I wouldn't be too keen to get rid of them rats," the turnkey advised. "A few days on prison victuals and you'll be thinking they're a right little delicacy."

And there they languished, cold and dank, to the sound of water dripping from the walls and moans of other inmates who cried for mercy or the relief of death.

"Well, today went well, don't you think?" Archer said.

"At least we're not dead," Gareth replied

Jongarrat glared at him.

"Yeah, so what's your next plan then?" the dwarf demanded.

*I remember my dread when Macayle was sick,
but Edrid looks ten times worse.*

*It would be so easy just to stay here and help Otillie
rebuild her village.
We've done our bit and Redbone's country is
wonderful — and peaceful now the
Starkmen are gone.*

"I've seen men in better shape who didn't live," Redbone announced as he examined Edrid's savaged wrist. The Prince of Palo Innes lay on a cot in the squire's lodge. Beatrice scolded him for being tactless when she saw the concern and grief on Henry and Macayle's faces.

"I'll do my best," he said.

Of course everyone knew that, but they also knew it might not be enough. Although the wound had stopped bleeding, the stump still ended in rugged nodes that seeped yellow grume. Henry and Macayle hovered around Edrid who was deathly pale, clammy with fever, and groaned pitifully when the pain became too much to bear even in his coma. Anvil Cornfoot and Otillie stood by the door, out of the way, but on hand if needed. The rescued islanders made themselves useful around the village and in the paddocks while they waited for their prince. A few of Otillie's people had left, but most stayed to witness Julian negotiate a deal with the squire, making relations between the two villages more friendly, a good outcome especially as the two communities were so close together. Although most injuries were minor, dwarf medicine sped their healing and, frankly, the villagers were enjoying a few days off before returning to rebuild their homes.

"The wound is staunched well enough, but it festers and I fear infection. Were this pus clear, I'd be less worried. I must sever these enflamed welts and suture them so they will heal cleanly." Redbone said. "Anvil, you'll need to bring me healing fungus from the forest–you know where–also mandrake root, vervain, nightshade, wild garlic and… mistletoe... yes… and osier sap…that should do the trick. Take Henry and Macayle to help you, they're only underfoot here."

In a way it was a relief to leave the cabin and have something to do. Otillie joined them as she knew where to find forest herbs just as well as the dwarves. They were gone for hours, perhaps longer than necessary, but Anvil wanted to keep Henry and Macayle away from the cabin until he was sure Redbone and Beatrice had completed their work. Finally, with four sacks full of herbal prophylactics, they returned to find Edrid in distress from the pain and shock of his operation.

"Just in time," Redbone said. "We'll need those medicines to blend a poultice to deter infection and brew a calming philtre."

"He looks bad," Henry said glumly. "It'll take some powerful magic to save him."

"Magic?" Redbone said. "Dunno about that, but the forest is always a source of wonder if you know where to look and how to apply its gifts. I suppose anything is magic if you don't understand it. We have some potent medicine now, but it's not always successful."

Beatrice frowned at him again.

"I'm not one to give false hope, wife," he said.

"I know dear, but you can be such a grumble-bum at times."

"He must live," Macayle whispered as tears flowed down her cheeks.

"Most men would be done for by now, so he's got the will and that's a good sign."

The squire selected plants and fungus, pestling them to pulp in a crucible while Beatrice added more ingredients to a simmering pot that soon gave off a pleasing aroma. Redbone applied the paste to Edrid's stump and Beatrice let her potion seep in drops between his lips, after which he rested more easily. She then brought a bowl of icy water from the creek to douse his fever.

"Now it's just a matter of waiting," Redbone said.

"And hoping," Macayle added, taking over nursing duties from Beatrice and holding Edrid's good hand when she wasn't sponging his brow. She stayed with him far into the night until she dozed fitfully. Beatrice woke her gently and showed her a spare bed where she immediately fell asleep again. The squire's goodwife then examined Edrid's stump, gasped and called her husband.

"The poultice should have taken effect," he said after checking the wound, "yet putrilage persists. We must try something more astringent."

Henry and Otillie slept in a barn adjoining the squire's lodge and awoke early. They were jerked awake by a scream from the room where Edrid lay. They raced inside to find Macayle, ashen faced and staring at Edrid's stump. The dressing was gone and in its place a seething mass of maggots covered the entire wound.

"They're disgusting," she wailed. "Get them off him."

Henry hesitated, how could so many grubs have attacked the wound so quickly and how could he remove them? Pick them off one-by-one or wash them away? Would he get them all and what damage had they done already done.

"Don't touch them," Redbone said sternly from behind him.

"But…"

"Their purpose is to clean the wound. The worms will only consume rotten flesh, in that way removing any cankerous tissue. We must attend him vigilantly and only remove them when their job is done. It's probably best you two get some breakfast and stay outside. I'll call you if there's any change. Otillie and Beatrice can manage here."

Although Beatrice later suggested it was touch-and-go for a time, the maggots proved their worth. Once the source of infection was removed, Edrid's recovery was remarkable. The squire's first-rate surgery healed neatly while Beatrice's soothing brews eased his pain and restored his strength. Macayle remained by his bedside and didn't stop kissing him for ages. Although he was disappointed her affections lay with the prince, Henry was overjoyed to see his friend's recovery. In a week Edrid was on his feet, although he fell over a few times.

"You know I never realised how much a hand weighs," he declared. "Why, I'm clear off balance."

"Just as well you didn't lose a whole arm then," Anvil Cornfoot said.

"You'll get used to it," Henry added.

"I suppose so, but swordplay will be difficult."

"We'll practise tomorrow if you feel up to it, just a little to start. It'll be exercise to build up your strength as well. Meantime, I've got something to do."

Edrid nodded and Henry left him to be mothered by Beatrice and smothered by Macayle, but he had an idea what might help. Henry owed Edrid after all he lost his hand saving Henry's life. Redbone's village included a cordwainer's shop where he sent

Otillie with instructions for the leather-master while he made his way to the forge and asked the owner if he could use his equipment and furnace for the day. The smith said he'd be pleased to help and they set to work. Otillie joined Henry at dusk and they took their handiwork to Redbone's lodge. Edrid was sitting at the main table enjoying his first square meal since being wounded and beamed when they arrived.

"I haven't even thanked you for saving my life." Henry said. "Especially after what happened to you."

"Don't mention it, old boy," Edrid said. "We got my people back, finished off the Starklanders, and we'd never have done it without you. I should have stood up to Crag Daniek from the very beginning. I guess the hand was the price I had to pay for my own failure."

"But if it wasn't for me, you'd be…"

"Nonsense, if it wasn't for you the Starkmen would still be a menace. And don't worry, I don't dread living out my time with one hand, the other was a useful trinket, but by-and-large overrated. Anyway, it's Otillie you need to thank. She's the one who killed Crag Daniek."

Henry smiled, squeezed her hand and mouthed thank you. She returned his smile, blushing a little, but it pleased her when he held her hand.

"In that case," Henry said, "Otillie and I have made something for you. Well, we got a lot of help from the dwarves."

Henry placed a bag on the table and produced a leather sleeve, lined with otter pelts. He gently slipped it over Edrid's forearm and fastened the straps that fitted above his elbow and across his shoulder to prevent the sleeve falling off. It was a perfect fit, but Edrid looked puzzled, unable to guess its purpose until Henry produced several metal devices from the sack. He attached the first, a hook, onto bayonet clips on the sheath.

"See how easily it fits," Henry was pleased with himself. "You exchange the parts depending on what you need. I've done a hammer, a spike, and even a glove stuffed with goose down that you can wear under your robes for ceremonies. I bet a prince has lots of ceremonies. I can fashion all sorts of devices when you decide what you need. The otter pelt can be replaced if it wears out or gets feral. What do you think?"

Edrid raised his arm and examined the hook then flexed his muscles inside the sleeve which twinged, but would improve with time.

"Hmmm," he smiled, "I think it will do very well, Henry. Thank you…and you too Otillie. Yes, I reckon I'll get used to this pretty quickly. You might even be able to craft something I can attach a shield to. Then I'll be right back in business."

"You'll have to take it off at night so you don't poke your eye out," Macayle said. "And now we'll have to think of a tough warrior name for you."

"Edrid the Hook," Otillie suggested, but no one was sure about that.

"The Claw…"

Edrid didn't like it.

"Hammer Hand."

Not that either.

The discussion went back and forth for a while, until Redbone suggested Edrid Iron Fist, which met general approval.

"Oh, very tough," Macayle said.

"I don't feel all that tough," Edrid admitted.

He still tired easily and turned in early with Beatrice and the girls fussing over him and seeing him comfortably settled. Henry, Redbone, and Anvil Cornfoot took their beer tankards and sat on the porch, listening to the chorus of insects in the lingering twilight. Bron lay at Henry's feet, gnawing on a gammon bone.

"Now, what am I going to do?" he asked no one in particular. "Ayla wasn't at Glam, so where is she?"

"No mystery there, boy," Anvil Cornfoot said. "She's been taken to Dambar. You heard Crag Daniek say so with his dying breath, didn't you? That's where they trade human beings hereabouts."

"I suppose that's what he meant. It didn't make sense at the time."

"Nothing made sense then."

"Dambar's not for the faint-hearted, Henry," the squire said. "The slave trade isn't a pretty business. Sometimes our people are caught and sold as freaks to amuse the city gentry. We try to keep raiders out with the treaty, that's why the penalties for violations are so severe. Starkmen are one thing, but Dambar is quite different.'

"You have to admit we took Glam pretty well," Henry said with a smug grin.

"Yes, and I don't mean to rain on your parade, but the Starkmen were stupid, drunk, and taken by surprise. On a battlefield, they'd have cut you to shreds."

"We could surprise Dambar."

"Not going to happen, Henry. Dambar is strong, fortified, and guarded by a cohort of disciplined, well-trained troops."

"You defend your treaty against them, though."

"But for how long? We've been successful in past skirmishes, but I fear it'll only be a matter of time before we're sorely pressed.

Duke Percival and Count Maslovaric's avarice won't stay quenched for ever."

"So you're waiting to be invaded?"

"We'll make 'em pay," Anvil Cornfoot said. "You've seen us do it."

"Against half-a-dozen thugs."

"Didn't do you any harm, did it?"

"Yes, sorry, don't think I'm not grateful, but if Dambar sends an army...?"

"Maybe we have some time," Redbone considered. "Trade is Dambar's main focus and an army is expensive to maintain. The merchants know they need protection, but aren't happy about paying for it. But the cohort will come eventually, I'm sure. The trouble is we have so little information from the city. We can't send spies there, we sort of stand out, don't we?"

Henry could see things getting a lot more complicated than simply rescuing Lady Ayla. Grander designs were afoot and his quest had stalled. Edrid was understandably not as ardent as before and Macayle's attention had turned from finding her mother to tending the prince, possibly her prince. But, they hadn't rescued all his islanders, along with a number of Otillie's people. Many still laboured to their deaths in the Nadia Mines. The dwarves had worries of their own and, although they were his allies, what were their chances against the Dambar cohort?

Also the price of the quest was mounting; most people involved had suffered some loss. Anshelm was gone, Otillie's dad murdered while other villagers were slain at Glam and now Edrid crippled. The risks could only grow worse and what right did he have to ask them to sacrifice more? If only Gareth and his warriors would show up, someone else could take charge. Maybe it would be best to press on alone, find Gareth, and tell him about Dambar. The chief would know what to do and Henry could bring valuable intelligence back to the dwarves. Yes, that's what he'd do. He'd leave before dawn and be well away before anyone noticed and tried to stop him or confuse him with their protests. Enough had been done on his behalf; it was time to continue alone, he was practically a man now and should no longer rely on others to support his dreams.

With Edrid asleep and the evening chores complete, Beatrice and the girls joined them. They brought a pitcher of ale and refilled the men's beakers. They settled on the porch, enjoying the evening and they talked of other things. Redbone explained how the forest stretched for countless leagues to the east where mysterious folk lived hidden in its wooded depths.

"It falls to me and dwarves to try and protect the land from thoughtless exploitation. It's not an easy balance. The trouble is where there is bounty, men multiply and overuse the land, causing famine. Folk starve and die until their numbers reduce sufficiently for the land to heal itself. Once it does, men proliferate once more and the whole vicious cycle begins again. Sometimes the land is damaged beyond repair. Unab desert is just such a case. In bygone times is was rich woodland, but men came with their goats and saws, felling trees and grazing the grasslands bare until simooms swept the soil away leaving barren rock. I fear the same for our forest if we can't defend it."

"Do other people live in the forest then?" Otillie asked.

"Oh, many, dear," Beatrice said. "Some we see, and some we only sense or hear about, and the squire must try and protect them all. Our children are grown now with families of their own and some have moved to other villages, but there is a song we sang to them about mysterious folk they might come across. I'm sure they sing it to their children too."

"Perhaps you'll sing for our guests, love," Redbone said. He went inside and returned with a lute, tuning the strings while Anvil produced a fife from his tunic and they began to play. Beatrice clapped lightly to keep time as she sang in a lilting contralto:

Dwarf folk drawn from time gone by
To fill this land by and by
Elf and Pixie
Shy and tricksy

Gnomes underground do dwell
And care for men none too well
Dread troll and ogre
Make hearts no bolder

Fay goblins shield your home they say
Though you'll not see them today
Satyrs charm the trees
Faeries glide the breeze

Wee folk no man shall spy
Gazing as you pass by
But stop and hearken maybe
To sense those ones so free.

"It's to do with your senses," Redbone said, when Beatrice finished. "Mostly we use them all at once, but if you separate them, they're more powerful. You can appreciate the nightingale's song in a forest after dark because you can't see. In battle there is noise all around, but can you actually remember hearing it? Learn to use your senses in isolation and it's amazing what you'll discover."

They played and sang as twilight turned to night and stars filled the sky. As Henry gazed upwards, he thought of the legendry folk in Beatrice's song and the wonders he'd seen since leaving Hollowford. In fact, the lyrics didn't seem so fanciful to him at all. Who knew what lived in the land or beyond, for that matter? Dean Merrick had once said mysteries just need to be explored and understood for magic to become science, so nothing was impossible if you were determined enough to achieve it. Maybe that applied to finding Lady Ayla too. The squire's ale was a heady brew and Henry grew drowsy. It was time to turn in; he wanted to be far away by morning.

Henry went with regrets, but there was no turning back. Leaving his friends was painful, but he still had Bron for company. She seemed happy to be on the move again, bounding ahead before returning and then racing off again. She was a wild creature, after all, and back in her element. They were gone before first light, and even though Bron managed with ease, Henry had to take care following the trail south, which made slow progress, so by morning he hadn't gone as far as he'd hoped. But with daylight, he quickened his pace so Bron was happy to lope along beside him until she stopped abruptly, turned, and snarled a warning, although Henry saw nothing.

"Call your dog off," Anvil Cornfoot cried as he jogged along the path and drew alongside Henry. He didn't seem out of breath, but Henry remembered how easily he moved about the forest.

"Going somewhere?" the dwarf asked.

"Yes, to see if I can meet Chief Gareth on the trail and tell him about Lady Ayla. If he comes all the way up here, he'll have made the journey for nothing and just have to turn around."

"True enough. I'd better come too and make sure you don't get lost."

"It might be dangerous."

"No doubt about that."

"You'll just be an observer, I presume?"

"Absolutely."

"It's a long way, isn't it?"

"Sure is, so you'll be glad of company, even it's only a grumpy midget like me."

"You caught up quickly."

"No, I heard you leave and followed straight off. I thought I'd better wait for day break so your dog didn't have a go at me."

"She's not a dog, she's a wolf."

"Whatever."

Anvil Cornfoot suggested they press on at an easy pace so they'd not tire and go further in the long run. They camped early that afternoon, allowing time to forage for food and Bron to hunt as usual, bringing home a brace of pheasants. They were tough and chewy, but Henry didn't mind returning to meals of freshly killed meat that had not been hung or tenderised. He slept well and awoke at first light. The blue fire smoke filled the glade and swirled through dawn's sunbeams that streaked into the forest. Anvil Cornfoot crouched by the fire, chewing an apple from the supply he'd brought.

"Why didn't you wake me for my guard duty?" Henry said.

"No need, take a look."

A lone horseman, who stood like a motionless sentinel silhouetted against the sunrise.

"What… A challenge..?"

The rider drew his left arm from under his cloak and raised its shining hook above his head.

"No, a guardian," Edrid said.

"And he's not alone," Anvil Cornfoot added as Macayle and Otillie emerged from the shadows.

"You didn't really think we'd let you go without us again?" Otillie said.

"We started together and we'll finish together," Macayle added.

"What about your arm?" Henry said, turning back to Edrid. "It's barely healed."

"Mere bagatelle as I said, old boy. No way we're going to let you conquer Dambar all by yourself. Definitely a job for Iron Fist, wouldn't you say? And the squire was kind enough to lend me one of his horses. She's more used to a plough or sulky, but we're getting along fine. Her name's Gwen."

"I don't think we'll be conquering anywhere with just four of us, an observer, and a horse."

"Maybe not, but take a look back along the trail."

Julian marched ahead of the village folk and islanders who were armed with weapons taken from Glam and provisioned for a long journey. He stepped in front of Henry and vigorously shook his hand.

"You've given us back our self-respect, Henry," Julian said. "We've tasted freedom and like it, so we're prepared to fight to keep it."

Henry was certainly pleased, but how could these men and women–brave no doubt–beat trained professionals? That was the rub. Extra man-power might be enough leverage to obtain the release of Ayla and the other captive slaves, but it could also antagonise the Dambar merchants and Duke Percival to set the cohort loose.

"What about restoring your village?" Henry asked.

"It'll have to wait. No point in putting things to rights, if someone is just going to turn up and tear it all down again," Julian said.

"It'll be dangerous…'"

"You don't say, but we have allies."

Sure enough in moments they heard the tramp of feet and saw Squire Redbone leading a company of dwarves towards them, and what a sight. They were dressed in leather helmets, chain mail sarks, and carried spears, shields, and short swords. They proudly marched in threes with heads erect as sharply as any military unit. On the squire's command, his column crunched to a halt in precise unison.

"Surprise!" Redbone declared.

Henry nodded.

"You're right, you know. The Starklanders were only sub-contractors for Dambar slavers. Now they're gone, the cohort will come. We assembled a quick quorum of village leaders and decided we're going to have to stop 'em once and for all."

"Looks like you've got quite a battalion now, Henry," Edrid said. "So lead on, colonel. We await your orders."

Henry was lost for words, so he simply drew Hornet-Sting. The blade flashed in the sunlight as he raised the sword high.

"Then onward to Dambar and glory!" he cried.

The army roared, brandished their weapons, fell into ranks of three and followed Henry southwards.

Once we join forces with Chief Gareth and Archer, Henry thought, everything will be fine.

I'm not a colonel or a general or whatever.
How do I give orders, and what if they decide to disobey?
What do I do then?

Cross that bridge when I come to it, I guess.
It's too late to go back now.
And go back to where?

Chapter 25
Girls of the Seraglio

All this time, Ayla was being held prisoner and, frustrating as it was, her situation wasn't entirely uncomfortable. The soldiers had taken her through a maze of streets and alleyways to the Duke's palace inside the city keep. Encircled by a high wall, it appeared accessible by only two gates attended by female guards. These women carried spears and swords although they wore no helmets or armour, but simple leather tunics, skirts, and boots. The escort merely nodded and handed her over, and the sentries led the way into a different world. If she thought Olgaric's home was luxurious, it hardly compared with her new surroundings. She entered a tranquil courtyard adorned with gardens and jingling fountains shaded by arching jacarandas that cast a carpet of mauve bracts over the cobblestones. The city babble was entirely shut off as the gate clanged behind her and the temperature dropped in a zephyr that flowed through the branches.

A grand, marble structure stood before her, a tall white palace, studded with arched windows and soaring minarets. A wide, paved stairway led to an ornate gate that formed the palace entrance. One of the guards hurried away, while Ayla stood in silence, but she didn't have to wait long. A few moments later, two women stepped through the gate and down the stairway. Both were dressed as soldiers, but wore ornamental brooches, golden torques, and chains that marked their rank. The leading woman was dressed entirely in black. Ayla recognised the style of jewellery as the talismans Henry had found. So Dambar was where they'd come from.

The woman in black approached and stood uncomfortably close to Ayla, scrutinising her with piercing eyes. She was about Ayla's age and just as striking, but her loveliness was etched with cruelty as a smile crossed her crimson lips.

"Madam," Ayla said. "I don't know who you are, or why I have been brought here…"

"You dare to address me?" the woman arched her eyebrows.

"I dare to address whom I please…"

The woman's gloved palm slapped across Ayla's face with such suddenness and force she nearly fell, but recovered and launched herself forward, only to be restrained by the guards.

"Dear me," the woman purred, "I do hope they haven't brought me a harridan, but of course it may be fun beating the waywardness out of her." She turned to her companion. "Take her and prepare her, Aurelia. That fool Olgaric really has no idea how to present a girl, whatever he might think. I mean, just look at that shift, I'm sure we can do better than that. I will tell the duke another one has arrived, although she seems a bit old for his taste."

A bit old! I'll wring her scrawny neck first chance I get.

The woman stalked away leaving Ayla to be gently, but firmly guided by Aurelia to the inner palace apartments. The guard captain was a doe-eyed teenager who looked impossibly young and benign to be in charge of the duke's personal guards.

"It's best to do exactly what the Duchess Zalina says," she advised. "She's the duke's wife and pretty much has the last say."

"Prepare me for what..?"

"That rather depends on the duke. Whatever he wants, really."

Ayla was beginning to have a very bad feeling about the duke.

"She procures women for him?"

"It's complicated," Aurelia said. "Zalina likes to…use people…men and women alike, just as long as she's in charge."

"And if I refuse?"

"I wouldn't advise that. The personal guards have been chosen for their looks, no doubt, but don't be fooled. We're better trained than all the cohort scum put together. Look, it may not be so bad. The duke is…fickle…you just have to know how to distract him."

Ayla would have asked more, but she was taken into a large chamber where about forty bored girls lounged on sedans, played cards, chess, dice, the occasional musical instrument, or simply gossiped. The room was beautifully appointed with velvet drapes, mosaic floors, and ornate panelling and furniture. The tables were laden with fruit, wine, sweetmeats, and tasty savouries. The girls were all stunning beauties who were mostly teenagers, although some women in their early twenties were among the harem. They were dressed from practically nothing to fine gowns with no particular theme or similarity. A dozen men attended their every whim and although they were tall and fit looking, their familiarity with the girls was puzzling, and when Aurelia instructed a pair of them to bathe and prepare Ayla, she was appalled.

"But they're…"

"Eunuchs, my dear," Aurelia smiled. "Fear not, your virtue is safe…well, for the moment anyway."

Ayla's arrival created a good deal of giggling interest from the harem girls who were always looking for new sources of amusement. They eyed her golden hair curiously as they were all raven brunettes from southern lands. Their skins ranged from olive to ebony compared to Ayla's fairness. She was led to a beautifully tiled bathing pool with a bubbling spar in its centre and rose and jasmine petals floating on the surface. Before she realised it, she had been gently stripped and led to the centre of the pool, which was delightfully cool. Several of the other girls shamelessly joined her. One of the eunuchs poured fragrant oils into the pool while the other gently massaged her shoulders and legs.

"Relax, my darling," he crooned. "You are so tense, but we'll soon attend to that. We don't wish to see our ladies tense, now do we?"

He was right and she was in the hands of an expert. After she'd bathed, he led her to a divan where he stroked away the built up tension of the last weeks. She smiled for the first time since being captured and allowed herself to simply drift off to sleep. She awoke with a yelp and a stinging leg.

"What..?"

"Oh sorry, my darling," the eunuch said, "but dear me, we are not smooth at all, are we?"

"There hasn't exactly been time for personal touches in the bottom of a pirate ship or being dragged across the desert."

"True, so true, sweetie, but the duke does like his girls to be so smooth."

She stared at him.

"Yes," he said apologetically, "the wax stings a little, but we have the finest soothing balms, and you'll look delicious, my pet."

"Smooth… where?"

"Why everywhere, precious," he beamed.

"No...?"

"Oh, yes."

Duke Percival d'Ibin, last scion of the declining House of Trey, did not appear to be in any particular hurry to meet Ayla. Affairs of state must have preoccupied him. At first she had baulked at the thought of the eunuchs' attention, but they explained gently that she could either enjoy being pampered or be pampered forcibly, which was so undignified and they did like their ladies to be dignified at all times. In the days that followed, Ayla was bathed, massaged, preened, manicured, dressed and redressed, while her hair was combed endlessly. All the harem girls offered to do this as golden hair fascinated them. Their primary occupation, other than grooming, was gossip and they chattered incessantly, but it was from this chatter that Ayla began to gather information about Dambar and its hierarchy.

True, Duke Percival was the official sovereign of Dambar and Unab, but he was indolent, absent-minded, and prone to moods. It was Zalina who controlled Percival and the city, but it wasn't long before she discovered Count Maslovaric controlled the duchess. Aurelia was her chief source of accurate intelligence. Because Ayla was a stranger, the guard captain befriended her and asked endless questions about Hollowford and the peninsula. In turn, she confided in Ayla and it wasn't long before she was aware of some of the city's most intimate secrets.

Much of Aurelia's dissatisfaction was to do with her lover Jagar, a cohort subaltern. Zalina insisted her personal guards remain single as a sign of their total allegiance to her. Also all guards had taken a life-long oath to remain in service, which had seemed a good deal at the time as the deal included light duties, good food and lodging, and a reasonable salary. But the trouble with life-long agreements is that someone always changes their mind. Mostly it was Duchess Zalina who regularly dismissed guards for misdemeanours, often accompanied by savage punishments, a hundred bastinado strokes being one of her favourites, which usually left the victim crippled, if not dead. Zalina often threatened exile or deportation to the mines, but she preferred the sensuality of witnessing physical torture so a reign of terror kept discipline sharp among the palace guards.

Ayla noted every detail. Fear bred discontent and discontent bred…well…

Zalina was also in the habit of caressing the harem girls. Whereas some seemed not to mind, and even invited her intimacy, others tensed at her touch and it was these who gave her the greatest pleasure. She revelled in their discomfort and especially targeted Ayla, who received several canings for her lack of response. The eunuchs who'd been forced to administer the punishment apologised to her afterwards, but said it was more than their lives were worth to disobey the duchess. Ayla forgave them readily enough when they administered healing balms. She felt they were holding back on the strokes as much as they dared and the welts faded without leaving a mark.

"Just go along with her," Aurelia finally advised. "It's your distress she craves. Pretend to enjoy yourself and she'll leave you alone. You're no fun if you're compliant."

It was sound advice and Zalina grew bored, turning her attention elsewhere. It seemed she could be as contrary as the duke. As seraglio life dragged on, Ayla grew bolder and explored the palace as far as she could. Occasionally she was discovered beyond the permitted bounds and had to be shepherded back to the seraglio with a few stern warnings, but she was never punished. She suspected Aurelia had ordered her guards to treat her leniently. But, she gathered little further information. The palace was a labyrinth of passages, chambers, courtyards, gardens and, most of all, walls, but there were a couple of narrow alleyways that led from the keep. Unfortunately, they were always guarded, with no way of squeezing past the sentries in such a tight space. Escape seemed impossible.

She discovered many pleasant surprises right there in the harem. The girls identified new fruit varieties that fascinated her and some tasted delicious. She loved pineapples, peaches, apricots and thought oranges were the nectar of the gods, but mangoes proved too strong and stringy for her taste. She really liked dates and enjoyed coffee, after getting used to its bitterness. Even so, she considered peninsula apples were the best. But the meat dishes cooked with a pungent mixture of spices took her breath away and meals served from Gareth's kitchen seemed bland by comparison. And Dambar wines were superb.

I'll be fat as a fool if I don't watch out, she thought, and carefully rationed her food. Especially as she had grown used to the pleasure of dressing in the superb selection of elegant and sensual gowns available to the seraglio girls. They could wear pretty much what they pleased as it seemed Duke Percival liked them to surprise him.

And then one day he summoned Ayla.

Aurelia and two guards escorted her to Percival's majestic throne room and, if she thought the seraglio was magnificent, this was even more splendid. Dambar itself ranged from the abject poverty of its beggars to Percival's regal opulence. Ayla had never seen such grandeur as she gazed about her. The drapes, marble tiles, statues, fountains, and furnishing were all made of fine cloth, exotic wood and inlaid with colourful stones. The intricate workmanship of Henry's medallions sparkled from every corner.

How could so much wealth be in one small place? Not that the throne-room was small, in fact it was huge with high, vaulted ceilings decorated in swirling cameos interspersed with gargoyles and other sinister mouldings.

Ayla was uncertain what the duke would be like, as reports from the harem girls varied and were generally unreliable. He was seated on an ebony throne carved with lions and padded with crimson, leather cushions. He certainly didn't look particularly threatening dressed in garish robes and a foppish, feathered hat that was a size too large. But his eyes blazed with a disturbing intensity as he studied Ayla's every detail. He was alone; the equally splendid throne beside him was empty. The duke wasn't much older than Ayla, but inbreeding and a hedonist's life had taken its toll. He simply looked unhealthy.

"Do you like it?" the duke beamed, waving his arms about him.

"It is indeed magnificent, your grace," Ayla replied, recovering her composure. She was a chief's lady after all and not an ignorant peasant.

"Chose it all myself," he said. "No expense spared, but hey, I'm the duke, I can have anything I want, what?"

"I don't doubt it, lord."

"Oh, do call me Percy in private. All the other girls do. Come here, sit down,' he invited, patting the throne beside him.

"Surely that's for the duchess…er…Percy?"

"Yes, I know, and she'd be livid if someone else sat there, so it'll be our little secret, won't it?"

Ayla sat. The throne was hard and uncomfortable, but it made her sit with a straight back. A regal posture was undoubtedly a good image for monarchs holding court.

"Now I do hope we'll be friends," the duke crooned patting her knee. "Very good friends."

"I warn you I will not submit willingly, Percy. I have a husband and no need to be unfaithful."

"Technically I suppose you do, but the point is moot considering your present situation. Anyway, I have plenty of younger girls for that sort of thing."

Well that's a relief, but grossly insulting all the same.

"You keep those girls simply for your pleasure?"

"Is it so wrong to have pretty things around you? I do so love pretty things, you know, don't you?"

"I believe it is wrong to keep people against their will."

"Do you not have slaves where you come from then?"

True, Gareth's household had three slave girls, although they had been bought from a shady drummer who'd found them in Velma's back streets and were probably better off with the chief. Ayla had cleaned them up, fed them, provided warm, comfortable quarters and put them to work. She had never seen Gareth mistreat them and she certainly had not. Also she ensured Faranden kept his grubby hands to himself. Gareth had agreed they were free to leave when they chose to marry; indeed, one of the girls was betrothed but preferred to remain in service until she was ready to start her own family. Of course, there were also cases like the tattooed girl Thayer had taken from the battle with Velma's horde, along with the other captives who'd have to make themselves useful around Hollowford to pay for the trouble they'd caused. Many would see that as salvation rather than enslavement.

"Well, yes, but they're treated differently," Ayla admitted, but the duke had lost interest.

"I suppose it is just a matter of degree. Now, Aurelia tells me you have studied the stars," the duke continued. "I would have you assay my future. I wish to know what the heavens predict."

"I fear I shall disappoint you then, lord..." He frowned. "...er...Percy, for I am a student of astronomy not astrology. I know many claim to foresee events from sky portents, but I have only once seen evidence of it. The skies were ablaze the night I was captured and lost my daughter."

The ache returned, now she remembered the heart-wrenching shock of Macayle vanishing below that bleak morning tide. Had she reappeared? She wasn't sure, but she must keep that sliver of hope alive or she would die of despair. Duke Percival saw the profound sadness in her eyes and seemed moved by her sorrow.

"Look, we can talk later, I'm sure I'll be fascinated by the stars and planets. I have an apothecary somewhere who has put together lenses in a tube and you can see for miles. Tell you what, I'll get him to set his apparatus up in one of the high towers and one night we'll have a look together, how's that?"

She nodded, but tears glistened in the corners of her eyes.

"Now you pop back with the other girls and I'll see you later."

Aurelia took Ayla's arm and led her away.

"He didn't seem so bad," Ayla sniffed. "He was quite kind really."

"Don't let him fool you. Sometimes he's like that, but he can be cruel as a snake, especially when the duchess and Count Maslovaric get in his ear. He doesn't seem to have a mind of his own when they're around. And he didn't set you free, did he?"

It was only a matter of days before Ayla was summoned once more, but this time Count Maslovaric stood at the duke's right with Zalina seated on the throne to his left, and Ayla knew how dangerous they could be. Other than Aurelia, the only other person in the room was a handsome officer who Ayla thought must be

Jagar judging by the glances he cast at Aurelia. He was armed in typical Dambar fashion with a spear, shield and falchion.

"Is she to your liking, my lord?" Zalina asked, seemingly unaware that the duke had already met Ayla.

He turned to Zalina who patted his hand.

"Yes my dear, she is charming and her hair is divine," he said.

"But she must be over thirty," Zalina purred through a strained smile.

There she goes again. I swear I'll crown the next person who says anything about my age. It's as if I'm in my dotage; wait till Gareth gets his hands on the lot of 'em.

"Alas, we must keep these pleasantries for later," Count Maslovaric said. "This woman is from Grambak, your grace. A place surrounded by sea and marshland which we have hitherto had no interest in, but it may be time for that to change. I suggest we question her in detail about her homeland, thus better preparing us for invasion."

He wasn't the slightest bit worried about revealing his plans in front of Ayla as she was nothing but an inconsequential slave. But this was news to her. Invasion? Well, people had tried that before and lived to regret it. Indeed many had not lived to regret it.

"You won't get anything from me," Ayla said, standing defiantly erect.

"We get everything from everyone," Maslovaric hissed.

"Oh, hush now, my dear count," the duke said, "I don't think we need any unpleasantness. I do so dislike unpleasantness. It makes my head ache abominably."

"As you wish, your grace," Maslovaric oozed. "Of course you are right as always."

You oily toad, Ayla though, you think I can be so easily intimidated?

"Now, my dear," the duke continued, "we really would like to know all about you. I'm sure it'll be awfully interesting, and I do so like to be interested. The count and I have discussed how useful you can be to us."

"I'm still not going to tell you anything that will threaten my homeland."

"Oh, but I think you will," Maslovaric sneered.

"Not ever!"

"Tell her please, my dear count," Zalina sighed.

"You will answer all our questions, because, you see, your beloved husband and four of his yokel buffoons are languishing in our gaol right now and what happens to them may well depend on your cooperation."

"But first we're going to have fun," Percival declared. "I do so love having fun more than anything else in the world."

Doubt, doubt and more doubt.
Count Maslovaric holds all the cards,
And deals them ruthlessly.

Chapter 26
The Dambar Pit

While Ayla languished in luxury, the peninsula five languished in gaol and soon lost track of time. With nothing on their minds but boredom, inactivity, poor food, and poorer sanitation, depression set in. They were men of action and idleness was as sure a killer as any enemy. Their clothing was tattered and soiled and the stench of stale sweat seeped from their pores while their hair hung in matted hanks infested with lice and fleas and their skin faded to a decaying pallor. The turnkey and his lackeys enjoyed taunting them. The gaolers led a dreary life, so they gained their amusement where they could. Curiously, they stopped short of beatings, which they inflicted enthusiastically on other inmates. Possibly Count Maslovaric had ordered the prisoners to remain unharmed or, the turnkey with only two bruisers for back up, simply wasn't game to venture into a cell containing five ill-tempered warriors.

Eventually Maslovaric returned leading a company of spear-toting guards. His cloaked silhouette framed the cage bars.

"Well, hello there, Gareth," the count greeted. "How do these quarters suit you? A bit cramped I suppose and pooh, you stink worse than a pox-ridden tribesman's armpit."

Gareth leapt at the bars.

"You treacherous, black-hearted…"

"Oh, my, my, we are in a snit, aren't we? But that's the spirit I want to see. You're going to need it, you know. I've decided you're not bound for the mines or galley-decks…yet."

Gareth continued ranting and demanding what had become of Ayla, but Maslovaric wasn't in a helpful mood.

"But things are going to get better…before they get worse," he said enigmatically, and they were left alone to consider their surroundings once again. They heard Maslovaric issuing instructions to the turnkey, although he was at the far end of the chamber and no one made out what he was saying. Shortly, the gaoler clanked open the cell bolts with a huge key attached to a chain he wore around his waist. The troops nervously entered the cage and pressed the peninsula men against the far wall at spear-point, where they expected to be butchered out of hand. To their surprise, the turnkey's minders placed two buckets of fresh drinking water on the cell floor along with a hamper of fruit, meat, and bread. Maslovaric appeared satisfied and left without a further word leaving two guards manning the chamber door.

While they ate, they noticed other men were being hustled from remote cells into the surrounding barracoons. Soon, over a score of miserable souls were packed into the cages.

A lone black-skinned man sat in the barracoon beside them with his back against the bars and, although he'd eyed them suspiciously when he arrived, he showed no further interest. Jongarrat could just reach across and nudged him in the back, but the man didn't respond. Undeterred, the dwarf continued to prod him.

"What's the matter with you, I know you ain't dead," Jongarrat hissed.

"You will be if you don't stop prodding me, midget," the stranger snarled, without moving.

"I guess I'm safe enough behind these bars."

"You reckon, eh?"

"Tell me then."

"You really don't know why you're here?"

"No, who are you and what are all these men doing here?"

"My name is Ebony Vy, and we have all been specially chosen. Most prisoners are used as mine or galley slaves, but these men are tribesmen, vagrants, or cohort deserters. We're here for the sports."

"I don't mind a game or two," Serlequin commented. "Me and Kimball here are good at weight-lifting and tug-o'-war."

"I don't think we're talking about the same sporting idea," Ebony Vy said, even managing a smile. "We are to amuse the duke and his cronies. The Dambar Pit lies through that gate at the end of this hall. We are expected to fight there. Sometimes we're armed, sometimes not, sometimes it's man-to-man, sometimes against wild beasts. It depends on the duke's fancy…or the duchess's. That's why men don't speak much in here. It's easier to kill a stranger. I have fought a dozen times and remain unbeaten, but it's just a matter of time," he added dully.

"Has anyone tried to escape?" Archer asked.

"A few," Ebony Vy conceded, "but they're all caught in the end and then it's a slow and painful death. At least it's quick in the pit…well, most of the time."

"The city's a warren of nooks, alleys, and passages. There're plenty of places to hide."

"If you dodge the cohort you'd most likely get lost and who'd give you sanctuary anyway? So good luck with that."

"We met your father on the plains," Gareth said. "He's worried about you."

"There isn't much else he can do."

"He thinks you're just being held as a hostage, if he knew the truth, well..."

"Like I said, there isn't much he can do."

Gareth's men had inspected the barracoon for weaknesses, but they persisted in rattling the bars, attempting to dig under the foundations, and trying to pry the lock, but even Serlequin and Kimball's strength proved useless.

"It's all been tried before," Ebony Vy said in a bored voice. "It'll take an elephant to move those bars."

"Elephant?"

"Never mind, you'll never move them."

Servants brought all the prisoners a decent supper and breakfast the following morning to "sharpen them up" according to Ebony Vy. Just before noon the following day, a cheerful young subaltern entered the barracoon chamber, followed by the usual force of cohort regulars. He rattled a set of keys across the cage bars.

"Come on gents, on your feet. Let's be having you," he bellowed. "Them first," he added as he unlocked the cage where the peninsula warriors were held. The portcullis to the far end of the chamber rose and the prisoners were herded into the arena beyond to the roar of an expectant crowd. Word had got out that the games were on and the stadium was full to the bleachers. The sun blazed down and five men shaded their eyes against its unaccustomed glare as they moved slowly into the ring centre where their weapons lay in a random pile.

"Help yourselves," the subaltern invited. "You're going to need 'em."

"What for?" Gareth demanded.

The subaltern stared for a moment.

"You ain't been here before, have you? No, of course not. Well, this is the duke's circus. That's him, sitting up there with all his posh hangers-on who've come to see a good stoush."

All Gareth saw was a sea of jeering faces and flailing arms.

"Fight who?"

"Right now, I'm going back to let that mob out of their cages, then they'll come boiling through that gate and try to chop you to pieces. Simple really."

"All of them?"

"Yep."

"They outnumber us four-to-one."

"They certainly do. Rather you than me, I must say."

The subaltern strode jauntily back through the portcullis, whistling as he went.

Duke Percival lounged on a divan, propped by velvet cushions, surrounded by his toadies, and shovelled titbits into his mouth, washing them down with claret. He grew bored with the tumblers, mummers, jugglers, and troubadours who provided warm-up entertainment. Count Maslovaric had sensed the royal discontent and sent a young subaltern named Jagar to get the main act underway. The count had insisted Ayla accompany him and stand by his side.

"You can see what's going to happen here," Maslovaric whispered in her ear. "Now we'll see just how good your noble chief and his yokels are."

"They'll make mincemeat of your trash."

"Possibly, but you don't really think it'll be a fair fight, do you?"

Ayla stared at him.

So that's your game, is it? She though. *Gareth can take anything you throw at him, you villain. I'll just tell you a pack of lies. You won't know the difference anyway.*

"Very well," she said. "Spare them and I'll answer your questions."

"Oh, that won't be necessary. There isn't much I don't know already from Captain Aurelia. You can't honestly think she befriended you because she likes you, can you? Zalina ordered her to spy on you, and who do you think put that idea into the duchess's head? Anyway, with the peninsula's top chief out of the picture, I don't expect much resistance. So let's settle back and enjoy the show."

How could I have been such a trusting fool, but Aurelia's grievances seemed so genuine?

The count secretly had other ideas about how Ayla was going to amuse him, but that would have to wait. Zalina often required him to perform additional court duties, but her cruelty and perversity were so predictable she'd become boring, and he craved something new. But matters-of-state were at hand, so he turned to Percival and they discussed the value of extending their influence into Grambak.

"Exact a regular tribute at the very least," the duke suggested.

"Colonisation I think, your grace," Maslovaric replied, knowing full well that Unab needed to expand its territory. Dambar was sucking the country dry and Lake Naida's level dropped each year as the population used more than it could replenish from the remote mountain catchments. The control of distant lands would undoubtedly bring much-needed resources to the city. Sorting out those troublesome pygmies in the north was also on the agenda, and hang their wretched treaty as well as most of the dwarfs along with it.

"But enough of business," Percival said, "they're coming out and the fun is about to begin, and I do so love to have fun."

"Now we'll see what your precious Gareth is made of," Maslovaric said.

"A hundred of you," Ayla hissed.

"Oh, look at that jolly little fellow. I wager a hundred florins he's first to go," the duke declared, clapping his hands only to be imitated by his sycophants until a thunder of applause spread throughout the arena.

"Nice to be out in the sunlight again," Archer commented as he balanced Skull-Crusher and Avenger in his grip. "The weapons could do with a honing, but all-in-all, not too bad."

"Quick, to the gate," Gareth hissed. "We'll get 'em as they bunch through the door."

But, they were met by spear points as the cohort troops forced them back to the centre of the arena, so they stood back-to-back in a defensive block and waited. The soldiers parted before the screaming, desperately-manic horde charged through the portal straight into the fight. Steel scraped against steel in a shower of sparks, the clash of metal and shrieks of men. Goresax struck down two men in a heartbeat and Archer took another. Kimball's axe cleaved a man from skull to groin. Serlequin's range with a staff was awesome and he crowned a swordsman who went down and lay still. Jongarrat was perceptively agile and skewered an enemy belly, ripping the flesh apart as entrails slithered onto the dust. The gladiator clutched his gut with a look of stunned amazement before dropping face-first into the dirt.

The attack stalled as the gladiators circled the peninsula warriors with new respect. A few made lunges, but rewarded with wounds, the fight ground down to a tense stalemate and the crowd grew restless. They hadn't paid good money to see men dancing around each other.

"Get on with it!"

"Go at it with a will, you pansies!"

"Cowards!"

"Call us cowards, would they?" Archer said, darting forward and slicing into one of the less cautious opponents. The others backed off until a company of cohort troops encouraged them at spear-point, impaling a couple of men just to let them know they were serious. With no choice remaining, the gladiators renewed their attack with suicidal vigour. And suicide it was. They may not have been the most virtuous of men, but they weren't natural warriors either, rather reluctant conscripts, shepherds and desert traders and no match for the peninsula men to whom combat was second nature. But some gladiators broke through and drove the defenders apart into several individual brawls. Some thought Jongarrat was the easiest target and surged around him, but he dodged them all, inflicting several wounds before Serlequin and Kimball came to his aid and finished off his attackers. Goresax lived up to its name and soon Gareth's wrists ran red with blood. Archer weighed into the melee, wielding sword and axe in both hands. They eventually dealt with another three or four men and a pitifully small group of survivors was driven against the arena wall. A couple threw down their weapons and pleaded for mercy, although Ebony Vy stood his ground, bloody from several wounds, but urging the others to meet their deaths like warriors with sword in hand.

Gareth was not averse to finishing off wounded enemies who'd aggrieved him or risked more trouble if they lived, but he had no argument with these men other than they'd all been forced together in Percival's pit.

"You must kill us now," Ebony Vy said matter-of-factly.

"It's over," Gareth said.

"Can't you hear them baying for blood? We were ill-matched. You bested us fair-and-square. Death is the price we must pay, the mob always decides."

"I decide who dies by my sword."

The chant from the crowd grew to a roar. They unanimously held out their fists with thumbs pointing down.

"You seem in an uncommon hurry to die," Archer observed.

"Like I said, it's only a matter of time," Ebony Vy said, barely audible in the jeers from the mob that suddenly fell silent when Gareth turned and marched to the wall under Duke Percival's pavilion. The bewildered cohort troops parted before him. He lifted Goresax and pointed the blade at Percival, not in a salute, but a challenge.

"There is no fight left here," he cried. "No spectacle for your blood-lust. No honour!"

And then he saw Ayla.

"That is so annoying," Duke Percival complained. "They've spoilt everything and now our people are upset and I do so like them to be happy. They cause trouble when they're unhappy. All those idiots had to do was kill a few worthless ruffians, was that so much to ask? Go and get your fellows to finish 'em off will you, my dear count?"

"Ayla, I'm coming for you," Gareth yelled from the pit as he began to clamber over the arena wall. It wasn't a great height and he would have managed it, but the cohort troops, who were no longer confused, thrust their spears at his throat, stopping him in his tracks. Archer and the other Grambak men moved to join him, but met the same line of bristling spear-points.

Seeing Gareth trapped, Ayla dashed from the duke's pavilion and down the steps that led to the arena wall. To the cheers of the crowd, she leapt over the barricade into the pit and raced into Gareth's arms. The troops were once again baffled and raised their weapons. The crowd's roaring subsided to a hushed murmur before erupting into cheers and applause once more, apparently they appreciated romance as much as mayhem.

"I found you," Gareth sighed, "I couldn't bear to lose you. My family is my life."

"I knew you'd come," Ayla said, "only my heart breaks for Macayle..."

"But, she is safe at home. Henry pulled her from the waves and she recovered from her ordeal."

Ayla clung to him as tears rolled down her cheeks. She didn't notice he stank and knew she could face whatever challenges lay ahead knowing her daughter was alive and out of danger. But their reunion was short-lived.

"How touching," Maslovaric hissed. "It'll make killing that buffoon even sweeter."

"Oh, not now," Percival said peevishly. "That will only upset the crowd. We'll have to spare them after all."

"What would you have me do with them, your grace?"

"Take the woman back to the seraglio and do whatever you think best with the others."

"After a week in the mines, those oafs will be begging us to bring them back and butcher whoever we want."

It took six soldiers to drag Ayla from Gareth, bashing him to the ground in the process. She screamed, kicked, gouged, and wrestled every inch of the way back to the harem chamber. The troops flung her inside and slammed the doors, retiring scratched and bruised, but relieved to be rid of such a spitfire. Ayla threw herself onto a couch in a tantrum and there was nothing the others girls could do to console her. But in time she remembered Crag Daniek's words–don't blubber, woman–and Hollowford girls were tough. So her grief turned to frustration, and then to anger. She was damned if she'd let a pack of poncy, trumped-up bullies ship her husband and friends off to die in their labour camps. It was time to get even. For that she needed a plan and some help, and she thought she knew just where to get it.

Count Maslovaric issued instructions for his men to round up any gladiators fit enough to live. Those too badly hurt were disposed of with minimum care and no ceremony at all.

"Throw 'em all back in the cages," the count commanded. "I'll have the seneschal arrange for their branding and transportation tomorrow."

Gareth and Archer helped Ebony Vy limp back to captivity, while Serlequin, Kimball and Jongarrat also aided as many as they could. About a dozen men, although cut up, managed to make it on their own. As their numbers were so reduced, all the survivors were dumped into the same barracoon, leaving the other cages empty, although they knew many other prisoners were incarcerated in cells along the chamber's adjoining passages. The turnkey was delighted to see his favourites return and promised they'd receive special treatment. They checked Ebony Vy's condition, but in truth, with no medicine or dressings, there was nothing much anyone could do other than bathe his wounds, which was risky judging by the fetid water supply. Because of their disgrace, fresh rations and water were no longer forthcoming. Cohort troopers returned with their weapons and dumped them in a corner.

"Guess you won't be needing that stuff, no more," the turnkey laughed over the clatter of metal as spears and swords landed in a messy heap. "Next bunch might put up a better fight, but you won't be around to see it."

Archer and Gareth ignored him and returned their attention to Ebony Vy.

"How're you feeling?" Archer asked as they made the nomad as comfortable as possible.

"Like camel crap, actually."

"Sorry about cutting you up, it was sort of a heat-of-the-moment thing. No offence intended."

"None taken, but I fear it's all through with us anyway. We'll all be off to the mines in a day or two."

"We haven't given up hope," Gareth said. He might have been presumptuous speaking for his men, but their determined looks confirmed his point.

"You'll only last a year if you're fit, but believe me, you'll be better off dead," Ebony Vy insisted, "and I haven't heard of anyone escaping from the mines."

"That's the point, we're not just anyone."

Still how I wish Chief Gareth would arrive.
What's keeping him?
I know it's a long walk,
but how difficult can it be?
I'd even be pleased to see Faranden.

Chapter 27
The Catacombs

Dambar was abuzz over the extraordinary events at the pit that day. The inns were packed with customers, who all had an opinion on the subject, along with tavern hussies, pimps, barmen, bouncers, and drunken beggars. Wives gossiped as they did their chores while their children, armed with wooden swords, sparred with streets urchins, re-enacting the contest until their mothers called them in before someone was hurt. Ultimately, the city factors and mercers returned home before nocturnal vagabonds crept from their hovels to waylay unwary stragglers. The cohort night watch tended to be indifferent to petty theft and generally ineffective as a police force. So with the steamy heat of day past, Dambar settled for the night.

Percival's seraglio was also settling just prior to midnight. The girls prepared for bed as usual, overseen by sleepy eunuchs while disinterested guards patrolled the palace precincts. Spats were common enough among the courtesans, but were seldom long or spiteful, so when a minor squabble escalated into a full-scale brawl, everyone was taken by surprise. Well, that's what it looked like and it seemed the girls were split into roughly even-numbered sides. The palace echoed with shrieks, squeals, and the crash of furniture and broken pottery. Cushions were the prime weapons of choice and soon down sprayed from split seams and filled the room along with an amount of shredded night wear. Indeed close inspection of the fracas would have revealed it was nothing more than a mass pillow-fight, although a few old scores were settled with a sharp elbow-jab here and there.

The eunuchs let the melee take its natural course, but finally decided it was time to wade in and sort it out with their usual, jocular firmness. Suddenly, the girls joined forces and turned on their minders, overwhelming them by sheer numbers. Finally, one bemused fellow escaped to warn the palace guard and a detachment was sent to restore order while others left their posts to investigate as well. At the melee height, no one noticed a lone figure in the shadows edging behind a row of colonnades before slipping through the seraglio portal.

Thank you, ladies. A job well done.

Ayla fled down a stairwell and headed for the gaol. She'd remembered the way to the arena and knew from what the girls had told her of the city layout. The cells were directly under the bleachers. A few girls had even accompanied Zalina on her sojourns to watch miscreants being made to pay for their crimes. Apparently, the duchess enjoyed the girls' distress as much as watching torture-victims suffer. But they explained the gaol was manned by only two or three men and that was a very useful piece of information. Her only plan was to join Gareth and escape with him. She'd seen the Grambak men fight in Percival's pit and once released they'd surely be unstoppable. It wasn't the best plan and not exactly thought through, especially when Ayla ran headlong into Aurelia. The guard captain was off-duty and alone, but she'd heard the commotion in the seraglio and was on her way to discover what it was all about. It was hard to judge who was the most surprised.

"What are you doing here, Ayla?"

There was no satisfactory answer to that one. Although Ayla

had armed herself with a long-bladed knife from the supper platter, which might prove lethal in the right hands, it was no match for Aurelia's falchion.

"I trusted you and you spied on me to that viper, Maslovaric. I thought you were my friend," Ayla snapped as the best means of defence seemed to be attack in this case.

"Ayla, it wasn't like that. He and Zalina just asked about you that was all. They seemed curious more than anything else. I didn't know what they were planning, please believe me. I am your friend. Do you know how hard it is to trust someone in Dambar? The palace guard is a nest of deceit, disloyalty and back-stabbing– literally sometimes. It was wonderful to meet someone without an ulterior motive.'

"I want to escape, that's an ulterior motive."

"I know. That's what all the fuss is about, isn't it?"

"What are you going to do about it?"

"Prove my friendship. Go, I didn't see you, I'll delay the search as long as possible, but sooner or later Zalina will discover you're missing and we'll have to come looking. I don't know what you're planning, and I don't want to. You know it won't be pretty if Zalina catches you."

"She'll get me eventually if I stay. I'm just not cut out to be one of Percival's concubines."

"No, it's not for everyone, is it?" Aurelia grinned.

"I'll kill myself before I let them take me," Ayla said revealing the knife tucked into her waist-sash.

Aurelia drew her own razor-sharp stiletto and Ayla braced, ready to challenge.

"No, you won't" Aurelia smiled. "It's not your way, but I bet you'll go down fighting. Take my dagger. It'll be of more use. Now go, before we're spotted."

They embraced, Ayla's lips brushed Aurelia's cheek, and she was gone.

The palace guard captain was not the only one drawn to the midnight disturbance. Duchess Zalina heard the uproar and was in the mood to mete out punishment. She spotted Aurelia and trailed her to the seraglio steps, quickly ducking out of sight when Ayla appeared. Although they spoke in whispers, Zalina was close enough to eavesdrop and emerged from the alcove that had concealed her after the two women parted. The barbarian woman could wait, so she followed Aurelia.

Ayla kept to the shadowy alley-ways left unattended now the palace guard had been decoyed to the seraglio. But, in the dark wall-lined streets, finding her way was proving difficult. The very dimness that protected her was also confusing and she feared she'd lose her way. She dodged a night patrol and, other than a few vagrants, no one was about. She quizzed one bleary individual, who stank of booze and inadequate personal hygiene, but he thought she was a reincarnation of his dead wife. He was so surprised he promised to mend his drunken ways at once, which although gratifying, was hardly useful. Her next encounter was with a lone, tipsy, off-duty soldier who gave her directions and offered to escort her. She politely refused saying she was on an errand for Duchess Zalina and hurried on with a knife ready in each hand, but he didn't follow her.

As she expected, the doorway to the cells was guarded by two cohort troopers, neither of whom had been recruited for their intelligence. However, she was at a loss as to how to get past them. Her opportunity arose almost immediately when one sentry ambled away to the shadows followed by the splash of liquid on cobblestones. With no time to waste, she boldly approached the remaining guard.

"I have a message from her grace, Duchess Zalina. Open the door please."

"It's a bit late, ain't it?"

"The duchess doesn't keep regular hours. I just do what I'm told, and you'd better do the same if you know what's good for you."

"Where's your authority. I gotta see the royal mark."

It was unlikely many of the cohort troops could read, but they all recognised the Duke's seal stamped onto their orders. Without it, he would have to check, and she had no time for that. Her advantage was that he was half asleep and unsuspecting. She drove Aurelia's stiletto to the hilt through his neck, severing his jugular. To make sure, she wrenched the knife free and stabbed him again. He dropped his spear and slumped to the ground. He died instantly, but the clatter as he hit cobblestones alerted his companion. Ayla heard his hurrying footsteps. There was no time to draw the dead man's sword so she grabbed his spear, turned, and drove it into the second sentry's belly, killing him with his own body momentum as he ran onto the point.

Sorry, boys, wrong place at the wrong time, but desperation makes savages of us all. I've had enough of being pushed around by Dambar louts.

Ayla wasted no time. There was nothing she could do about the sentries and two dead soldiers lying in the street were going to draw attention sooner rather than later. She edged the heavy wooden door open and squeezed through the crack. The gaol was dimly lit with torches along the walls, but after the darkness outside her eyes adjusted easily as she assessed her options. The caged prisoners all appeared asleep as did the turnkey's two assistants, who were both slumped over a table beside their wine jugs. Keys hung on a rack behind the sleeping gaolers.

Good, nice and peaceful, now for those keys.

She crept forward, but stopped suddenly as the turnkey stepped from a shadowy alcove and grabbed her, cruelly digging his fingers into her arm. She gasped, frozen to the spot.

"Well, missy," he leered. "Whatcha doin' here? One of them harem sluts come down to try a bit of rough, are yer?"

His foul breath hissed in her ear, but she smiled and fluttered her eye-lashes coyly.

"Oh, it's so boring at the palace, and the duke, well…"

As her knee slammed into his groin, he doubled over, gagging on his mucus-filled vomit. Ayla took no chances and slashed the sentry's sword across the turnkey's face, shattering his cheekbone to crimson pulp. He thumped to the stone slabs but still writhed around, so she struck him again, ensuring his silence.

You, I'm not sorry about! I know a worthless piece of trash when I see one.

Her heart stopped when one of the minders stirred, but he simply belched and slept on. She cut the keys from the turnkey's belt and it didn't take long to locate Gareth. Archer was awakened by the scuffle and saw her approaching.

"Ayla," he hissed, "we're over here."

There were some anxious moments as she tried several keys before finding the right one and throwing the door open. The prisoners surged out without a word while Ayla clung to Gareth.

Serlequin and Kimball neutralised the two heavies, clubbing them senseless with some of the torture instruments at hand. Archer took the keys and opened all the cells embedded along the passageways, encouraging anyone fit enough to join the breakout. He was surprised how many men were held captive as their numbers swelled to over fifty. Many armed themselves with swords, spears and axes from the prison arms racks; others made use of anything heavy, blunt or sharp that came to hand.

"There's another sword and spear outside," Ayla gasped, "I had to deal with a couple of guards."

"Impressive," Gareth said. "You never cease to amaze me."

He'd never been more proud of her, but there wasn't time to reflect. It was time to leave.

"That's not the only surprise I've got for you if we ever get out of here," she said with a wink.

They gathered their weapons from the discarded pile, fretting about the neglect, but they'd just have to make do with what they had.

"And they call us barbarians," Gareth muttered. "No respect for good craftsmanship at all."

There were also enough surplus weapons, including a dozen shields, to adequately arm the remaining escapees.

"Now, let's find a way out of here," he said. "Bring some torches to light the way."

The duke was not a happy man. He was ready to retire when the trouble started and now he was seated in his throne room instead of been snuggled under the sheets with a couple of his favourites. Zalina sat beside him and Count Maslovaric stood in his usual place. Aurelia knelt before him flanked by a pair of palace guardswomen.

"This is all very disturbing," the duke whined, "I so dislike being disturbed. What are we to do about the seraglio, my dear?"

"A few cane cuts across all their bare bottoms should pull the little strumpets into line," Zalina suggested with relish as the duke nodded absently.

"And what about this one?" he asked, having heard the whole story from Zalina.

Betrayal by one of his guards was far more disturbing than any wayward antics from his harem. He was unhappy and disappointed rather than angry. He genuinely liked Aurelia.

"What do you have to say for yourself? This is very serious indeed…"

"I've told you everything," Zalina butted in, "She disobeyed my orders. There can only be one punishment."

"Yes, yes, but let the girl speak in her defence."

"I took pity on her," Aurelia whispered.

"Really," Zalina pounced. "It is not your place to pity anyone. You have disobeyed me and that is an end to it. Is that not so, your grace?"

The duke looked truly pained and stared at the crown of Aurelia's bowed head.

"I'm sorry," he said. "See to it if you please, Count."

Ducal justice in Dambar was summary, swift and acute, but Maslovaric had a final, cruel ace to play. He was well aware of Aurelia's relationship with Jagar and now the subaltern stood at attention, his face ashen and glistening with sweat. Maslovaric detested intimacy in the ranks, it was bad for discipline and a damn nuisance all round. It was high time to set an example. If it wasn't for Zalina's vagaries he'd get rid of the guardswomen altogether.

"Kill her, subaltern," Maslovaric hissed. "Now!"

Jagar hesitated.

"What are you waiting for?" Zalina purred. No one kept secrets from her in the palace and she too knew that Jagar was Aurelia's lover. It was just the sort of emotional anguish that delighted her.

Jagar had no choice but to march in front of Aurelia pressing the spear point lightly over her heart, as his chest heaved in grief and trepidation. She raised her pleading eyes welling with tears.

"Quickly, beloved," she whispered. "I know you have the skill and I shall suffer little. This way one of us will live. Farewell, my love, please hurry before my courage fails."

Jagar's grip tightened on the spear as he pulled the point away from Aurelia and, spinning on his heels, he hurled the missile with all his strength straight at Duchess Zalina. The point impaled her heart, dragging it through her backbone. At such short range the force completely buried the spear haft into Zalina's breast with the quivering point protruding behind her throne. Her heart dangled from the lance, pulsated a few times before stopping as Zalina's sightless eyes gazed ahead and the last breath gasped from her gaping mouth.

No one moved, not even Maslovaric.

"I say," Percival blurted, "was that meant for me?"

Jagar grabbed Aurelia's arm and shoving the guardswomen aside they bolted from the throne room.

For once, Maslovaric stood as dumb-struck as the duke. Neither of them was particularly sorry to see the last of Zalina, and each secretly breathed a sigh of relief that they weren't Jagar's target. The count admitted he was lucky to be standing slightly behind the duke's throne, which was probably all that saved him. "If you'll excuse me, your grace, I'd better rouse a company of the cohort and round 'em up."

"Alive, if possible, my dear count," Percival said. "We'll have to set an example of course, something public and befitting."

"As you wish, your grace. I will deal with it personally."

And he swept from the room.

Gareth took stock of his army, all of whom agreed they'd rather die in battle than return to slavery. Ebony Vy knew many of them and others said they were captured from far away Palo Innes. There was no time to fill them in on the fate of their prince, they had to keep moving and hope to be away into the desert before dawn where, hopefully, tribesmen would help them. Ebony Vy explained that although the cohort had a company of cavalry, they were essentially a plodding, infantry unit.

They ran into two night-watch patrols that only numbered four or five men each and were easily overwhelmed. Their main problem was no one knew their way to the main gate. They'd killed or maimed everyone in their path and not thought to ask. So Gareth ordered his men to capture the next person who came along and use them as a guide. He was starting to worry that no one would show up, when they bumped headlong into Jagar and Aurelia. To everyone's surprise, Ayla and Aurelia rushed into each other's arms and clung together as if their lives depended on it.

"Beats me," Gareth shrugged, staring Jagar down. "Why,

you're the young whelp from the pit, ain't you?"

"Yeah, sorry about that. Orders are orders I guess, but now I'm in deeper trouble than you ever were."

"Oh, really?"

"I just killed the duchess."

Information was exchanged in a couple of brief sentences.

"Ayla, I never thought you'd do it," Aurelia gushed, "but Zalina found out and wanted to kill me. Jagar saved my life and we're on the run too."

"Join the club," Jongarrat muttered.

"Maslovaric thinks he's only after Ayla and us," Jagar said. "He doesn't know about the breakout yet, but it won't be long before he calls out the entire cohort. I'll lead the way."

"Can we trust him?" Jongarrat asked.

"I do," Ayla said.

"Have you got a better idea," Gareth asked. "Lead on, Jagar."

"We'll go through the catacombs," Jagar said.

"Tunnels?"

"There's a network of sewer channels under the city with access ducts for slaves to use when clearing blockages. It's cold, wet and stinks, but we won't meet anyone and there's a passageway that comes out close to the main gate. Come on, there's an entry point in the next street."

Count Maslovaric soon realised that two platoons were not enough to scour the city for three fugitives. He wasn't particularly worried about Ayla, she'd turn up somewhere, but Jagar and Aurelia knew every corner of Dambar and who knows where they'd go to ground. It was time to raise the hue-and-cry and assemble more troops, especially when he came across a night watchman who staggered towards him with a rag pressed to the side of his head, staunching the blood flowing from his severed ear. The trooper collapsed at Maslovaric's feet. His eyes blazing in terror, but not because he'd just escaped a massacre. He was about to give the count bad news, which he never received well.

"Lord," the wretched man stammered, "prisoners have broken out of the dungeon. They're rampaging through the city killing everyone."

"And you couldn't manage that rabble?" Maslovaric growled.

"They're no rabble, lord. They seem to be under orders and fight like demons. That big, red-headed fellow from the pit leads them. He sliced my ear off and the others trampled over me thinking I was dead."

To one-ear's surprise Maslovaric's didn't seem angered by the news, but simply interested to embrace a new challenge. He was a hard man to understand.

"Gareth, eh? It appears he's a worthy adversary after all," the count said, turning to his officers. "Rouse the whole garrison and get them over to the main gate and secure the postern. No prizes for guessing where that scum's heading. Take this fellow to the surgeon and tell him to gather his assistants, we'll have business for them tonight no doubt. Send a runner to the gates and warn them. Someone advise his grace I've declared martial law and the city is in lock-down!"

Illuminated by torchlight, the fugitives sloshed through the tunnels, which were every bit as disagreeable as Jagar predicted. For most of the time, they travelled on raised walkways, but in places they waded knee-deep in effluent-laden slush that rushed under the city. They reached a set of steps that led upwards to a wide, stone passage that opened into a square where the main gates stood about fifty paces ahead. Two wooden bars held the gates shut from the inside and once the gates were opened, they'd need to raise an iron portcullis from a mechanism in one of the towers beside the portal. The gate was designed to keep attackers out, but was equally efficient at keeping people in; it was also brightly lit by a dozen torches and several glowing braziers. To complicate matters, a full platoon of heavily-armed guards patrolled the gate and the walls above. They all carried loaded crossbows and were relieved every hour so they remained alert and ready.

"How do we get across there and deal with them?" Archer asked. "We'll lose too many if we rush 'em headlong."

"I'll have to try and divert them," Jagar said, "They won't know I'm a wanted man yet."

Aurelia wanted to go with him, but he explained the duke's personal guard rarely ventured from the inner palace walls and her presence might arouse suspicion. While the fugitives hid in the passage shadows, Jagar crossed the courtyard to the gates. The sentries snapped to attention and Jagar began to speak and, although Gareth couldn't make out what was being said, it seemed to be complicated. The guards were asking questions so Jagar's story–whatever it was–didn't appear to convince them. Ultimately it didn't matter when they heard the thump of marching feet and two full companies tramped from separate directions towards the gate.

"Arrest that man!" yelled the leading officer, confusing the sentries. They knew and respected Jagar, who took the opportunity to bolt back to the fugitives while the cohort formed in ranks barring any way through the gate. Gareth, Archer, and Jongarrat still hugged the shadows of the passageway remaining unseen, but they had a clear view of the main gate. The remaining escapees grew restless in the dark, but Kimball and Serlequin kept them in order.

"Damn, they were quick," Jagar panted, "but there's no way out now."

"What about over the wall?" Gareth said.

"Too high, we'd break every bone in our bodies. We don't have ropes."

"Another gate?"

"There is a postern on the far side of the city, but it is small and easily defended. If the guards are here, they'll also have blocked that exit too. We'll never get this number of people through, it'd be slaughter."

"We're trapped then?" Gareth surmised.

At that moment Count Maslovaric led two more companies into the square. Now troops not only blocked the gate, but also any escape into the city side streets and alleys.

Squire Redbone says
The Dambar Cohort is nothing but a big armadillo.
Whatever that is.
Trouble is we'll never break through
a solid shield wall anyway.

Even if we did, I don't like our chances in
hand-to-hand combat
What was it Archer said? –
'beat you enemy anyway you can.
Be sly and have conviction.'
Conviction we've got, so we'll just have to think of
something sly.

Chapter 28
Spies

The journey south through Unab was uneventful, except for frequent training sessions to hone the villagers' fighting skill that improved remarkably as their confidence and fitness developed. The dwarves were naturally warlike and proved good instructors. The battalion often sighted horsemen who usually kept their distance and appeared curious rather than hostile. Redbone went to meet one group, returning with Gunthred Vy and a dozen riders. After the preliminary civility, the nomad leader confirmed that Ayla had been taken to Dambar and Gareth was after her, although he'd lost track of the peninsula men when a wild dust storm swept through the southern desert. The name Count Maslovaric kept recurring. He was the man to deal with; he ran Dambar; he was as mean as a snake; don't trust him for a moment; don't turn your back on him for a second. The nomads joined Henry's battalion as they travelled by moonlight and rested in the heat of the day, but gave no indication that they intended to become allies. Gunthred Vy obviously thought there was safety enough in numbers for him to now approach Dambar.

"Will the tribes unite against Maslovaric?" Henry asked as they sheltered under makeshift canvases.

"Unlikely," Gunthred Vy admitted. "Each tribe has its individual grievances with Dambar, but in truth we spend more time fighting each other than the cohort. They'll most likely tag along at a distance and see which way the wind blows."

When they reached a ridge overlooking Dambar, it was some hours before dawn and the city stood as a mighty silhouette against the waning moon dotted with specks of light from the sentries' torches.

"Right, get some rest," Henry called, and everyone collapsed pretty much where they stood. They were expert at erecting shelters against the morning sun by then and soon the army was bedded down. There was no wood for fires, so breakfast would be dried meat and stale bread, but their water supply was lasting well.

"So, we're here," Anvil Cornfoot said matter-of-factly. "What now?"

"Find out where Lady Ayla is and negotiate her release, I guess. It's a pity we haven't run into Chief Gareth."

"You have to consider he may not have made it this far," Edrid said, immediately regretting the hasty words when he saw Macayle's alarm. "But he's probably inside the city doing the ground work for us right now," he added hastily.

"Best to reconnoitre first," Redbone suggested.

"Good idea, I'll take Julian if you and Edrid can keep everyone behind the ridgeline out of sight. They need the rest and we shouldn't take more than a day."

There was no objection, having reached Dambar, no one was in a hurry to go barging in until they knew what they faced. Everyone turned in, except Macayle, who stood staring at the city. Edrid joined her and gently placed his right arm around her shoulder. She tensed for just a second then relaxed and leant against him.

"Sorry," he said, "I wasn't very sensitive. I'm sure your dad'll be fine. I mean, it's not like he's a sissy or anything."

She smiled as she took his hand.

"We're going into the city," she announced.

"Are we? Henry will never allow that, it might be dangerous."

"Henry won't know and anyway, when do I have to do what Henry says? I'm the chief's daughter, not him."

"He'll be mad."

"No doubt, but you'll stand up to him. You'll have to show some gumption if you think you're going to marry me."

"Marry...?"

She turned and kissed him in a long, passionate embrace.

"Of course, silly. Do keep up," she whispered. "But, just watch where you put that spike, big boy."

They waited until the camp was asleep then packed food and water and a small purse of coppers the Palo Innes folk had looted at Glam and shared out. They saddled Gwen and walked until they were well clear before Edrid mounted and Macayle leapt astride behind him. They cantered towards the city. Anvil Cornfoot heard them go, but did nothing to stop them, deciding they were as good at spying as anyone. He'd wait a while before telling Henry though.

Edrid and Macayle reined up some distance in front of the main gate. They pulled their hair up and tied it under their cloak mantles. A fiery redhead and blond hair stood out in a sea of black, so they thought it best to keep their crowns from view. Most Unab travellers stayed well covered as protection against the sun's fury anyway. It was daybreak when they reached Dambar and a number of people had gathered around the gate protesting to be let in. They all claimed to be legitimate traders and delays were bad for business. A guard yelled from the battlement that the gate would be closed all day and they must go around the city wall to the postern. So they trooped around Dambar's perimeter and finally came to a small, single gate where a queue formed as soldiers questioned everyone. By the time Edrid and Macayle reached the gates the guards were bored and careless. They dismounted and led Gwen forward.

"What seems to be the trouble?" Edrid asked when ordered to stop.

"Riot in the city," the sentry replied, "Some slaves are running amok. What's your business anyway?"

"I'm a trader from the north."

"I don't see nothin' to trade."

"Just a fact-finding mission, my friend, checking out local markets, you know. I have a caravan under guard on its way, but I thought I'd come along ahead with my servant and investigate any possible opportunities."

"Your timing's bad then. With all the unrest in the city, the markets are disrupted, but I don't think it'll last long and things'll be back to normal. Good luck then."

Edrid nodded his thanks. Macayle glared at him as they passed through the postern

"Servant," she hissed, "I'll give you servant, you great lummox."

"You know you're beautiful when you're mad," Edrid grinned.

They stabled Gwen at an inn close to the postern, as it looked like they'd travel faster on foot through Dambar's congested streets. Edrid thought it wise to keep the horse near the gate in case they needed a quick get-away. They had no difficulty finding their way to the main portal; the slave rebellion was on everyone's lips. Townsfolk were either rushing as far away from trouble as they could, or heading towards it to see the fun. Watching the cohort make mincemeat of a bunch of rebels was as good as a show at the pit any day. It proved a struggle, but Edrid and Macayle finally pushed their way to a vantage point. They couldn't stand there for long. Cohort officers tired of the crowd's distraction and sent detachments of troops to move everyone on. Taking advantage of the confusion, the two spies ducked behind a produce-wagon to wait for the square to clear. The plaza emptied except for three ranks of troops standing before them, led by a resplendently dressed officer. He marched towards a tunnel opening a few yards away.

"Gareth," Maslovaric called (Macayle's heart skipped). "I know you're in there, so here's the deal. You can't stay holed up in there forever, unless you really like eating rats. You might as well give up. I've sent masons to brick up all the catacomb entrances; this is the only way out. I'm not going to waste men down there (an audible sigh through the cohort ranks). We'll just wait it out until you starve to death."

"You'll kill us anyway, Maslovaric," Gareth yelled from the tunnel (Macayle's heart skipped again). Her father's ensuing tirade would have normally caused her to blush, but not now.

"That's your dad all right," Edrid whispered. "Looks like a stalemate, we'd better get back to let Henry know."

"You go," Macayle said, "I'll stay and keep an eye on things here."

"Are you mad?"

"I've got water and some food, I'll be fine. If anything happens, I can sneak back and warn you. No one will see me, I promise."

He wasn't happy, but he knew how stubborn she could be (and he still wanted to marry her), but she had a point. Someone had to report back to Henry and having a spy inside the walls made sense. It was a simple matter to get lost in the throng, so moving through the city undetected wasn't a problem. He heaved a sigh, squeezed her hand and slipped unnoticed into an alley and made his way back to the inn without further trouble.

Edrid paid for the stable and rode to the postern. Details of the rebellion had spread and the guards were not as amiable or casual as before. One strode in front of Edrid and ordered him to stop.

"Leaving so soon?" the sentry queried. "It's as hot as blazes out in the open this time of day.'"

"I think I'll come back when things have settled down," Edrid replied.

"Fair enough, but I've got to search everyone leaving. It's the count's orders."

"As you see, I have nothing," Edrid declared spreading his arms, revealing his sword. There was nothing suspicious about that, many Dambar citizens carried arms, but his mantle slipped slightly revealing just enough of his blond hair to attract attention.

"Hey, you got yella hair. You're one of them damned slaves," the guard cried. "Pull yer hood back and let's have a look at yer."

The guard rushed him, but Edrid booted him clear and dug his heels into Gwen's flank. The animal wasn't a trained saddle horse, but only bucked once before bounding through the postern where another guard charged with a raised spear. Edrid clung to the reins and was unable to draw his sword to deflect the lance, which caught in his hook. Pain screamed up his arm as he wrenched free and slashed at the trooper's face. The man howled and fell to his knees, clutching his wounded cheek seeping blood from a scar he'd be able to brag about to his grandchildren. A volley of crossbow bolts whistled past, but Edrid was out of range before the sentries had time to reload.

"Arrest that man!" an officer yelled, and a platoon of men raced through the postern, but soon returned as they had no chances of catching even a draft horse. The guard commander sent word to the palace stables, where a troop of cavalry hastily leapt astride their thoroughbreds and clattered into the streets of Dambar. Edrid was half a league away when they thundered through the postern, but Gwen was tiring in the oppressive heat. Edrid thought he was safely away and dismounted, until he noticed a cloud of dust coming from the city. He clambered back into the saddle.

"Come on, old girl," he urged the horse. "Not far now."

But Gwen proved recalcitrant and refused to move. She was going no further however hard Edrid dug his heels into her flanks. He could make a run for it, but knew he'd be overtaken on foot.

"You nag," he yelled. "If you don't budge I'll eat you, I promise!"

Gwen was unimpressed and simply stayed put as the cavalry swept up the ridge behind him.

"I'm sorry, but I warned you," Edrid said, once again using the hook, he stabbed the animal's rump. She reared and whined, but lurched forward in an unsteady canter. The wound wasn't serious but left blood droplets staining the sand in their wake. The troopers were coming fast and the distance between them rapidly closed. They carried short bows rather than crossbows and soon a volley of arrows flashed towards Edrid. The arrows thwacked into the sand around Gwen's hooves. She baulked and slowed just as another arrow dug into her shoulder. The poor animal's foreleg gave way and she crashed forward, sending Edrid tumbling. He scrambled to his feet, spitting sand with grit stinging his eyes. He raced back to Gwen wallowing in a sand drift struggling to regain her feet. Edrid grabbed the reins trying to coax the beast up, but fumbled with only one hand.

Dammit Henry, you'd better come up with something more useful than this wretched hook!

But, by then it was too late. The troopers were almost upon him.

"Take him alive," their sergeant yelled. "The count'll want to question him."

Edrid had other ideas. Drawing his sword, he crouched, ready to meet them head on. The troopers slowed to a trot, then a walk, and almost casually surrounded Edrid.

"Give it up," the sergeant said. "That nag's done for; you might just as well come quietly."

"You'll have to kill me first," Edrid hissed.

The sergeant shrugged.

"Have it your own way then," he said turning to the trooper beside him. "Shoot him; one slave dead or alive probably won't make any difference to the count anyway."

The man raised his bow, but his horse reared just as he released the arrow. Bron had come from nowhere and latched onto the animal's fetlock. The trooper was nearly tossed off and the shot flew wide. The horse bucked again as Bron leapt clear of its hooves, leaving bleeding teeth marks.

"Trouble is, he's not a slave," a calm voice said as an arrow drove into the sergeant's shoulder and he slumped in his saddle, clutching the half-buried shaft. Henry stalked over the ridge nocking a second arrow. Otillie, the dwarves, and the entire battalion followed. A pair of troopers fell to arrows as the others wrenched at the reins, turned their horses, and galloped away. Another tumbled from the saddle just before they were out of range. A band of tribesmen appeared to the cavalry's flank and galloped towards them, but were too far away to intercept the retreating horsemen and gave up the chase.

Otillie and Redbone rescued Gwen and gave her a drink. Her injuries proved superficial after they extracted the arrowhead, while Henry checked Edrid for damage.

"Are you all right?" Henry cried. "Where's Macayle? What the blazes were you thinking, you idiot?"

"I'm fine, she's okay. She's still safely hidden in the city, and boy, have I got news for you."

Edrid explained the situation within the city.

"We have to rescue our people," Henry said, and there was no argument there, but there was one insurmountable obstacle.

"Big problem, Henry," Edrid said. "Maslovaric'll know we're here once those troopers get back to Dambar. How are we going to get through the gate?"

"That mightn't be an issue"' Gunthred Vy advised. "If I know the count, his pride and arrogance won't let him leave you outside the city. He'll bring the cohort to you."

"Are we strong enough to meet him?" Henry asked.

The nomad chief shrugged.

"You'll need a plan," he said.

"I've got an idea and those crossbows of yours are our secret weapon."

"The cohort has crossbows too."

"Yes, but I'm sure you're much better shots."

All quiet at the gates of Dambar.
Count Maslovaric is pacing in front of his troops.
He's not a patient man.
He will deal with the rebels himself
although his subordinates are quite capable
of handling a few miscreants.
He wants to be present when justice is administered.
and he'll wait it out unless…

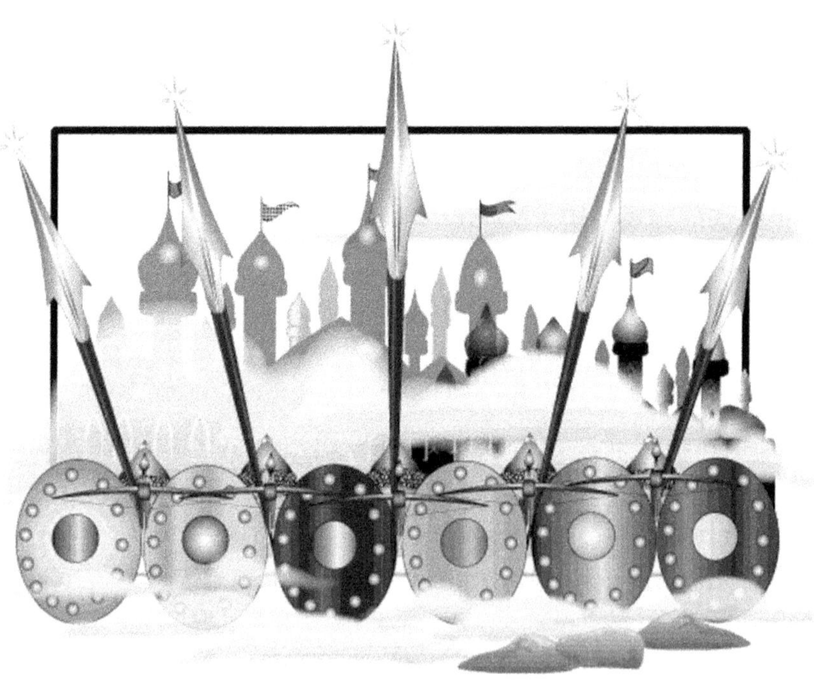

Chapter 29
Cohort

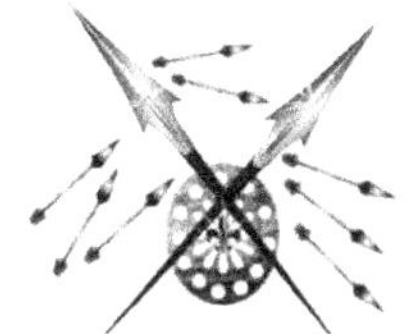

It wasn't long before the city burghers sent a delegation to Duke Percival complaining that the city lock-down was ruining their businesses and that it was high time he and the count dealt with the matter. The duke, who tended to agree with the last person he spoke with, ordered a sedan chair to carry him to the main gate. He was accompanied by a detachment of his guardswomen. Reaching the gate, he ordered Maslovaric to get on with it.

"We'll smoke 'em out then," Maslovaric said, turning to his officers. "Find some wagons and fill them with straw, rubbish, horse dung if need be; anything that'll burn."

A platoon was sent foraging, but it would be some time before they gathered sufficient material for the job. Eventually, three wagonloads of anything combustible were drawn up in front of the tunnel. The rebels might just retreat further into the catacombs, but with all the entrances walled up, it wasn't going to be pleasant. Smoke was already swirling from the wagons and drifting into the tunnel. His soldiers were reluctant to get too close to the entrance and Maslovaric was about to threaten bastinado when a sentry hailed from the battlements above the gate.

"Patrol coming, my lord, I think you should see this."

Maslovaric heaved a what-now sigh and marched up the spiral steps beside the gatehouse to the battlement ramparts. It irritated him when the duke followed and, now he was here, Percival seemed to be taking an uncharacteristic interest in town security. The patrol clattered to a halt below the portcullis, demanding to be let in, but it was the view beyond that drew Maslovaric's attention. An army of several hundred men and women marched on Dambar. They may not have been particularly uniform, but they were all well-armed and advanced with a determined confidence that troubled the count. He saw the troop sergeant bore an arrow-wound, and three riderless horses milled around behind the patrol.

"Might be a rag-tag lot, but they look ready for business," Maslovaric said, "and damned if there ain't a bunch of those pygmies with 'em. They're small, but I know they can fight if that's what they've come for."

"Open the gates and let those fellows in," the duke said.

"What?" Maslovaric snapped.

"You heard me, let the troopers in, then take the cohort and shoo those people away." Percival insisted. "They are unsightly and I do so dislike unsightliness."

"And the slaves in the catacombs?"

"Forget about them, my ladies will stand guard until you get back. I shall send to the palace for reinforcements."

Maslovaric could manipulate Percival on most occasions, but he knew the duke could be stubborn and even prone to tantrums. Best quickly scatter the rabble at the gate, then sort out the escapees.

"Very well, your grace," Maslovaric said. "Open the gate!"

In the gatehouse, men hauled on chains and oiled pulleys as the portcullis clanked upwards. Another team removed the massive locking bars and pushed the gates open. Maslovaric issued orders and the cohort tramped out of Dambar. The cavalry patrol dismounted and joined the ranks, leaving their wounded sergeant to stagger into the city to find medical attention.

Macayle witnessed the scene in disbelief, but knew time was vital. She'd heard an officer send a messenger to bring all available guardswomen to the gate, so she must act before they arrived. In the hustle and excitement no one noticed her creep from cover, edge along a wall, and dash behind the wagons cluttering the tunnel entrance. She was instantly blinded as she rushed into darkness. It would take a few minutes for her eyes to adjust and the smoke didn't help, so she stopped before she blundered into anything.

Gareth saw a silhouetted figure through the haze in the tunnel mouth against the outside sunlight and thought an attack was imminent.

"To arms, men," he whispered. "I think the fight is on."

There was a clatter of weapons and the rebels advanced. Gareth raised Goresax to strike the first attacker who stood as a featureless shadow before him.

"Daddy, where are you?" Macayle cried.

He lowered the blade, his palms sweating as he realised he'd nearly killed his daughter.

What was she doing here? And she only called him "daddy" when she was really frightened or wanted to twist him around her little finger.

Ayla rushed passed Gareth and clung to Macayle, but there was no time for tears, hugs or kisses. Macayle couldn't speak for a moment after discovering her mother, if not safe, at least well. It was baffling, but explanations would have to wait.

"You have to leave now," Macayle blurted. "The gates are open... Henry has an army outside... Must join up with him… More guards are on the way... We don't have time to spare... The troops are moving out to meet Henry… Hurry...I love you...oh… I'm going to marry Edrid..."

"Henry, how did he get here? How did you get here?"

"Marry Edrid?" Ayla said.

"Nice boy," Gareth explained, "but, we'll talk about it later."

Now that his family was together, nothing was going to stop Chief Gareth. He turned to his rebels.

"Men with shields to the front, everyone else fall in behind. Form a shield-wall once we're in the open. Straight through the gates and kill anything that gets in our way.'

With a roar of battle cries the rebels surged from the tunnel, pushing the blazing wagons aside. They provided an effective smoke-screen and the rebels took full advantage of it. The shield wall was met by a few crossbow bolts that hammered into wood and iron, but caused no injuries. Jagar, Aurelia, and Archer protected one flank while Kimball, Serlequin, and Jongarrat held the other. They swept the guardswomen aside, who were outnumbered, choking in the smoke, and confused when they saw their ex-captain and a cohort officer charging past. So the rebels surged out of Dambar onto the plains beyond.

Henry led his battalion towards the city, but called a halt a quarter of a league short of the wall when they saw the cohort stream through the gate. The troops fanned out in two long ranks, but their numbers were less than Henry had imagined. Once formed, they slowly advanced as a solid barrier of shields. Henry formed his people in three ranks: crossbows in front, bowmen next, and the remaining horde stretching in a line behind.

"We're about evenly matched," he said to no one in particular.

"I'd say so," Edrid agreed. "So what's your plan, colonel?"

"Negotiate first…"

"And if that doesn't work?"

"I'm still working on that."

"We'll not breach that shield wall," Anvil Cornfoot observed.

"Then we'll have to out-manoeuvre them. They're cumbersome and inflexible. Tell everyone to drink plenty of water," Henry ordered, remembering his thirst after his first battle. "It's going to be hot work and we might have to do some running. Our bowmen are in position. That's Maslovaric leading them, isn't it?"

Gunthred Vy nodded.

"Then I'd better go and talk to him. Remember, have the archers ready."

He turned to his army.

"Take heart," he yelled, "remember you've proved yourselves before. Freedom isn't a right; you must defend it all the time. There's always someone who wants to take it from you unless you fight them off."

"Very inspirational," Edrid muttered as a roar rose from the rebels.

The two forces halted fifty paces apart and Henry stepped forward to meet Count Maslovaric, who came straight to the point.

"I'm a busy man. I really don't have time for this," he snarled. "Why are you here?"

"I'm Henry of Hollowford and I've come to get my chief, Gareth, his wife Ayla, and all the northern folk you're holding prisoner."

"Well, Henry of Hollowford, what if I choose not to do that?"

"You'll regret it."

"What, from that lot?" Maslovaric waved dismissively at Henry's people.

"They've fought before and won. Don't under-estimate them."

"You think a rabble can beat my trained soldiers?"

"Soldiers? They're just gaol-sweepings and gutter-trash who can't make a living any other way. They're not so good, when push comes to shove."

There was a certain element of truth in Henry's claim, although it was a bold bluff nevertheless. Henry'd had enough of this man he'd only known for a few minutes. He was the source of all Henry's trouble. Druid Urdec, Olag Black Axe, Crag Daniek, and the Starkmen were all small-fry, just links in a sinister chain. Maslovaric was the puppet-master. He'd caused the deaths of Otillie's dad and Anshelm. He was responsible for Edrid's missing hand. He was to blame for all that misery and Henry's blood ran hot. He was plain sick-and-tired of it.

"Best case is you'll lose a lot of men," Henry continued calmly, despite his rage. "It'd be much easier to just give us what we want."

Maslovaric considered for a moment. A few slaves here and there wouldn't make much difference. He needed to quickly return the city to normal to satisfy the duke and his infernal merchants, who were easy enough to manipulate individually, but could be difficult as a group. However, there was a principle involved. Here he was being faced down by a stripling who irritated him immeasurably, but possibly provided an answer.

"Tell you what," Maslovaric said, "there's no need for a bloodbath. I challenge you to fight it out man-to-man. Just you and me. You win; you get the prisoners. I win; your lot shove off and never bother me again."

Henry hesitated. "Very well," he agreed.

"Are you mad?" Edrid hissed in his ear. "Do you honestly think you can beat him? You can't trust him an inch."

"Maybe, maybe not, but can he trust me?"

Henry and Maslovaric were about evenly matched in strength and stature while Henry's skill-at-arms had developed with plenty of match-practice. Impossibly rash maybe, but Henry was undaunted by Maslovaric, and how good was he anyway? No one had actually seen him fight, although Redbone seemed pretty sure the count was a master swordsman.

"Just keep everyone alert and watch out for treachery," Henry added.

Maslovaric turned and handed his cloak to one of his officers.

"I'll play with the kid for a while, if he's not dead in five minutes, finish him off and the rest will scatter without a leader."

But Henry had ideas of his own, remembering what his mentor had taught him all those weeks ago. Sly and committed, Archer had said.

"Maslovaric!" Henry called.

The count turned and stared in horror as he saw Henry draw his bow string and release an arrow that slammed through Maslovaric's chest. Henry instantly nocked another arrow, aimed and shot the officer beside the dead count.

"Nice one, Henry," Edrid said, "I think you just started a war."

Anvil Cornfoot and Redbone also knew the battle was on, and there was no turning back now. Their eyes met for an instant as they exchanged nods.

"Second row, fire!" Anvil Cornfoot yelled and a hail of missiles lanced almost vertically skywards and showered death onto the cohort. The troops raised their shields to protect themselves from above.

"Front row fire!" Redbone bellowed.

The first rank was kneeling and armed with crossbows. They levelled the weapons about chest-high and aimed. A spray of deadly bolts sliced into the suddenly exposed cohort, just as Gareth and the rebels slammed into the undefended rear, causing bloody havoc. Normally the cohort would have closed ranks and formed a square, but with their leader dead they were in disarray, although some officers struggled to keep order. Even after the first two lethal archery volleys, the troops facing Henry's force still bristled with spears, making a frontal assault suicidal. When the rear ranks turned, they blocked Gareth's attack. It looked as if the cohort had regained control, until tribesmen struck from the sides. Ever the opportunists, they darted in at full gallop with scimitars flashing as they hacked into the cohort's unprotected flanks.

The fight dissolved into a rout as the cohort broke formation, their best defence, and fled back to Dambar. It was still a difficult business, tackling heavily armed and armoured men, and a number of former slaves fell after becoming too reckless. Gareth led half his party around one flank while Archer took the rest the other way to join Henry's battalion. They found him leading his people, who harried the cohort all the way to the gates and drove them through. Gone was the boy. Henry now stood in total control as a man doing serious damage with Hornet-Sting.

Gareth and Archer stared in disbelief.

"Long story!" Henry bellowed and even seemed to be enjoying the fight, so the peninsula men charged back into the melee. Macayle, sword in hand and feeling dangerous, saw Edrid and dashed to his side before they joined Otillie, Ayla, and Aurelia, added their contribution to the cohort's woes.

As the rebels forced their way into the city, Jagar spotted Duke Percival, who still stood on the ramparts.

"Gareth!" he bellowed over the clash of iron and screams of the victors and vanquished. "Take the gate house. Stop them lowering the portcullis!"

Both Gareth and Archer saw the danger. If the gate was closed with half the rebels inside the walls and half still outside, it spelt disaster. The cohort then had a chance to reform and turn on those trapped by the portcullis with no help from those on the other side. Kimball and Serlequin followed them, battering down the gate-house door, and slaughtering the guards within. There was no time for clemency. Archer jammed Skull-Crusher into the hoist mechanism, effectively locking it before following the others back to the confusion in the square. The cohort scattered through side streets, desperately seeking hiding places. The rebels were in danger of splintering into small groups to track them down. Archer and Gareth bellowed for everyone to stick together and stay in the square. Their strength lay in numbers; it was their only advantage, so the leaders regrouped the battalion and gave up the chase.

Henry had no idea who Jagar was, but with Bron at his heels, bolted after him to the rampart where the cohort officer proved why he'd been promoted. No one stood before him and Henry had little to do but follow in his wake. The duke nervously backed away as Jagar approached brandishing his falchion. He grabbed Percival's collar and pressed the sword point under his chin drawing a fleck of blood.

"Make me kill Aurelia, would you?" Jagar hissed.

"It was Zalina's idea… You saw that," Percival stammered. "Mercy… I didn't want to kill her."

"You could have stopped it…"

"Actually I wouldn't be in too much of a hurry to finish him off," Henry said. "I take it this is Duke Percival and no friend of yours."

"What of it?" Jagar snapped.

"Take a look; you might want a bit of leverage."

Sections of the palace guard poured into the square and along the ramparts. They were all armed with short bows and had arrows aimed into the milling rebels at the gate. A rather severe and nervous young officer held her arm aloft, ready to give the order to fire. Some of the rebels might escape through the gate, but it'd be a massacre.

"Wait!" Jagar roared. "Hold your fire or I swear I'll run Duke Percival through."

All heads turned to him and doubt crossed the young officer's face. In that moment of uncertainty, Aurelia stepped forward and stood before her. They spoke quietly for a few moments and the young guard commander relaxed and signalled her troops to lower their weapons. The two captains embraced as the guardswomen heaved a collective sigh of relief and the rebels erupted into cheers. The battle was over.

Jagar pushed Percival ahead of him and held his hand out to Henry who shook it firmly.

"Jagar, cohort lieutenant. Nice to meet you."

"Henry, rebel colonel it seems. The pleasure's all mine, I'm sure."

"Can you hold onto this fellow for me? If he gives any trouble, set your dog on him. I think I'm needed to help Aurelia and Gareth negotiate a truce."

"Hopefully a peace, and she's not a dog, she's a wolf," Henry said.

Jagar passed Otillie on the steps as she raced to Henry, wrapped her arms around him, and squeezed so tightly he could hardly breathe.

"We did it, Otillie," he gasped. "Thank you, you're wonderful. We couldn't have done it without you."

"Yes, we did, didn't we? Not bad for a couple of country bumpkins. You surprised us all, but I wouldn't have waited for Maslovaric to turn around. I'd have shot him in the back."

"I wanted him to see it coming."

"He was so arrogant. I don't think he believed anyone could beat him, silly man."

"I suppose someone will always come along who will beat you in the end."

Archer stomped to the rampart and slapped Henry's shoulder.

"Well done," he said, "I'm proud of you, boy."

"Boy?"

Archer grinned.

"I'm proud of you, Henry."

It's not going to be as it was, is it?
We see each other differently now.
Nothing will ever be the same again.

For good, bad or indifferent, I simply have no idea.
But I now know I will fight to the death
to defend our land.
And…I don't mean my death…

Chapter 30
Palo Innes

A battlefield is not an ideal venue for reunions. Indeed Jongarrat didn't meet his brother until after the rebels reorganised themselves. Gunthred Vy was unaware his son had taken part in the breakout and, although he was delighted to have the lad back, he cursed the duke for breaking his word and condemning Ebony Vy to the pit. Percival claimed he knew nothing about it and said Maslovaric was entirely to blame—but he would say that, wouldn't he? Jagar managed to stop the nomad chief killing Percival out of hand and he eventually calmed down. The tribesmen were disinterested once they realised they weren't going to get any loot out of the city and promptly bid the rebels good day. They returned in small groups to the desert.

Redbone and Anvil Cornfoot rather lost the big picture once they finally found Jongarrat. The dwarf contingent headed for the nearest inn and proceeded to drink it dry. There was little for them to do as dusk approached anyway. Jagar and Aurelia took charge and ordered the palace guard platoons to comb the city and round up any cohort troopers they found and return them to their barracks. Jagar insisted they were to be treated well, as he intended to reorganise all Dambar military into an effective defence unit and police force. He no longer wanted city dross in the cohort ranks, but motivated, loyal soldiers.

The rebels took over the palace and Ayla insisted Gareth take a bath and, after crawling around the catacombs, needed one herself. She took him to where she had first experienced seraglio life and posted a pair of eunuchs at the entrance to ensure complete privacy for a few hours. His reaction to her new-found smoothness remains unknown. The seraglio courtesans were free to go. Some returned to their families while others, who'd become used to luxury and didn't mind boredom, wished to stay. Although the duke no longer ruled, he was still a wealthy man.

"What are you going to do with Percival?" Archer asked Jagar.

"I think most folk are over the urge to kill him, he's pretty harmless if he stays out of bad company. We're going to send him on a trade mission to the east. He'll be away for at least a year or two, and travel broadens the mind. He can take any of his girls who want to go."

Dambar citizens took the invasion of their city with relief more than anything else. The burghers and merchants were not concerned with war or conquest, they were simply traders and only interested in commerce. They formed a city council and appointed Jagar and Aurelia as duke and duchess to run city security. One of their first tasks was to commission Redbone and a team of dwarf engineers to tackle the water supply. They developed a number of recycling methods using wind driven pumps, tree plantings, aqueducts, and more efficient individual usage.

A rebel delegation entered the mines and released the slaves, bringing all the surviving dwarves, Palo Innes folk, and Otillie's people back to Dambar. Some were weak and ill, but responded well to care and good food. They even discovered the missing Burgal children who were used in the tiniest crevices where no one else would fit. The emancipation of slaves proved less difficult than anyone expected. The city fathers formed a consortium to take over the mines and encouraged investors. Freed labourers were paid and given the choice whether they wished to stay or not. Working hours were halved and ample food provided. The sites were improved with accommodation proposed for miners and their families. The new owners claimed the system would be more profitable as the miners worked harder, especially for bonuses, and the overheads were less than the duke's old taxes. The mine guards were each given five years at the galley oars to reflect on their misdeeds.

After the rebels had occupied Dambar for a week, despite the luxury, it was time to leave. Gareth, along with everyone else, just wanted to go home.

"You're welcome to stay and help with the work here," Redbone said to Jongarrat.

"No, I'll head back to the peninsula. Guilda and I get along fine, I kind of miss her."

You can always come back home for a visit."

"I'd like that. I hope sailing suits me, because I ain't going over Zilek Gorge again."

Gareth returned the two medallions to Henry, who was now a rich man with three brooches, including the one he'd taken from Olag.

"You know, no one even noticed them all this time," Gareth said, "but they're yours, Henry. You earned them and so much more."

Henry thought of giving one to Macayle as a wedding gift, but Edrid had looted two from Maslovaric's cloak and presented one each to Macayle and Ayla. Technically they were Henry's as he'd killed the count, but Edrid had lost a hand and Henry didn't begrudge his friend for getting on the right side of his future mother-in-law. So he gave one to Otillie and would take another home for Thayer and, dammit, he'd keep one for himself.

Ayla had one task to perform before they left. Accompanied by Macayle and Otillie, she marched to Olgaric-y-Islad's house. The trader was packing ready to sneak off to Skinner's Landing and lie low for a few weeks. Ayla kicked his door open and the three women barged inside. Macayle and Otillie grabbed Olgaric, holding him rigid while Ayla pulled out Aurelia's stiletto.

"P…p…pweath…" the slaver begged supplemented by a measure of drool.

"I'm thinking we might put you to work in the seraglio, but first we'd have to ensure your behaviour. Just a quick snip should do it…"

Olgaric's face turned white and tears gushed down his cheeks, blubbering incoherently for mercy.

"Wouldn't make any difference, you're hardly a man anyway, you snivelling wretch. Lucky for you the harem has been abolished and the girls free to do what they please."

She slammed the knife into the floor between Olgaric's sandaled feet where a pool formed from the yellow stream flooding down his inside leg. Ayla held out her hand as Macayle slapped a pair of thick, falconry gauntlets into her palm. She deliberately pulled the gloves on and planted a vicious left jab onto Olgaric's nose followed by a right hook that landed with a crack across his face. Otillie and Macayle let the slaver drop with a broken nose and dislocated jaw. Ayla peeled the gauntlets from her hands and tossed them beside the trader who crawled to her feet begging forgiveness.

"Oh, show some backbone just for once," Ayla sighed. "Thank you ladies. I believe we're done here."

The three women strode through Olgaric's front door.

Jongarrat shook hands with his brother and they parted with a brief smile. Loaded with provisions, Henry and the battalion bade Jagar, Aurelia, and the dwarves, who were staying, goodbye before journeying north. Gwen wouldn't let Edrid anywhere near her and attempted a few sharp kicks. Edrid was quick enough to dodge, but agreed he'd bear a grudge too if someone had stabbed him. The Burgal children's need was greater anyway, so they took turns on horseback. Anvil Cornfoot led his people until they reached their forest where the dwarves melted into the trees and were gone. Cornfoot shook everyone's hand.

"Thank you," Henry said. "You were brilliant."

"Hey, I was just an observer, remember."

"Yeah, right. We're going on to Glam. With luck, Edrid's people will fix the boats and we can sail home."

"Plenty of timber for repairs."

"At least there're no more Starklanders to worry about."

"We didn't get 'em all, you know."

"Some escaped?"

"A few always do. Dunno how many though."

"You didn't tell me."

"No time, and what would you have done: chase down the villains or save Edrid?"

Henry nodded as Anvil turned to Jongarrat and held out his hand.

"I might come over and visit if those boats work," Cornfoot said. "You didn't turn out so badly after all."

"Mellowed with age, I guess," Jongarrat smiled and they parted as friends.

When they reached Otillie's village, those who'd remained had started repairs and Julian was confident they'd have the place back in order before winter. Otillie was at a loss. Although many of the young people had returned, with her home ruined and her dad gone, nothing much remained for her. Henry sensed Otillie's sadness and placed his arm around her shoulder.

"Bit of a mess, isn't it?" he said.

"I don't really know where to start," she sniffed.

"Why start at all?"

"Of course I've got to start."

"What I mean is why don't you come with us to Hollowford? Aunt Thayer would love to have a girl around and you'd like it there. We're very friendly when we aren't fighting bad people."

"Do you mean that?"

"I wouldn't have it any other way."

It wasn't as if she had much to pack, so she wished Julian luck before she and Henry followed the others north. Otillie walked with a spring in her step and felt happier now than she had ever been.

The wolf-ships were not too badly damaged; the hulls were blackened, but not deeply charred, as moisture had prevented the fire taking hold. Edrid assayed they'd be repaired in a week, but one of the ships was missing and Henry recalled Anvil Cornfoot's warning that some Starklanders had escaped. They must have taken to the high seas, but it was pointless to worry now.

In the hands of experienced sailors and with a stiff following wind, the voyage across Black Water was fast and uneventful. Edrid had trouble managing the steer-board with only one hand and his hook, but worked it out in the end. The sea still amazed

Henry, while Otillie was thrilled and luckily not prone to sickness. Ayla was indifferent and said that once they landed she never wanted to set foot in a boat again. Gareth and Archer were both ill, but after the first day found their sea legs and spent the remainder of the voyage learning the ropes, while Jongarrat said he preferred a good forest any day.

They beached at Tremill Broch, but no one was there. After mooring the wolf-ships, Gareth led everyone ashore, weapons at the ready and alert for danger. Although scorch marks remained, much of the settlement had been repaired and there were signs that it had been occupied recently–very recently. Fires still burned and a meal was half eaten in the main hall. Open books, scrolls, parchments, vellum and quills still wet with ink lay on the desks and lecterns.

"This is puzzling," Gareth said.

"Maybe not," Archer replied, wading across the causeway to the mainland where a few nervous heads peered through the reeds and scrub.

"Come out, we're not raiders," he yelled returning his sword to its scabbard. "Chief Gareth is home, so you'd better come and greet him before he gets cranky."

Dean Merrick led a group of rather sheepish scholars back to the island.

"Don't worry, I'd have done the same after last time," Archer grinned, slapping Merrick on the shoulder. The scholars were of course overjoyed to see Ayla and Macayle safely home. They were their favourite students and brightened the Broch during their visits. After a short time, with everyone talking at once, they reboarded the boats and rowed into Ita Cay lagoon and glided southwards to Anshelm's hut. Henry once more felt a great pang of regret as they passed the empty shack and a tear slipped down Macayle's cheek as she touched the scrimshaw pendant she'd carried for so long. Edrid placed his arm around her.

"He'll be pleased you have his carving to remember him by," he whispered. "And he cooked damn fine fish chowder.

So they journeyed on to Hollowford, where the celebrations really began and lasted for days, including countless toasts to Faranden's memory.

Thayer was delighted with her new brooch and welcomed Otillie into her household. The tattooed girl she'd captured during the fight with Olag's villains had settled in well and worked part time in Clem Foster's tavern. She'd even made friends with many of the Hollowford lasses and a couple of local lads were showing an interest. Edgar forgave Henry for running off, admitting he was pleased to see him back now his house was filling up with females.

But, it was time for Edrid and the islanders to leave, before the autumn storms, and they returned to their ships. Edrid and Gareth had spent hours deep in discussion over the forthcoming nuptials. Most importantly, Ayla liked her prospective son-in-law. The islanders would return in spring for the wedding that promised to be a grand affair. A chief's daughter and a prince didn't get married every day and there was much to prepare. Macayle moped, as half a year away from her darling was more than she could bear.

"Just be patient, young lady," Gareth admonished. "The time will pass quickly enough."

After a tearful goodbye, she sulked in her room as Henry, Bron, and Archer accompanied the islanders back to the wolf-ships. Although Henry and Archer brought mounts, they led them as Edrid's people went on foot and were in no particular hurry. It took the remainder of the day to prepare the ships and they planned to set sail at dawn, as navigating the reef at night was foolish.

As the sun rose, Henry and Edrid stood on the beach.

"See you next spring," Henry said, pumping Edrid's hand.

"I look forward to it and I'll think of some fancy gadgets you can make for my arm."

"You bet."

There was no need for further words. They both knew they would remain true friends for life, so with a brief nod to Archer, Edrid boarded the leading ship and they cast off. The current bore them quickly northwards and soon the vessels disappeared.

Henry and Archer mounted their horses and headed for Hollowford. They hadn't gone far when they came upon Bruno ambling towards town. They knew Gareth had bought him from Edgar for Macayle to ride, but there was no sign of her and they were alarmed at first, until the realisation dawned on them.

"No," Henry gasped.

"She wouldn't...?" Archer said.

"She did before."

And a note in her saddlebag confirmed their fears. They galloped back to the beach, but it was hopeless. The islanders were long gone and they would never catch up.

The wolf-ships glided past Tremill Broch before the crews hoisted the sail, but Macayle didn't reveal herself until they were far into open water.

"Not again!" Edrid sighed.

"Aren't you glad to see me, sweetheart?" she whispered coyly.

"Worried I wasn't coming back?"

"Daddy would kill you if you didn't."

"He'll kill me anyway."

"Not if you behave yourself, so now you'll just have to be patient 'til spring."

There was no turning back. The tides and wind had swept them well out to sea and beating back to Tremill Broch was out of the question. The islanders were secretly pleased that their beautiful, young princess was coming home with them.

"Anyway, you don't expect me to come and live on Palo Innes without seeing it first."

"Don't worry, you'll love it. It's the best place in the world."

And this time she knew Anshelm's scrimshawed whale bone around her neck meant good fortune.

Jongarrat returned to Guilda's hut while Kimball and Serlequin casually bade everyone farewell, as if nothing particularly interesting had occurred, and disappeared into the forest. They'd managed to hang onto the seeds they'd harvested in Unab and planned to grow the stuff to sell at the Velma market. Thayer voiced her disapproval and said she'd speak to the boys' mother and see what she had to say about the matter. Life in Hollowford quickly returned to normal with everyone busy preparing for harvest time, although Henry found settling back to a routine difficult. He was distracted for much of the time, which tried Edgar's patience.

Then Archer appeared at the forge as they were having lunch and Thayer added a plate for him.

"I dunno what I'm going to do with the lad," Edgar complained. "His head's in the clouds most of the time these days."

"I might have the answer," Archer said. "Chief Gareth was discussing who might replace Faranden and Henry's name came up…"

"Me!"

"No one has done more to earn Gareth's trust and you've grown into a great, burly lout just like Faranden."

Henry couldn't believe it; he'd be a warrior, but what about the forge? What about Edgar? He was not only Henry's uncle, but his master as well. There was a long pause as all eyes turned to Edgar who remained silent as if enjoying Henry's dilemma. Finally the blacksmith spoke.

"Well, do you want the job or not?"

The task of returning Burgal's children fell to Archer and his new deputy-reeve as they'd been to the west coast before. Bron accompanied them, of course, and Otillie came along to see what the peninsula looked like. They were glad to leave Hollowford as Gareth was in a foul mood over Macayle, but Ayla assured the town that he'd calm down before the wedding or she'd have something to say about it. Otillie loved the majesty of Enta Geweore and it seemed the bandits had learnt their lesson and stayed away. Burgal was in a joyful mood when they arrived and reunited the children with their families, but there was something else.

"Folk seem happier around here," Henry observed.

"You brought our kids back, why shouldn't they be?" Walter said.

"No, I mean generally."

"That's probably down to you two, and that hound as well."

"Oh? And she's not a dog, she a wolf."

"Well, Urdec went soft in the head when you left and folk started questioning how things were around 'ere. Why, he took the best of everything and left us the scraps. Said it's what the gods wanted, but we didn't see no good come of it. So folk just stopped takin' notice of 'im, and what's 'e gonna do about it anyway? There was a lot o' rantin' an' ravin' till we got sick of it and a bunch of lads ran him out of town and he ain't been seen since. Urdec couldn't do nothin' and now you've brought our young'uns back, seems we don't need a druid at all. 'E's out in the bog somewhere, who cares?"

The autumn storms were upon them when they returned, just in time, in Archer's opinion. They stopped at Guilda's hut and Otillie enchanted the old woman as much as she had delighted Thayer. They spent the night and were awoken by wolves baying close by. The pack had returned and Bron snarled as she stalked from Guilda's hut. Henry followed ahead of the others. The pack was at the gate led by a male who stood with its back arched and fur bristling. Bron crouched beside Henry, who stood only a few paces in front of the alpha male.

"You know why they're here, don't you?" Jongarrat said from the doorway.

"Yes," Henry replied.

He knelt and stroked Bron's back.

"It's up to you, girl," he whispered in her ear. "He knows you're worthy and loyal, but I shall miss you."

He leant forward and placed his hands on the ground and looked up into the wolf's eyes.

Okay, you're the boss, if that's the way you want it.

Bron hesitated, uncertain and divided, and then she loped towards the pack leader, but did not lower her head in submission.

"Atta girl, let him know you're his equal," Henry called, rising to his feet. "Now go, but I'll look for you when the snow melts. I expect you'll have a family to show me then."

The alpha male nuzzled her side, acknowledging her status, followed by the rest of the pack, who each accepted her as the male's consort. Then they turned and bounded away with Bron leading beside her new mate. As they approached the tree line, she stopped and howled one last farewell before vanishing into the forest, leaving five figures standing by Guilda's hut staring into the distance. Otillie silently reached for Henry's hand.

"Come on," Archer said at last. "Breakfast is ready, fresh baked bread and porridge laced with honey. Let's tuck in before we head home."

A lone wolf-ship had been hauled onto the shingle at Skinner's Landing and would stay there until the winter storms abated. Its crew sat it out, brawling, boozing, and whoring. Evil Queig had gathered the few survivors from Glam and taken the best wolf-ship to sea. But it was hard going with only a dozen men, so now he was recruiting, and he had plenty of takers. One upshot of the Dambar cohort's reform was that those unsuitable were dismissed. Many had trouble turning their hands to employment other than banditry, but the cohort's newly formed cavalry hunted outlaws mercilessly. So when word got out that a ship was looking for a crew with no questions asked, what better way to escape than by sea. By spring, Queig reckoned, he'd be ready to set sail and plunder anywhere he pleased.

THE END

The Author

Richard Marman was born in Swindon, UK. His father was a RAF pilot who had served with distinction during WWII. His family moved from base to base after the war, including four years in Germany. They immigrated to Fremantle in 1962. Richard attended six primary and three secondary schools, so he is familiar with the 'new kid on the block' status.

After school, Richard joined the Royal Australian Air Force and trained as a pilot. He served for nine years, including a tour in Vietnam and a significant time flying in New Guinea. In 1975 Richard left the RAAF to fly with Ansett Airlines until the company closed in 2001 at which time he was a Boeing 767 captain. Afterwards he trained Singapore Airlines cadets on Lear Jets until 2007.

Leaving aviation behind, Richard completed a Diploma of Visual Arts at Tewantin TAFE and a Bachelor of Arts at the University of the Sunshine Coast, majoring in creative writing and graphic design. Many of Richard's book ideas have stemmed from University projects.

Richard lives on Queensland's Sunshine Coast with his wife Judy. They have twin daughters living interstate.

For more information visit:

www.richardmarman.net and www.richardmarman.com

If you read only one book set against WWI during its centenary anniversary, make it *McAlister and the Great War*. This novel, splashed across a truly global canvas, explores many fascinating and thrilling historical incidents that occurred during the tragic conflict.

The McAlister Line Reader Reviews

'...Masterfully handled and quite eloquent...wonderful.'

'I like this book [McAlister's Way] it covers issues that need to be addressed.'

'Waiting for the sequel'

'*McAlister's Spark* is a fast-paced, action-riddled amazing read you will struggle to put down.'

'A great action read for teenagers and great graphics...a great literary effort.'

'...with pirates and secrets set amongst the northern tropics, you're in for a delightful read. With a good sense of place and the voice to the detail it's [*McAlister's Way*] a very fast-moving action story that will have you wanting more.'

'*McAlister's Way* is a fast-paced, page-turning read — the kind of read where you lose track of time. Absolutely enveloping! Highly recommended!!'

'Through the non-stop action and the integration of history, new cultures and wars the reader is kept engaged from beginning to end on a literary roller coaster ride they won't soon forget.'

Wave and Web Series

Illustrated for Rita Hayward   **Illustrated for Elle Burton**

The dreaded dragon, Brimstone is terrorising the sleepy village of Oak Tree, so it's up to Prince Roger and his sister Princess Crystal to hunt down the fiery beast.

They are aided and hindered — as the case may be — by an evil knight, a mysterious good-guy, the local sheriff, loyal men-at-arms, forest brigands, a pair of trusty — and not so trusty — chargers, ogres, trolls and Oak Tree's citizens with a bunch of attitude.

There are thrills, spills, romance and a heap of rollicking good fun to be had by all.